The Golden Book II

Khan's Legacy

Donald J. Wright

About the author

My career, spanning over four decades, has been a testament to the power of strategic vision and leadership. From the vibrant sales floors of Bashinski's Gems and Jewelry to the strategic boardrooms of Reeds Jewelers and Friedman's Incorporated, I have navigated the complicated landscape of diamonds, gems, and the buying sector with a blend of scientific precision and creative flair. My passion for storytelling is not just a personal interest but a reflection of my professional journey. It is beyond the sparkle of a well-cut diamond, weaving narratives that resonate with the heart and mind—my passion is clear in my published five nonfiction books and the twenty-plus novels. As an author, I understand the value of legacy, and it's the timeless beauty of a family heirloom or the enduring impact of a well-told tale. My books are more than just collections of words. They are vessels of 'knowledge, experience, and imagination' destined to inspire and enlighten. I hope you find these sources of information and entertainment too.

Contents

1. Chapter 1: The Sister's Message   1

2. Chapter 2: Dangerous Reunion   7

3. Chapter 3: The Second Box   17

4. Chapter 4: Old Friends, New Enemies   28

5. Chapter 5: The Mongolian Connection   37

6. Chapter 6: Escape from Virginia   50

7. Chapter 7: Stopover in Istanbul   66

8. Chapter 8: Crossing into Mongolia   82

9. Chapter 9: City of Shadows   99

10. Chapter 10: The Guardian's Test   119

11. Chapter 11: Preparing for the Mountain   135

12. Chapter 12: The First Assassin   147

13. Chapter 13: Into the Khentii Mountains   161

14. Chapter 14: The Watchers   175

15. Chapter 15: The False Tomb   183

16. Chapter 16: Storm Sanctuary   192

17. Chapter 17: The Underground Path   213

18. Chapter 18: The Rival's Arrival   231

19. Chapter 19: Unlikely Alliance   239

20. Chapter 20: The River of Death   255

21. Chapter 21: The Hall of Warriors   272

22. Chapter 22: The Three Trials   280

23. Chapter 23: Betrayal in the Dark   287

24. Chapter 24: The Final Gate   294

25. Chapter 25: The Burial Chamber   300

26. Chapter 26: The Khan's Curse   306

27. Chapter 27: Collapse   315

28. Chapter 28: The Mountain's Judgment   321

29. Chapter 29: The Guardians' Blessing   328

30. Chapter 30: Unfinished Business   335

31. Chapter 31: The Reckoning   343

32. Chapter 32: New Beginnings   351

33. Epilogue: The Next Mystery   359

34. Coming Soon: The Golden Book III — The Wolf of Em-   366
    pire

Also by Donald J. Wright   368

Chapter 1: The Sister's Message

The nightmares always started the same way—with golden light reflecting off dark water.

Barry Curtis jerked awake, his T-shirt damp with sweat despite the October chill seeping through the cabin windows. For a moment, he was back in that flooded chamber, the golden map illuminated by his dying flashlight, Blossom's hand slipping from his grasp as the water rose.

"Damn it," he muttered, swinging his legs off the bed.

The digital clock read 3:17 AM—the witching hour, as his grandmother used to call it. When the veil between worlds was thinnest. Maybe that's why Blossom's absence felt most acute in these pre-dawn hours, the emptiness beside him like a physical wound that refused to heal.

Eighteen months. Eighteen months since he'd returned from the Solomon Islands alone. Eighteen months of waking to this gnawing hollowness.

Barry padded barefoot across rough pine floorboards to the kitchen of his small Virginia cabin. The place was remote enough that his nearest neighbor was a twenty-minute drive away—exactly as he wanted it. He'd purchased it with the advance from his book, a sanitized account of the

Solomon Islands expedition that had made the New York Times bestseller list for three consecutive weeks.

The Emperor's Sunken Legacy: A Lost Japanese Treasure and the Price of Discovery.

The critics had loved it. "A gripping adventure that doubles as a thoughtful meditation on historical preservation," the Washington Post had written. "Curtis deftly navigates colonial exploitation, wartime atrocities, and modern archaeological ethics," said National Geographic.

What none of them knew—what no one could ever know—was what he'd left out. The golden map fragments. The true nature of the Red Lotus Society. How Blossom Hirata had died protecting secrets that went beyond mere historical artifacts.

He poured bourbon into a glass, not bothering with ice. The amber liquid caught the moonlight streaming through the kitchen window, another unwelcome reminder of gold. Of treasure. Of everything that had been lost.

His laptop sat on the kitchen table, its power light pulsing softly like a mechanical heartbeat. On impulse, he opened it, squinting against the sudden blue light. He'd been avoiding email for days, ignoring his publisher's increasingly agitated messages about the promotional tour for the paperback edition.

Fifty-seven new messages. Most would be fan mail forwarded by his agent—amateur historians offering theories, adventure seekers asking for tips on expedition planning, and film producers seeking rights. He'd stopped responding months ago.

But one subject line stopped his scrolling cold: She always said you would understand the jade key.

Barry's hand froze on the trackpad. The jade key. Not a phrase anyone would know unless...

The sender's address was unfamiliar: s.hirata@cybertech.au.

Hirata.

His heart hammered against his ribs as he double-clicked the email. It opened to reveal a brief message:

Professor Curtis,

You don't know me, but my sister Blossom spoke of you often. I need to meet urgently. Mother was killed two weeks ago—same method as Nakamura's men used on the others. The Red Lotus has reorganized under new leadership.

I know about the map. ALL of it.

I'm flying to Washington tomorrow. I'll be at the National Museum of Asian Art at 2 PM, Thursday, near the Mongolian artifacts.

Come alone. Trust no one.

—Sakura Hirata

P.S. This email will delete itself after reading. I've included decryption instructions for future communications attached below.

Barry read it twice, then a third time, the bourbon forgotten. Blossom had mentioned a sister once, younger by several years, estranged. They hadn't spoken in nearly a decade, she'd said. Something about opposing life choices.

He scrolled down to find a complex set of encryption protocols, far more sophisticated than anything a civilian should have access to. Whoever Sakura Hirata was, she moved in different circles than her archaeologist sister.

As promised, when he refreshed his inbox, the email had vanished without a trace.

Barry stood and moved to the window, staring out at the dark outline of the Blue Ridge Mountains. He'd come here to disappear, to nurse his grief and guilt in isolation. To keep the secrets that had cost so much.

And now this.

His gaze drifted to the fireplace, to the loose stone in the hearth beneath which he'd hidden the waterproof case. Inside lay the five golden sheets they'd recovered, inscribed with ancient Mongolian script and detailed maps to what Blossom had believed was the greatest archaeological find of the century: the true burial site of Genghis Khan.

The sheets that men had killed for. That Blossom had died for.

He hadn't looked at them since returning. Couldn't bear to. But he'd memorized every intricate line, every symbol. The lost tomb of the greatest conqueror in history, hidden for eight centuries through misdirection and myth.

Barry took a long swallow of bourbon, welcoming the burn. The Red Lotus reorganized. Blossom's mother was murdered. And now her sister is coming to America with knowledge that should have died in those flooded ruins.

He glanced at the calendar on the wall. Today was Tuesday. Thursday was less than forty-eight hours away.

His first instinct was to run—pack up the gold sheets and disappear deeper into the mountains. But Blossom's face flashed in his mind, her final words echoing: Promise me they won't get it. Promise me you'll protect it.

If the Red Lotus had killed her mother, they wouldn't stop with Sakura. And if she truly knew about the map, she was already marked for death.

Barry moved to his closet and pulled out the dusty go-bag he'd prepared upon returning to the States. Inside were cash, multiple IDs, a satellite phone, and a Glock 19 that he'd never had to use. He hoped he wouldn't have to now.

Dawn was still hours away as he began packing, his mind racing through contingencies. The cabin had been secure, but now it felt exposed, vulnerable. He'd need to implement the evacuation protocol he'd established—the one Blossom had insisted upon before they'd even left for the Solomon Islands.

"We're disturbing something powerful, Barry," she'd said. "Something that's stayed hidden for centuries. There will be ripples."

She'd been right, of course. There had been ripples. Waves, really. And now, eighteen months later, they were still coming.

As he worked, Barry felt something shifting inside him—a sensation almost forgotten. Beneath the grief and guilt, the old fire was rekindling. The thrill of the hunt. The scholarly obsession with unveiling history's secrets.

And something else, something he was almost ashamed to acknowledge: relief. Relief that his self-imposed exile was ending. That he would no longer face the ghosts alone.

By the time morning light filtered through the trees, Barry had made his decision. He would meet Sakura Hirata. He would hear what she knew.

And then, perhaps, he would finally fulfil his promise to her sister.

He brewed coffee and carried a mug to the porch, watching the mist rise off the mountains. Birds called in the distance, and somewhere, a deer moved cautiously through the underbrush.

Barry pulled out his phone and dialed a number he hadn't used in over a year.

"Jim? It's Curtis. I need a favor." He paused, listening to the surprised response from his former boss at the university. "No, I'm not coming back to teaching. This is... something else. Something related to the Solomon Islands."

Another pause.

"Yes, I know what I wrote in the book. But there are things I left out. Things that matter now."

He took a deep breath, feeling the weight of his next words.

"I need everything you can find on a woman named Sakura Hirata. And I need to know if there have been any reports of Red Lotus activity in the past six months."

As Jim's voice rose with questions, Barry's gaze drifted to the mountains again. Somewhere on the other side of the world were more mountains—the Khentii range of Mongolia, where legend said the greatest conqueror in history was secretly buried.

And if what Blossom had discovered was true, those mountains held secrets far more valuable than gold.

"I can't explain over the phone," he said finally. "But I think it's starting again. All of it."

He ended the call and stood watching the sunrise, feeling like a man awakening from a long, dark sleep—uncertain of what the new day would bring, but knowing that, for better or worse, his isolation was over.

The sister was coming. And with her, the past he'd tried so desperately to bury.

Chapter 2: Dangerous Reunion

The National Museum of Asian Art stood like a fortress of marble and glass against the late October sky. Barry arrived forty minutes early, positioning himself on a bench with clear sightlines of all entrances. He'd chosen a spot near the Mongolian exhibition but not directly in it—close enough to observe without being obvious.

Three days of minimal sleep had left him hypervigilant. Twice now, he'd spotted the same dark sedan circling the blocks near his hotel. Coincidence, perhaps, but Barry Curtis no longer believed in coincidences.

He wore a navy blazer over a gray shirt, casual enough to blend with the Thursday afternoon museum crowd but formal enough not to draw attention. The Glock 19 pressed uncomfortably against his lower back, concealed by the blazer. He hadn't carried a weapon in public before the Solomon Islands. Now it felt as necessary as his wallet.

Jim's information on Sakura Hirata had been sparse but revealing. Thirty-two years old, four years younger than Blossom had been. No criminal record. Double major in computer science and linguistics from the University of Sydney. Currently employed by CyberShield, an Australian cybersecurity firm with government contracts. Three years of competitive judo in college. A brief engagement broken off two years ago.

What the file didn't contain was a photograph. Barry had no idea what to expect beyond the obvious family connection.

At precisely 1:58 PM, she walked in.

Barry almost missed her at first. Where Blossom had moved with an archaeologist's careful deliberation, cataloging the world around her, this woman glided with athletic efficiency. Nothing wasted, nothing telegraphed. She wore a charcoal pantsuit that somehow managed to look both professional and ready for combat, her black hair cut in a sharp bob rather than Blossom's flowing curls.

But the eyes—those were unmistakable. The same amber-flecked brown that had captivated him the first time Blossom had challenged his translation of a Heian-period scroll.

Sakura didn't look around searching for him. Instead, she moved directly to the central display case housing Mongolian artifacts, her gaze never lingering too long in one place. She knew she was being watched—either by him or by others.

Barry waited, counting to one hundred in his head. Only then did he rise, adjusting his blazer to ensure the weapon remained concealed, and approached.

"The ceremonial daggers are remarkable," he whispered, standing beside her but looking at the display case. "The craftsmanship suggests Song Dynasty influence."

She didn't startle or turn. "The curators mislabeled them. They're Jurchen, not Mongol. Jin Dynasty."

Her voice was lower than Blossom's, with a hint of an Australian accent that eighteen years in Sydney had layered over her native Japanese. She still hadn't looked at him directly.

"I'm sorry about your mother," Barry said.

Now she turned, studying him with those familiar yet utterly different eyes. Where Blossom's had sparkled with discovery, Sakura's calculated risk.

"I never thanked you properly," she said, "for trying to save my sister."

Barry felt the familiar stab of guilt. "I didn't try hard enough."

"That's not what she told me." Sakura's gaze flicked past his shoulder, scanning the room. "We need to move. Second floor, east wing. Pre-modern Japanese collection."

She walked away without waiting for a response, moving through the crowd with the same efficient grace. Barry followed, maintaining distance, his own eyes searching for watchers. The museum was moderately busy—a school group clustered near a display of Chinese calligraphy, couples wandering hand-in-hand, solitary art students sketching in corners.

And a man in a gray suit who seemed too interested in his phone while positioned for optimal sightlines of the main hall.

Barry diverted to a display of ceremonial masks, pretending interest while watching the man's reflection in the glass. When the man adjusted his position to maintain visual contact, Barry's suspicions were confirmed.

They were being watched.

He continued toward the east wing, taking the stairs rather than the elevator. On the second floor, the crowd thinned considerably. Sakura stood before a display of samurai armor, her posture seemingly relaxed, but Barry could see the tension in her shoulders.

"There's a man in a gray suit," he said quietly as he joined her. "Professional. Government training, if I had to guess."

"I spotted him when I entered. There's another by the south entrance. Woman, red blouse, camera but no tourist behavior." Sakura's eyes never left the armor display. "Are you carrying?"

"Yes."

"Good. Did you bring it?"

"Not here." Barry studied the intricate lacework on the samurai helmet. "It's secure."

"The golden map." She said it matter-of-factly, not a question. "Blossom wrote to me about it before you both left for the Solomon Islands. Her insurance policy, she called it."

"You were in contact? She told me you hadn't spoken in years."

A flicker of something—pain, regret—crossed Sakura's face. "We reconciled shortly before her last expedition. In secret."

"Why the secrecy?"

"Because she knew I worked adjacent to intelligence communities. Because she'd discovered something that certain governments would kill to possess." Sakura moved to the next display case, maintaining the appearance of casual museum visitors. "Did she tell you what the map truly leads to?"

"The burial site of Genghis Khan."

"That's only part of it." Sakura lowered her voice further. "The tomb contains the complete Altan Debter—the Book of Gold. The secret history of the Mongol Empire, including military technologies they acquired from conquered civilizations: Chinese siege weapons, Persian engineering, Byzantine naval designs. Knowledge that disappeared after the empire fractured."

Barry felt a chill despite the museum's carefully regulated temperature. "That's speculation. No historian has ever confirmed the Book of Gold even existed."

"The Red Lotus believes it exists. That's why they've hunted our family for three generations." Her eyes met his directly now. "They killed my mother two weeks ago in her Sydney apartment. Made it look like a home invasion, but it was the same method used on my grandfather in 1982. Precision knife wound severing the carotid artery. No defensive wounds. No forced entry."

"I'm sorry," Barry said again, inadequately.

"Save it." Her tone wasn't unkind, merely practical. "Grief is a luxury I can't afford right now. Neither can you."

She was right, of course. Barry studied her profile, so similar to Blossom's yet fundamentally different. Where her sister had radiated intellectual curiosity and warmth, Sakura projected calculated competence and control.

"You mentioned new leadership," he prompted.

"Kenji Yamamoto." Sakura practically spat the name. "Nakamura's protégé. Younger, more tech-savvy, better connected politically. He's restructured the Red Lotus into smaller cells with specialized functions. Less of a traditional yakuza approach, more like a modern terrorist network."

"How do you know all this?"

"Because I've been hunting them too." Her gaze hardened. "After Blossom died, I used my contacts. Took a leave of absence from CyberShield. Followed money trails, weapons purchases, mysterious deaths connected to archaeological sites across Asia."

She moved again, leading them toward a less populated section of the exhibition. A scroll painting of Mount Fuji dominated the wall, its subtle gradations of ink creating the illusion of mist around the sacred peak.

"Three months ago, I traced a shell company in Singapore that purchased specialized ground-penetrating radar equipment. The same company later hired four former Chinese military personnel with excavation experience." Sakura's voice remained steady, professional. "They're preparing for an expedition. They know something we don't."

Barry processed this information, his academic mind automatically categorizing and connecting facts. "The map fragments we recovered weren't complete," he admitted. "There were references to additional markers needed to pinpoint the exact location within the Khentii Mountains."

"That's why I'm here." Sakura glanced around before reaching into her jacket pocket, partially withdrawing a small object before concealing it again. "My mother left me this. Her note said it was time for the 'second key' to be used."

Barry caught only a glimpse, but it was enough. A jade puzzle box, similar to the one Blossom had decoded to find the original map fragments, but with different inlay patterns.

"A second box," he breathed. "Blossom never mentioned..."

"She didn't know. Our family separated the keys generations ago. Insurance against any one person having too much knowledge." Sakura's eyes flicked to the left. "Gray Suit is coming up the stairs. We need to move."

Barry nodded, maintaining a casual posture while mentally mapping the museum layout. "Service corridor past the restrooms. Leads to administrative offices and eventually a staff exit."

They moved unhurriedly toward the restrooms, Barry fighting the urge to look back. The museum suddenly felt like a trap—too many blind corners, too many places for watchers to hide.

"If they make a move," Sakura said softly, "I'll engage. You get clear with the box."

"I'm not leaving you to face them alone."

A ghost of a smile touched her lips, so like Blossom's that it physically hurt. "I'm not my sister, Professor. Fighting is what I do."

They rounded the corner toward the restrooms. The service corridor door was marked "Staff Only," with a keycard reader beside it.

Sakura reached into her pocket and withdrew what looked like a hotel key card. "Electronic skeleton key. Military grade."

"Definitely not standard issue for a cybersecurity consultant," Barry observed.

"I told you. I've been hunting them too." She swiped the card, and the light blinked green.

As they slipped through the door, Barry caught movement in his peripheral vision—Gray Suit, reaching inside his jacket while speaking into what appeared to be a Bluetooth device.

The service corridor was narrow and utilitarian, a stark contrast to the elegant exhibition spaces. Fluorescent lights buzzed overhead, illuminating beige walls and linoleum flooring.

"We may have a problem," Barry said, explaining what he'd seen.

Sakura nodded, unsurprised. "They've been watching you for days: hotel, restaurant choices, museum visit patterns. Standard surveillance before an approach."

"How do you know that?"

"Because I've been watching them watch you." She moved quickly down the corridor, checking doors as she went. "I needed to be sure you weren't compromised."

The implication stung. "You thought I might be working with them?"

"I considered all possibilities." Her tone was unapologetic. "Blossom trusted you. But people change in eighteen months. Especially after trauma."

A door ahead opened, and a museum employee with a clipboard emerged. He frowned at them. "This area is—"

Sakura flashed what appeared to be an official ID. "Homeland Security. Art Crimes Division. The museum director is aware of our inspection."

The man hesitated, then nodded and continued past them. Barry caught only a glimpse of the ID before it disappeared back into Sakura's pocket.

"That was a fake," he whispered when the employee was out of earshot.

"Of course it was. But confidence sells more than authenticity." She tried another door, finding it unlocked. "In here."

The room was a small storage area filled with crates and conservation supplies. Sakura closed the door behind them and withdrew the jade puzzle box fully now.

It was exquisite—larger than the one Blossom had possessed, with intricate carvings of mountains and rivers flowing across its surface. Inlaid mother-of-pearl caught the light, forming what appeared to be astronomical symbols.

"I've tried to solve it," Sakura admitted. "But this is where I need you. Blossom said you were brilliant with these puzzles. That your understanding of historical context made connections others missed."

Barry took the box gingerly, feeling its weight—solid jade, cool to the touch. His fingers traced the patterns, his mind already analyzing potential mechanisms.

"The original box had a specific sequence," he murmured. "Based on the lunar calendar of the Mongol Empire. This appears different... possibly solar alignments?"

He rotated the box, studying it from all angles. The craftsmanship was extraordinary, the jade polished to a translucent gleam in places.

"We don't have time for a full analysis now," Sakura said, checking her watch. "Gray Suit will have called for backup. We need to—"

The door handle turned.

They froze. Sakura immediately positioned herself between Barry and the door, her stance shifting subtly into what he recognized as a combat-ready posture. Her hand moved toward her waistband.

The door opened to reveal a janitor with a mop cart. The elderly man blinked at them in surprise.

"Sorry, didn't know anyone was in here," he mumbled, backing out.

When the door closed, Barry released a breath he hadn't realized he was holding. "We need to get somewhere secure to examine this properly."

Sakura nodded. "My hotel is compromised if they've been watching you. Your hotel too."

"I have a safe house," Barry said. "Jim Beasley—my former department chair—keeps an apartment in Alexandria. He's out of the country at a conference."

"Can you trust him?"

"With my life. He helped me after I returned without Blossom."

Sakura considered this, then nodded. "We'll need to evade surveillance first. Split up, use public transportation, multiple transfers."

"I know the drill." Barry carefully tucked the jade box into his inner pocket. "What about the watchers?"

"Leave that to me." Sakura moved to the door, listening. "Take the service exit to the loading dock. There's a metro station three blocks east. Make at least two line changes before heading to Alexandria. I'll meet you at the safe house in two hours."

"How will you find it if we split up?"

She almost smiled. "Professor, I found you after eighteen months of isolation. Trust me to find an apartment in Alexandria."

Barry hesitated, studying her face—so familiar yet so foreign. "Blossom would have told me if you'd reconciled. We didn't have secrets."

Something flickered behind Sakura's eyes. "Everyone has secrets, Professor. Even Blossom. Especially Blossom." She checked the corridor through a crack in the door. "Clear for now. Go."

As Barry moved past her toward the exit, she caught his arm. Her grip was strong, assured.

"One more thing," she said quietly. "If I don't arrive within three hours, take the box and disappear. Use whatever contingency plan you've already established. Don't look back."

"I'm not going to abandon you."

"This isn't about me or you." Her eyes hardened. "It's about keeping the map from Yamamoto. About honoring what Blossom died for." She released his arm. "Three hours. Not a minute longer."

Barry nodded reluctantly and slipped into the corridor, moving quickly toward the exit sign at the far end. Behind him, he heard Sakura going in the opposite direction—toward the exhibition space, toward Gray Suit and his colleagues.

Creating a diversion, he realized. Drawing their attention to give him time to escape with the box.

The loading dock door opened onto an alley behind the museum. Cold autumn air hit his face as Barry emerged, scanning for threats before setting off toward the metro station at a deliberate pace—not running, which would attract attention, but not dawdling either.

His mind raced faster than his feet. A second jade box. A reorganized Red Lotus. A sister who moved like an operative and spoke of hunting killers.

And somewhere in the mountains of Mongolia, if the legends were true, the greatest archaeological find in history waited—along with secrets that powerful people would kill to possess.

As he descended into the metro station, Barry touched the bulge in his jacket where the jade box rested. He thought of Blossom's final moments, of promises made in desperation.

Three hours, Sakura had said. He checked his watch and quickened his pace.

The hunt had begun again.

Chapter 3: The Second Box

The safe house in Alexandria was a third-floor apartment in a pre-war building with peeling crown molding and unreliable heating. Barry reached it first, using the circuitous route he'd planned—three subway transfers, a bus, and finally a quarter-mile walk through back streets, doubling back twice to ensure he wasn't followed. The autumn evening had turned bitter, an unseasonable chill settling over the Potomac like a shroud.

Every car that slowed near him sent adrenaline coursing through his system. Every pedestrian who maintained pace behind him for more than a block became a potential threat. Eighteen months of isolation had done nothing to dull the hypervigilance that had followed him home from the Solomon Islands.

The apartment smelled of dust and old books—Jim's natural habitat. Barry swept it methodically, checking windows, closets, potential hiding places, the cold metal of the Glock comforting against his palm. Only when satisfied did he secure the door with the additional deadbolt Jim had installed after Barry's return.

He checked his watch: two hours and seventeen minutes since leaving the museum. Sakura would arrive soon—if she'd evaded capture.

If she was who she claimed to be.

Barry removed the jade puzzle box from his jacket, setting it on the kitchen table under the harsh fluorescent light. Its intricate carvings seemed to shift in the uneven illumination, mountains flowing into rivers, constellations rearranging themselves. He forced himself to step back, to breathe. The academic in him wanted to dive in immediately, but experience had taught him caution.

He prepared instead drawing the blinds, positioning a chair to face the door, laying out paper and pencils for notes. From his bag, he withdrew a small leather kit containing specialized tools: a magnifying glass, calipers, soft brushes, and dental picks. The tools of archaeology repurposed for a more urgent excavation.

A floorboard creaked in the hallway outside.

Barry froze, hand moving to the Glock. His ears strained against the silence, catching the subtle shift of weight on aged wood. Not the heavy tread of the building's elderly superintendent. Something lighter, deliberate.

Three precise knocks followed.

He moved silently to the door, weapon ready. "Yes?"

"The jade key opens doors beyond perception." Sakura's voice, reciting the phrase they'd agreed on during their brief planning at the museum.

Barry checked the peephole before disengaging the locks. Sakura slipped inside like a shadow, her movements economical. She wore different clothes now—dark jeans, a black turtleneck, a leather jacket—and carried a small backpack. Her hair was tucked beneath a cap.

"Any problems?" he asked, securing the door behind her.

"Minor. Lost two tails on the Metro. A third was more persistent." Her eyes scanned the apartment, assessing. "This place is insufficient. Single entry point, predictable layout, minimal escape routes."

"It's temporary." Barry returned to the table, where the box was waiting. "Did anyone follow you here?"

"No." Her certainty was absolute. Then, noticing his expression, "I've done this before, Professor. Extensively."

"So I'm gathering." Barry gestured to the backpack. "Shopping trip?"

"Necessities." She set it down and withdrew items methodically: a satellite phone, different from the model Barry owned; a slim laptop; what appeared to be signal jammers; a handgun smaller than his Glock but no less lethal-looking; and various electronic devices he couldn't identify.

"That's not standard consumer technology," he observed.

"No," she agreed without elaboration, setting up one of the devices near the window. "We have approximately ninety minutes before we need to relocate. The box?"

Barry indicated the jade puzzle sitting on the table. "I've only had a preliminary look. It's definitely connected to the one Blossom had, but more sophisticated. The inlay work suggests the same craftsman created it, but later in his career. More confident techniques."

Sakura approached, her demeanor shifting subtly. For a brief moment, Barry glimpsed the scholar beneath the operative—the same intellectual curiosity that had animated her sister.

"The original box used lunar calendar alignments," she said, leaning over the intricate jade surface. "Blossom's notes mentioned a twelve-fold sequence."

"Yes. This appears to use solar alignments instead, but with..." Barry trailed off, studying a particular pattern along the edge. "Wait. These aren't just decorative. They're coordinates."

Outside, a car door slammed. Both of them tensed, Sakura's hand moving instinctively toward her weapon.

"This neighborhood," Barry explained, forcing his heart rate to slow. "People coming home from work."

Sakura nodded but didn't relax. "Work quickly."

Under the harsh kitchen light, Barry examined the box through his magnifying glass. The jade had the translucent quality of the finest imperial specimens, allowing light to penetrate just enough to reveal deeper layers of carving within.

"The surface patterns are misleading," he murmured, tracing one finger along a mountain ridge that transformed into a river valley. "They're meant to distract from the actual mechanism."

He carefully rotated the box, studying each face. Unlike Blossom's puzzle, which had been cubic, this one had subtle irregularities—faces that weren't quite parallel and edges that were slightly uneven.

"It's not geometrically perfect," he said, more to himself than to Sakura. "Intentional imperfection."

"Like wabi-sabi," she said. "Japanese aesthetic principle. Beauty in imperfection."

"Yes, exactly. But the Mongols wouldn't have followed that concept. This suggests Japanese craftsmen were involved in its creation." Barry's mind raced through historical connections. "There were Japanese captives brought to Karakorum during the attempted Mongol invasions. Skilled artisans were often spared to serve the Khan."

A thin smile crossed Sakura's face. "You sound like her. The same connections, just... appearing from nowhere."

The comparison stung in its accuracy. Barry refocused on the box, finding an almost invisible seam along one edge. "Pressure here might trigger a mechanism, but without knowing the correct sequence..."

"The wrong sequence might damage the contents," Sakura finished. "Or trigger a failsafe."

"You think it's booby-trapped? After eight hundred years?"

"Our family doesn't take chances with secrets." She checked her watch. "Eighty-three minutes."

The pressure of time sharpened Barry's focus. He examined the astronomical symbols inlaid in mother-of-pearl. "These aren't random. They show specific celestial alignments." He traced the pattern. "Summer solstice... winter solstice... equinox..."

A memory surfaced—Blossom in his university office, lamplight catching her glasses as she traced similar patterns on an ancient Chinese star chart. "The Mongols navigated by the stars more accurately than Europeans would for centuries," she'd explained. "They understood that the heavens move in perfect cycles. Press the right points in the right sequence..."

Barry positioned his fingers on four specific inlaid stars. "The Four Guardians of Heaven—Azure Dragon, White Tiger, Black Tortoise, Vermilion Bird. They mark the four cardinal directions in East Asian astronomy."

He pressed them in sequence—east, west, north, south—applying gentle but firm pressure. Something inside the box shifted with an almost imperceptible click.

"That's the first layer," he murmured.

The building's heating system kicked on with a metallic groan, making them both tense again. Somewhere down the hall, a door opened and closed. Footsteps passed their apartment without slowing.

Barry returned to the puzzle, finding that one face of the box now had a slight give. Pressing it revealed a second layer of mechanisms—tiny wheels carved from jade, nested within each other like the interior of a watch.

"Astronomical calculator," he said, excitement temporarily overriding caution. "Similar to mechanisms found in Song Dynasty devices. You align the celestial bodies..."

His fingers worked delicately, rotating the wheels to match the positions shown in the inlaid constellations. Each correct alignment produced another subtle click from within.

Sakura had gone completely still, watching his hands with focused intensity. "How did you learn to do this?"

"Your sister taught me," Barry said simply. "She helped me solve the first box in hours. It would have taken me days to understand it without her help and motivation."

A final wheel clicked into place, and one entire face of the box slid open with a whisper of jade against jade. Inside lay a velvet pouch, its once-rich crimson faded to rust with age.

Barry's fingers trembled slightly as he withdrew it. The fabric felt fragile, threatening to disintegrate at his touch. Carefully, he placed it on the table and folded back the ancient velvet.

Three sheets of gold gleamed under the fluorescent light, each no thicker than a leaf, covered in dense script that matched the fragments he'd hidden beneath his cabin's hearth.

"My God," he breathed.

Sakura leaned closer, her composure finally cracking. "The missing pieces."

Barry didn't touch them directly, instead using a soft brush to gently separate the sheets. The gold was incredibly thin, hammered to the point of translucence, allowing light to filter through the etched characters. Like the previous fragments, these combined texts in ancient Mongolian script with precise diagrams and maps.

"The original fragments showed the general region," he explained, voice hushed with reverence. "The Khentii Mountains of northern Mongolia. But the specific location was missing—a deliberate omission in case the map was seized."

"And these provide the exact coordinates," Sakura said, not a question.

"More than that." Barry indicated markings along the edge of one sheet. "These are astronomical alignments—specific dates when certain stars would be positioned directly above the burial chamber. Like a celestial key."

A sound from the hallway—the elevator arriving at their floor. Both froze, listening as the doors opened and closed, followed by footsteps moving away from their door.

"Seventy-one minutes," Sakura murmured, returning to the gold sheets. "Can you read it?"

"Parts of it. The script is archaic, uses characters that fell out of use centuries ago." Barry pointed to specific sections. "This references 'the mountain that guards the sky lord.' And here—' enter only when the celestial hunter stands above the wolf's tail.'"

"Astronomical timing again," Sakura nodded. "When certain stars align."

"This is incredible," Barry whispered, academic excitement momentarily overriding his caution. "If authentic, this is the most significant—"

"It's authentic," Sakura interrupted flatly. "My family has guarded these secrets for generations. People have died protecting them." Her gaze met his, unflinching. "Blossom died protecting them."

The room suddenly felt colder. Barry looked down at the golden sheets, remembering the cost of the fragments he already possessed. The flooded chamber. Blossom's hand slipping from his. Her final words, lost beneath dark water.

"We need to document these quickly and secure them," Sakura continued, practical again. "I have a specialized camera in my pack."

As she turned toward her backpack, a subtle click sounded from the apartment door.

They both froze.

It wasn't the sound of a key. It was the infinitesimal noise of a lock pick finding its target.

Sakura moved first, silently gathering the gold sheets and returning them to their velvet pouch. She thrust them at Barry while drawing her weapon in one fluid motion. No words were needed—her eyes directed him toward the bedroom while she positioned herself beside the entrance, gun aimed at the door.

Barry quickly but carefully tucked the pouch into his inner pocket, securing the jade box in his bag. His own weapon felt suddenly inadequate as he backed toward the bedroom door, eyes fixed on the apartment entrance.

The handle turned slowly, silently.

Sakura had flattened herself against the wall, becoming nearly invisible in the shadow beside the door frame. Her posture had changed completely—coiled energy, ready to strike.

The door opened a fraction of an inch.

Then everything happened at once.

The door exploded inward with concussive force. A cylindrical object bounced across the floor—a flash-bang grenade. Barry ducked behind the bedroom doorway as blinding light and deafening sound filled the apartment.

Through ringing ears, he heard the distinctive report of Sakura's pistol—three shots in rapid succession. A man screamed. Something heavy crashed against a wall.

Barry risked a glance around the door frame. The apartment entrance was filled with smoke. Dark figures moved through it—two, then three. Sakura had somehow crossed the room and engaged them in hand-to-hand combat, her movements a blur of practiced violence.

She drove an elbow into one attacker's throat, simultaneously sweeping the legs from beneath another. The third man—massive, with hands like sledgehammers—caught her arm and slammed her against the wall hard enough to crack plaster.

Barry raised his Glock and fired twice. The shots sounded distant through his damaged hearing. The first missed; the second caught the big man in the shoulder, spinning him away from Sakura.

"Out! NOW!" Sakura shouted, her voice muffled by the ringing in his ears.

Barry backed toward the bedroom window, keeping his gun trained on the melee by the door. Sakura had recovered, executing a perfect spinning kick that connected with an attacker's jaw with an audible crack.

But more dark figures were pushing through the doorway—five, six, all in tactical gear, all armed. Too many.

In the bedroom, Barry threw open the window. Fire escape. Three floors up. The cold night air rushed in, carrying the distant sounds of traffic and sirens.

He looked back toward the living room in time to see Sakura slam her palm into an attacker's nose, driving cartilage upward with killing force. Blood sprayed across the wall. She caught his eye across the chaos and jerked her head toward the window—Go!

Barry hesitated, unwilling to leave her against such odds.

In that moment of indecision, one of the attackers spotted him. The man raised what looked like a compact submachine gun.

Barry ducked as bullets tore through the doorframe, sending splinters flying. He fired back blindly, emptying his magazine toward the doorway before scrambling onto the fire escape.

Cold metal bit into his palms as he descended as quickly as he dared, the golden sheets and jade box weighing against his chest like stones. Two flights down, his foot slipped on frost-slick metal. He barely caught himself, wrenching his shoulder painfully.

A crash above—someone following through the window. Barry looked up to see a black-clad figure emerge onto the fire escape, weapon raised.

No time for the stairs. He vaulted over the railing, dropping the remaining distance to the alley below. The impact drove through his knees and ankles with jarring force. He rolled awkwardly, pain flaring in his left ankle, but forced himself upright.

Gunfire sparked off the metal stairs above him. Barry limped deeper into the alley, desperate for cover, for distance, for time.

Behind him, glass shattered—another window. He risked a glance back to see Sakura diving through a different apartment window onto the fire escape, pursued by two attackers. Even at a distance, he could see blood darkening her left sleeve.

She caught sight of him and gestured urgently eastward before engaging her pursuers on the narrow fire escape. Her movements were economical, brutal—nothing like Blossom's gentle precision.

Barry forced himself to turn away, to follow her direction. East would take him toward the river. Potential escape routes, but also fewer witnesses, more isolated areas where they could be cornered.

His ankle protested with each step as he emerged from the alley onto a residential street. The normal rhythms of the neighborhood continued around him—lights in windows, television sounds, a couple walking a dog who gave his disheveled appearance a wide berth.

None of them were aware of the violence unfolding just yards away. None of them understood what had been unleashed.

Barry moved as quickly as his injury allowed, staying close to buildings, avoiding direct light. His mind raced faster than his limping gait. The attackers had found them too quickly. Known exactly where to look.

They'd been betrayed. But by whom? Jim? Impossible. The man had been like a father to him after Blossom's death.

A tracking device? Perhaps. But there hadn't been time to plant one at the museum.

Unless...

Barry stopped, hand going to his jacket pocket where the jade box had been. Had Sakura known? Had she led them deliberately into a trap?

No. She'd fought too fiercely, taken too many risks.

But someone had known. Someone had given them up.

Sirens wailed closer—multiple units, converging on the apartment building. Barry forced himself to keep moving, each step sending pain lancing up his leg. He needed to reach the rendezvous point they'd established during planning.

If we're separated, meet at the pier. Two hours. No longer.

The night had turned colder, his breath clouding before him as he limped eastward. Every shadow concealed potential threats. Every passing car might hold enemies. The golden sheets pressed against his chest seemed to burn with unnatural heat, as if the knowledge they contained was too potent to be contained.

Behind him, gunfire erupted again—short, professional bursts. Then the silence was more terrifying than the shots.

Barry quickened his pace despite the pain, the weight of history and legacy driving him forward. The knowledge in his possession had already cost too many lives—Blossom, her mother, perhaps now Sakura.

He wouldn't let those sacrifices be in vain.

The river appeared ahead, black water reflecting city lights. The pier would be half a mile south. Barry checked his watch—damaged in the fall, the face cracked and frozen at 9:17.

No way to know how much time had passed. No way to know if Sakura had escaped. No way to know if the men in tactical gear were still hunting him through Alexandria's quiet streets.

Only the certainty that the game had changed. The stakes raised. The danger multiplied.

Barry touched the pocket containing the golden sheets, feeling their weight—not just physical, but historical. The burial site of history's greatest conqueror. The Book of Gold with its ancient secrets.

Knowledge worth killing for. Knowledge worth dying for.

He limped toward the river, pain and fear driving each step, the night closing around him like a vise.

Chapter 4: Old Friends, New Enemies

The safe house in Arlington looked like every other suburban rental property on the quiet residential street—beige siding, small front yard, absolutely forgettable. Which was exactly the point. Barry Curtis sat at the kitchen table, staring at the encrypted satellite phone Jim Beasley had provided during their hasty extraction from his destroyed apartment twelve hours earlier.

Sakura emerged from the bedroom, where she'd been treating the cuts on her arms from their escape through the shattered window. She'd found clean clothes in the safe house's emergency supplies—dark jeans and a gray sweater that made her look younger, less like the hardened cybersecurity expert who had fought off Red Lotus assassins with deadly efficiency.

"Any word from your contact?" she asked, pouring herself coffee from the machine that had been mysteriously stocked and ready when they arrived.

"Jim's been in meetings since dawn," Barry replied, checking his watch. "He should be calling back soon."

The silence stretched between them, filled with the weight of everything that had happened. Barry found himself studying Sakura's face, looking for traces of her sister in the line of her jaw, the way she held her shoulders. But where Blossom had been warm and open, Sakura carried herself like a coiled spring—controlled, watchful, ready for violence.

"You don't trust him," she observed.

"I trust Jim with my life. I've done it before." Barry set down his coffee cup. "But this situation... it's bigger than what we faced in the Solomon Islands. The Red Lotus has had eighteen months to regroup, and now they have someone new calling the shots."

"Yamamoto." Sakura's voice carried a note of cold hatred. "My mother's research indicated he was Nakamura's most promising student. Younger, more ruthless, with connections throughout the Japanese underworld."

Before Barry could respond, the satellite phone chirped with an incoming call. The display showed only a series of numbers, but Barry recognized Jim Beasley's emergency protocol.

"Talk to me, Jim."

"We've got problems, Barry. Plural." Jim's voice carried the strain of a man who hadn't slept. "First, the good news—I can get you the resources you need for a Mongolia operation: weapons, equipment, transportation, clean papers."

"And the bad news?"

"The bad news is that the Red Lotus isn't your only problem. You remember Sarah Blackwood?"

Barry felt his stomach drop. He remembered her very well—the MI6 agent who had been Blossom's handler during the Solomon Islands operation. Blonde, professionally competent, with the kind of ice-cold demeanor that marked the best intelligence operatives. She had disappeared after Blossom's death, and Barry had assumed she'd been reassigned to another operation.

"What about her?"

"She's gone rogue. Officially, she resigned from MI6 six months ago for 'personal reasons.' Unofficially, she's been selling intelligence to the highest bidder ever since."

Sakura leaned closer to hear the conversation, her expression growing darker with each word.

"How does this affect us?" Barry asked.

"Because she knows everything about your previous operation. Every detail of your encounter with the Red Lotus, every piece of intelligence Blossom gathered, every weakness in your operational profile." Jim paused. "And three days ago, someone matching her description was spotted in a high-end hotel in Hong Kong, meeting with known Red Lotus financiers."

Barry closed his eyes, feeling the walls closing in around them. "She's working for Yamamoto."

"It gets worse. My contacts in the intelligence community say she's been asking questions about Mongolian archaeological sites. Specifically, sites connected to Genghis Khan's burial legends."

Sakura reached across the table and activated the phone's speaker function. "Mr. Beasley, this is Sakura Hirata. How much does Blackwood know about the map?"

"Miss Hirata. I'm sorry for your loss." Jim's voice softened momentarily before resuming its professional tone. "As for the map, she knows your sister found something significant in the Solomon Islands. She was Blossom's handler, so she would have been briefed on all recovered materials."

"But she doesn't know about the second puzzle box," Sakura said. "My mother kept that secret even from her."

"Maybe. But don't count on it. Blackwood is one of the best intelligence officers MI6 has ever produced. If there were clues to a second map, she would have found them."

Barry stood and began pacing the small kitchen, his mind racing through implications. "Jim, we need to assume she knows everything. That means she knows about the astronomical alignments, the seasonal access windows, probably even our planned route into Mongolia."

"Agreed. Which is why I'm recommending a completely different approach."

"I'm listening."

"Instead of trying to slip into Mongolia undetected, we go loud. I can arrange official cover through the State Department—an archaeological survey mission with full Mongolian government approval. Hide in plain sight."

Sakura shook her head. "That won't work. If Yamamoto has government connections, he'll learn about our mission within hours of the paperwork being filed."

"She's right," Barry agreed. "And if Blackwood is feeding them intelligence, they'll be waiting for us."

Jim was quiet for a moment, and Barry could hear him typing on a keyboard. "Okay, alternative plan. I've got a contact in the smuggling community—someone who specializes in getting people and equipment across borders without official notice. A Turkish national named Yusuf Kaplan. He's expensive, but he's never lost a client."

"What's the route?"

"Turkey to Georgia, then through Russian airspace to Kazakhstan. From there, overland to Mongolia through routes the border guards don't monitor closely. It'll take longer, but it keeps you off the official radar."

Barry considered the options. Every choice carried enormous risks, but doing nothing meant leaving Sakura and her remaining family members exposed to Red Lotus assassination attempts.

"There's something else," Jim continued. "My investigation into the British connection has turned up some interesting information. Blackwood wasn't just Blossom's handler—she was part of a larger MI6 operation focused on recovering lost treasures from former colonial territories."

"What kind of operation?"

"The kind that officially doesn't exist. Black budget, minimal oversight, designed to acquire culturally significant artifacts before their countries of origin could claim them." Jim's voice carried a note of disgust. "Turns out our British allies have been running their own treasure-hunting operation for decades."

Sakura's expression hardened further. "So when my sister found the map, Blackwood saw an opportunity to claim the Khan's treasure for Britain."

"Or for herself. The timeline suggests she started planning her defection shortly after the Solomon Islands operation ended. My guess is she realized the treasure was too valuable to share with her government."

Barry returned to the table, his decision crystallizing. "Jim, set up the meeting with your smuggler contact. We're going to Mongolia, but we're going to do it our way."

"Barry, you need to understand what you're walking into. This isn't just about competing treasure hunters anymore. Between the Red Lotus, Blackwood's mercenaries, and whatever government interests might be involved, you're looking at a potential shooting war in one of the most remote regions on Earth."

"Then we'd better get there first."

Jim sighed audibly through the encrypted connection. "All right. But I'm sending backup. I've got a small team of contractors who owe me favors—former Special Forces, experienced in international operations. They can provide security and extraction support if things go sideways."

"No." The refusal came from Sakura, sharp and immediate. "Too many people mean too many chances for information leaks. Yamamoto has demonstrated an ability to infiltrate operations before they begin."

"She's right," Barry agreed. "This has to be a minimal footprint operation. Just the two of us, with whatever local support we can arrange once we're in-country."

"You're making a mistake," Jim warned. "The intelligence suggests Yamamoto is mobilizing a substantial force. We're talking about professional operatives with military-grade equipment. You two won't stand a chance in a direct confrontation."

Barry looked across the table at Sakura, seeing his own determination reflected in her dark eyes. "Then we'll have to make sure it doesn't come to a direct confrontation. We find the tomb first, document everything, and get out before they know we were there."

"And if the tomb is empty? If someone else got there first?"

"Then at least we'll know the truth." Barry picked up the satellite phone. "How long do you need to set up the extraction route?"

"Forty-eight hours for the paperwork and advance payments. Seventy-two hours to get you to the departure point in Istanbul."

"Do it."

After Jim disconnected, Sakura remained seated at the kitchen table, staring at the second puzzle box they had recovered from her mother's house. The jade surface seemed to glow in the morning sunlight streaming through the safe house windows.

"There's something I haven't told you," she said quietly.

Barry felt his heart sink. After everything they'd been through, more secrets were the last thing they needed.

"What is it?"

"My mother wasn't just hiding information about the map. She was hiding information about Sarah Blackwood." Sakura opened her laptop and began typing rapidly. "After Blossom's death, my mother conducted her own investigation. She had contacts in the intelligence community—people who owed favors to our family."

A series of photographs appeared on the screen—surveillance images of Sarah Blackwood meeting with various individuals in locations around the world: Hong Kong, Singapore, Dubai, and London.

"Blackwood didn't go rogue six months ago," Sakura continued. "She's been selling information for over a year. Including intelligence about Red Lotus operations."

Barry studied the photographs, noting the timestamps and locations. "She's been playing both sides."

"Worse than that. Look at this." Sakura clicked on another file, revealing financial records that showed substantial payments flowing into numbered accounts associated with Blackwood's name. "She's not just selling information. She's actively coordinating attacks."

The final piece of evidence was a communication intercept—an encrypted message between Blackwood and an unknown recipient, dated three days after the attack on Barry's apartment.

"The Curtis extraction was successful. Both targets are mobile and proceeding as anticipated. Recommend advancing the timeline for Phase Two operations."

Barry felt the world shift around him as the implications hit home. "She let us escape. The attack on my apartment wasn't meant to kill us—it was meant to force us into the open, make us reach out for help."

"Which means she knows about this safe house. She knows about Jim Beasley. She probably knows about the smuggling route he's arranging." Sakura closed the laptop with a snap. "We're walking into a trap."

Before Barry could respond, the satellite phone rang again. But this time, the caller ID showed an international number he didn't recognize.

"Don't answer it," Sakura warned.

Barry hesitated, then activated the phone's speaker function and answered without identifying himself.

"Dr. Curtis." The voice was unmistakably British, professionally modulated, with the kind of accent that spoke of expensive education and intelligence training. "I believe we need to talk."

"Sarah Blackwood."

"Very good. I was beginning to wonder if your academic reputation was deserved." There was amusement in her voice, the confidence of someone who held all the cards. "I have a proposition for you."

"I'm listening."

"You want to reach Genghis Khan's tomb. So do I. But we both have a problem—Kenji Yamamoto and his Red Lotus organization are mobilizing substantial resources to beat us there."

Barry caught Sakura's eye, seeing his own skepticism reflected in her expression. "And you're suggesting we work together?"

"I'm suggesting we acknowledge reality. You have the map fragments and the historical expertise. I have the resources and intelligence capabilities. Separately, we'll both lose to Yamamoto's superior numbers and funding."

"What makes you think we'd trust you after everything you've done?"

Blackwood's laugh was cold and professional. "Because you don't have a choice, Dr. Curtis. Yamamoto's people are already in Mongolia, establishing base camps and conducting preliminary surveys. While you've been playing games with safe houses and encrypted phones, he's been building an operation that would make a military invasion jealous."

Sakura leaned toward the phone, her voice deadly calm. "You killed my sister."

"No, Miss Hirata. I failed to protect your sister. There's a difference." For the first time, Blackwood's voice carried a note of something that might have been regret. "Blossom was a remarkable operative and a good person. Her death was... regrettable."

"Regrettable?" Sakura's hand moved instinctively toward the knife she carried.

"Yes. Because it was unnecessary, she could have survived if she'd been willing to share what she'd found. But she chose loyalty to you and your mother over her own survival."

Barry felt the temperature in the room drop several degrees as Sakura processed this information. "You're saying you gave the Red Lotus the information they needed to find her."

"I'm saying the intelligence community is a complex ecosystem, Miss Hirata. Sometimes good people die because they refuse to adapt to changing circumstances."

That was enough. Barry reached for the phone's disconnect button, but Blackwood's next words stopped him cold.

"Dr. Curtis, if you hang up now, Sakura's aunt and uncle in Kyoto will be dead within six hours."

Sakura went completely still, her face draining of color.

"You see," Blackwood continued conversationally, "Yamamoto isn't content to simply beat you to the treasure. He wants to eliminate the Hirata family line entirely. Consider this call a professional courtesy—and an opportunity for all of us to survive what's coming."

Barry looked at Sakura, seeing the same terrible calculation in her eyes that he was making in his own mind. They were trapped between enemies who wanted them dead and an ally who couldn't be trusted.

"What are you proposing?" he asked finally.

"Simple cooperation. I provide transportation, equipment, and intelligence support. You provide the expertise needed to locate and access the tomb. We split whatever we find."

"And after we reach the tomb?"

"After we reach the tomb, Dr. Curtis, we'll discover whether we're partners or competitors. But first, we have to survive long enough to get there."

The line went dead, leaving Barry and Sakura alone in the safe house that no longer felt safe at all.

Chapter 5:
The Mongolian Connection

The Georgetown University campus felt exposed, too open after three days of hiding in a series of increasingly dilapidated safe houses. Barry limped slightly as they approached Healy Hall, his ankle still tender from the fire escape fall. Beside him, Sakura moved with the hypervigilant precision of a hunted animal, her eyes constantly scanning rooftops, windows, and passing vehicles.

"This is a mistake," she murmured, adjusting the scarf that concealed the bruising along her jaw. "Too public. Too predictable."

"Which makes it temporarily safe," Barry countered. "They've hit three properties connected to me. They'll expect us to go deeper underground, not walk onto a university campus in broad daylight."

He didn't add his growing suspicion: that whoever had betrayed them at the Alexandria apartment was still tracking them through means he couldn't identify. Every hiding place had been compromised within hours. Moving constantly seemed their only defense.

The golden sheets and jade box were no longer with them—secured in a bus station locker across town, the key hidden beneath a specific brick in the National Cathedral's garden wall. A precaution that felt simultaneously paranoid and insufficient.

"Tell me about Dr. Batbold again," Sakura said as they climbed the stone steps to the imposing Gothic building.

"Erdene Batbold. Fifty-eight. Visiting professor of Central Asian Studies. Mongolian national with dual American citizenship." Barry kept his voice low despite the crowd of students flowing around them between classes. "He's published extensively on the reign of Genghis Khan, focusing on separating historical fact from mythology."

"And you trust him because...?"

"I don't trust anyone right now." The words came out harsher than intended. Three nights of minimal sleep had frayed his nerves. "But he's the foremost expert on Mongol burial practices, and he once helped Blossom authenticate artifacts from the period. If anyone can verify what we've found and help us understand its significance, it's him."

Sakura's skepticism was palpable, but she followed him into the building. The marble corridors echoed with footsteps and voices as students hurried to classes or gathered in small discussion groups. Normal academic life continued around them, oblivious to the deadly game unfolding in their midst.

Barry led them to the fourth floor, each step sending a dull throb through his injured ankle. The Department of History's corridor was quieter, lined with office doors bearing nameplates and academic cartoons. Dr. Batbold's temporary office was at the far end—a converted storage room allocated to visiting scholars.

Barry knocked three times, then twice more after a pause—the agreed-upon signal.

"Enter," called a deep voice from within.

The office was cramped but meticulously organized, bookshelves lining every available wall space. Maps of Mongolia and the broader Central Asian steppes covered what little wall remained visible. Behind a desk piled with scholarly journals sat Erdene Batbold—a broad-shouldered figure, despite his advanced years, with a weathered face that spoke of a life divided between academia and fieldwork. His silver hair was pulled back in a short ponytail, and wire-rimmed glasses perched on a nose that had been broken at least once.

He rose as they entered, his keen eyes assessing them both before settling on Barry. "Professor Curtis. You look like a man who has seen the horsemen of the apocalypse."

"Something like that." Barry closed the door behind them. "Thank you for agreeing to meet on such short notice."

"Your message mentioned Blossom Hirata." Batbold's expression softened slightly. "I owed her a great debt. She authenticated the Ürümqi scrolls when others dismissed them as forgeries." His gaze shifted to Sakura. "And this must be the sister she spoke of."

Sakura tensed. "She mentioned me?"

"Only in passing. That you had chosen a different path." Batbold gestured to the chairs across from his desk. "Please, sit. Though I suspect this is not a social call."

They sat, Barry positioning himself to keep the door in his peripheral vision. Sakura did the same with the window, which overlooked an internal courtyard four stories below.

"We need your expertise," Barry began carefully. "And your discretion."

"Those often go hand in hand in our profession." Batbold removed his glasses, polishing them with a handkerchief. "What exactly have you found, Professor Curtis?"

Barry hesitated, measuring his next words. "Evidence regarding the burial site of Genghis Khan."

The change in Batbold was subtle but immediate—a slight stiffening of his posture, a narrowing of his eyes. "That is... a significant claim."

"Not a claim. Evidence." Barry leaned forward. "Golden map fragments with astronomical alignments pointing to a specific location in the Khentii Mountains."

Batbold replaced his glasses with deliberate slowness. "And you believe these fragments are authentic?"

"Blossom authenticated them before her death. And they've already cost multiple lives."

The Mongolian professor's face remained impassive, but his knuckles whitened where they rested on the desk. "People have searched for the Khan's burial site for eight centuries. The Japanese. The Russians. Even the Nazis. All failed."

"Because they didn't have the complete map," Sakura interjected. "We do."

Batbold studied her with new intensity. "And how did you come to possess such a thing, Ms. Hirata?"

"Family legacy. Protected across generations." Her tone made it clear she would elaborate no further.

A heavy silence filled the small office. Outside, rain began to patter against the window, distorting the view of the courtyard below. The weather matched the darkening mood within.

"If what you say is true," Batbold finally said, "you are in grave danger. Not just from whoever is pursuing you, but from my own government."

Barry exchanged a glance with Sakura. "Explain."

Batbold rose and moved to the window, looking out at the rain. "Genghis Khan is not merely a historical figure to Mongolians. He is our national identity personified. Our pride. Our soul." He turned back to face them. "For centuries, foreign powers have sought his burial site—not to honor him, but to plunder his legacy."

"We're not treasure hunters," Barry insisted.

"Perhaps not. But the Mongolian government established the Burkhan Khaldun Special Protection Area in 2021 specifically to guard what many believe is the general region of the burial site." Batbold's expression hardened. "They monitor all archaeological expeditions in the area. Foreign researchers require special permits that are rarely granted. The military patrols the most sacred areas."

Sakura leaned forward. "You're saying the government knows the location?"

"No. They know the approximate region, as scholars have for centuries. The Khentii Mountains, likely near Burkhan Khaldun—the most sacred peak." Batbold returned to his desk, lowering his voice. "But specific coordinates? No. If they possessed those, they would have excavated already, despite traditional taboos against disturbing the great Khan's rest."

"Then why the military presence?" Barry asked.

"Because they fear exactly what you represent—outsiders with the means to locate and potentially plunder our greatest historical treasure." Batbold removed a leather-bound book from his desk drawer and placed it before them. "This is a restricted governmental report on all known expeditions to search for the tomb since 1990. Twenty-seven attempts, most illegal. All prevented."

Barry opened the book, finding photographs of excavation equipment seized by Mongolian authorities, maps with restricted zones clearly marked, and surveillance photos of Western and Asian researchers being detained.

"Jesus," he murmured.

"The stakes are higher than you realize," Batbold continued. "This isn't merely archaeological. It's geopolitical. Chinese authorities have made quiet overtures about joint excavation rights, claiming a historical connection through the Yuan Dynasty. The Russians have their own claims based on the later Mongol Empire's reach. Even the Japanese—"

"The Red Lotus," Sakura interrupted. "You know about them."

It wasn't a question. Batbold's expression confirmed her suspicion.

"The Aka Hasu Society," he nodded grimly. "They've sent three expeditions in the past decade alone. Their interest is... concerning."

"They're not after archaeological fame," Barry explained. "They believe the tomb contains the Altan Debter—the Book of Gold. The secret history and military knowledge of the Mongol Empire."

"Which they intend to use," Sakura added. "Their new leader, Kenji Yamamoto, has modernized their approach. Better technology, better connections, better weapons."

Batbold's eyebrows rose slightly. "You seem remarkably well-informed about a supposedly secret society, Ms. Hirata."

"They murdered my sister and my mother." Her voice was flat, emotionless. "I've made it my business to know everything about them."

The office fell silent again, broken only by the increasing tempo of rain against the window and the distant rumble of thunder. The storm that had been threatening all morning was finally breaking.

"I understand your personal stakes," Batbold said eventually. "But you must understand mine. The Khan's resting place is one of the most significant cultural heritage sites in Mongolian history. If it exists—if you truly have the means to locate it—then it belongs to the Mongolian people."

"We agree," Barry said quickly. "Any artifacts, any historical knowledge—all of it should return to Mongolia."

"Yet you came to America with this discovery, not to Ulaanbaatar."

"Because we're being hunted," Sakura snapped. "Because people are dying. Because the Red Lotus has resources inside multiple governments—possibly including yours."

Batbold considered this, fingers steepled beneath his chin. The rain had intensified, drumming against the window with growing urgency. Lightning flashed, briefly illuminating the courtyard below.

"What exactly do you want from me?" he asked finally.

Barry leaned forward. "Authentication of what we've found. Help interpreting the astronomical alignments and geographical markers. And..." he hesitated, "a secure contact in Ulaanbaatar. Someone we can trust when we go to Mongolia."

"When?" Batbold's eyebrows rose. "Not if?"

"The Red Lotus is closing in," Sakura said. "We can't keep running. We need to find the tomb before they do."

Batbold fell silent, his weathered face unreadable. He opened a drawer and withdrew what appeared to be an ancient bronze seal, placing it on the desk between them.

"This was given to me by my grandfather," he said quietly. "A family heirloom passed through generations. It bears the mark of the Borjigin clan—the Khan's direct lineage." He met Barry's eyes. "My ancestors served the great Khan. Some say they were entrusted with knowledge of his final resting place."

Barry stared at the seal, its patina speaking of immense age. "You know more than you've published."

"There are some things that shouldn't be written." Batbold's voice had dropped to nearly a whisper. "Some knowledge that can only be passed directly, protected from those who would misuse it."

The implication hung in the air between them. Barry felt a familiar scholarly excitement rising beneath his fear—the historian's thrill of touching hidden knowledge.

"Will you help us?" he asked.

Before Batbold could answer, Sakura's posture changed. She straightened, head tilting slightly toward the window.

"What is it?" Barry asked, instantly alert.

"Reflection in the building across the courtyard. Fourth floor, second window from the left." Her voice was calm, professional. "Someone with binoculars."

Barry didn't turn to look. "Could be a student, a professor—"

"With military-grade tactical binoculars? In a maintenance room?" Sakura's hand moved subtly toward her concealed weapon. "We've been compromised. Again."

Batbold's expression darkened. "How would they know to find you here?"

"That's the question that's kept us alive the past three days," Barry said grimly. "Someone is tracking us, but we haven't figured out how."

A new tension filled the small office. Barry assessed their options—one door, one window, four stories up. No good escape route.

"We need to move," Sakura said, rising smoothly. "Now."

Batbold held up his hand. "Wait." He opened another drawer and withdrew a small leather pouch and a folded paper. "If what you say is true, if you truly possess the map to the Khan's resting place, then you must have this."

He handed the paper to Barry. "My contact in Ulaanbaatar. Tuguldur Sechen. He operates a guide service for the Khentii Mountains, but was once a member of Mongolian intelligence. He can be trusted—to a point."

"And this?" Sakura asked, indicating the leather pouch.

"Insurance." Batbold placed it in her hand. "A talisman that marks you as operating with the blessing of the Borjigin clan. It may mean nothing to foreigners, but to certain Mongolians in the region, it grants protection."

Lightning flashed again, followed almost immediately by a deafening crack of thunder. The storm was directly overhead now, rain lashing against the window with violent intensity.

Sakura moved to the door, checking the corridor through a narrow opening. "Clear for now."

"Go," Batbold urged. "Use the east stairwell. Less trafficked. I will create a distraction."

"Come with us," Barry insisted. "If they've identified your connection to us—"

"My place is here." Batbold's resolve was evident. "Besides, an old Mongolian professor attracts less attention than two foreigners fleeing a building."

Barry hesitated, then extended his hand. "Thank you."

Batbold clasped it firmly. "Honor the Khan's rest. Ensure that what you find returns to Mongolia. That is all the thanks I require."

Sakura had the door open wider now, scanning the corridor. "Still clear. We need to—"

The window exploded inward in a shower of glass and rain. The concussive force of the blast threw them all to the floor as smoke filled the small office. Through ringing ears, Barry heard Sakura shouting, saw her draw her weapon, and return fire through the shattered window.

Batbold lay crumpled against his desk, blood streaming from a gash in his forehead. Barry crawled toward him as more gunfire erupted—this time from the corridor. The door splintered under automatic weapons fire.

"Professor!" Sakura shouted over the chaos. "Second exit!"

Barry looked around wildly, seeing nothing but smoke and debris. Batbold grabbed his arm with surprising strength, pulling him closer.

"Behind the map," the Mongolian gasped, blood bubbling at his lips. "Maintenance access. Go!"

Barry saw it then—a large map of the Mongol Empire mounted on the wall concealed a small maintenance door. He ripped the map aside to reveal the narrow entrance.

"Sakura! Here!"

She was crouched by the shattered window, returning controlled bursts of fire toward unseen attackers in the building across the courtyard. At his call, she backed toward him, still firing.

"Get Batbold!" she ordered.

Barry turned to the fallen professor, but one look told him it was too late. A large shard of glass had pierced Batbold's chest. His eyes were fixed and staring, blood pooling beneath him.

"He's gone," Barry shouted over the gunfire.

"Then don't waste his sacrifice!" Sakura grabbed his jacket, shoving him toward the maintenance door. "Move!"

The narrow door opened to a dusty utility corridor barely wide enough for their shoulders. Pipes ran along the ceiling, and the air smelled of mildew and forgotten spaces. They moved as quickly as the confined space allowed, the sounds of gunfire and shouting diminishing behind them.

"Batbold," Barry gasped as they ran. "He knew more than he was telling us."

"They all do," Sakura replied grimly. "Everyone in this game has their own agenda."

The utility corridor ended at a metal ladder leading down. They descended rapidly, emerging into a basement maintenance area filled with humming machinery and pipes wrapped in asbestos. Distant alarms were sounding now—the university responding to gunfire in an academic building.

"Which way?" Barry asked, disoriented in the labyrinthine basement.

Sakura pointed to a faded emergency exit sign. "There. Should lead to the service entrance."

They pushed through the heavy door into the ongoing storm. Rain lashed them immediately, soaking through their clothes as they emerged into a loading dock area. Campus security vehicles were already converging on the main building, lights flashing through the downpour. In the distance, police sirens wailed.

"This way," Sakura pulled him toward a service road that led away from the main campus. "Stay in the tree line."

They ran through the deluge, feet splashing through puddles, the wet foliage providing minimal cover. Barry's ankle protested each impact, but adrenaline dulled the pain. Behind them, more sirens joined the chorus—police, possibly ambulances.

Another man dead. Another connection severed. The pattern was becoming sickeningly familiar.

"How did they find us?" Barry gasped as they reached the relative shelter of a campus parking structure. "It doesn't make sense."

Sakura didn't answer immediately. Instead, she pulled him between parked cars and began methodically checking his clothing, patting down seams and crevices.

"What are you—"

"Hold still." Her hands moved with professional efficiency, checking his collar, the lining of his jacket, and his belt. Finally, she found what she was looking for—a device no larger than a button battery sewn into the lining of his jacket collar.

She held it up, expression grim. "Tracker. Military grade. Activated by body heat."

Barry stared at the tiny device. "When? How?"

"The museum, most likely. Professional brush pass when we were separated." She crushed the device beneath her heel. "They've been following your jacket, not you."

The realization hit him like a physical blow. "Batbold. If I'd figured this out sooner—"

"Don't." Sakura's voice was sharp. "Guilt doesn't help us survive. Focus on what matters now."

What mattered now. Barry forced himself to compartmentalize, to push aside the image of Batbold bleeding out on his office floor. "The contact in Ulaanbaatar. The talisman."

Sakura nodded, producing the leather pouch Batbold had given her. It had survived their escape, though dampened by the rain. She opened it carefully to reveal an ancient bronze medallion on a leather cord, with intricate knotwork surrounding what appeared to be a falcon or eagle design.

"The mark of the Borjigin clan," Barry murmured. "Genghis Khan's family emblem."

"Will it actually help us in Mongolia?"

"If Batbold was telling the truth about his lineage, possibly." Barry took the folded paper from his pocket, now damp but still legible. "Tuguldur Sechen. Our contact in Ulaanbaatar."

Sakura took the paper, memorizing the information before carefully refolding it. "We need to assume Yamamoto knows about him too now."

"Then we need to reach him first."

The sirens were closer now, multiple vehicles converging on the university. They couldn't stay here much longer.

"We've lost the advantage of secrecy," Sakura said, calculation in her eyes. "We need to change strategy. Move faster. Get to Mongolia before they can mobilize their full resources."

"After what just happened? They'll be watching airports, train stations—"

"Not all routes." Her expression was cold and determined. "I have contacts who can get us out of the country undetected. But we need to move now, tonight."

Barry hesitated, the academic in him reflexively wanting to analyze, to plan. But Batbold's blood was still drying on his hands, and the jade box and golden sheets remained hidden across town, vulnerable.

"The artifacts," he began.

"We retrieve them, then disappear." Sakura was already moving toward the far end of the parking structure. "From this moment, Professor Curtis ceases to exist. The man who walks into Mongolia will be someone else entirely."

The rain continued to pound the concrete around them, washing away footprints almost as quickly as they were made. Thunder rolled across the sky like distant artillery. Through a gap in the structure, Barry could see emergency vehicles surrounding Healy Hall, their lights pulsing red and blue through the downpour.

Another death. Another escalation. The consequences of knowledge that had remained hidden for eight centuries.

Barry followed Sakura into the storm, leaving behind the last vestiges of his academic life. Ahead lay Mongolia, the Khentii Mountains, and the tomb of history's greatest conqueror.

And hunting them every step of the way, the shadows of the Red Lotus, closing in like storm clouds over the steppes.

Chapter 6: Escape from Virginia

The safe house in Arlington smelled of mildew and desperation. Rain lashed against boarded windows, each drop a metronome counting down the little time they had left. Barry stood in the cramped bathroom, scrubbing Dr. Batbold's dried blood from beneath his fingernails with surgical intensity. The pink-tinged water swirled down the rust-stained drain, but the memory remained—another death, another life sacrificed to the knowledge they carried.

"They're moving faster than anticipated," Sakura's voice came from the doorway. She'd changed into nondescript clothing—dark cargo pants, a gray thermal shirt, and a black windbreaker—the uniform of someone who wished to disappear. "Police bulletins describe us as 'armed suspects' in connection with a shooting at Georgetown. Your face is already circulating."

Barry turned off the water but didn't turn around. "And yours?"

"Grainy CCTV footage only. My face was partially concealed."

"Small mercies." He dried his hands on a threadbare towel, finally facing her. "How long can we stay here?"

"Six hours, maximum. The property belongs to a defunct shell corporation three layers removed from anyone who might connect to us." Sakura moved back into the main room, a spartan space containing only a folding table, two metal chairs, and a mattress on the floor. "But we should assume nowhere is truly secure."

Barry followed, wincing as his injured ankle protested. The adrenaline that had carried him through their escape from Georgetown had faded, leaving raw pain in its wake. "We need help."

"We have no one to trust."

"Jim Beasley," Barry insisted, lowering himself carefully into one of the metal chairs. "My former department chair. He's helped me before, after the Solomon Islands. He has connections—diplomatic, academic, intelligence community."

Sakura's expression hardened. "The same Jim who knew you were meeting Batbold? The meeting that was somehow compromised?"

The implication hung in the stale air between them. Barry wanted to deny it, to defend the man who'd been like a father to him after his return without Blossom. But the evidence was damning—every move they'd made had been anticipated, every sanctuary breached.

"I need to hear his voice," Barry said finally. "I'll know if he's involved."

Sakura considered this, calculation visible behind her eyes. "One call. Untraceable. One minute maximum." She withdrew a burner phone from her backpack. "If I sense anything wrong, I end it."

Barry nodded, taking the phone with fingers that weren't quite steady. He dialed Jim's private number from memory, holding his breath as it rang once, twice, three times.

"Department of History, Professor Beasley." Jim's voice sounded strained, tired.

"Jim, it's me." Barry kept his voice low, controlled.

Silence for two heartbeats, then: "My God, Barry. Where are you? The police were here. They're saying you're involved in Batbold's murder. There's footage of—"

"I didn't kill him, Jim. You know I wouldn't." Barry closed his eyes, listening not just to the words but to the tone, the cadence, searching for any hint of deception. "Batbold was helping us translate something. The people who killed Blossom found us."

"The Red Lotus." Jim's voice dropped to a whisper. "Barry, this is bigger than before. Diplomatic channels are buzzing. The Mongolian Embassy is involved. There are rumors about government agents and international antiquities theft."

"We need help, Jim. Safe passage. New identities."

Sakura tensed visibly at this, her hand moving toward the phone, but Barry shook his head slightly. Trust me, his eyes pleaded.

A long pause on the line. "The Fitzroy Protocol," Jim said finally. "Remember when we discussed it after you returned? For worst-case scenarios?"

Barry's breath caught. The Fitzroy Protocol—a contingency plan Jim had put in place after Barry's return from the Solomon Islands. Named after a 19th-century explorer who had famously disappeared in Africa only to reemerge years later under a new identity. They'd discussed it only once, in hushed tones, in Jim's book-lined office with the door locked and classical music playing to thwart any listening devices.

"I remember," Barry confirmed.

"Twenty-four hours. The arrangements will be waiting at the third location we discussed. After that, you're on your own." Jim's voice cracked slightly. "Barry, are you sure about this? Once you activate Fitzroy, there's no coming back to your old life."

Barry looked around the decrepit safe house, at Sakura's vigilant posture, at his own blood-flecked cuffs. "My old life ended in a flooded chamber in the Solomon Islands, Jim. I just didn't admit it until now."

"God help you then." A pause. "Be careful who you trust, Barry. Even those closest to you."

The line went dead. Sakura took the phone, removing the battery and SIM card in one practiced motion before crushing them under her boot.

"Well?" she demanded.

"He's not compromised," Barry said with certainty. "The Fitzroy Protocol is something only he and I know about. A contingency plan for extreme circumstances."

"Specifics."

"New identities. Untraceable funds. Transportation routes that bypass normal security checkpoints." Barry rubbed his temples, feeling the weight of the decision settling on him. "It means abandoning everything—my career, my home, any hope of returning to my former life."

"You've been living as a ghost already," Sakura observed dispassionately. "At least now it will be official."

The truth of her words stung. Since Blossom's death, he'd merely been going through the motions, a shadow of his former self. Perhaps this final severing was simply acknowledging what had already happened.

"Twenty-four hours," he said. "We need to reach the storage facility in Alexandria, where the third drop point is located."

"Too risky. Alexandria will be crawling with authorities after what happened at Georgetown."

"We have no choice. It's the only way to access the Fitzroy Protocol."

Lightning flashed outside, momentarily illuminating the room through gaps in the boarded windows. Thunder followed almost immediately, the storm directly overhead.

"Fine." Sakura checked her watch. "We move at 3 AM. Less surveillance, reduced police presence due to shift changes." She reached into her pack and withdrew a small medical kit. "Now let me see that ankle."

Barry extended his leg reluctantly. Sakura knelt, cutting away his sodden sock with efficient movements. The ankle had swollen considerably, with mottled purple bruising spreading across the joint.

"Grade two sprain," she diagnosed, hands probing with clinical detachment. "You're lucky it's not broken."

"Doesn't feel lucky," Barry winced as she manipulated the joint.

"Pain means you're still alive." She began wrapping the ankle with practiced precision. "Dead men feel nothing."

As she worked, Barry studied her—the controlled movements. This hypervigilance never fully abated even in relative safety, the tactical assessment that seemed to run continuously behind her eyes. So different from Blossom, whose enthusiasm and warmth had drawn people in. Sakura kept the world at a calculated distance.

"Who trained you?" he asked abruptly.

Her hands paused fractionally before continuing their work. "Multiple sources."

"That's not an answer."

"It's the only one you're getting for now." She secured the bandage with medical tape. "Rest. I'll take first watch."

Barry didn't move. "No more evasions, Sakura. If we're going to survive this, we need truth between us. All of it."

Her eyes met his, unflinching. "Truth is a luxury, Professor. One we can't afford until we're safely out of the country."

"Batbold died because we weren't prepared. Because we didn't have all the information." Barry leaned forward, ignoring the pain as he shifted his weight. "What aren't you telling me?"

For a moment, he thought she would maintain her silence. Then something shifted in her expression—a calculation made, a decision reached.

"I haven't been working alone," she admitted. "I have... a partner. Someone who shares my interest in stopping the Red Lotus."

"Who?"

"His name is Takashi Ishida. Former Japanese Intelligence. Now private contractor."

The revelation hung between them, its implications expanding like ripples in still water. "Intelligence," Barry repeated. "Espionage."

"Among other specialties." Sakura rose, moving to check the perimeter seals on the boarded windows. "He approached me after my mother's murder, offered resources, information."

"And what does he want in return?"

"The same thing I want. To destroy the Red Lotus." She turned back to face him. "And to ensure the Khan's legacy doesn't fall into dangerous hands."

Barry processed this new information, connecting dots that suddenly aligned. "The sophisticated tracking countermeasures. The military-grade equipment. The safe houses." He shook his head. "You've been reporting to him all along."

"Coordinating," she corrected. "There's a difference."

"Does he know about the golden sheets? The map fragments?"

"He knows we have information leading to the tomb location. Not the specifics."

Barry stood despite his ankle's protest, anger providing temporary relief from pain. "You've put us both at risk. If this Ishida has government connections—"

"Former government," Sakura interrupted. "He was forced out three years ago for questioning certain political relationships, including connections between Japanese officials and the Red Lotus."

"So he's a rogue agent with a vendetta. That's supposed to reassure me?"

"He has resources we need. Connections in Mongolia that Batbold couldn't provide." Sakura's tone remained measured, reasonable. "And he has a plane waiting in West Virginia. Small airstrip, minimal security. It's our best chance to leave the country undetected."

Barry paced the small room, mind racing through implications. "And once we reach Mongolia? What then? Does Ishida expect to claim the discovery? To control what happens to the artifacts we find?"

"His priority is ensuring the Red Lotus doesn't obtain whatever weapons technology might be contained in the Book of Gold."

"And what's your priority, Sakura?" Barry stopped, facing her directly. "Revenge for your sister and mother? Archaeological integrity? Or something else entirely?"

A flicker of genuine emotion crossed her face—the first Barry had seen beyond her professional mask. "My priority is finishing what Blossom started. Protecting what our family has guarded for generations." Her voice dropped. "And yes, ensuring that those responsible for her death answer for it."

The raw honesty in her tone resonated with something in Barry's own chest—the grief and rage he'd suppressed for eighteen months, buried beneath academic detachment and isolation.

"We need to be clear with each other," he said finally. "No more secrets. No more separate agendas. If we're doing this together, we're truly together."

Sakura studied him for a long moment before nodding once, decisively. "Agreed. Starting now—full disclosure."

"Starting with this Ishida. I want to know everything about him before we get on his plane."

"Fair enough." She reached into her pack again, withdrawing a slim laptop. "I'll show you his dossier. Everything I have."

As she booted up the computer, a notification pinged on her satellite phone. Sakura checked it, her expression darkening immediately.

"What is it?" Barry asked.

"Local police bulletin. They've found the bus station locker." She looked up, eyes hard. "The golden sheets and jade box are gone."

Barry felt the floor drop from beneath him. "Impossible. No one knew about that location except—"

"You and me," Sakura finished. "And whoever has been tracking our movements despite all countermeasures."

The implications were staggering. Either one of them was compromised, or they were dealing with surveillance capabilities far beyond what they'd anticipated.

"We need to move. Now." Sakura was already packing, movements swift and economical. "Forget 3 AM. If they've found the artifacts, they'll be closing in on this location next."

Barry moved to help, ignoring the throbbing pain in his ankle. "The Fitzroy Protocol—"

"Still our best option, but we need a new approach." She handed him a small backpack. "Essentials only. Be ready to run in three minutes."

As they hastily packed, the satellite phone pinged again. Sakura checked it, her face revealing nothing.

"Ishida," she explained. "He's tracked unusual communications between multiple agencies: FBI, Homeland Security, and a Japanese diplomatic channel known to be used by Red Lotus sympathizers."

"They're coordinating," Barry realized. "Official and unofficial channels working together."

"They're squeezing the net. Roadblocks on major arteries leaving the DC area. Surveillance teams at train and bus stations." She paused. "And Jim Beasley was just taken into custody for questioning."

The news hit Barry like a physical blow. Jim, arrested because of his connection to them. Another life disrupted, possibly destroyed. The cost of the knowledge they carried continued to mount.

"The Fitzroy Protocol might be compromised," he acknowledged grimly.

"Ishida has an alternative. The extraction team is en route to a location twenty miles from here. They can have us on the plane within three hours."

Barry hesitated, weighing options that all seemed to lead to deeper entanglements with forces beyond his control. "Do we have a choice?"

"There's always a choice, Professor." Sakura's voice was flat. "Survive on someone else's terms, or die on our own."

Outside, the storm intensified, rain hammering against the boarded windows like bullets. Thunder crashed overhead, and for a brief moment, the power flickered, plunging them into darkness before sputtering back to life.

"How do we get past the roadblocks?" Barry asked, shouldering his pack.

"We don't." Sakura moved to a corner of the room, pulling back a section of stained carpet to reveal a hatch in the floor. "We go under. Maintenance tunnels connect this building to the old industrial complex two blocks east. From there, we can access the storm drainage system."

"The drainage system? In this weather?" Barry gestured toward the window where rain continued to lash against the boards. "Flash flooding—"

"Is a risk we'll have to take. The alternatives are worse." She lifted the hatch, revealing a rusty ladder descending into darkness. The smell of damp earth and stagnant water rose from below. "Ishida's people will meet us at the eastern outlet, near the abandoned paper mill."

Barry peered into the abyss, doubt gnawing at him. "And you trust these people? Ishida's extraction team?"

"I trust their professionalism." Sakura checked her weapon one last time before securing it in a waterproof holster. "The rest is irrelevant."

A crack of thunder directly overhead shook the building. Through gaps in the boarded windows, Barry caught glimpses of the storm-ravaged night—tree branches whipping in the wind, rain falling in horizontal sheets.

"The tunnels will be flooding already," he warned.

"Then we move quickly." Sakura handed him a waterproof flashlight. "Stay close. Follow my exact path. The structural integrity of these tunnels is questionable at best."

She descended the ladder first, disappearing into the darkness below. Barry took one last look around the safe house—another temporary shelter about to be abandoned, another fragile sanctuary breached.

The golden sheets were gone. The jade box seized. All they had left were the knowledge in their heads and the coordinates committed to memory. And now they were about to place their lives in the hands of a former Japanese intelligence agent with unknown motives.

Barry lowered himself onto the ladder, his injured ankle screaming in protest as he put weight on it. Below, Sakura's flashlight illuminated a narrow tunnel with crumbling concrete walls, a stream of murky water already flowing along its base.

"Faster," she called up. "Water's rising."

He descended into the darkness, pulling the hatch closed above him. The sound of the storm became muffled, replaced by the ominous gurgle of water seeping through the ancient infrastructure.

The tunnel stretched before them, a throat of concrete and brick swallowing them into the earth. Sakura moved with confident purpose, but Barry couldn't shake the sensation of entering a tomb—perhaps a fitting symmetry, given what they sought half a world away.

"Eighteen minutes to the first junction," Sakura said, her voice echoing oddly in the confined space. "After that, we follow the main drainage pipe east for approximately half a mile."

They waded forward, the water already ankle-deep and rising. Barry's injured joint throbbed with each step, but he forced himself to maintain pace. Their flashlight beams carved twin tunnels through the absolute darkness, revealing glimpses of a forgotten underworld—maintenance markings faded to ghostly smudges, rusted pipes running along cracked ceilings, and occasional side tunnels branching off into impenetrable blackness.

"Who built these?" Barry asked, partly from academic curiosity, partly to distract himself from the claustrophobic pressure.

"Cold War era," Sakura replied without slowing. "Part infrastructure, part civil defense. Most were abandoned by the 1970s."

The water continued to rise, now approaching their knees. The current was strengthening too, pushing against them as they moved forward. Behind them, an ominous rumbling grew—the sound of water under pressure seeking release.

"It's rising too fast," Barry warned, fighting to maintain his footing on the slippery tunnel floor.

"We're almost at the junction." Sakura increased her pace. "Once we're in the main drainage pipe, we'll have more clearance."

A sudden surge of water hit them from behind, nearly knocking Barry off his feet. He caught himself against the tunnel wall, the rough concrete scraping his palm raw.

"Flash flood," Sakura confirmed what they both already knew. "Run."

They abandoned caution, splashing forward as the water level rose with terrifying speed. Ahead, the tunnel widened into a junction chamber, where multiple conduits converged. Sakura pointed to a maintenance platform built into one wall, elevated about four feet above the current water level.

"There!"

They made for it as another surge hit, water now at mid-thigh and powerful enough to threaten their balance with each step. Barry's ankle gave out just as they reached the platform. Sakura caught him, her strength surprising as she hauled him up beside her.

They crouched on the narrow platform, watching as the water continued to rise below them, carrying debris—branches, trash, a child's forgotten toy swirling in the murky current.

"How much higher will it get?" Barry asked, trying to keep his voice steady.

Sakura's flashlight played across the chamber, revealing water marks on the walls well above their current position. "We need to keep moving. This platform won't stay dry for long."

She indicated a larger tunnel opening on the opposite side of the chamber, about twenty feet away. "That's our route east. There's a maintenance walkway along the side."

"And how do we cross this?" Barry gestured to the churning water between them and their escape route.

Sakura was already removing a coil of thin, high-tensile rope from her pack. "I'll secure a line."

Before Barry could protest, she had secured one end to a rusted but seemingly solid pipe behind them. Then, with a runner's burst of speed, she leapt from the platform across the churning water, landing with athletic precision on a narrow outcropping near the larger tunnel.

She secured the other end of the rope to a metal bracket, creating a handhold across the gap. "Your turn, Professor."

Barry eyed the distance, the roiling water, his injured ankle. The academic in him calculated the physics, the probabilities, the likely outcomes—none favorable.

"Trust the rope," Sakura called. "Not your ankle. Upper body strength."

Another surge of water rose below them, splashing onto the platform. They were out of time and options.

Barry gripped the rope with both hands, his knuckles white. Taking a deep breath, he pushed off from the platform, his body swinging out over the churning water. His injured ankle dragged uselessly as he pulled himself across, hand over hand, muscles burning with the effort.

Halfway across, the metal bracket on Sakura's end groaned, bending slightly under the tension. The rope dipped, lowering Barry closer to the surging water below.

"Keep moving!" Sakura urged, bracing herself against the bracket to reinforce it.

Barry redoubled his efforts, adrenaline masking the fire in his shoulders and arms. Three more pulls and he was within reach of the outcropping. Sakura grabbed his jacket, hauling him the final distance to safety just as the bracket gave way completely.

They collapsed against the tunnel wall, breathing heavily. The rope's end slithered away into the churning water like a dying snake.

"That was our only rope," Barry noted between gasps.

"We won't need it again." Sakura was already recovering, checking her pack to ensure nothing had been lost. "The maintenance walkway runs the entire length of this main pipe."

The walkway in question was a narrow concrete shelf built into the side of the larger tunnel, barely wide enough for single-file travel. Below it, stormwater thundered eastward, carrying increasing amounts of debris.

"Half a mile on this?" Barry eyed the treacherous path dubiously.

"Unless you'd prefer to swim." Sakura was already moving ahead, flashlight illuminating their precarious route. "Stay close to the wall. Test each step before committing your weight."

They proceeded cautiously, the roar of water filling the tunnel, making conversation impossible. Their flashlight beams caught glimpses of a parallel world beneath the city—junction boxes with faded warning labels, century-old brickwork intersecting with more modern concrete repairs, and the occasional service ladder rising toward distant manhole covers.

The walkway narrowed in places, forcing them to sidle along with their backs pressed against the curved wall of the tunnel. In other sections, portions had crumbled away entirely, requiring precarious leaps across gaps with certain death flowing beneath.

Time lost meaning in the thunderous darkness. It might have been twenty minutes or two hours when Sakura finally raised her hand, signaling a halt. Ahead, their flashlights revealed a larger chamber where the tunnel opened into what appeared to be a collection basin. Daylight—or what passed for it during the ongoing storm—filtered down through a massive grate about thirty feet above.

"The outlet," Sakura shouted over the water's roar. "The extraction team should be waiting topside."

She consulted a small GPS device, confirming their position before pointing to a maintenance ladder built into the far wall of the basin. "That's our way up."

The final challenge lay before them—crossing the collection basin where multiple water flows converged into a churning maelstrom. The walkway ended at their position, with no visible continuation to the ladder on the far side.

"Now what?" Barry asked, exhaustion making his voice sharp.

Sakura's flashlight played across the upper sections of the chamber, revealing a series of pipes running across the ceiling. "Up and over."

Before Barry could protest, she was already climbing a service access built into the wall, making for the overhead pipes. He followed more slowly, his injured ankle and exhausted arms making each movement a study in controlled agony.

The pipes were slick with condensation, but wide enough to provide a precarious path across the basin. Sakura moved across them with gymnastic precision, while Barry followed with academic determination, focusing on each movement to the exclusion of all else—hand here, foot there, balance, shift, repeat.

They reached the far side as another surge of water crashed into the basin below, sending spray high enough to dampen their clothes. The ladder before them rose toward the distant grate and whatever awaited them above.

"You first," Sakura insisted. "I'll follow and secure our exit."

Barry didn't argue, saving his remaining strength for the climb. The ladder rungs were slippery with moss and corrosion, threatening to give way with each step. Above, the storm still raged, rain pouring through the grate in miniature waterfalls.

He reached the top, pressing against the heavy metal grate. It didn't budge.

"It's locked," he called down.

Sakura climbed up beside him, examining the mechanism. "Standard municipal lock. Give me space."

She produced a small tool from a waterproof pouch and worked it into the locking mechanism. After several tense moments, something clicked. Together, they pushed upward, the grate rising with a groan of protesting metal.

Rain lashed their faces as they emerged into the storm-battered night. They were in an industrial yard surrounded by the crumbling remnants of the abandoned paper mill. No lights, no vehicles, no sign of the promised extraction team.

"Where are they?" Barry shouted over the wind, helping Sakura secure the grate behind them.

She checked her satellite phone, frowning at the screen. "Signal's blocked. Electromagnetic interference."

Barry scanned their surroundings, the hairs on the back of his neck standing on end. "Or signal-jamming technology."

Sakura's posture changed instantly, a weapon appearing in her hand as she pushed Barry toward the minimal cover of a collapsed loading dock. "Move. Now."

They had barely reached the shelter when bright lights suddenly illuminated the entire yard—vehicle headlights, powerful handheld spots, the unmistakable red dots of laser sights dancing across the rain-soaked ground around them.

"Federal agents!" a voice boomed through an amplified speaker. "You are surrounded. Surrender your weapons and exit with your hands visible."

Sakura pressed Barry deeper into the shadows, her eyes calculating distances, angles, and possible escape routes. Finding none.

"Your Japanese friend sold us out," Barry realized, the betrayal a dull ache beneath his physical exhaustion.

"No." Sakura's certainty was absolute. "This isn't Ishida's style. This is someone else. Someone who's been one step ahead from the beginning."

The amplified voice came again: "Professor Curtis. Ms. Hirata. You have thirty seconds to surrender before we deploy tactical teams."

Barry met Sakura's eyes in the reflected glare of the encircling lights. "What now?"

For the first time since meeting her, Sakura Hirata looked uncertain. "I don't know."

The storm raged around them, rain washing away any trace of their desperate journey through the underworld. Beyond the blinding lights, shadowy figures moved into position—the noose tightening, options vanishing.

The countdown had begun.

Chapter 7: Stopover in Istanbul

I stanbul unfolded beneath them as the plane banked sharply, revealing the glittering confluence of the Bosphorus and the Golden Horn. Hagia Sophia and the Blue Mosque punctuated the skyline like sentinels from another age, their minarets piercing the haze of early evening. In another life, Barry might have admired the historian's view in him, recognizing the palimpsest of civilizations layered across the ancient city.

Now, he saw only potential threats. Escape routes. Surveillance points.

"Thinking like a hunted animal already," he muttered to himself, rubbing his eyes. Three days of minimal sleep had left him raw, nerves frayed to breaking point.

Beside him, Sakura stared out the window with a calculated assessment rather than wonder. "A two-hour layover is too long," she said quietly. "We're exposed."

Their flight from West Virginia had been a masterpiece of evasion—Jim's contact piloting them in a private charter to a small airstrip in Quebec, then separate commercial flights under their new identities, converging in London before this final leg to Istanbul. Each transition executed with meticulous precision, each new boarding pass and customs check a moment of heart-stopping tension.

Yet despite every precaution, Barry couldn't shake the sensation of being pursued—invisible eyes tracking their movement across continents, the net drawing tighter with each passing hour.

"Did Ishida confirm our contact?" he asked as the plane touched down with a jarring thud.

Sakura nodded once. "Yusuf will meet us at a carpet shop near the Grand Bazaar. He has our passage to Mongolia arranged."

"And we can trust him?"

Her expression remained neutral. "Ishida says he's reliable. Which means he's likely dangerous, amoral, and expensive—but professional."

The plane taxied to the gate with excruciating slowness. Barry checked his watch—a new one purchased at Heathrow, untraceable—calculating time zones, distances, the hours slipping away while their pursuers closed in.

"They'll have people watching the airports," he murmured. "Standard procedure."

"Not looking for Daniel Pierce and Mei Lin Wong," Sakura reminded him, using their cover identities. "We bypass passport control since we're in transit. Immigration won't flag us."

It sounded reassuring. It wasn't.

As they disembarked, Barry maintained the deliberate slouch he'd adopted for Daniel Pierce—a Canadian geology consultant with chronic back pain, according to his elaborately crafted background. Beside him, Sakura's transformation into Mei Lin Wong was more dramatic—colored contact lenses turning her eyes dark brown, subtle makeup altering the contours of her face, her posture and gait now suggesting academic diffidence rather than coiled combat readiness.

Istanbul International Airport engulfed them in its cavernous modernity—all gleaming surfaces and towering digital displays—a stark contrast to the ancient city beyond. They moved through the transit concourse, bypassing the main immigration channels as Sakura had predicted.

"Keep moving," she murmured. "Security cameras at two o'clock, nine o'clock, and directly overhead."

Barry resisted the urge to look up. "You think facial recognition—"

"Standard practice at international hubs now. Our identities should withstand digital comparison, but minimizing exposure is still prudent."

They navigated the crowded terminal, threading through masses of travelers from across the globe. Every face became a potential threat, every lingering glance a possible recognition. Barry's injured ankle throbbed with each step, the painkillers he'd taken during the flight wearing off too quickly.

Near the terminal's exit, Sakura abruptly veered toward a coffee kiosk. "We're being watched," she said conversationally, as if discussing the weather. "Man by the currency exchange. Blue jacket, reading a newspaper. Hasn't turned a page in six minutes."

Barry didn't look directly but caught the figure in his peripheral vision—middle-aged, nondescript, utterly forgettable except for his unnatural stillness amid the flowing human current.

"Blackwood's people?" he asked.

"Possible. It could also be Turkish intelligence. They monitor transit passengers with connections to Mongolia, especially since the antiquities smuggling crackdown last year." Sakura ordered two coffees in flawless Turkish. "Change of plans. We separate here."

"What? No—"

"Two targets are easier to track than one. I'll create a diversion, draw attention. You proceed to the meeting point." She handed him a small paper with an address written in precise script. "Memorize it, then destroy it."

Barry committed the address to memory before tearing the paper into tiny fragments and dropping them in a nearby trash receptacle. "How will you find me?"

"I'll be right behind you." She handed him one of the coffees. "If I'm not at the meeting point in thirty minutes, proceed without me. Yusuf will know what to do."

Before Barry could protest further, Sakura brushed her lips against his cheek in a convincing display of casual affection. "Make it convincing, Daniel," she whispered, using his cover name.

Then she was moving away, vanishing into the crowd with practiced ease. Barry watched her go, fighting the instinct to follow. Instead, he sipped the bitter Turkish coffee and ambled toward the terminal exit, affecting the mild disorientation of a first-time visitor.

Outside, Istanbul assaulted his senses—the heavy aroma of spices and exhaust fumes, the cacophony of honking horns and merchants' calls, the press of humanity flowing through streets laid down by Roman engineers sixteen centuries earlier. The ancient and modern collided at every corner, creating a disorienting tapestry that even Barry's historian's mind struggled to process in his exhausted state.

He flagged down a taxi, giving the driver an address three blocks from the actual meeting point—another security measure ingrained by days of constant vigilance. The taxi lurched into the chaotic traffic, its driver launching into a rapid monologue in heavily accented English about Istanbul's attractions, seemingly oblivious to Barry's tension.

Through the smudged rear window, Barry scanned for signs of pursuit. Nothing obvious—no vehicles maintaining consistent distance, no motorcycles weaving through traffic with too much purpose. Yet the sensation of being watched persisted, raising the fine hairs on the back of his neck.

The taxi dropped him near the entrance to the Spice Bazaar, its ancient stone archways funneling tourists and locals alike into the labyrinthine market beyond. Barry paid in cash and limped into the crowd, using the dense human traffic as cover while he assessed his surroundings.

Three blocks to the meeting point. Three blocks of exposure, of vulnerability. He checked his watch—twenty-two minutes until Sakura's deadline.

He moved deliberately, maintaining Daniel Pierce's pained slouch while navigating the narrow streets. The evening call to prayer began to sound from minarets across the city, the muezzins' amplified voices creating an otherworldly chorus that momentarily transcended his fear.

Two blocks now. The streets narrowed further, ancient buildings leaning toward each other across the cobblestones, creating shadows despite the lingering summer light. Merchants called out to him from tiny shops overflowing with leather goods, ceramics, textiles—the commercial lifeblood of Istanbul flowing through capillaries too small for modern vehicles.

A flicker of movement reflected in a shop window caught his attention—a figure moving with too much purpose, too directly toward him. Barry's pulse quickened. He cut suddenly into a side alley, its entrance partly concealed by hanging carpets displayed for sale.

The alley opened into a small courtyard surrounded by workshops where artisans still practiced crafts unchanged for centuries. Barry crossed quickly, exiting through another narrow passage that twisted back toward the main street. A classic evasion technique: changing direction while maintaining overall progress toward the objective.

One block remained. The streets here were still older, dating back to Ottoman times, and barely wide enough for two people to pass without touching shoulders. Perfect for ambush. Terrible for escape.

Barry reached for the Glock concealed beneath his jacket, then stopped himself. Drawing a weapon here, in these crowded streets, would only escalate the situation. Instead, he increased his pace, ignoring the complaints from his injured ankle.

The carpet shop appeared ahead—a narrow storefront with intricate kilims and sumptuous carpets hanging from every available surface. Above the door, a faded sign in Turkish, English, and Arabic proclaimed, "Mehmet's Fine Carpets—Established 1842."

Barry checked his surroundings once more before entering. No obvious surveillance. No familiar faces in the crowd. Perhaps his paranoia was just that—imagination fueled by exhaustion and stress.

A bell jangled as he pushed open the shop door. Inside, the space was a riot of color and texture—hundreds of carpets stacked floor to ceiling, hanging from rails, draped across every surface. The air smelled of wool, silk, and the faint sweetness of apple tea.

"Welcome, welcome!" A corpulent man with an impressive mustache emerged from behind a particularly large stack of carpets. "You are American? English? I have the perfect carpet for you!"

"Canadian," Barry corrected automatically. "I'm looking for Yusuf."

The shopkeeper's effusive demeanor vanished instantly. His eyes, previously wide with commercial enthusiasm, narrowed to calculating slits. "No, Yusuf here. Only carpets. Perhaps you could try next door?"

Barry remained in place. "Jim Beasley sent me."

The name acted like a key turning in a lock. The shopkeeper's expression shifted again, not returning to his previous affability but settling into something more genuinely neutral.

"Wait here," he said simply, disappearing behind a curtain at the rear of the shop.

Barry used the moment to scan the shop for exits—the front door, the curtained doorway the shopkeeper had used, and a small window near the back that might accommodate a person in desperate circumstances. Force of habit now, cataloging escape routes wherever he went.

The curtain parted again, revealing not the shopkeeper but a much younger man—lean, with close-cropped hair and the hypervigilant eyes of someone accustomed to danger. He wore expensive Western clothing that somehow failed to conceal his coiled physical presence.

"You are late," the man said without preamble, his English carrying only the faintest trace of an accent. "Where is the woman?"

"Creating a diversion. She'll be here shortly." Barry studied the man. "You're Yusuf?"

A curt nod. "Your documents are ready. Transport arranged. But the price has increased."

"Why?"

"Because now two groups are hunting you, not one." Yusuf gestured toward the back room. "Come. It is not safe to speak here."

Barry hesitated, glancing at his watch. Twelve minutes until Sakura's deadline.

"She will find us," Yusuf said, reading his concern. "If she is still alive."

The casual brutality of the statement struck Barry like a physical blow. He followed Yusuf through the curtain into a back room that contrasted sharply with the shop's chaotic display. Here, everything was ordered with military precision—modern communications equipment on sleek desks, maps covering one wall, multiple computer monitors displaying what appeared to be security feeds from around the bazaar.

"Your operation seems... extensive for a carpet merchant," Barry observed.

Yusuf offered the ghost of a smile. "Carpets are like information. Many layers. Many patterns. Value depends on who is buying." He gestured to a chair. "Sit. You look ready to collapse."

Barry sank into the offered seat, his ankle throbbing in relief. "You mentioned two groups hunting us."

"Yes. The Japanese—they arrived three days ago. Six men, professional, staying at separate hotels, communicating through encrypted channels." Yusuf manipulated one of the computers, bringing up surveillance photos. "Red Lotus, yes?"

Barry nodded, recognizing the calculated dispersion of forces—a trademark of operational security. "And the other group?"

"British. Or pretending to be." Yusuf displayed another set of images—four individuals moving with the disciplined casualness of military personnel attempting to appear civilian. "Arrived this morning. Established surveillance at the airport, train station, major hotels."

"Blackwood," Barry confirmed grimly.

"The woman, yes. She leads them." Yusuf brought up a clearer image—Sarah Blackwood herself, exiting a black SUV near the Grand Bazaar, her auburn hair now platinum blonde, but her imperious bearing unchanged. "Very professional. Very dangerous."

Barry studied the images, a knot forming in his stomach. "How did they know we'd come through Istanbul?"

"Limited routes to Mongolia that bypass normal security protocols." Yusuf shrugged. "They know your destination. They know you need alternate travel arrangements. Istanbul is a logical waypoint."

"And now they're both here. Converging."

"Yes. Making my job more difficult. Hence, higher price." Yusuf named a figure that would have shocked Barry a week ago. Now, it seemed merely another cost of survival.

"Agreed," he said without haggling. Jim's emergency funds would cover it, barely.

Yusuf nodded, satisfied. "Good. Now—"

The security monitors flickered simultaneously, several screens momentarily displaying static before resetting. Yusuf tensed, fingers flying across a keyboard.

"Someone is probing our system," he muttered. "Very sophisticated. Not typical local authorities."

Barry rechecked his watch. Eight minutes until Sakura's deadline. "We need to move. If they've located this place—"

"They have not. Not yet." Yusuf's confidence seemed unshaken. "My security protocols are... substantial."

As if in direct contradiction, the front door's bell jangled. Both men froze, eyes turning to a monitor showing the shop's interior. The corpulent shopkeeper was greeting a Western couple, tourists by their appearance and demeanor, interested in a small kilim displayed near the window.

"Legitimate customers?" Barry asked.

"Perhaps." Yusuf studied the feed with narrowed eyes. "Mehmet will handle them. If they are more than they appear, he will signal."

On screen, the shopkeeper's performance was flawless—the same effusive welcome, the same practiced sales patter. The couple seemed genuinely interested in the carpets, asking questions about provenance and materials.

Barry's attention shifted to another monitor—an exterior view of the street outside the shop. "There," he pointed to a figure loitering across the street, apparently examining goods at a leather seller's stall. "He's watching the entrance."

Yusuf zoomed the camera, the image sharpening to reveal a man Barry recognized from the surveillance photos. "Blackwood's team. Ex-military. British special forces, most likely."

"How many exits does this building have?" Barry asked, tension coiling in his gut.

"Three. Front door, service entrance to the alley behind, and rooftop access to adjacent buildings." Yusuf was already gathering documents from a safe concealed behind a painting—the oldest trick in the world, yet still effective. "We use the roof. Most flexible escape route."

"I need to wait for Sakura," Barry insisted. "Four more minutes."

"If she is coming, she will find an alternative approach." Yusuf handed him a thick envelope. "New passports. Mongolian visas. Currency. Satellite phone numbers. Memorize them, then destroy that paper."

Barry accepted the envelope, tucking it inside his jacket. "And our transportation to Mongolia?"

"Private cargo flight. Departs from the military airfield near Ankara at midnight. We must reach it before—"

The security monitors flashed again, this time going completely dark for several seconds before returning with a different image on each screen—the same symbol, a stylized lotus blossom rendered in blood red against a black background.

"Red Lotus," Barry breathed. "They've hacked your system."

Yusuf's calm finally cracked. "Impossible. My security—"

"Is compromised." Barry was already on his feet, ignoring his ankle's protest. "They're coming. Both groups. Now."

As if confirming his words, the front door's bell jangled again. On the single functioning monitor, they watched four men enter the shop—not bothering with the pretense of carpet shopping, moving with tactical precision to secure the space.

"Blackwood's team," Yusuf confirmed, already moving toward a concealed door at the back of the room. "Roof. Now."

They slipped through the hidden exit into a narrow stairwell that smelled of centuries of cooking odors permeating into ancient stone. Barry followed Yusuf upward, each step sending spikes of pain through his injured joint, each moment expecting the sounds of pursuit from below.

"What about the shopkeeper?" Barry gasped as they climbed.

"Mehmet has been in worse situations." Yusuf's tone suggested this was a significant understatement. "He will claim ignorance, offer carpets, waste their time."

They emerged onto a rooftop bathed in the golden light of late afternoon. Istanbul spread around them in a breathtaking panorama—minarets and domes punctuating the skyline, the Bosphorus glittering in the distance, the ancient city pulsing with life beneath a sky streaked with crimson and gold.

Barry had no time to appreciate the view. Yusuf was already moving across the rooftop toward an adjacent building, separated by a gap of perhaps six feet—trivial for someone uninjured, potentially catastrophic for Barry's damaged ankle.

"I can't make that jump," he admitted, hating the weakness.

Yusuf assessed the situation with cold efficiency. "Then we find another way." He led them toward a different edge of the roof, where the gap to the next building was narrower but the drop steeper if they missed.

Below, shouts erupted from the stairwell—pursuit, closing fast.

"No choice now," Yusuf said grimly. "Jump or be caught."

Barry looked at the gap—barely four feet, but with a three-story drop to unforgiving cobblestones below. Physics and probability calculations raced through his academic mind, none favorable given his condition.

"Professor Curtis!"

The voice came from behind them—not from the stairwell but from another section of the rooftop. Barry spun to see Sakura emerging from a different access point, her disguise partially abandoned, a fresh cut bleeding along her cheekbone.

"Sakura!" Relief flooded him, quickly replaced by renewed urgency. "They've found us. Both groups."

"I know." She moved toward them with lethal grace. "I've been leading Yamamoto's men on a chase through the bazaar. They're two minutes behind me. Maybe less."

Yusuf reassessed immediately. "New plan. Follow me."

He led them not toward the adjacent rooftop but to a small shed-like structure near the center of their current roof. Inside was a maintenance hatch leading to a metal ladder.

"Service access to water cistern," he explained, already descending. "Ottoman era. Connects to ancient underground water system."

They followed him down the ladder into darkness that smelled of damp stone and centuries of stillness. Yusuf activated a powerful flashlight, revealing they stood in a vast underground chamber supported by marble columns—a Byzantine cistern repurposed during Ottoman times and apparently forgotten by modern Istanbul.

"The Yerebatan Saray—the Sunken Palace—gets all the tourists," Yusuf explained as he led them along a narrow walkway beside black water. "But Istanbul has dozens of ancient cisterns beneath the old city. Most unmapped, unknown except to a few."

Their footsteps echoed in the cavernous space, the flashlight beam revealing carved column capitals and fragments of ancient statuary half-submerged in the still water. In other circumstances, Barry's historian's heart would have thrilled at this glimpse of hidden history. Now, he focused only on the path ahead, on escape.

"Where does this lead?" Sakura asked, her own flashlight sweeping the darkness for potential threats.

"Eventually, to the Golden Horn. But we exit before that." Yusuf moved with the confidence of intimate familiarity. "There is an access point near the spice market. From there, we take a boat."

They proceeded in tense silence, the only sounds their footsteps on ancient stone and the occasional drip of water from the vaulted ceiling high above. Barry's mind raced with questions—how Sakura had found them, how both enemy groups had converged so quickly, what awaited them in Mongolia if they managed to escape Istanbul alive.

After what seemed like hours but was likely only fifteen minutes, Yusuf halted before another ladder rising into darkness. "Here. This emerges in the storage room of a spice merchant. Friend of mine."

"They'll be watching the spice market," Sakura pointed out. "Logical cordon around the area."

"Yes. But not expecting emergence from below." Yusuf patted a bulge beneath his jacket that Barry now recognized as a concealed weapon. "Besides, the market is crowded. Good cover for extraction."

No better options presented themselves. Yusuf ascended first, pushing open a trapdoor and exchanging rapid Turkish with someone above before signaling them to follow. Barry climbed painfully, emerging into a storeroom pungent with the aroma of hundreds of spices—cardamom, saffron, cumin, scents he couldn't identify, all mingling in a heady perfume that momentarily overwhelmed his senses.

An elderly Turkish man waited beside the trapdoor, his face deeply lined but his eyes sharp with intelligence. He and Yusuf conferred briefly before the old man gestured toward a beaded curtain leading into the main shop.

"Hasan says the market is busy, good for us," Yusuf translated. "But he has seen strangers asking questions, showing photographs. Both European and Asian men."

"The net is tightening," Sakura observed dispassionately. "What's our extraction plan?"

"Hasan's nephew has a boat at a small dock near the Egyptian Spice Bazaar. He can take us downriver to a private airfield." Yusuf checked his watch. "If we move now, we can still make the midnight flight."

The old spice merchant handed them each a shopping bag filled with purchases—ordinary tourist items, the perfect prop for blending into the market crowd. With a nod of thanks, they moved through the beaded curtain into the sensory assault of the spice market at full swing.

The narrow aisles teemed with humanity—tourists haggling over exotic spices, locals shopping for everyday ingredients, merchants calling out their wares in multiple languages. The air was thick with competing aromas, the noise a blanket of sound that could conceal their movements.

"Stay close," Yusuf instructed. "Act like tourists. Interested in goods, not in a hurry."

They moved through the crowded market, pausing occasionally at stalls to maintain their cover. Barry found the performance excruciating—each delay another opportunity for discovery, each moment in the open another vulnerability.

Halfway through the market, Sakura's hand suddenly clamped on his arm. "Three o'clock," she murmured. "Red jacket. Yamamoto's man."

Barry risked a glance in the indicated direction. A Japanese man in a red windbreaker was moving methodically through the crowd, his attention too focused, his movements too precise for a casual shopper.

"And at our six," Yusuf added quietly. "Woman with blonde hair. Blackwood herself."

Barry felt the blood drain from his face. Sarah Blackwood had entered the market from the opposite direction, her recently platinum hair visible above the crowd. She moved with predatory purpose, scanning faces with experienced efficiency.

"They're converging," Sakura assessed. "Closing the net from both sides."

"They don't know each other," Barry realized suddenly. "Blackwood and Yamamoto's people—they're not coordinating. They're competing."

Understanding dawned in Sakura's eyes. "We can use that."

Without explaining further, she suddenly separated from their group, moving purposefully toward the Japanese operative in the red jacket. Barry started to follow, but Yusuf held him back.

"Wait," the smuggler advised. "Watch."

Sakura approached the Japanese man with the confident stride of someone with purpose. She spoke to him briefly—Barry couldn't hear the words over the market's din, but the man's reaction was immediate. His head snapped toward where Blackwood was advancing through the crowd, his hand moving instinctively toward what was likely a concealed weapon.

Chaos erupted almost instantly. The Japanese operative spoke urgently into what appeared to be a communication device concealed in his sleeve. Within seconds, three more Asian men materialized from different points in the market, converging toward Blackwood's position.

Blackwood spotted them immediately, her training evident in her instant response. She signaled to her own team, who emerged from the crowd with practiced coordination. Two opposing forces, now aware of each other, squared off in the middle of a crowded spice market.

"Now we go," Yusuf urged, pulling Barry toward a side exit as the first shouts erupted behind them. "Quickly, while they are occupied with each other."

They slipped through a service exit into a narrow alley just as the sounds of conflict intensified behind them—raised voices, a woman's scream, the crash of a stall being overturned. The diversion was working perfectly.

Sakura rejoined them seconds later, materializing from another exit with the silent efficiency that still unnerved Barry.

"What did you tell him?" he asked as they hurried through the warren of ancient alleys.

"That Blackwood was CIA, here to intercept their operation." Sakura's smile was cold. "Amazing how quickly professionals become unprofessional when they think they've been compromised."

They emerged onto a small street running parallel to the waterfront. Yusuf led them toward a decrepit dock where a weathered fishing boat bobbed in the choppy water of the Golden Horn. A young Turkish man waited impatiently, gesturing for them to hurry aboard.

As they clambered onto the boat, Barry cast one last glance toward the spice market. Police vehicles were already converging on the scene, lights flashing against the deepening twilight. In the chaos, two deadly forces had neutralized each other, at least temporarily.

The boat's engine sputtered to life, pushing them away from the dock and into the busy waterway. Istanbul receded behind them, its skyline now silhouetted against the sunset, minarets like dark needles against a blood-red sky.

"They'll regroup quickly," Sakura warned, breaking the momentary relief. "Both teams. And now they know we're here, heading for Mongolia."

Yusuf nodded grimly. "And they have resources we do not: private jets, government connections. They will reach Ulaanbaatar before us."

"Then we need an advantage they don't have," Barry said, his mind already working through possibilities. "The exact coordinates from the combined map fragments. The astronomical alignment dates."

"And Batbold's contact," Sakura added. "Tuguldur Sechen. If he's legitimate, he could get us to the site before they can mobilize search parties."

The boat cut through the darkening waters, carrying them away from immediate danger but toward greater peril. Behind them, Istanbul's lights began to twinkle against the twilight. Ahead lay Mongolia, the Khentii Mountains, and the tomb of history's greatest conqueror.

And converging from all sides, forces powerful enough to reshape history if they reached it first.

Barry touched the pocket containing the golden sheets, their weight a constant reminder of what was at stake, of what Blossom had died protecting, of what might await them in the sacred mountains of Mongolia.

The race was truly on.

Chapter 8: Crossing into Mongolia

The cargo plane shuddered violently as it descended through a pocket of turbulence, its aging Soviet-era frame groaning in protest. Barry gripped the frayed canvas of his jump seat, knuckles white, as the aircraft lurched again. They were flying deliberately low—beneath radar coverage—on the final approach to a remote airstrip in China's Inner Mongolia region, three kilometers from the Mongolian border.

"Fifteen minutes!" the pilot shouted over the deafening engine noise, his Uzbek accent thick enough to nearly obscure the words. Yusuf's "reliable transportation" had materialized as a weather-beaten Antonov cargo plane, its exterior markings deliberately obscured, piloted by a man who introduced himself only as Dmitri.

The cabin held no comforts—no insulation against the bone-rattling cold at this altitude, no proper seating beyond military-style jump seats bolted to the metal walls, no windows except the small porthole beside the cockpit through which Barry had glimpsed the endless expanse of the Gobi Desert unfolding beneath them. The cargo bay stank of machine oil, aviation fuel, and fear.

Sakura sat opposite him, seemingly unbothered by the violent turbulence, her eyes closed in what might have been meditation or merely tactical assessment. The bruise on her cheek from Istanbul had darkened to a livid purple, stark against her pale skin. She hadn't spoken since takeoff six hours earlier, retreating into the inscrutable silence that Barry had come to recognize as her defense mechanism.

The plane banked sharply, eliciting another chorus of metallic protests from its frame, then began a steep descent that pressed Barry hard against his seat.

"We're being followed," Yusuf announced, emerging from the cockpit with a grim expression. "Chinese military aircraft. J-11 fighter. Keeping distance but tracking us."

"Have they challenged us?" Sakura asked, her eyes snapping open, instantly alert.

"Not yet. But we are off the approved flight path. Matter of time." Yusuf checked the ancient altimeter mounted on the cabin wall. "Plan changes. No landing at the airstrip. Too risky."

Barry felt his stomach drop faster than the plane. "Then how—"

"Low drop," Yusuf said matter-of-factly. "Over border zone. Less monitored section."

"Drop?" Barry repeated incredulously. "As in parachute?"

"No parachute. Too visible on radar." Yusuf was already moving toward the rear of the cargo hold, uncovering equipment that had been concealed beneath tarpaulins. "Zip line deployment to ground. The plane maintains an altitude of thirty meters. Very fast exit."

"That's insane," Barry protested. "We can't possibly—"

"Choice is this or Chinese military detention," Yusuf interrupted flatly. "I have experienced both. The zip line is preferable."

The plane banked again, descending even more rapidly now. Through the tiny cockpit window, Barry glimpsed a vast emptiness—the lunar-like landscape of the Gobi stretching to the horizon, with no signs of human habitation visible in any direction.

"Seven minutes!" Dmitri called from the cockpit, his voice tight with tension.

Yusuf was already assembling the equipment with practiced efficiency—heavy-duty harnesses, thick gloves, and what appeared to be a winch mechanism that would attach to the cargo door.

"This is standard smuggler escape protocol," Sakura observed, moving to help him. "Risky but effective."

"You've done this before?" Barry asked, shock momentarily overriding his fear.

"Similar deployment in Yemen," she replied without elaboration. "The principle is sound if the equipment is reliable."

"Very reliable," Yusuf assured them, though his rapid movements belied his confident tone. "Used by special forces in several countries."

Barry's mind raced through calculations of physics, probability, and survival rates—none encouraging. Thirty meters above ground, moving at aircraft speed, dropping on a steel cable into a desert with no medical facilities within hundreds of kilometers. The academic in him cataloged all the ways this could go catastrophically wrong.

"Chinese radar has locked on!" Dmitri shouted from the cockpit. "Military channel requesting identification!"

"Now we hurry," Yusuf said, tossing harnesses to both of them. "Put them on. Quickly."

Barry fumbled with the unfamiliar equipment, his fingers clumsy with cold and fear. Sakura moved to help him, her own harness already secured with practiced ease.

"Focus on what matters," she said quietly, tightening his straps with efficient movements. "Blossom. The map. What waits in the mountains? That's why we're here."

The mention of Blossom steadied him somehow, a reminder of purpose beyond mere survival. He nodded, drawing a deep breath that tasted of metal and adrenaline.

"J-11 has visually acquired us!" Dmitri's voice had risen an octave. "They're signaling for a forced landing!"

"Three minutes to drop zone," Yusuf replied, moving to the cargo door's manual release mechanism. "Get ready."

The plane dropped altitude rapidly, engines screaming in protest. Barry's ears popped painfully as the pressure changed. Through the cockpit portal, he could now see individual rocks and scrub brush below—terrifyingly close.

"They're arming weapons systems!" Dmitri shouted.

Yusuf slammed his palm against the cargo door release. Metal screeched against metal as the hydraulic system engaged, the rear door slowly lowering to reveal the desert floor rushing past beneath them—so close that Barry could distinguish individual stones.

Wind howled through the cabin, the temperature plummeting further as the plane maintained its perilously low altitude. Yusuf secured the winch system to the door frame, rapidly feeding out a heavy metal cable that trailed behind the aircraft like a lifeline.

"Anchor deployed!" he shouted over the wind's roar. "When I signal, clip your harness to the cable and go! Do not hesitate! Do not stop! Keep your legs up until final approach to ground!"

The plane banked slightly, aligning with what appeared to be a dry riverbed—slightly softer terrain for their landing. Through the open cargo door, Barry glimpsed a line of distant mountains—the border with Mongolia, their destination so close yet separated by this final, terrifying obstacle.

"Chinese fighter moving to intercept!" Dmitri's voice crackled through the intercom. "Thirty seconds!"

"Now!" Yusuf shouted, gesturing toward the open door.

Sakura moved without hesitation, clipping her harness to the cable and launching herself into the void. Barry watched in horror as she vanished from sight, the cable singing with tension as it carried her toward the rushing ground below.

"Your turn!" Yusuf urged, physically positioning Barry at the threshold. "Now!"

Barry felt the cold metal of the carabiner click into place on his harness. The desert floor blurred beneath him, wind tearing at his clothes, his face, his resolve. Every instinct screamed against stepping into nothingness.

"Go!" Yusuf shoved him firmly between the shoulder blades.

Then he was falling, suspended, flying—all at once. The cable sang as his weight hit it, his body accelerating along its length toward the ground with terrifying speed. Wind roared in his ears, drowning out even his own involuntary shout of terror. The desert floor rushed up to meet him with increasing velocity.

Remember to keep your legs up until final approach, his mind supplied uselessly as the ground expanded beneath him. But how did one define "final approach" in this scenario? When was the right moment to—

Impact. Barry hit the ground with bone-jarring force, his injured ankle collapsing beneath him. Momentum carried him forward in an uncontrolled tumble across sand and rocks, each impact a new explosion of pain, until he finally rolled to a stop in a cloud of dust.

For several seconds, he simply lay there, mentally cataloging his body parts to ensure nothing was broken. Remarkably, despite the violence of his landing, he seemed largely intact—bruised, battered, his ankle screaming in renewed protest, but alive.

Twenty meters away, Sakura was already on her feet, detaching her harness and scanning their surroundings with tactical precision. Above them, the cargo plane banked sharply, climbing rapidly as it released the cable entirely. In the distance, the glint of sunlight on metal revealed the pursuing Chinese fighter.

Yusuf landed more gracefully than Barry had, rolling to absorb the impact before springing to his feet with practiced ease. He unclipped rapidly, surveying the terrain.

"No time to rest," he announced, pulling Barry to his feet. "The border is three kilometers that direction." He pointed toward the distant mountains. "Chinese patrols will be here within minutes once the plane is intercepted."

"Can you walk?" Sakura asked, eyeing Barry's ankle with clinical detachment.

"I'll manage." Barry tested his weight gingerly. The pain was significant but bearable—fear and adrenaline providing temporary analgesic effects. "What about our equipment?"

In answer, Yusuf hefted the waterproof backpack that had somehow remained secured to his body throughout the descent. "Essential supplies only. Documents. Water. Emergency medical. Satellite phone." He nodded toward a larger pack on Sakura's back. "Your friend carries weapons and navigation equipment."

Without further discussion, they set off toward the distant mountains, moving as quickly as Barry's injury allowed across the unforgiving terrain. The landscape offered no cover, no concealment—just endless expanses of rock and sand beneath a sky of merciless blue. They were completely exposed, visible to any surveillance aircraft or patrol that might come looking for the foreigners who had so dramatically violated Chinese airspace.

"The plane?" Barry asked as they trudged forward, the sun beating down with increasing intensity as morning advanced.

"Dmitri will claim mechanical difficulties forced him off course," Yusuf explained. "He has prepared documentation, a believable story. The Chinese will detain him briefly, then release him. Standard procedure."

"And the fighter saw us drop," Barry pointed out. "They'll send ground forces."

"Yes. Which is why we must reach the border quickly." Yusuf checked his GPS unit. "Mongolian border guards are more... flexible in their enforcement. Especially with proper incentives."

They maintained a grueling pace despite the difficult terrain and rising heat. Barry's ankle protested with each step, but he pushed through the pain, focusing instead on the mountains growing incrementally larger before them. Mongolia. Their destination. The next stage of their desperate journey.

After an hour of silent progress, the distant thrum of helicopter rotors froze them in place. Sakura's head snapped up, her eyes narrowing as she scanned the horizon.

"Chinese Z-10 attack helicopter," she identified, pointing to a dark speck approaching from the east. "Search pattern. They're looking for us."

"No cover," Yusuf observed grimly, stating the obvious. The terrain around them remained brutally exposed—not even a boulder large enough to hide behind. "We run for the border. Now."

They abandoned all pretense of caution, breaking into an outright sprint toward the mountains. Barry gritted his teeth against the fire in his ankle, forcing his body forward through sheer willpower. The helicopter's drone grew louder, its search pattern bringing it inexorably closer to their position.

"They've spotted us," Sakura announced, her voice eerily calm. "Banking toward our position."

Barry risked a glance over his shoulder. The helicopter had indeed changed course, now moving directly toward them with deliberate purpose. Even at this distance, the distinctive profile of the Z-10 was unmistakable—the Chinese military's primary attack helicopter, armed with a 23mm cannon and air-to-ground missiles.

"The border is one kilometer ahead," Yusuf gasped, pointing toward a line of marker posts barely visible in the distance. "International incident if they fire on us in Mongolian territory."

"If they care about international incidents," Barry countered, his breath coming in ragged gasps as they ran.

The helicopter was closing rapidly now, the thunderous beat of its rotors drowning out all other sound. Through the shimmering heat haze, Barry could make out figures in the cockpit, the ominous swivel of weapons systems tracking their movement.

Five hundred meters to the border. The helicopter descended to just thirty meters above the ground, pacing them. A voice boomed from its loudspeakers—Chinese commands that none of them paused to translate.

Three hundred meters. The first warning shot kicked up sand ten meters to their right—a deliberate miss, a final warning.

"They won't fire directly on us," Yusuf shouted over the rotor noise. "Too many diplomatic complications. Keep moving!"

One hundred meters. The border markers were clearly visible now—concrete posts spaced at regular intervals along an otherwise invisible line drawn across the desert. Beyond them, the terrain began to rise toward the mountains proper, offering the first hint of potential cover in the form of rocky outcroppings.

The helicopter hovered directly above them, rotors driving sand and debris into painful clouds that tore at exposed skin. Another burst of gunfire—closer this time, the rounds impacting just meters from their position. Not aiming to kill, but to stop.

"Now!" Yusuf urged as they crossed the invisible line between border markers. "We are in Mongolia! They cannot legally—"

The helicopter pilot apparently disagreed with this assessment. Another burst of gunfire stitched the ground directly in their path, forcing them to veer sharply to avoid being hit. The message was clear: legal niceties would not prevent the Chinese military from completing their mission.

"Split up!" Sakura commanded, veering right toward a jumble of rocks that offered the first real cover they'd seen. "Make them divide their attention!"

Barry followed her lead while Yusuf broke left, creating a triangular pattern that forced the helicopter pilot to choose which target to pursue. The aircraft hovered momentarily in indecision before banking toward Yusuf—perhaps identifying him as the leader of their group.

Sakura and Barry reached the relative shelter of the rock formation just as another burst of gunfire pursued Yusuf across the open ground. The smuggler zigzagged with practiced skill, making himself a difficult target while drawing fire away from them.

"He's buying us time," Sakura observed coolly, already assessing their options. "There." She pointed toward a narrow ravine that cut deeper into the foothills. "That leads toward higher terrain. The helicopter will have difficulty following in a confined space."

"What about Yusuf?" Barry protested.

"He knows extraction protocols. He will rejoin if possible." Her tone brooked no argument. "We move now while they're focused on him."

Reluctantly, Barry followed her lead, scrambling into the ravine as the sound of gunfire continued behind them. The narrow passage twisted between wind-carved rock formations, offering blessed concealment after the exposed desert crossing. They moved as quickly as the difficult terrain allowed, climbing steadily into a more mountainous landscape.

The helicopter's rotor beats gradually faded behind them, though whether because it had broken off pursuit or simply because distance and terrain now muffled the sound, Barry couldn't tell. After twenty minutes of grueling ascent, Sakura finally called a halt in a sheltered overhang that offered both shade and a vantage point of the path they'd traveled.

Barry collapsed against the rock wall, his ankle throbbing in time with his racing heartbeat, sweat soaking his clothes despite the cooler temperature at this elevation. He fumbled for his water bottle, taking careful sips despite his body's demand for more.

"Think they'll follow us into the mountains?" he asked when he'd caught his breath.

"Not with a helicopter. Terrain too dangerous." Sakura scanned the horizon with methodical precision. "They may send ground units. Depends on how badly they want us."

"And Yusuf?"

"If he escaped, he'll make for our designated rendezvous point." She checked her GPS unit. "We're still two days from Ulaanbaatar overland. We need to find transportation."

"In the middle of nowhere?"

"Nomadic herders maintain seasonal camps throughout this region. Some have vehicles." Sakura's practical assessment left no room for doubt. "We'll find something by nightfall."

The casual confidence in her voice struck Barry suddenly as familiar—reminiscent of Blossom's unwavering certainty when faced with seemingly insurmountable challenges. For the first time, he glimpsed a genuine similarity between the sisters beyond their physical features.

"You've done this before," he realized aloud. "Not just similar deployments like you mentioned. This specific journey. To Mongolia. To the mountains."

Sakura's expression remained neutral, but something shifted behind her eyes—a calculation made, a decision reached.

"Yes," she admitted finally. "Six years ago. I tried to find the tomb."

The revelation hung between them in the thin mountain air.

"Alone?" Barry asked.

"With a team. Private expedition." She looked away, her gaze fixed on the distant horizon. "I was young. Arrogant. Thought I could succeed where generations had failed."

"What happened?"

"We got close. Too close." Her voice had taken on a distant quality, as if recounting events that had happened to someone else. "Found markers in the Khentii range matching family legends. Ancient stone formations aligned with specific celestial positions."

"The same coordinates on the golden sheets," Barry surmised.

She nodded. "But we lacked the complete map. The astronomical timing. The final keys." Her expression hardened. "And we weren't alone in our search."

"The Red Lotus."

"Yes. Though I didn't know who they were then." She took a careful sip from her water bottle. "They attacked our camp at night. Three of my team were killed. The rest scattered. I barely escaped with my life."

Barry absorbed this new information, recalibrating his understanding of Sakura and her motivations. "And your mother? You said in the outline that she discovered the Red Lotus was still active because of your attempt."

"When I returned, I told her everything. I showed her photographs of the men who attacked us." Sakura's voice remained steady, but her knuckles whitened around her water bottle. "She recognized one of them. An associate of Nakamura's from decades earlier. Someone who should have been dead or imprisoned."

"She realized the society had continued underground," Barry concluded.

"More than that. She realized they were watching our family. Had been for years." Sakura's eyes met his directly. "After my failed expedition, she began investigating. Quietly. Carefully. She discovered they'd infiltrated academic institutions, government agencies, even law enforcement—positioning themselves to seize any information about the tomb's location."

"And that's why they killed her when the second jade box was discovered."

Sakura nodded once, her expression unreadable. "She knew they would come eventually. She left me instructions for contacting Blossom's 'associate' if anything happened to her." A ghost of a bitter smile touched her lips. "She never specified that associate was her other daughter."

The pieces aligned in Barry's mind with devastating clarity. "You and Blossom reconciled in secret because you both realized the danger was real. That the Red Lotus was active and hunting for the tomb."

"Yes. After years of estrangement." Something like regret flickered across Sakura's features before vanishing beneath her composed exterior. "Too little, too late."

The admission carried such weight that Barry found himself responding with his own confession. "I dream about her death every night," he said quietly. "The water rising in that chamber. Her hand slipping from mine. Her final words lost as she went under."

Sakura's gaze sharpened. "What were her final words? What did she say?"

Barry closed his eyes, the memory surfacing with painful clarity. "She said, 'It returns to Mongolia. Promise me.' Then something else I couldn't hear as the water..." He couldn't finish the sentence.

"She knew," Sakura whispered. "Even then, dying, she was protecting the secret. Ensuring the map returned to its origin point."

"I thought she meant we should abandon the search. That the cost was too high." Barry opened his eyes, meeting Sakura's gaze directly. "But she meant the opposite, didn't she? That we needed to complete it. To find the tomb before others could exploit it."

"That would be Blossom," Sakura agreed, a genuine emotion finally breaking through her composed exterior—a complex mixture of pride and grief. "Seeing the mission through to the end."

They sat in silence for several moments, the shared understanding of Blossom's sacrifice creating a tentative bridge between them. For the first time since meeting Sakura in the museum, Barry felt he was glimpsing the real person beneath the operative's calculated exterior.

"We should move," she said finally, rising with fluid grace despite their ordeal. "Still several hours before nightfall. We need to put more distance between us and the border."

They continued their journey through the increasingly mountainous terrain, the landscape transitioning from desert to rocky steppe as they moved deeper into Mongolia. By late afternoon, they spotted the first signs of human habitation—a small encampment of traditional gers (yurts) nestled in a protected valley, horses and goats grazing on the sparse vegetation nearby.

Sakura approached the camp with diplomatic care, speaking to the herders in halting Mongolian phrases supplemented with universal gestures. Barry watched in fascination as she negotiated with the family patriarch—an elderly man with a weather-beaten face and evaluating eyes. Money changed hands, followed by a meal of fermented mare's milk and dried meat that Barry forced himself to consume out of respect for their hosts.

By nightfall, they had secured transportation—an aging Russian UAZ jeep with questionable suspension but apparently reliable mechanics. The nomadic family seemed unsurprised by the arrival of foreigners seeking discrete transportation; such transactions were likely common in this border region where official crossings were sparse and heavily monitored.

They departed at dawn the following day, bouncing along barely visible tracks that the herder had assured them led eventually to a main road connecting to Ulaanbaatar. Sakura drove with focused intensity, her eyes constantly scanning the horizon for threats while Barry consulted maps and the GPS unit, confirming their route.

"Yamamoto will have people watching Ulaanbaatar," he observed as they navigated a particularly rough section of terrain. "All major entry points, hotels catering to foreigners, transportation hubs."

"Yes. And Blackwood's team as well." Sakura maneuvered around a boulder with practiced skill. "We'll need to enter the city carefully. Establish secure contact with Batbold's associate before revealing ourselves."

"Tuguldur Sechen," Barry recalled the name from Batbold's final instructions. "The guide who was once Mongolian intelligence."

"A man with connections in both worlds," Sakura noted. "Useful if he can be trusted."

"If," Barry emphasized. After all they'd experienced, trust had become a scarce commodity.

They reached the main road by mid-afternoon—a weathered two-lane highway stretching across the steppe toward the distant silhouette of Mongolia's capital city. Traffic was sparse—occasional trucks hauling goods, battered cars carrying locals, the rare tourist vehicle marked by its relative newness.

As they approached the outskirts of Ulaanbaatar, the landscape transformed again—gers giving way to concrete apartment blocks, traditional herders replaced by city dwellers in Western clothing. The capital rose before them like an architectural battleground where Soviet-era brutalism clashed with modern glass towers and centuries-old Buddhist temples.

"We'll approach Sechen's office from secondary streets," Sakura decided as they entered the city proper. "Less surveillance. Easier to spot tails."

They abandoned the jeep in a crowded market area and continued on foot through increasingly narrow streets. The address Batbold had provided led them to a modest building in the older section of the city—a two-story structure wedged between a traditional tea house and what appeared to be a tourist shop selling cashmere products.

A weathered sign identified it as "Khentii Expeditions - Professional Guide Services." The windows were dark despite the business hours posted on the door.

"Something's wrong," Sakura murmured, her posture shifting subtly into combat readiness.

Barry felt it too—an absence where there should have been presence, a stillness that spoke of disruption rather than peace. "Could be closed temporarily. Out on an expedition."

"No." Sakura nodded toward the door, which Barry now noticed was slightly ajar. "No guide leaves their office unsecured in a city like this."

They approached cautiously, Sakura moving to one side of the entrance while signaling Barry to stay back. She pushed the door open with a careful touch, revealing a darkened interior. No response came from within—no greeting, no challenge, only silence.

Sakura withdrew a small flashlight from her pack, its beam cutting through the gloom as she stepped cautiously inside. Barry followed, every sense heightened to painful acuity.

The office appeared ordinary at first glance—a reception desk, maps of the Khentii Mountains decorating the walls, photographs of smiling tourists on horseback displayed in frames. A doorway behind the desk led to what was presumably Sechen's private office.

"Blood," Sakura said quietly, her flashlight illuminating droplets on the wooden floor—small, dark spatters leading toward the inner doorway.

They followed the trail with mounting dread, pushing open the second door to reveal a scene of calculated violence. The private office had been methodically ransacked—drawers emptied, maps torn from walls, computer equipment smashed. But it was the figure slumped over the desk that commanded their attention.

Tuguldur Sechen—Barry assumed it must be him—had died where he worked. A precision wound to the throat had ended his life with professional efficiency, the blood pooling beneath him now darkened to the color of old rust. He had been dead for at least a day, possibly longer.

"Red Lotus," Sakura assessed clinically, examining the wound without touching the body. "Their signature technique. Clean. Minimal struggle."

Barry forced himself to approach, academic detachment providing thin armor against the horror before him. The dead man appeared to be in his fifties, with the weathered features of someone who had spent a lifetime in Mongolia's harsh elements. His expression was one of surprise rather than fear—death had come unexpectedly despite his alleged intelligence background.

"They beat us here," Barry said unnecessarily. "They knew we were coming."

"Yes. But they were looking for something specific." Sakura indicated the targeted nature of the destruction—maps and files related to the Khentii range had received particular attention. "Information about the mountains. About potential tomb locations."

Barry's gaze caught on something incongruous—a pattern in the blood on the desk that didn't match the natural pooling from the wound. Moving closer, he realized with a chill that someone had used the dead man's finger to write in his own blood.

"Sakura," he called softly. "Look at this."

The message was brief, written in ancient Mongolian script that few modern people could read. But Barry recognized it immediately from his academic work on Central Asian languages.

"The Khan's spirit protects his own," he translated, the words seeming to hover in the air between them.

"A warning," Sakura said.

"Or a challenge." Barry studied the careful brushstrokes. "This wasn't written by someone in a hurry. They took their time. Wanted us to find it. To understand it."

"They know we're coming. That we have the map." Sakura's expression hardened. "This was left specifically for us."

The implications chilled Barry to his core. Their enemies were not just ahead of them but waiting for them, anticipating their movements with unsettling accuracy. Even here, in Mongolia's capital, they had found no safety—only another death, another warning.

"We need to leave," Sakura decided, already moving toward the door. "This location is compromised. Probably under surveillance."

"Where do we go?" Barry asked, the desperate nature of their situation suddenly overwhelming. "Our contact is dead. We have no allies in this city. Yamamoto's people are watching every move."

Sakura paused at the doorway, her silhouette framed against the fading daylight beyond. For a brief moment, uncertainty flickered across her features—a rare crack in her professional facade.

"We go to the mountains," she said finally. "Directly. Without guides, without support. It's the last thing they'll expect."

"That's suicide," Barry protested. "The Khentii range is vast. Harsh terrain. Unpredictable weather. We'd need supplies, transportation, local knowledge—"

"All of which they'll be watching for us to acquire." Sakura's expression hardened into resolve. "We find another way. One they won't anticipate."

As they slipped out of the office of the dead man, Barry felt the weight of the golden sheets against his chest like a physical burden. The map that had cost so many lives. The secret that had drawn killers across continents. The legacy that Blossom had died protecting.

And now they faced their greatest challenge yet—finding the tomb of history's greatest conqueror while hunted by enemies on all sides, in a land as unforgiving as Genghis Khan himself.

The race had entered its final, desperate phase.

Chapter 9: City of Shadows

Ulaanbaatar unfolded around them like a fever dream—a disorienting collision of eras where Soviet concrete monoliths loomed over traditional gers, where Buddhist prayer flags fluttered alongside neon advertisements, where nomadic herders in traditional deels walked past teenagers in designer jeans. In the gathering twilight, the city took on an otherworldly quality, streetlights creating pools of harsh illumination amid deepening shadows.

They had abandoned the area near Sechen's office immediately, weaving through back alleys and side streets with practiced urgency. Barry's historian's eye couldn't help but note the irony—they were fugitives in the capital city founded by the grandson of the very man whose tomb they sought.

"We need somewhere to regroup," Sakura murmured as they paused in the shadow of a crumbling apartment block. "Somewhere they wouldn't expect."

"Not a hotel," Barry agreed, scanning the street with newfound paranoia. "They'll be watching all accommodation catering to foreigners."

The problem seemed insurmountable. In a city where they knew no one, where their only contact lay dead in his ransacked office, where enemies with seemingly unlimited resources monitored every conventional option—where could they possibly find sanctuary?

"There," Sakura nodded toward a weathered Buddhist temple tucked between newer buildings, its ancient architecture almost apologetic beside the encroaching modernity. "Gandan Monastery. Tourists visit by day, but locals seek sanctuary at all hours. We can blend with worshippers while we plan our next move."

They approached the temple complex cautiously, Sakura purchasing incense sticks from a vendor to complete their disguise as spiritual tourists. The main temple hall was largely empty at this hour, the few present visitors, either foreign backpackers or devout locals, were lost in prayer. The scent of sandalwood and butter candles hung heavy in the air, centuries of devotional smoke having seeped into every wooden beam and painted surface.

"This is temporary at best," Barry whispered as they knelt before a towering statue of the Buddha, maintaining their cover. "We need real allies. Resources. Transportation to the mountains."

"Working on it," Sakura replied cryptically, her eyes scanning the temple's shadowed corners with professional assessment.

They remained in the temple for nearly an hour, moving periodically between different shrines to avoid drawing attention. As genuine worshippers departed and the backpackers drifted away, the cavernous space gradually emptied until only a few monks remained, attending to evening rituals with practiced efficiency.

"We should go," Barry murmured. "Before they close for the night."

"Wait." Sakura's attention had fixed on something across the temple—a figure partly concealed in shadow, watching them with undisguised interest. "We're being observed."

Barry tensed, hand instinctively moving toward the weapon concealed beneath his jacket. "Red Lotus?"

"No." Sakura's assessment was immediate and certain. "Different posture. Different purpose." She rose smoothly from her kneeling position. "He wants us to follow."

"Follow? That's exactly what—"

"If he meant us harm, he wouldn't reveal himself," she cut him off. "This is an invitation."

The figure—a Mongolian man of indeterminate age, dressed in a modernized version of traditional clothing—made a subtle gesture before slipping through a side door that Barry hadn't previously noticed. Without waiting for further discussion, Sakura moved to follow, leaving Barry little choice but to accompany her or be left behind.

The doorway led to a narrow corridor illuminated by bare bulbs that buzzed with unstable electricity. The passageway smelled of incense, old books, and something indefinable that Barry associated with places of ancient power. Their mysterious guide moved ahead with unhurried confidence, occasionally glancing back to ensure they followed.

"This could be a trap," Barry hissed as they descended a worn stone staircase that appeared significantly older than the surrounding structure.

"Could be salvation," Sakura countered pragmatically. "We're out of options either way."

The staircase terminated in another corridor, this one lined with weathered wooden doors. Their guide stopped before one, rapped a distinctive pattern against the ancient wood, and waited. A moment later, the door swung inward to reveal a room that seemed to exist in another century entirely.

Oil lamps cast flickering light across walls lined with scrolls, manuscripts, and maps of varying antiquity. A low table dominated the center, surrounded by cushions in the traditional Mongolian style. The air held the distinctive scent of airag—fermented mare's milk—and burning juniper.

Three people awaited them inside. An elderly woman with silver hair pulled into an intricate braid, her face a tapestry of wrinkles yet her eyes startlingly clear. A middle-aged man with the weathered features of someone who had spent a lifetime in Mongolia's harsh climate. And dominating the space by presence rather than physical size, a man perhaps in his early forties, his bearing so regal that Barry immediately understood he was the leader.

"Professor Curtis. Ms. Hirata." The leader addressed them in flawless English, his voice a rich baritone that seemed to resonate within the chamber. "We've been expecting you."

Barry exchanged a glance with Sakura, whose expression had shifted into careful neutrality—her version of surprise.

"You have us at a disadvantage," Barry replied carefully.

"A common condition for those who seek the Great Khan's resting place." A smile touched the man's lips without reaching his eyes. "Please, be seated. You've traveled far and faced much to reach this point."

Warily, they accepted the invitation, taking cushions opposite their hosts. The elderly woman poured airag into small bowls, offering them with a ceremonial nod that Barry recognized from his academic studies of Mongolian customs. To refuse would be a grave insult.

He sipped cautiously, fighting not to grimace at the sour, slightly alcoholic taste. Beside him, Sakura consumed hers with the practiced stoicism of someone accustomed to maintaining cover at any cost.

"You know why we're here," she said, placing her empty bowl on the table with deliberate care. "How?"

"The signs have been gathering for months," the leader replied cryptically. "Strangers asking questions in the mountains. Expeditions with hidden purposes. Technology deployed where it does not belong." His gaze sharpened. "And then the death of Erdene Batbold in Washington. News travels quickly in certain circles."

"You knew Batbold," Barry realized.

"He was one of us. Though his path took him to academic circles in the West, his heart remained with the true guardians." The man gestured to himself and his companions. "I am Temujin. These are my associates, Altan and Khulan."

The name landed with deliberate weight. Temujin—the birth name of Genghis Khan himself. Either an extraordinary coincidence or a carefully chosen identity.

"You claim to be guardians," Sakura observed, her tone neutral yet probing. "Of what exactly?"

"Of Mongolia's greatest secret. Of the Khan's eternal rest." Temujin leaned forward slightly, the lamplight casting dramatic shadows across his angular features. "Of the knowledge that, in the wrong hands, could reshape or destroy our world."

Barry felt a chill at the words, so closely echoing what he and Sakura had come to believe about the tomb's contents.

"For nearly eight centuries, my ancestors have protected the sacred mountains," Temujin continued. "First with swords and arrows, later with secrets and misdirection. We are the Köke Tengri Sakigchid—the Guardians of the Blue Sky."

"You're descendants of Genghis Khan," Barry surmised, the historian in him momentarily overriding his caution. "From his unbroken lineage."

Temujin inclined his head slightly. "From his fourth son, Tolui, through lines that history has forgotten or ignored. We preserve what others seek to exploit."

"Yet you reveal yourselves to us," Sakura noted. "Why?"

"Because you carry the golden sheets." Temujin's statement was not a question but a certainty. "Because you have solved the jade puzzles that have confounded others for centuries. Because the time of concealment is ending."

Barry's hand moved instinctively toward his inner pocket, where the golden fragments rested in their protective case. "How could you possibly know—"

"The death of your companion's sister in the Solomon Islands did not go unnoticed," Temujin interrupted, his gaze shifting to Sakura. "Nor did your own expedition six years ago, Ms. Hirata. We have watched your family for generations, just as we have watched all who seek the tomb."

The revelation struck Barry with physical force. These people had known about Blossom, about Sakura's previous attempt, about the very existence of the golden map fragments that he had believed secret from all but a handful of people.

"If you've known all along," he challenged, anger momentarily overriding caution, "why didn't you intervene? When Blossom was killed. When Batbold was murdered. When Sakura's mother—"

"We are guardians, not gods," the elderly woman—Khulan—spoke for the first time, her voice carrying the gravelly texture of great age. "Our reach extends primarily to the sacred mountains themselves. Beyond Mongolia's borders, we can only watch and record."

"So you've been watching us stumble toward you," Sakura concluded, a dangerous edge entering her voice. "Watching people die while you remained hidden."

"We've been waiting," Temujin corrected. "To see if you would reach us. To see if you were worthy of the knowledge you seek." His expression remained impassive. "Many have sought the tomb. Few have deserved to find it."

"And you judge worthiness?" Barry couldn't keep the skepticism from his tone.

"The mountains judge," the third guardian, Altan, spoke with quiet certainty. "We merely interpret their will."

The conversation had taken a turn toward the mystical that made Barry profoundly uncomfortable. He was a historian, an academic—he dealt in evidence, in documentation, in verifiable facts. Yet something in Temujin's unwavering gaze suggested the man absolutely believed what he was saying.

"The Red Lotus Society has reached Ulaanbaatar," Sakura redirected the conversation to immediate concerns. "Their leader, Kenji Yamamoto, is mobilizing resources for a major expedition. They've already killed our contact, Tuguldur Sechen."

"We know." Temujin's expression darkened. "Sechen was not one of us, but he was an ally. His death will be answered for." He exchanged glances with his companions before continuing. "The Red Lotus is not your only concern. The British woman and her mercenaries arrived yesterday. They've established a base camp near the airport, importing specialized equipment disguised as geological survey tools."

"And both groups are watching the city," Barry added. "Every hotel, every transportation hub, every outfitter who might supply an expedition."

"Which is why you sought sanctuary in the temple," Temujin nodded. "A wise choice, though temporary."

"We need to reach the mountains," Sakura stated flatly. "Before either group can mobilize their full resources. We have the map, the astronomical alignments, everything needed to locate the exact site."

Temujin studied them both with unsettling intensity, as if peering beneath their skins to examine their very souls. The silence stretched uncomfortably before he finally spoke again.

"Perhaps. But possessing a map does not guarantee safe passage to the destination." He rose with fluid grace, gesturing toward a door at the rear of the chamber that Barry hadn't previously noticed. "Come. There is something you must see before we proceed."

They followed him through the door into a second chamber, this one larger and dominated by an enormous map of the Khentii Mountains that covered an entire wall. Unlike modern topographical maps, this one appeared hand-drawn on aged parchment, with annotations in classical

Mongolian script so ancient that even Barry, with his linguistic expertise, could decipher only fragments.

"The sacred mountains as they truly are," Temujin explained, approaching the map with reverent steps. "Not as modern cartographers understand them, but as they exist in the realm of spirit and truth."

Barry examined the map with scholarly interest, noting discrepancies between this representation and the official surveys he'd studied. Certain peaks appeared more prominent, valleys deeper, features marked that didn't exist on any modern map.

"These formations," he indicated, clusters of symbols near a particularly imposing mountain. "What do they represent?"

"The fallen," Khulan answered, her weathered finger tracing the symbols. "Those who sought the tomb and found only death. Expedition after expedition, century after century. The mountains keep their own counsel about who may approach the Khan's rest."

"You're suggesting some supernatural defense," Sakura's tone carried polite skepticism. "Some mystical force that protects the tomb."

"I suggest nothing," Temujin replied evenly. "I merely state what we have observed across generations. The mountains permit some to pass while claiming others. Weather changes with impossible suddenness. Equipment fails without explanation. Experienced guides become disoriented in terrain they've navigated dozens of times."

He indicated a specific region on the map, a valley nestled between three distinctive peaks. "Here, in 1934, a Japanese expedition vanished completely—thirty-seven men with modern equipment, gone without a trace. Here," his finger moved to another location, "a Russian team in 1978 turned back after three members died in separate accidents on perfectly clear days."

"Coincidence," Sakura suggested. "Harsh conditions. Inadequate preparation."

"Perhaps." Temujin seemed untroubled by her skepticism. "Yet consider this—in eight centuries, with hundreds of attempts, not one expedition has reached the true burial site. Not one." His eyes locked with Barry's. "Do you believe in coincidence on such a scale, Professor?"

Barry had no ready answer. His academic training insisted on rational explanations, yet his experiences since discovering the golden map fragments had repeatedly challenged his understanding of what was possible.

"The Japanese expedition in 1934," he said instead, recalling details from his research. "They were funded by the Imperial government. Early precursors to the Red Lotus."

Temujin nodded approvingly. "You know your history well. Yes, they sought the tomb not for knowledge but for power—specifically, the military secrets believed to be contained in the Altan Debter."

"Just like Yamamoto now," Sakura concluded.

"With greater resources and more dangerous technology." Temujin returned to the first chamber, gesturing for them to follow. "Which is why we must determine if you are worthy to attempt the journey."

"Test us how?" Barry asked warily.

"The tests are threefold—mind, body, and spirit," Altan spoke with the gravity of reciting ancient doctrine. "As they have been since the guardianship began."

"We don't have time for ritual challenges," Sakura objected. "Every hour we delay gives our enemies an opportunity to advance."

"Without our guidance, you will never reach the tomb before they do," Temujin countered calmly. "Without our blessing, the mountains themselves will resist you. This is not negotiable."

Barry and Sakura exchanged glances, an entire conversation passing silently between them. They had come too far, risked too much to turn back now. Whatever tests these self-proclaimed guardians required might be their only path forward.

"How long will these tests take?" Barry asked reluctantly.

"For some, a lifetime," Khulan said with cryptic severity. "For you? We shall see."

"Rest tonight," Temujin offered more practically. "You are safe here—this compound lies beneath the temple but connects to tunnels that run throughout the old city. The Red Lotus does not know of its existence."

"And Blackwood?" Sakura pressed.

"The British woman seeks local guides with experience in the Khentii range. So far, she has found none willing to assist her." A cold smile touched Temujin's lips. "Our influence among the people remains strong."

With that cryptic assurance, they were shown to Spartan but clean quarters—a small chamber with two sleeping pallets, a washing basin, and a single oil lamp. The door had no lock, Barry noted with unease. They were guests, but perhaps also prisoners, dependent on their hosts' goodwill.

"What do you think?" he asked Sakura once they were alone, keeping his voice low despite the thick walls.

She completed a methodical inspection of the room before answering. "They're legitimate. Or at least, they believe they are." She tested the solidity of one wall with careful pressure. "The compound is extensive. Older than the temple above. Multiple escape routes based on the air circulation patterns."

"That's not what I meant," Barry clarified. "Do you believe their claims? About being descendants of Genghis Khan? About guarding the tomb for centuries?"

Sakura paused in her security assessment, considering the question with unusual thoughtfulness. "The Hirata family has protected knowledge of the golden map for generations," she said finally. "Is it so difficult to believe others might have their own legacy of guardianship?"

"And the tests? The claims about the mountains having their own defenses?"

"Mysticism often conceals practical realities." She sat on one of the pallets, checking her weapons with habitual care. "Perhaps the 'mountain's judgment' is simply their way of describing their own protective measures. Perhaps they themselves ensure that unworthy expeditions fail."

It was a rational explanation, yet Barry found himself troubled by Temujin's absolute conviction. "And if they judge us unworthy?"

Sakura met his gaze directly. "Then we find another way. As we always have."

Despite his exhaustion, sleep eluded Barry that night. The windowless chamber's absolute darkness created a disorienting timelessness, while his mind raced with the implications of all they'd learned. These guardians represented yet another faction in the increasingly complex web surrounding the Khan's tomb—their motives still unclear, their trustworthiness unproven.

When the door finally opened, admitting a slice of lamplight and the silhouette of their original guide, Barry realized he had no idea whether it was morning or still the middle of the night.

"It is time," the man said simply.

They were led through a different series of corridors than they had traversed the previous evening, descending deeper beneath the city. The air grew cooler, the walls changing from finished stonework to rough-hewn rock that suggested they had entered natural caverns adapted for human use.

Eventually, they emerged into a vast underground chamber that took Barry's breath away. Towering columns of natural stone rose to a ceiling lost in shadows, while ancient petroglyphs covered the walls—hunting scenes, celestial symbols, and warrior figures that predated even the rise of the Mongol Empire.

In the center of the chamber stood Temujin and his fellow guardians, now joined by perhaps twenty others—men and women of varying ages, all with the distinctive features of ethnic Mongolians, all regarding the newcomers with unreadable expressions.

"The council is gathered," Temujin announced as Barry and Sakura were brought before them. "The testing will commence."

"What exactly should we expect?" Barry asked, eyeing the assembled guardians warily.

"Three challenges, as is traditional," Temujin explained. "First, the test of mind—to prove you understand what you seek. Second, the test of body—to prove you have the strength to reach it. Third, the test of spirit—to prove you are worthy of finding it."

He gestured toward an elderly man who stepped forward, carrying what appeared to be a wooden box inlaid with silver.

"The first test begins now," Temujin declared. "Khoyor Ünen, Negen Khudal—Two Truths, One Lie."

The box was opened to reveal three small objects resting on faded silk—a carved wooden horse no larger than Barry's thumb, a tarnished silver arrowhead, and what appeared to be a fragment of aged parchment with faded writing.

"These three artifacts are connected to the Great Khan," Temujin explained. "Two are genuine. One is false. Identify the falsehood, and the first test is passed."

Barry approached carefully, academic instincts immediately engaged by the challenge. This was familiar territory—authentication of historical artifacts, the precise kind of analysis he had performed countless times in his career.

The carved horse was exquisite in its detail, the wood darkened with age and handling. The arrowhead showed distinct Mongol craftsmanship of the 13th century, its distinctive shape matching examples he had studied in museums. The parchment fragment contained script that appeared to be an early form of Mongolian writing.

"May I?" he asked, gesturing toward the artifacts.

At Temujin's nod, he carefully examined each item, conscious of the silent guardians watching his every move. The horse figurine showed appropriate wear patterns, the wood itself of a species native to the region. The arrowhead's tarnish appeared genuine, not artificially applied as would be the case with a modern forgery.

The parchment, however... He studied the writing carefully, his expertise in Central Asian languages triggering warning signals in his mind.

"This is the falsehood," he declared, pointing to the parchment. "The script is accurate for the period, but the linguistic structure is wrong. This sentence—" he indicated a specific line, "—uses a grammatical form that didn't develop until the 15th century, well after Genghis Khan's time."

A murmur ran through the assembled guardians. Temujin's expression revealed nothing as he turned to an elderly woman who appeared to be a scholar or record-keeper of their group. She examined the parchment carefully before nodding once.

"The first test is passed," Temujin announced without ceremony. "Prepare for the second."

The wooden box was removed, replaced by a younger guardian carrying what appeared to be traditional Mongolian wrestling garments—the zodog and shuudag worn in bökh competitions for centuries.

"The test of body," Temujin explained, "is as old as our people. You will face a guardian in hand-to-hand combat. Victory is not required—only that you demonstrate the strength and skill necessary for the journey ahead."

Barry felt his stomach drop. While physically fit for an academic, he was no match for these people who had likely trained in traditional wrestling since childhood. He glanced at Sakura, whose expression had shifted to focused calculation.

"I will undertake this test," she said, stepping forward before Barry could protest.

Temujin considered her for a moment, then nodded. "Tradition permits the stronger to stand for both when two seek the same goal. Prepare yourself."

Sakura was escorted to a side chamber to change, returning minutes later in the traditional wrestling garments that had been adapted for her smaller frame. Despite the unfamiliar clothing, she moved with the confident grace that Barry had come to recognize as the mark of her extensive combat training.

Her opponent was a guardian perhaps ten years her junior—a powerfully built man with the hardened physique of someone who had lived a life of physical challenge. He towered over Sakura by at least a foot, outweighing her by a considerable margin.

The match began without fanfare, the two circling each other in the traditional opening of Mongolian bökh. The young guardian moved with surprising speed for his size, attempting to grapple with Sakura in a hold that would have immediately ended the contest for most opponents.

But Sakura was not most opponents. She slipped his grasp with fluid precision, redirecting his momentum in a technique Barry recognized from Japanese judo rather than Mongolian wrestling. The guardian recovered quickly, adapting his approach to counter her different style.

What followed was a physical chess match of extraordinary skill—two combatants from different traditions testing, probing, seeking advantage. The guardian's raw strength was formidable, but Sakura's speed and precision kept her from being overwhelmed. When he managed to grasp her arm in what should have been a decisive hold, she executed a complex counter that momentarily reversed their positions.

The assembled guardians watched in appreciative silence, clearly recognizing the high level of skill on display. Even Temujin's impassive expression had shifted to one of professional assessment.

The match continued for perhaps ten minutes—an eternity in the intensely physical contest—before the guardian finally succeeded in executing a throw that sent Sakura to the ground. By traditional rules, this would mark his victory, as her upper body had touched the earth.

Sakura accepted the defeat with dignity, rising to bow to her opponent in the Japanese tradition. He returned the gesture with the Mongolian equivalent, respect evident in his bearing.

"The test of body is complete," Temujin declared. "You have demonstrated the necessary skill and strength for the journey ahead."

Barry released a breath he hadn't realized he was holding. Though Sakura had technically lost the match, she had clearly impressed the guardians with her abilities—exactly as Temujin had said was the true purpose of the test.

After Sakura had changed back into her regular clothing, Temujin led them to yet another area of the vast underground complex. This chamber was smaller, illuminated by a circle of butter lamps whose flames burned with unnatural steadiness in the still air. In the center stood a simple stone altar bearing a single object—a human skull transformed into a ceremonial cup, its surface yellowed with age and polished by countless hands.

"The final test," Temujin announced. "The test of spirit."

Barry eyed the skull cup with scholarly recognition and personal apprehension. The use of kapala—ritual vessels made from human craniums—was well documented in certain Buddhist and shamanic traditions of the region. What concerned him was what might fill such a vessel.

"This test you must both undertake individually," Temujin continued. "The kapala contains the airag of truth—mare's milk fermented with herbs known only to the guardians. It reveals the heart's intention to those who know how to interpret the signs."

"A truth serum," Sakura translated skeptically.

"Of a kind far older and more revealing than your modern chemicals," Khulan responded, her ancient voice carrying surprising authority. "My ancestral line has prepared this mixture for twenty-seven generations. It does not compel truth—it reveals essence."

Barry exchanged an uneasy glance with Sakura. The implications were disturbing—whatever this concoction contained, it apparently had psychoactive properties that would leave them vulnerable before these people they barely knew.

"We have no guarantees of your intentions once this test is complete," Sakura pointed out with characteristic pragmatism. "We would be at your mercy."

"You have been at our mercy since entering this place," Temujin countered calmly. "Had we wished you harm, it would already have befallen you."

"And if we refuse?" Barry asked.

"Then our interaction ends here. You will be escorted back to the temple and released." Temujin's expression remained neutral. "What happens afterward is not our concern. The Red Lotus and the British mercenaries will continue their search. You will continue yours. The mountains will judge you all."

The choice was no choice at all. Without the guardians' assistance, they faced nearly impossible odds—outnumbered, out-resourced, in unfamiliar territory where their enemies had already established operations.

"I'll go first," Barry decided, stepping forward before Sakura could object.

Khulan lifted the kapala with reverent hands, offering it to him with formal ceremony. The liquid within was milky white with hints of green—herbs or other substances suspended in the fermented mare's milk. The scent that rose from it was earthy, ancient, with notes of aromatics he couldn't identify.

Barry accepted the vessel, conscious of the dozens of eyes watching his every reaction. Whatever this substance contained, it represented their only path forward. Pushing aside his apprehension, he raised the kapala to his lips and drank.

The taste was initially familiar—the sour tang of airag that he had sampled the previous evening—but beneath it lay complexity: bitterness, sweetness, and something ineffable that seemed to spread across his tongue like liquid fire. He drained the vessel as custom required, returning it to Khulan's waiting hands.

For several moments, nothing happened. Then the chamber began to shift around him—not violently, but with a dreamlike quality that suggested the boundary between perception and reality was thinning. The guardians' faces became simultaneously more defined and more symbolic, as if each were both an individual and an archetype.

"What do you seek in the sacred mountains?" Temujin's voice seemed to come from everywhere and nowhere.

"The tomb of Genghis Khan," Barry heard himself answer, the words emerging with perfect clarity despite the strange alteration of his consciousness.

"Why do you seek it?" The question penetrated deeper than its simple phrasing suggested.

In his altered state, Barry understood that superficial answers would not suffice. The drug was indeed revealing essence—stripping away the layers of rationalization and self-deception that humans typically interpose between their actions and their true motivations.

"For knowledge," he began, but the answer felt incomplete even as he spoke it. "For history..." Still not the full truth. "For redemption," he finally admitted, the word tearing from somewhere deep within him. "To fulfill my promise to Blossom. To ensure her death wasn't meaningless."

The admission hung in the strange, altered space between himself and the guardians. He felt exposed, vulnerable—not just to their judgment but to the truth he had been avoiding since returning from the Solomon Islands.

"And if finding the tomb requires sacrifice?" Temujin's voice probed deeper. "If you must choose between the discovery and another life? Between historical knowledge and human cost?"

The question struck at Barry's core, at the decision he had failed to make in that flooded chamber when Blossom's hand had slipped from his grasp. Had he prioritized securing the map fragments over saving her? Had he hesitated that crucial fraction of a second because part of him valued the discovery more than her life?

"I won't make that mistake again," he vowed, unsure if he was speaking aloud or only in his mind. "No discovery is worth another death. No historical knowledge justifies such a cost."

Whether his answer satisfied the guardians, he couldn't tell. The chamber continued to shift around him, time stretching and compressing in unpredictable patterns. He was vaguely aware of Sakura taking the kapala, of her own questioning, but the details eluded him as the substance carried him deeper into altered consciousness.

When clarity finally returned—minutes or hours later, he couldn't tell—Barry found himself seated on the stone floor of the chamber, Sakura beside him in a similar position. The guardians had formed a circle around them, their expressions solemn but no longer impenetrable.

"The testing is complete," Temujin announced. "The council will deliberate."

The guardians withdrew to the perimeter of the chamber, speaking in hushed tones that didn't carry to where Barry and Sakura waited. The aftereffects of the airag mixture lingered in Barry's system—a heightened awareness coupled with a strange emotional rawness, as if layers of protective callus had been temporarily stripped away.

"What did you see?" he asked Sakura quietly.

She didn't immediately answer, her expression more vulnerable than he had ever witnessed. "Truth," she finally said. "My truth. About Blossom. About why I'm really here." She met his gaze directly. "And you?"

"The same," he admitted. "Things I've been avoiding since the Solomon Islands."

Before they could elaborate further, Temujin approached, the council having apparently reached its decision.

"The tests are passed," he announced without preamble. "You may proceed to the sacred mountains with our guidance."

Relief flooded through Barry, though practical concerns quickly tempered it. "And the Red Lotus? Blackwood's mercenaries?"

"They have already departed for the mountains," Temujin confirmed grimly. "The British team left yesterday with hired local guides—not from our people, but experienced enough to be dangerous. The Japanese group departed this morning with more substantial resources—vehicles, equipment, armed personnel."

"Then we're already behind," Sakura concluded, her professional demeanor reasserting itself as the drug's effects faded.

"They follow false paths," Altan spoke up. "Routes that appear promising based on incomplete information."

"The golden sheets you carry," Khulan added, "combined with our knowledge of the true approaches, will give you an advantage they do not possess."

"When do we leave?" Barry asked, already calculating time frames, distances, and the complex astronomical alignments that the map indicated would be necessary to locate the tomb's entrance.

"Tonight," Temujin decided. "Under cover of darkness, through routes our enemies do not monitor. We have prepared supplies, transportation, and everything necessary for the journey."

"There is one thing you should understand before we proceed," Khulan added, her ancient eyes fixing on them with unsettling intensity. "Many have reached the mountains. Some have even found promising sites, caves, evidence of ancient Mongol presence. But none—not in eight centuries—have found the true burial chamber."

"Because of your guardianship?" Sakura asked.

"Partly," the old woman acknowledged. "But also because of the mountain itself. The Khan's final resting place is protected by more than human vigilance." She leaned forward, her voice dropping to a near whisper. "The sacred peaks have claimed dozens of expeditions. Entire teams vanished without trace. Others were driven mad by what they encountered. These are not mere stories to frighten children—they are accounts recorded by our order across generations."

"What exactly are you suggesting?" Barry pressed, scholarly skepticism warring with the undeniable evidence of strangeness he had encountered since finding the golden map fragments.

"That you prepare yourselves for the possibility that forces beyond ordinary understanding protect some mysteries," Temujin answered. "The Great Khan conquered half the known world. Do you imagine his final resting place would be guarded by anything less formidable than his living armies?"

The question hung in the underground chamber, unanswerable yet undeniable. Whatever lay ahead in the Khentii Mountains—whatever forces, natural or otherwise, protected history's greatest conqueror—they would face it within hours.

The race for the tomb had entered its final and most perilous phase.

Chapter 10: The Guardian's Test

Dawn broke over Ulaanbaatar in streaks of blood-orange and amber, the first rays of sunlight illuminating the golden roof of Gandan Monastery, where their strange journey had begun the previous day. But Barry and Sakura were not there to witness it. They had spent the night in the underground complex, a warren of ancient chambers and passages that existed beneath the city like a shadow realm—unknown to tourists, invisible to satellites, forgotten by all but those who served as its custodians.

They had been separated before dawn, led to different sections of the complex by silent guardians who offered no explanation. Now, as the sun climbed higher over the Mongolian capital, Barry stood alone in a circular chamber carved directly from bedrock, its walls adorned with petroglyphs so ancient they predated even the rise of Genghis Khan.

"The testing continues," Temujin announced, entering the chamber with four other guardians. "Last night, you passed the preliminary trials. Today, you face the true Guardian's Test—the same challenges that have determined worthiness for eight centuries."

Barry noted the guardians carried items of obvious ceremonial significance—a sword with a hilt wrapped in faded blue silk; a wooden box inlaid with silver and turquoise; a scroll case made from what appeared to be human bone; and a small clay vessel sealed with wax bearing an impression he couldn't quite discern.

"Where is Sakura?" he asked, uneasy at their separation.

"Undertaking her own trials," Temujin replied, his expression revealing nothing. "Your paths diverge here but will reconverge if both prove worthy."

"And if one of us fails?" Barry pressed.

Temujin's gaze was impassive. "Then that one does not proceed to the sacred mountains."

The implications were clear. Their partnership, their shared quest, could end here if either failed to meet the guardians' mysterious standards. After all they had endured together, they might be forced to separate at this critical juncture—or worse, both be turned away when they were so close to their goal.

"The Trial of Mind begins," Temujin declared, gesturing to the guardian holding the bone scroll case.

The container was opened with reverent care, a yellowed parchment extracted and unrolled upon a stone table that Barry hadn't noticed before. The script was ancient Mongolian, faded to near illegibility in places, the characters archaic even to his trained eye.

"Translate," Temujin instructed simply.

Barry approached cautiously, academic instincts already engaged despite his apprehension. The text appeared to be a riddle or poem, written in a dialectical variation of 13th-century Mongolian that incorporated shamanistic terminology largely lost to modern scholarship.

"This is pre-standardized script," he observed, fingers hovering above but not touching the fragile document. "Before Khubilai Khan's reforms. There are elements of Uighur and ancient Turkic mixed with early Mongolian."

"Translate," Temujin repeated, unmoved by the academic observation.

Barry focused, drawing on years of specialized linguistic training. The text swam before his eyes, characters shifting between recognizable forms and inscrutable symbols. Gradually, patterns emerged, meanings crystallized.

"It speaks of a mountain that guards the sky lord," he began slowly, "a place where heaven and earth meet. Where the Blue Wolf howls at the eternal stars." He paused, struggling with a particularly obscure passage. "Something about... the path that is not a path. The door that is not a door. Only when the celestial hunter stands above the wolf's tail will the way open."

Temujin's expression remained unreadable. "Continue."

Barry wrestled with the next section, the dialect shifting subtly into what appeared to be a ritual invocation. "Those who approach with... impure intentions? No, with conquest in their hearts... will find only death. The guardians of stone and wind will..." He hesitated, uncertain of a particular glyph.

"Will what?" Temujin pressed.

"Will 'unmake' them," Barry decided finally, the translation feeling inadequate for the ominous connotation of the original text. "The next part is heavily damaged, but it seems to describe astronomical alignments—specific configurations of stars that mark the true path."

The guardians exchanged glances, a silent communication passing between them that Barry couldn't interpret. Temujin nodded once to the guardian holding the wooden box, who stepped forward and opened it.

Inside lay objects that Barry initially took for game pieces—small carved figures representing celestial bodies. The sun, moon, and various stars were rendered in materials ranging from polished obsidian to what appeared to be jade and lapis lazuli.

"Demonstrate the alignment described in the text," Temujin instructed, indicating a circular stone depression in the chamber floor that Barry now realized was a model of the night sky.

Here was a challenge that tested more than translation—it required understanding of ancient Mongolian astronomical concepts that differed significantly from both Western traditions and modern science. Barry carefully selected the pieces, placing them in the depression according to his interpretation of the text.

The sun positioned at the western quadrant. The moon in its third quarter phase. The celestial hunter—Orion in Western astronomy, but with a different configuration in Mongolian tradition—aligned above the wolf's tail, which he identified as a specific star cluster in Ursa Major.

His hands moved with increasing confidence as the pattern emerged, his academic knowledge fusing with intuitive leaps that surprised even him. When the final piece was placed, the assembled guardians leaned forward with unmistakable interest.

"The alignment occurs three times per year," Barry explained, pointing to specific configurations. "But only once when combined with the solstice position described here. That would be... four days from now."

Temujin's eyebrow raised fractionally—the first genuine reaction Barry had observed from him. "You understand the timing. But do you understand the warning?"

Barry considered the ominous phrases from the text. "It suggests that the tomb is protected by more than human guardians. That the mountain itself—or some force within it—passes judgment on those who approach."

"And do you believe this, Professor?" Temujin's question carried unexpected weight. "You, a man of science and historical fact?"

It was a trap, Barry realized—not a test of knowledge but of perspective. His academic training had instilled in him skepticism toward supernatural claims, yet his experiences since discovering the golden map fragments had repeatedly challenged the boundaries of conventional explanations.

"I believe," he said carefully, "that our ancestors often used mystical language to describe natural phenomena they couldn't otherwise explain. But I also believe there are forces in this world that modern science hasn't fully accounted for." He met Temujin's gaze directly. "I don't dismiss the warnings. Whether they describe natural dangers, human guardians, or something else entirely, only a fool would ignore them."

A faint smile touched Temujin's lips. "A diplomatic answer. Let us see if your actions match your words."

He gestured to the guardian holding the clay vessel, who broke the wax seal and poured its contents—a fine blue-gray powder—into a small bronze brazier. When ignited, the powder produced a thick smoke with an acrid, medicinal scent that rapidly filled the chamber.

"Breathe deeply," Temujin instructed as the guardians donned elaborately carved wooden masks. "The Blue Smoke reveals truths hidden even from oneself."

Barry hesitated, remembering the disorienting effects of the ceremonial airag from the previous day's ritual. This seemed to be escalating from tests of skill and knowledge to something more invasive—a chemical alteration of consciousness that left him deeply vulnerable.

"Refusal ends your journey here," Temujin stated flatly, reading his hesitation.

With reluctance born of necessity, Barry inhaled the pungent smoke. The effect was immediate and profound—not the dreamlike quality of the previous concoction, but a hyper-clarity that seemed to sharpen every sense to painful acuity. Colors intensified, sounds separated into distinct layers, and time itself seemed to stutter and fragment around him.

The chamber dissolved, replaced by a windswept mountainside rendered with hallucinatory vividness. Barry found himself standing before a narrow cleft in a sheer rock face, a darkness beyond that seemed to swallow light itself. From within came whispers in a language older than any he had studied, carrying meaning that bypassed linguistic centers and spoke directly to primal instinct.

Approach and be judged.

He took a step toward the opening, then another, drawn by academic curiosity and something deeper—the same compulsion that had driven him since finding the first golden fragment. The darkness seemed alive, watching, evaluating.

What do you seek, scholar?

The question resonated not in his ears but within his mind. Barry found himself answering truthfully, unable to dissemble in this altered state.

"Knowledge. Understanding. The truth of what happened to Blossom."

Truth demands sacrifice. Knowledge requires surrender. Are you prepared to lose everything you believe to find what you seek?

The question struck at his core identity as an academic, as a rationalist. What would remain of Barry Curtis if his fundamental understanding of reality were shattered? If the frameworks through which he interpreted the world proved inadequate or false?

"I seek truth regardless of the cost to my preconceptions," he heard himself answer.

Then approach and be unmade.

He stepped forward into the consumptive darkness. There was a sensation of falling, of dissolution, of identity unraveling strand by strand. Barry Curtis—professor, archaeologist, rational man of science—fragmented into constituent elements and reassembled in configurations that defied conventional understanding.

Visions assaulted him with relentless intensity. The tomb of Genghis Khan rendered in impossible detail—not as it might be, but as it was, hidden within the living mountain. The Book of Gold with its accumulated wisdom and terrible secrets. The guardians, through centuries, maintained their vigil against those who would exploit the Khan's legacy.

And other things, things that shook the foundations of his understanding. Shapes that moved through stone as though it were water. Winds that spoke with human voices. A presence within the mountain itself, ancient and aware, that had kept its secrets for eight centuries through means beyond human comprehension.

With sickening abruptness, the visions collapsed. Barry found himself on his knees in the underground chamber, gasping for breath, his body drenched in cold sweat. The guardians stood in a circle around him, their wooden masks now appearing as stylized wolves—the symbol of Genghis Khan's ancestry.

"You have witnessed," Temujin stated rather than asked, removing his mask to reveal an expression of grave assessment. "What did you see?"

Barry struggled to articulate experiences that defied conventional language. "The mountain. The tomb. Something... guarding it. Something that isn't human." He looked up, meeting Temujin's gaze with newfound understanding. "You're not the only guardians, are you?"

A subtle shift passed through the assembled figures—tension or recognition, he couldn't tell which.

"The Blue Sky Guardians serve, but we do not command," Temujin confirmed cryptically. "The mountain has its own will, its own purpose. We interpret. We prepare those who must approach. We warn those who must be warned."

He helped Barry to his feet with surprising gentleness. "The Trial of Mind is complete. You have demonstrated the necessary knowledge and perception. Now comes the Trial of Body."

Before Barry could fully recover his equilibrium, the chamber door opened to admit two guardians leading a figure he initially didn't recognize—a man with his head shaved to the scalp, body stripped to the waist, intricate blue markings painted across his chest and face.

With shock, he realized it was himself.

No—not himself. The figure was his height and build, but as it drew closer, subtle differences became apparent. This guardian was selected for his physical resemblance to Barry, prepared to serve as his proxy or opponent.

"The Trial of Body tests not just strength but harmony between intent and action," Temujin explained as the painted guardian took position in the center of the chamber. "For scholars unused to physical combat, we permit the trial by proxy—your mind directing another's body through the ritual of Sünsnii Khölgön."

"Soul Vehicle," Barry translated automatically, academic training asserting itself even through his disorientation.

"Yes. The blue smoke has prepared your consciousness. Now you must project your will into your champion and guide him through the combat trial."

Barry wanted to protest the impossibility of what Temujin suggested, but the lingering effects of the blue smoke had altered his perception too profoundly for conventional skepticism. He felt a strange doubling of awareness—still present in his own body but simultaneously sensing an opening, a receptivity, in the painted guardian standing before him.

"Focus your intention," Temujin instructed. "See through his eyes. Move through his limbs. Become the vessel and the will simultaneously."

Barry concentrated, focusing on the painted figure with an intensity that seemed to narrow the world to a single point. The strange doubling sensation intensified until, with dizzying suddenness, perspective shifted. He was still aware of his own body, seated on the stone floor, but now also inhabited the form of the painted guardian, experiencing dual consciousness with hallucinatory clarity.

The chamber door opened again, admitting a second guardian—this one larger, more heavily muscled, his body painted with red markings that stood in stark contrast to the blue designs on Barry's proxy.

"The combat begins," Temujin announced. "Victory is not required. Worthiness is demonstrated through courage, adaptability, and harmony between mind and vessel."

The red guardian attacked without warning, moving with a speed that belied his size. Barry's academic mind recognized the techniques of bökh—traditional Mongolian wrestling—but this knowledge meant nothing without the physical training to put it into practice.

Yet somehow, through the inexplicable connection established by the blue smoke ritual, he found himself responding. His consciousness guided the blue guardian's movements with increasing coordination—blocking, countering, and applying principles of physics and biomechanics that he had theoretically understood but had never personally executed.

The combat was unlike anything in his experience—simultaneously intellectual and visceral, strategic and instinctual. Through his proxy, Barry experienced the impact of blows, the strain on his muscles, and the measured expenditure of energy that professional fighters understood intuitively.

The red guardian was clearly superior in raw skill and strength. Still, the unusual nature of the contest created unexpected advantages. The blue guardian's movements were unpredictable precisely because they originated from Barry's untrained mind—combining academic knowledge of combat principles with improvisational responses that a traditionally trained fighter might never consider.

How long the contest continued, Barry couldn't tell. Time had become elastic, stretching and compressing according to no discernible pattern. Eventually, inevitably, the red guardian executed a decisive throw that sent Barry's proxy crashing to the stone floor. By traditional bökh rules, the match was over.

With jarring suddenness, Barry's consciousness snapped fully back into his own body. The painted guardian rose from the floor, bowing respectfully to his opponent before both withdrew from the chamber.

"The Trial of Body is complete," Temujin declared. "You have demonstrated necessary harmony between intention and action."

Barry rose unsteadily to his feet, his own body aching in precise correspondence to the impacts his proxy had sustained—phantom pain from a combat he had experienced yet not physically undertaken. Before he could question this impossible sensation, the chamber door opened once more.

Sakura entered, accompanied by Khulan and three female guardians. Her appearance shocked him—her face bore intricate patterns painted in white clay, and her clothing had been replaced by traditional Mongolian female warrior garb, which he recognized from historical depictions. Most startling was her expression—a controlled ferocity that suggested she had undergone trials perhaps more intense than his own.

"Your companion has completed her testing," Temujin announced. "The council will now deliberate."

The guardians withdrew, leaving Barry and Sakura alone in the chamber. For several moments, neither spoke, each assessing the other's transformed state.

"What did they do to you?" Barry finally asked, his voice hoarse from smoke inhalation and shouting commands his proxy had never physically heard.

"Tested my limits," Sakura replied, her tone suggesting vast understatement. "Combat trials against increasingly skilled opponents. Weapons tests with traditional Mongolian arms. And something... something I can't entirely explain." She touched the white markings on her face. "A ritual they called Khilengiin Büjig—the Dance of Rage. A combat trance similar to practices I've encountered in certain Japanese martial traditions."

"Did you also experience... visions?" Barry asked carefully.

A shadow passed across her features. "Yes. The mountain. The tomb. Things I can't rationally explain." Her eyes met his with unexpected vulnerability. "Things that challenge everything I thought I understood about reality."

The admission from someone as pragmatic as Sakura struck Barry with particular force. Whatever she had witnessed had shaken her foundational beliefs as profoundly as his own experience.

"They're preparing us," he realized aloud. "Not just testing our worthiness. Preparing us for what we'll encounter in the mountains."

"Yes." Sakura's expression hardened into resolution. "And based on what I saw, we need every advantage they can provide."

The chamber door opened again, admitting Temujin, Khulan, and the full council of guardians. They formed a semi-circle before Barry and Sakura, their expressions solemn.

"The testing is complete," Temujin announced. "The council has reached its decision."

Barry felt his heart rate accelerate. After all they had endured, would they be turned away now? Separated? Forced to abandon their quest when they were so close?

"You are found worthy to approach the sacred mountains," Temujin continued, "but not as you are. The final trial remains—the Trial of Transformation."

At his gesture, guardians approached bearing ceremonial items—clothing of ancient design, weapons of traditional Mongolian style, containers of ritual paints and unguents. Khulan stepped forward, her ancient hands carrying a small knife with a blade of polished obsidian.

"To seek the Khan's rest, you must be reborn in the old way," she explained, her voice carrying the weight of centuries. "The old name, the old self, must be sacrificed. Only then can you walk the true path without triggering the mountain's defenses."

Barry exchanged glances with Sakura, both recognizing the dangerous escalation this represented. They were being asked to surrender not just their physical appearance but their identities—to undergo a transformation whose full implications remained ominously unclear.

"The ritual leaves permanent marks," Temujin warned, perhaps sensing their hesitation. "The mountain recognizes those who have been properly prepared. It destroys those who approach under false pretenses."

"And our enemies?" Sakura asked practically. "Yamamoto and Black-wood? They've already departed for the mountains without your prepa-ration."

"They follow false paths that appear promising but lead only to empti-ness or destruction," Khulan answered. "They may find caves, ruins, arti-facts of the period—enough to convince themselves they approach the true site. But without the guardians' blessing, without the proper preparation, they will never reach the burial chamber itself."

"And if they force their way through?" Barry pressed. "With modern technology, explosives, ground-penetrating radar?"

Temujin's expression darkened. "Then the mountain's deepest defenses will awaken. The consequences would be... severe. Not just for them, but potentially for all who stand upon the sacred peaks."

The warning carried unmistakable gravity. Whatever protected the Khan's tomb—whether natural forces, human guardians, or something less easily categorized—it represented a danger beyond ordinary consider-ation.

"The ritual must begin now if you are to reach the mountains by the celestial alignment," Khulan urged. "Four days remain before the stars stand in the configuration you identified. If you miss this window, the next opportunity comes only after the winter snows."

By which time Yamamoto or Blackwood might have triggered whatever catastrophe Temujin hinted at. The choice was being stripped away by circumstance and urgency.

"We'll do it," Barry decided, looking to Sakura for confirmation.

She nodded once, decisively. "Whatever is necessary."

The guardians moved forward, surrounding them with a ceremonial purpose. Female attendants led Sakura toward one side of the chamber while male guardians directed Barry to the opposite wall. Screens were erected, creating separate ritual spaces.

"Remove your Western garments," an attendant instructed Barry. "All of them. Nothing from your old life can remain."

As he complied, Barry observed Temujin preparing a paste of blue pigment in a stone bowl, mixing it with what appeared to be blood and a powder ground from an unidentifiable substance. Khulan approached with the obsidian knife, its edge gleaming with unnerving sharpness in the lamplight.

"The first mark is made with blood and blade," she explained, her ancient eyes holding his with hypnotic intensity. "The name you have carried is cut away. The name you will carry is written in the old script."

The knife touched his chest, directly over his heart. Barry suppressed a gasp as the obsidian edge bit into his skin—not deeply, but enough to draw blood that Khulan collected in a small clay bowl.

"Baatar," she pronounced, mixing his blood with the blue pigment. "It means 'hero' in the old tongue. This will be your name until the journey ends."

The mixture was applied to the small wound and then in intricate patterns across his chest, shoulders, and face. Other attendants worked simultaneously, wrapping his lower body in traditional Mongolian garments, binding his feet in leather boots designed for the harsh mountain terrain.

Through gaps in the screen, Barry caught glimpses of Sakura undergoing a parallel transformation. Her ritual name was pronounced clearly enough for him to hear—"Sakura," meaning "moon" or "monthly," a name with connections to female warrior traditions in ancient Mongolia.

The ritual continued for what felt like hours, each element executed with meticulous attention to ancient protocols. Barry's head was partially shaved in the Mongolian warrior style of Genghis Khan's era, the remaining hair bound in a specific configuration. Protective amulets of bone, leather, and metal were secured around his wrists and neck, each inscribed with symbols whose meaning eluded even his linguistic expertise.

Finally, Temujin approached with a cup containing a liquid that steamed despite the chamber's cool temperature. "The final element. The essence that completes the transformation. Drink fully without hesitation."

The liquid burned like fire, going down, spreading through Barry's body with alarming speed. Unlike the previous ceremonial substances, this one didn't produce visions or altered perception. Instead, it created a hyperawareness of his physical form, as though every cell had awakened to its own distinct existence.

As the sensation peaked, Temujin and Khulan spoke in unison, their voices blending in a chant that seemed to resonate within Barry's very bones: "The old self is surrendered. The new self awakens. The mountain will know its own."

The screens were removed, revealing Sakura's—no, Sakura's—transformed appearance. Her hair had been similarly styled in the ancient manner, her face and exposed skin marked with white patterns that seemed to shift subtly in the lamplight. She wore the traditional deel of a Mongolian female warrior, adapted for practicality in the harsh mountain environment.

They regarded each other with mutual shock and recognition—familiar yet fundamentally altered, themselves yet not themselves.

"The transformation is complete," Temujin declared. "You are prepared to approach the sacred mountains. To walk the true path that remains hidden from those who come with conquest in their hearts."

"What exactly will we find there?" Barry—now Baatar—asked, his voice sounding strange in his own ears.

"That depends on what the mountain reveals to you," Khulan answered cryptically. "Some see only stone and wind. Others glimpse realities beyond ordinary perception."

"And the tomb itself?" Sakura—Sakura—pressed.

"Has remained inviolate for eight centuries for reasons you will understand only when you stand before it," Temujin replied. "But know this—the journey before you is treacherous in ways that transcend physical danger. The mountain does not merely guard the Khan's remains; it guards knowledge that humanity has not been ready to possess."

"The Book of Gold," Barry surmised. "The military technologies Yamamoto seeks."

"That and more," Khulan confirmed. "Secrets that could reshape the world or destroy it, depending on the intentions of those who discover them."

The weight of their responsibility settled on Barry with crushing force. They weren't merely racing to reach a historical discovery before their enemies; they were potentially preventing a catastrophe whose dimensions they couldn't fully comprehend.

"We depart at midnight," Temujin announced. "Rest now. Embrace your new identities. Let the old selves fade like mist before the morning sun."

As the guardians withdrew, leaving them alone in the chamber, Barry studied Sakura's transformed appearance more carefully. Behind the ritual markings and traditional garb, he caught a glimpse of something unexpected—uncertainty, perhaps even fear—in the eyes of this woman, who had faced every previous danger with calculating composure.

"Are you all right?" he asked quietly.

"I'm not sure," she admitted, touching the markings on her face with tentative fingers. "During the ritual, I experienced... something. A connection to this place, to these people, that makes no rational sense." Her eyes met his with troubling intensity. "I saw the tomb, Barry, not as a theoretical archaeological site, but as it exists at this moment. I saw the mountain's defenses. I saw what happened to those who approached with the wrong intentions."

A chill ran through him at her words. "What happened to them?"

Her expression darkened. "The mountain unmade them. Not killed—unmade. As though they never existed at all."

The statement hung between them in the ancient chamber, its implications too disturbing to fully process. Whatever awaited them in the Khentii Mountains transcended normal understanding of danger or discovery.

They were no longer merely Barry Curtis and Sakura Hirata, archaeologist and security expert on a quest to find a historical treasure. They had been transformed into Baatar and Sakura, initiates of an ancient order, prepared through rituals they didn't fully understand to face forces they couldn't entirely comprehend.

And somewhere ahead, in the sacred mountains of northern Mongolia, the tomb of history's greatest conqueror awaited—along with enemies willing to kill for its secrets and defenses capable of unmaking those who approached with conquest in their hearts.

Four days until the stars aligned. Four days to navigate a landscape both physical and metaphysical. Four days to reach a destination that had remained hidden for eight centuries despite countless attempts to uncover it.

The final journey was about to begin.

Chapter 11: Preparing for the Mountain

The storage chamber beneath Gandan Monastery smelled of leather, wool, and the sharp tang of metal—the scent of warriors preparing for battle, unchanged across centuries. Barry—no, Baatar now—ran his fingers over the equipment laid before him on rough-hewn wooden tables. The guardians had assembled an eclectic arsenal that straddled centuries: traditional Mongolian gear interspersed with modern necessities, ancient wisdom complementing contemporary technology.

"These have been prepared for your journey," Temujin explained, his hand sweeping over the assembled items. "Each selected with purpose, each blessed in the old way."

Baatar examined a curved knife with a polished bone handle, its blade inscribed with symbols he recognized as protective wards in ancient Mongolian script. Beside it lay a modern satellite phone, waterproofed and hardened against extreme conditions, incongruous next to tools that could have equipped Genghis Khan's own warriors.

"The mountain responds to intention and respect," Khulan added, her weathered hands smoothing a map drawn on cured leather rather than paper. "Modern tools used with proper reverence will be tolerated. But weapons of pure destruction—guns, explosives—these anger the ancient guardians."

Baatar caught Sakura's eye across the chamber, noting her skeptical expression even through the ritual markings that transformed her face. The rational parts of them—the parts still clinging to their identities as Barry Curtis and Sakura Hirata—struggled with these assertions that defied scientific understanding. Yet the experiences of the past twenty-four hours had shaken those rational foundations in ways neither could fully articulate.

"The combined maps," Baatar said, returning to concrete matters. "I need to study them before we depart."

Temujin nodded, guiding him to a separate alcove where a stone table stood illuminated by oil lamps. Upon it lay three distinct maps: the golden sheets they had carried from America, now removed from their protective case; the ancient leather map Khulan had presented; and a third rendered on silk, its surface shimmering in the wavering light.

"Together, they reveal what separately remains hidden," Temujin explained.

Baatar spread the golden sheets carefully, their thin metal surfaces catching the lamplight. Beside them, he arranged the leather map, noting points of correspondence and divergence. The silk map was last, its delicate surface decorated with astronomical symbols that appeared to shift subtly as the lamplight flickered.

"These markings," he said, pointing to a series of symbols along the edge of the golden sheets. "They're astronomical notations, but I couldn't fully decipher their significance without proper reference points."

"Because they are incomplete by design," Khulan confirmed. "The knowledge was divided, as all dangerous secrets must be." She indicated corresponding marks on the silk map. "These complete the celestial align-ment indicators. Together, they reveal not just where to seek the tomb, but when the entrance becomes accessible."

Baatar's academic training asserted itself as he began cross-referencing the notations across all three maps, his mind calculating stellar positions, seasonal variations, and geographical coordinates with increasing excite-ment.

"The alignment happens three times yearly," he muttered, half to him-self. "But only during the summer solstice period does it correspond with these terrestrial markers." His finger traced a specific mountain formation on the leather map. "Here—where these three peaks form a perfect triangle with the North Star at summer solstice."

"Yes," Temujin confirmed. "And that alignment occurs four nights from now. If you fail to reach the site by then, the entrance will not reveal itself again until next year."

"By which time our enemies might have found another way in," Sakura interjected, joining them at the table. She had been inventorying survival gear with methodical precision, her movements fluid despite the unfamil-iar traditional clothing. "Or worse, triggered whatever defenses guard the tomb without proper preparation."

"The consequences would be severe," Khulan agreed, her ancient eyes momentarily unfocused as though seeing distant possibilities. "The mountain's anger is not a simple thing. Its retribution extends beyond those who provoke it."

Baatar returned his attention to the maps, focusing on practical matters rather than cryptic warnings. "These markings show a specific approach route," he observed, noting a sinuous path marked in faded red on the leather map. "Through this valley, then upward along this ridge. But the golden sheets show a different path entirely."

"Because there are false paths," Temujin explained. "Dozens of them. Some lead to empty caves that appear promising. Others to dangerous terrain that has claimed many lives. Others still to... places that exist between realities."

"What does that mean?" Sakura asked sharply.

"There are locations in the sacred mountains where the boundary between worlds thins," Khulan said, her voice dropping to near-whisper. "Where those who enter may never return, or return... changed. The Khan's protectors created these deliberate misdirections, these traps for the unwary or unworthy."

Baatar might have dismissed such claims days earlier. Now, after the visions induced by the blue smoke, after experiencing consciousness transfer during the combat trial, such assertions occupied an uncomfortable space between superstition and possibility.

"The true path is revealed only when all three maps are considered together," Temujin continued practically. "And only when approached at the correct celestial alignment. This is why no expedition has succeeded in eight centuries. They lacked either the complete information or the proper timing—usually both."

Sakura leaned closer to the silk map, her trained eye assessing distances and terrain. "The route is challenging," she noted. "Exposed ridgelines, narrow passes, limited cover. If Yamamoto's forces are already in the area..."

"They follow false paths," Temujin assured her. "But yes, they could still pose danger if they detect your approach. The mountain's influence grows stronger near the sacred peaks, but is not absolute until you reach the inner sanctum."

"Meaning guns will still kill us in the outer approaches," Sakura translated bluntly.

"Yes," Temujin acknowledged. "Until you reach the boundary marked here." He indicated a line on the leather map rendered in blue pigment. "Beyond this point, weapons of metal and fire cease to function. Only traditional arms retain their power."

Baatar traced the route from their planned entry point to the boundary line, mentally calculating distances. "That's nearly fifteen kilometers of exposed terrain before we reach the protected zone. Plenty of opportunity for interception."

"Which is why speed and stealth are essential," Temujin agreed. "You depart at midnight, traveling under darkness until you reach the mountains' shadow. Vehicles will take you as far as this point." He indicated a location on the map, perhaps fifty kilometers from Ulaanbaatar. "Beyond that, you continue on horseback along routes rarely traveled."

"Horses?" Baatar questioned, his limited equestrian experience suddenly a concerning liability.

"The mountain knows them," Khulan said cryptically. "Modern vehicles disturb the ancient spirits, create... disharmonies that alert watchers both seen and unseen."

Sakura straightened, her expression shifting to professional assessment. "I need to make contact with my intelligence source," she stated. "If Yamamoto's team is already in the mountains, Ishida might have surveillance information we can use."

Temujin studied her with narrowed eyes. "Your Japanese contact. Can he be trusted?"

"As much as anyone in his profession," she answered carefully. "He opposes the Red Lotus and has provided reliable intelligence so far."

"And his interest in the tomb?"

"He wants to ensure the Book of Gold doesn't fall into Yamamoto's hands," Sakura replied. "Beyond that, his motives are his own."

Temujin exchanged glances with Khulan before responding. "You may use this." He produced a satellite phone different from the one included with their equipment. "It operates on frequencies shielded from standard monitoring. Make your communication brief. All electronic signals near the sacred mountains attract... attention."

Sakura accepted the device with a nod, withdrawing to a corner of the chamber for privacy. Baatar returned his focus to the maps, meticulously copying the most crucial information into a small leather-bound journal provided by the guardians. Electronic devices might fail; memory might falter under stress; but physical documentation had endured for centuries in Mongolia's harsh climate.

As he worked, Altan approached with bundles of clothing—additional layers designed for the mountain's unpredictable conditions. "The sacred peaks create their own weather," the guardian explained. "Sunshine can become a blizzard between one step and the next. Heat can turn to killing cold without warning."

"Natural weather patterns in mountain regions are often volatile," Baatar observed, the scientist in him seeking a rational explanation.

Altan smiled thinly. "Natural, yes. But not always governed by forces your meteorologists understand." He laid out the garments with methodical care. "These are woven with patterns that the mountain recognizes. They offer protection beyond their physical properties."

The clothing did indeed feature intricate designs woven or embroidered into the fabric—symbols that corresponded to certain protective motifs Baatar recognized from his academic studies of shamanic practices. He ran his fingers over a spiral pattern at the cuff of a heavy wool deel, feeling an unexpected warmth that seemed disproportionate to the material itself.

Across the chamber, Sakura's voice rose slightly, tension evident despite her controlled tone. Baatar glanced over to see her gripping the satellite phone tightly, her posture rigid with alarm.

"When?" she demanded. "How many?" A pause as she listened. "And their equipment? Understand. Yes. No further contact until we return. Maintain observation only."

She ended the call, her expression grim as she rejoined them at the map table.

"Yamamoto's expedition is larger than we anticipated," she reported without preamble. "Twenty-eight personnel, including specialized military contractors, ground-penetrating radar, and excavation equipment." Her finger stabbed at a location on the leather map. "They've established a forward base here, at the convergence of three valleys approximately thirty kilometers from the true site."

"That location," Khulan observed with evident concern, "is one of the false paths, but a dangerous one. A place where the veil thins unpredictably."

"They've already lost two men," Sakura continued. "According to Ishida's surveillance, they simply vanished while scouting the western ridge. No bodies recovered."

"The mountain tests those who approach," Temujin said, unsurprised. "But Yamamoto's force remains substantial. What of the British woman?"

"Blackwood's team is smaller but better equipped. Twelve operatives, all former special forces. They're approaching from the north, here." Sakura indicated another position, perhaps twenty kilometers from Yamamoto's base. "They're moving more cautiously, using local guides."

"Guides who will lead them in circles," Altan interjected with grim satisfaction. "No true Mongolian would reveal the sacred paths, even under threat."

"Blackwood's resources shouldn't be underestimated," Sakura countered. "She has satellite imaging, historical documentation from British imperial archives, and considerable experience in acquiring protected artifacts."

"Both forces represent serious threats," Baatar concluded. "But the celestial alignment remains our greatest constraint. Four nights from now, the entrance will reveal itself—but only if we're in position at precisely the right moment."

"And only if you approach with proper intention," Khulan reminded them. "The mountain knows what lies in the hearts of those who seek the Khan's rest. It... tastes their purpose."

The old woman's words sent an involuntary shiver down Baatar's spine. The rational part of him—the academic, the scientist—wanted to dismiss such claims as superstition. Yet the experiences of the past two days had systematically undermined his certainty about what was possible and what was merely mythological.

"We should review the supplies again," he suggested, retreating to concrete matters. "Ensure everything is properly secured for travel."

The next hours passed in methodical preparation. Clothing was carefully packed in waterproof satchels. Food—a combination of traditional Mongolian provisions and modern high-energy rations—was distributed for maximum efficiency. Water purification equipment, emergency medical supplies, climbing gear, and navigation tools were checked and rechecked.

Throughout the process, the guardians continued Baatar and Sakura's instruction—not just in practical matters of survival, but in the rituals and observances they would need to perform at specific points along their journey. Prayers to be spoken when crossing certain boundaries. Offerings to be left at ancient stone markers. Symbols to be drawn on rock faces to ensure safe passage.

"Superstitious nonsense," the scientist in Baatar wanted to declare.

"Essential protocols," the newly born Baatar accepted, the transformation of the ritual having affected him more deeply than he cared to admit.

As the hour of departure approached, Temujin called them to a final council in the main chamber. The full complement of guardians had assembled, forming a circle around a central fire that cast dramatic shadows across their solemn faces.

"Before you depart, there is one final matter," Temujin announced. "The sharing of blood and vision."

At his gesture, Khulan approached with the same obsidian knife used during their transformation ritual. "The mountain knows its own," she explained. "Those who share blood with the guardians receive certain... protections. Certain insights."

Baatar and Sakura exchanged wary glances. They had already undergone extensive ritual modifications to their appearances, consumed substances that induced visions and altered states of consciousness. This represented yet another surrender of autonomy, another step away from their original identities.

"Is this necessary?" Sakura asked, her pragmatic nature asserting itself.

"Not necessary," Temujin conceded. "But advisable. The sacred peaks are home to forces that respond to blood connection, to lineage. As outsiders, you would be... more vulnerable without this binding."

Khulan held the obsidian blade over the fire, its edge gleaming with ominous purpose. "The choice remains yours. But know that every protection refused increases the mountain's scrutiny."

After a moment's hesitation, Baatar extended his hand. "Proceed."

The blade was cool against his palm, the cut swift and precise. Khulan collected his blood in a small jade bowl, then performed the same procedure with Sakura. To this mixture, she added what appeared to be preserved blood from a sealed vial that Temujin produced from within his robes.

"The blood of the guardians, preserved through generations," he explained. "Containing traces from the Khan's own lineage."

Khulan mixed the contents with practiced motions, adding a powder that caused the liquid to momentarily phosphoresce with an eerie blue glow. She divided the mixture into two small cups carved from polished bone, offering one to each of them.

"Drink as the moon rises," she instructed. "When the night is deepest. When the boundary between worlds thins."

Baatar accepted the cup, fighting revulsion at its contents. His scientific mind cataloged all the potential health hazards of consuming human blood, even in this ritualistic context. Yet his transformed self—Baatar, initiate of the Blue Sky Guardians—recognized the significance beyond hygiene concerns.

"The final preparations are complete," Temujin declared. "You will depart when the midnight hour arrives. Until then, meditate upon your purpose. Clear your minds of doubt. Remember that the mountain tastes intention as clearly as a wolf scents fear."

The guardians withdrew, leaving Baatar and Sakura alone beside the fire. For several minutes, neither spoke, each processing the enormity of what lay ahead—not just a dangerous expedition, but a journey into realms of experience that challenged their fundamental understanding of reality.

"Do you believe any of this?" Sakura finally asked, her voice low, private. "The mountain's awareness. The forces beyond explanation. The rituals and blood magic."

Baatar considered the question carefully. "Three days ago, I would have dismissed it entirely. Now..." He stared into the dancing flames. "I've experienced things I cannot explain through conventional scientific frameworks. Witnessed phenomena that defy rational analysis."

"As have I," she admitted. "The visions during my trial... they showed me things that cannot possibly exist. Yet they felt more real than reality itself." Her hand unconsciously touched the ritual markings on her face. "And these transformations—they're affecting me in ways I don't fully understand. I feel... different. As though Sakura is receding and I am becoming more than just a role I'm playing."

"I feel it too," Baatar confessed. "As though the ritual reached something deeper than conscious identity. Something..." he hesitated, searching for words, "...ancestral. Primal."

Sakura's eyes reflected the firelight, their usual calculated assessment now mingled with something more vulnerable. "What if we can't go back?

What if Baatar and Sakura aren't just temporary identities but permanent transformations?"

The question hung between them, giving voice to fears that had been growing since the ritual. They had surrendered their former selves in exchange for access to the sacred mountains, but the full implications of that exchange remained disturbingly unclear.

"One problem at a time," Baatar decided pragmatically. "First, we reach the tomb before our enemies. Then we prevent whatever catastrophe might result from improper access to its contents. After that..." he attempted a smile that felt strange on his ritually marked face, "...we can worry about returning to our former selves."

Sakura nodded, her professional composure reasserting itself. "The immediate threats are tangible enough. Yamamoto's forces. Blackwood's mercenaries. The treacherous terrain. The deadline of the celestial alignment."

"And whatever truth lies behind the guardians' warnings about the mountain itself," Baatar added. "Whether supernatural or merely natural phenomena misinterpreted through cultural frameworks, the danger is real."

They lapsed into silence again, each contemplating the challenges ahead. Outside, night had fully descended on Ulaanbaatar, the ancient capital now hidden beneath darkness as it had been on countless nights since its founding by Genghis Khan's son. Somewhere beyond the city lights, the sacred mountains waited—and within them, the tomb that had remained hidden for eight centuries.

Four days until the stars aligned. Four days to navigate terrain that had claimed dozens of expeditions. Four days to reach a destination guarded by forces they still didn't fully comprehend.

And somewhere in those mountains, their enemies were already searching, already disturbing ancient equilibriums, already triggering defenses designed to protect history's most significant burial site.

The midnight hour approached, bringing with it the moment of depar
ture... and the final surrender of their former selves to the blood ritual that
would bind them to the guardians' ancient lineage.

The journey to the Khan's tomb was about to begin in earnest.

Chapter 12: The First Assassin

The safe house was an ancient ger nestled in the foothills thirty kilometers northeast of Ulaanbaatar. This traditional Mongolian dwelling had stood for generations, its weathered felt walls having witnessed the passage of centuries. Outside, the vast steppe stretched toward distant mountains barely visible in the predawn gloom. The air held a peculiar stillness that comes in the hours before sunrise, a silence so complete it seemed to press against the eardrums like physical pressure.

Baatar sat cross-legged beside the central hearth, studying the combined maps by the dim glow of coals. The blood ritual completed at midnight had left him changed in ways he struggled to articulate. His senses seemed unnaturally sharp, every sound and scent carrying information that registered on levels beyond normal perception. The ritual markings on his skin no longer felt foreign—instead, they pulsed with a subtle warmth that synchronized with his heartbeat.

More disturbing was the continued dissolution of his former self. Memories of Barry Curtis had taken on a dreamlike quality, as though they belonged to someone else entirely—a distant ancestor, perhaps, or a character

from a story he'd once read. Baatar felt increasingly natural, increasingly...
authentic.

"The horses sense something," Sakura announced, entering the ger with
predatory silence. She had been outside checking their mounts, five sturdy
Mongolian steeds provided by the guardians for the journey into the sacred
mountains. "They're restless. Ears pricked toward the west."

Baatar nodded, unsurprised. Since the blood ritual, his awareness had
extended outward in unsettling ways. He'd been sensing a disturbance for
the past hour—nothing concrete, merely a wrongness in the air, like the
electric tension before a devastating storm.

"How long?" he asked simply.

"Minutes, not hours." Sakura moved with fluid economy, checking
weapons arrayed near the entrance—traditional Mongolian blades and
bows alongside the limited modern equipment permitted by their ritual
preparations. The transformation had affected her even more profoundly
than Baatar, her movements now carrying an almost supernatural grace,
her eyes reflecting light like a predator's when she turned toward the dying
fire.

"Could be nomadic herders," Baatar suggested without conviction.

"No." Sakura's denial was absolute. "The wrongness tastes of metal and
malice." She touched the ritual markings on her face, fingertips tracing
patterns that seemed to shift beneath her skin. "The mountain's blood lets
me smell their intentions. Killers are approaching."

Two days earlier, such a statement would have triggered Barry Curtis's
scientific skepticism. Now, Baatar merely nodded, accepting her assessment as naturally as he accepted the evidence of his own enhanced senses.

"How many?"

"Five. Perhaps six." She selected a curved blade from their weapons,
testing its edge with practiced precision. "They move with purpose, trying
to mask their approach, but the steppe whispers their passage to those with
ears to hear."

Baatar rose, moving to the small window cut into the ger's wall. The landscape outside remained shrouded in darkness, the mountains to the north mere shadows against a marginally lighter sky. Nothing moved across the visible expanse of steppe, yet he felt the approaching threat as tangibly as an approaching thunderhead.

"Red Lotus," he surmised. "Yamamoto must have informants in Ulaan-baatar. Someone who detected our departure."

"Or our preparations triggered watchers we didn't recognize." Sakura had positioned herself beside the entrance, one hand resting on the curved knife at her belt, the other holding a weapon that seemed to occupy an impossible middle ground between ancient and modern—a throwing blade whose metal gleamed with unnatural luster in the dim light. "The guardians warned that the ritual would make us more visible to certain eyes."

Baatar crossed to his own weapons, selecting a bow of laminated horn and sinew that felt unnaturally comfortable in his hands despite Barry Curtis's complete lack of archery experience. The physical knowledge was there in his muscles, as though awakened by the blood ritual rather than learned.

"Options?" he asked, stringing the bow with practiced motions that came from somewhere beyond conscious memory.

"We could flee immediately. The horses are ready." Sakura's expression suggested this wasn't her preferred approach. "Or we spring their trap. Take one alive for questioning."

"The latter gives us valuable intelligence."

"And satisfies the blood debt owed for Batbold. For your sister." Sakura's eyes met his, something ancient and terrifying flickering behind them. "The mountain's justice demands balance."

The statement should have disturbed him. Instead, Baatar found himself nodding in agreement, the concept of blood debt feeling entirely appropriate. This too was part of the transformation—moral frameworks shifting along with identity, ancient imperatives superseding modern ethics.

"How do we proceed?" he asked, selecting arrows from a quiver of supple leather.

"They will attempt to surround the ger before attacking. Standard tactical approach." Sakura extinguished the remaining embers in the hearth with a practiced motion, plunging the interior into near-complete darkness. "I will exit first, create a diversion on the eastern side. You take position by the western wall, eliminate any who approach from that direction."

"And if their numbers are greater than we sense?"

Sakura's smile was visible even in the darkness, her teeth gleaming with unnatural brightness. "Then the ancestors receive more offerings tonight."

They moved to their positions with silent coordination, communicating more through intuition than planned strategy. Baatar positioned himself by the western wall of the ger, an arrow nocked but not yet drawn. Sakura crouched by the entrance flap, her body coiled like a predator prepared to spring.

For three heartbeats, nothing happened. Then Baatar felt it—a disruption in the night's energy, an intrusion of hostile intent into the harmonious patterns of the steppe. He sensed rather than saw movement approximately fifty meters from the ger, figures using the rolling terrain for concealment as they established a perimeter around the dwelling.

Sakura felt it too. Without verbal communication, she slipped through the entrance flap and vanished into the darkness, her movement so fluid it seemed more like shadow flowing than a human in motion.

Baatar counted silently, giving her time to circle behind their attackers before he provided his portion of the diversion. At precisely the count of thirty, he drove his knife through the felt wall of the ger, creating a viewing slit without exposing himself to outside observation.

Through this narrow aperture, he finally saw them—five figures in dark clothing moving with military precision through the tall grass surrounding the ger. Their equipment was modern yet minimal, optimized for stealth and combat rather than prolonged engagements. Even at this distance, Baatar recognized the distinctive movement patterns of Red Lotus operatives—the same efficient lethality he had witnessed in Washington and Istanbul.

A sharp whistle cut through the predawn silence—three notes in a pattern that seemed to vibrate in Baatar's bones rather than his ears. Sakura's signal. He drew the bow with practiced ease, the motion feeling as natural as breathing despite his lack of training, and loosed an arrow through the slit in the wall.

The projectile found its mark with uncanny precision, striking the nearest attacker in the junction between neck and shoulder. The man dropped silently, his collapse visible only as a sudden absence in the pattern of moving shadows.

Chaos erupted immediately. The remaining assassins broke formation, seeking cover while trying to identify the source of the attack. One fired a suppressed weapon toward the ger, bullets thudding into the felt walls with muffled impacts. Another threw something that landed just outside the entrance—a flash-bang grenade that detonated with concussive force, designed to disorient anyone inside.

But Baatar was no longer beside the wall. The moment he'd loosed his arrow, he'd moved to a new position, anticipating the counter-attack with intuition that felt simultaneously foreign and innate. The explosion's light penetrated the ger's fabric, casting bizarre shadows across the interior. Still, he remained unaffected by its disorienting purpose.

From somewhere in the darkness outside came sounds that raised the hair on Baatar's neck—a wet, tearing noise followed by a choked cry abruptly silenced. Then another. Sakura was among them.

He used the distraction to make his move, slipping through the entrance flap with the bow ready. The scene outside was one of controlled chaos. Two attackers already lay motionless on the ground, their forms crumpled in positions that suggested swift, efficient death. A third was engaged in desperate hand-to-hand combat with Sakura—though "combat" inadequately described the one-sided nature of the encounter.

She moved with impossible speed, her body flowing around her opponent's strikes like water around stone. The ritual markings on her skin seemed to writhe in the dim light, pulsing with faint luminescence that left blurred trails as she moved. Her knife found openings with surgical precision, each strike targeting nerve clusters and vulnerable anatomy rather than delivering immediately fatal wounds.

The fourth assassin had identified Baatar as he emerged and was bringing his weapon to bear—a compact submachine gun designed for close-quarters killing. Baatar's body reacted before his mind processed the threat, loosing another arrow with fluid precision. The projectile struck the man in the forearm, causing him to drop the weapon with a muffled curse in Japanese.

The fifth attacker was nowhere visible, either concealed in the darkness or already dispatched by Sakura's lethal efficiency.

The wounded assassin recovered quickly, drawing a blade from his belt and advancing on Baatar with obvious skill. This was no ordinary operative—his movements indicated extensive training in traditional Japanese martial disciplines, as well as modern combat techniques.

Baatar cast aside the bow, drawing his own curved knife in a motion that felt dictated by muscle memory he shouldn't possess. The two circled each other in the grass, measuring distance, assessing weaknesses.

"You are already dead," the assassin stated in heavily accented English. "The Red Lotus has bloomed across the sacred mountains. What you seek is already ours."

"The mountain has not yet rendered its judgment," Baatar heard himself respond in perfect Japanese, the language flowing from his lips despite Barry Curtis having no knowledge of it. "Your master violates ancient covenants. The price will be paid in blood."

The assassin's eyes widened fractionally—the only indication of surprise before he attacked with blinding speed. His blade sliced through the space Baatar had occupied a heartbeat earlier, meeting empty air as Baatar flowed aside with the same liquid grace Sakura had demonstrated.

The countering strike came not from conscious thought but from somewhere deeper—the muscle memory of warriors whose blood now mingled with his own. Baatar's knife found the gap between the assassin's ribs with precision that would have been impossible for Barry Curtis, penetrating just deeply enough to disable without killing.

The man collapsed to his knees, blood darkening his clothing but his eyes remaining defiant. Before Baatar could secure him, a shape materialized from the darkness—the fifth assassin, moving with desperate speed, a curved blade aimed at Baatar's unprotected back.

There was no time to turn, no possibility of evasion. Yet death did not come.

Instead, a wet, tearing sound broke the night's silence. The assassin froze mid-strike, his face contorting in shock as he looked down at the tip of a blade protruding from his chest. Behind him stood Sakura, her expression coldly detached as she withdrew her weapon with a practiced twist that ensured the wound would be fatal.

"Sloppy," she commented as the man collapsed. "Your awareness of your surroundings is improving, but still inadequate."

Baatar nodded, accepting the criticism without offense. "The blood ritual enhances, but does not complete the transformation," he acknowledged, the formal phrasing feeling natural on his tongue.

"One remains alive for questioning," Sakura observed, gesturing to the kneeling assassin Baatar had wounded. "The others have joined their ancestors."

Together, they secured the surviving assassin, binding his wounds to ensure he remained conscious, then restraining him with techniques that Barry Curtis should have found disturbing but Baatar accepted as necessary. The man's weapons were collected and examined—modern firearms with custom modifications, blades of exceptional quality, equipment that spoke of substantial resources and specific intent.

"These are not ordinary operatives," Sakura noted, examining a communication device recovered from one of the dead assassins. "Special deployment unit. Elite even within the Red Lotus hierarchy."

"Yamamoto commits significant resources to our elimination," Baatar agreed. "He fears what we might achieve."

They returned to the ger with their prisoner, securing him to a central post while Sakura rekindled the fire. Dawn was approaching, the eastern sky lightening to pearl gray, but inside the traditional dwelling, shadows still held dominion.

The assassin watched them with calculating eyes, his pain masked behind iron discipline. Despite his wounds and restraints, he maintained the dignified posture of a warrior who accepted his fate while revealing nothing to his captors.

"You wear the marks of the Blue Sky Guardians," he observed in Japanese, his gaze fixed on the ritual patterns adorning their skin. "Outsiders adopted into the blood lineage. An... unexpected development."

"Your master failed to account for many things," Sakura replied in the same language, her pronunciation flawless despite Sakura Hirata's Japanese being academic rather than native. "The mountain's influence extends further than he realizes."

"The mountain is stone and earth," the assassin countered. "Nothing more. Your superstitions will not protect you from what comes."

Baatar circled the bound man, studying him with detached curiosity. "You believe this because you have not yet approached the sacred peaks. Those who came before you have already discovered otherwise."

A flicker of something—uncertainty, perhaps even fear—crossed the assassin's composed features. "What do you mean?"

"Two of Yamamoto's advance scouts disappeared three days ago," Sakura stated flatly. "Not killed. Not captured. Vanished from existence while exploring the western ridge. Did your master share this information with his secondary teams?"

The assassin's momentary silence was confirmation enough.

"The mountain unmakes those who approach with conquest in their hearts," Baatar continued, the words emerging from some ancestral memory awakened by the blood ritual. "It does not merely kill—it erases. No body remains. No spirit transitions to the next realm. Complete dissolution of being."

"Superstitious nonsense," the assassin declared, but his conviction had weakened perceptibly.

"Then answer this," Sakura challenged, leaning close enough that the ritual markings on her face seemed to writhe in the firelight. "Why does your master seek the tomb with such urgency? Why commit elite resources to eliminate mere archaeologists? What does Yamamoto truly seek among the Khan's remains?"

The assassin's discipline held, but Baatar sensed the calculation behind his silence—weighing what could be revealed against what must be protected, measuring the value of information as currency for survival.

"You know nothing of our purpose," the man finally stated. "The Red Lotus serves greater imperatives than mere treasure hunting."

"The Book of Gold," Baatar surmised, watching the assassin's pupils dilate fractionally at the reference. "Not just historical documentation, but specific knowledge. Technical information. Weapon designs."

"The Khan conquered half the known world," Sakura added, picking up the thread with practiced coordination. "His armies incorporated the most advanced technologies from every civilization they encountered: Chinese siege engines, Persian astronomical calculations, Byzantine naval designs. All recorded in the Book of Gold for future generations."

The assassin's expression remained controlled, but sweat had begun to bead on his forehead despite the cool temperature inside the ger.

"Yamamoto doesn't seek historical artifacts," Baatar pressed. "He seeks applicable knowledge. Weapons that can be reproduced with modern materials. Strategic concepts that can be adapted to contemporary conflicts."

"You understand nothing," the assassin finally responded, his voice tight with controlled emotion. "The Book contains more than mere weapon designs. It holds secrets that transcend conventional warfare. Knowledge that could reshape the balance of global power."

"What knowledge?" Sakura demanded, her hand moving to the knife at her belt with deliberate intent.

The assassin hesitated, internal conflict visible in the tension of his jaw. When he finally spoke, his voice had dropped to a near whisper.

"The Khan's armies conquered territories stretching from the Pacific to Eastern Europe. In doing so, they encountered knowledge from dozens of ancient civilizations—some of which possessed understanding that has been lost to modern science." His eyes darted between them, measuring their comprehension. "Including principles of energy manipulation that your physicists are only beginning to rediscover."

"Be specific," Baatar commanded, a chill spreading through him despite the fire's warmth.

"The Book contains formulas for what you might call directed energy weapons," the assassin continued reluctantly. "Devices that could harness natural electromagnetic fields to devastating effect. The Chinese called it 'Heaven's Fire.' The Persians had similar technology, which they termed 'Lightning of the Gods.' Primitive by modern standards, but the underlying principles..." He shook his head slightly. "Yamamoto believes they can be adapted using contemporary materials to create weapons with no existing countermeasures."

The implications were staggering. If true, the Book of Gold contained not just historical curiosities but information that could create a devastat-

ing shift in military capability—particularly in the hands of an organization with the Red Lotus's nationalistic ideology.

"Your master moves with excessive forces," Sakura observed. "Twenty-eight personnel, specialized equipment, military contractors. For recovery of knowledge alone, this seems disproportionate."

"The primary expedition is prepared for extraction and immediate implementation," the assassin acknowledged, perhaps calculating that this
information was already known to them. "Engineers, physicists, materials
specialists—all chosen for their ability to translate ancient concepts into
functional prototypes. Yamamoto intends to demonstrate a working application within weeks of recovering the Book."

"Demonstrate to whom?" Baatar pressed.

The assassin's lips tightened, discipline reasserting itself. "I have said
enough."

"Japanese nationalist factions," Sakura surmised, watching the man's
face for confirmation. "Elements within the government and military are
sympathetic to Red Lotus ideology. Yamamoto seeks to prove the organization's value as more than mere historical preservationists. He wants to
transform it into a power broker with unique military capabilities."

The assassin's silence was confirmation enough.

"And the British woman?" Baatar asked. "Blackwood and her mercenaries. Where do they fit into this equation?"

"A complication," the assassin admitted with evident distaste. "She represents commercial interests rather than ideological ones. Corporations
that would weaponize the knowledge for profit rather than national resur-
gence." His eyes narrowed slightly. "The Red Lotus serves a higher purpose.
We seek to restore Japan's rightful place as a military power independent
of Western oversight."

"By threatening devastating weapons based on ancient Mongolian
knowledge," Sakura noted with irony. "Your nationalist vision requires
borrowed glory."

Anger flashed across the assassin's features before his training suppressed it. "The knowledge belongs to those with the vision to implement it. The Khan himself understood this principle—incorporating the innovations of conquered peoples into his own arsenal."

"And those who stand in your way?" Baatar asked quietly.

The assassin met his gaze without flinching. "Are removed. As you will be, regardless of the outcome of this interrogation. Yamamoto has deployed his full resources. The sacred mountains are surrounded. Every approach is monitored. Your journey ends before it truly begins."

A distant sound caught Sakura's attention—her head turning toward the entrance with predatory focus. "Reinforcements," she announced. "Two vehicles approaching from the southwest. Approximately three kilometers distant but closing rapidly."

Baatar moved to the entrance, confirming her assessment with his own enhanced senses. "Time to move," he agreed. "The horses are ready."

"And him?" Sakura nodded toward their prisoner.

The question hung between them—a test of how completely their transformation had progressed. Barry Curtis would have insisted on mercy, on civilized treatment even for an enemy. But Baatar felt older imperatives stirring in his blood, ancient codes of conduct that recognized different realities.

"The steppe will receive him," Baatar declared, the formal phrasing coming naturally. "His spirit will warn others who would violate the sacred mountains."

Sakura nodded, accepting the judgment without question. She approached the bound assassin, her movements conveying ritual purpose rather than mere pragmatism. "Your warning is received," she told him in formal Japanese. "Your death will have meaning as a message to those who follow."

To the assassin's credit, he met his end with the composed dignity of a warrior culture that stretched back centuries. No pleading, no desperate bargaining—only a slight inclination of his head in acknowledgment of the inevitable.

Sakura's blade moved with ceremonial precision, the killing stroke delivered with merciful efficiency. "May your ancestors receive you," she intoned as the light faded from his eyes.

They gathered their essential equipment with practiced speed, leaving behind anything that would slow their approach to the mountains. The sky had lightened to pale lavender in the east, the sacred peaks to the north now visible as jagged silhouettes against the dawn.

Outside, the horses sensed their urgency, stamping restlessly as Baatar and Sakura secured their minimal gear to the saddles. The animals were small but sturdy—traditional Mongolian stock bred for endurance and surefootedness in difficult terrain.

"The reinforcements will follow," Sakura observed, mounting her horse with fluid grace. "And they will alert Yamamoto's main expedition. Our advantage of secrecy is lost."

"But our knowledge is expanded," Baatar countered, settling into his own saddle with surprising comfort despite Barry Curtis's limited equestrian experience. "We understand the true stakes now. Not just archaeological preservation, but preventing weapons of devastating potential from falling into dangerous hands."

They rode north as the sun crested the eastern horizon, its first rays illuminating the steppe in shades of gold and amber. Behind them, dust clouds marked the approach of their pursuers. Ahead loomed the sacred mountains—their destination, their testing ground, and perhaps their final resting place.

The race for the Khan's tomb had entered its most perilous phase, with enemies converging from all directions, and the stakes had escalated beyond anything they had initially imagined. No longer merely a quest for historical knowledge, their journey had become a desperate effort to prevent catastrophic weaponry from falling into the hands of those who would reshape the global balance of power.

And somewhere in those mountains, ancient forces stirred—guardians beyond human understanding, awakened by the approaching conflict, waiting to pass judgment on all who dared disturb the Khan's eternal rest.

Chapter 13: Into the Khentii Mountains

The transition from steppe to mountains occurred with unsettling abruptness. One moment, they were riding across the undulating grasslands that had cradled Mongolian nomads for millennia; the next, the landscape fractured into hostile, angular forms—slate-gray cliffs rising like broken teeth from the earth, narrow valleys twisting between them like the spaces between vertebrae.

Baatar felt the change immediately. The air grew heavier, charged with an energy that made the fine hairs on his arms rise despite the protective layers of traditional Mongolian garments. Beside him, Sakura straightened in her saddle, head tilting as though listening to voices inaudible to ordinary senses.

"We've crossed the first boundary," she murmured. "The mountain knows we approach."

Their horses sensed it too. The sturdy Mongolian steeds that had carried them tirelessly across the steppe now moved with heightened alertness, ears flicking nervously at sounds beyond human perception. The lead mare—a dun-colored animal with unusual amber eyes—repeatedly stopped to paw at the stony ground, nostrils flaring as though testing the air for dangers invisible to her riders.

"They feel it stronger than we do," Baatar observed, stroking his mount's sweat-dampened neck. "The guardians said animals perceive the mountain's awareness more directly than humans."

"Some humans," Sakura corrected, her ritualized face turning toward the jagged peaks that loomed before them. "Those without preparation would notice nothing until too late."

The implication hung between them—that their blood-mingling with the guardians had attuned them to perceptions ordinarily beyond human range. Each hour that passed made this more evident. Baatar found himself noticing patterns in stone formations that seemed to shift when viewed directly; Sakura repeatedly tracked movements at the corners of her vision that vanished when she turned to face them.

They had been riding for two days since the encounter with the Red Lotus assassins. Their pursuers had maintained distance but never completely disappeared—dust clouds on the horizon, occasional glints of metal catching the sun, evidence of a determined force tracking their progress toward the sacred mountains.

"The map indicates we should follow this valley," Baatar said, consulting the leather-bound journal where he had transcribed the critical information from all three sources. "It leads to what the guardians called the Throat of the Wolf—a narrow pass between twin peaks."

Sakura studied the imposing mountains with trained assessment. "Tactically vulnerable. Perfect position for ambush."

"The only viable approach according to the guardians," Baatar reminded her. "False paths lead to... consequences."

The word inadequately conveyed the warnings they had received: stories of entire expeditions vanishing without trace, of experienced mountaineers found wandering in madness, of strange distortions in space and time that devoured the unwary. Before the blood ritual, Baatar might have dismissed such accounts as superstition or exaggeration. Now, with the mountain's presence prickling against his awareness like static electricity, skepticism felt dangerously naive.

They urged their horses forward, entering the valley that would lead them deeper into the Khentii range. Immediately, the temperature dropped several degrees, and shadows from the towering walls created a perpetual twilight despite the midday sun. The path narrowed, forcing them to proceed in single file, Sakura leading with predatory vigilance, Baatar following with the three pack horses trailing behind.

The silence was the first unsettling element—an absence so complete it felt deliberate rather than natural. No birds called. No insects buzzed. Even the wind seemed to hold its breath, creating an acoustic deadness that made their horses' hoofbeats sound unnaturally loud, like intrusions into a sacred space.

"Listen," Sakura whispered, drawing her mount to a halt.

Baatar strained his enhanced senses, at first perceiving nothing beyond the unnatural quiet. Then he caught it—a subtle vibration beneath the apparent silence, like a massive heartbeat conducted through stone rather than air. Regular. Deliberate. Alive.

"The mountain breathes," he murmured, the words emerging from ancestral memory rather than conscious thought.

They continued forward, the valley gradually narrowing until the stone walls rose nearly vertically on either side, creating a corridor barely wide enough for a single horse. Shadows deepened despite the sun being directly overhead, as though light itself were being absorbed by the ancient rock.

"Look," Sakura indicated marks on the valley wall—distinctive gouges in the stone that couldn't be explained by natural erosion.

Baatar dismounted to examine them more closely. "Tool marks," he confirmed. "Metal against stone. Recent, within the past few weeks."

"Yamamoto's advance team," Sakura surmised. "Or Blackwood's scouts."

"Either way, they passed this way before us." Baatar traced the marks with fingertips that detected more than merely physical information. "There's... wrongness in these. Disharmony. They struck the stone without proper reverence."

The observation would have sounded absurd to Barry Curtis, yet to Baatar it was simply evident—like noting that food had spoiled or water had been contaminated. The mountain remembered violations against it, recorded them in ways that transcended ordinary understanding.

They remounted and continued deeper into the valley, the path occasionally widening enough to ride side by side before constricting again. After an hour's journey, the sky above changed with alarming suddenness—clear blue replaced by rolling gray clouds that appeared from nowhere, gathering with unnatural speed.

"Weather shift," Sakura noted, eyeing the darkening sky with professional concern. "Too rapid for natural patterns."

"The guardians warned us," Baatar recalled. "The sacred peaks create their own climate. Sunshine becomes blizzard between one step and the next."

As if summoned by his words, the first snowflakes began to fall—not the gentle drift of ordinary weather, but sharp, stinging pellets driven by winds that howled down the valley with sudden fury. Within minutes, visibility shortened to mere meters, the landscape transformed into a howling white void.

"We need shelter," Sakura shouted over the wind's scream. "The horses can't continue in this."

Baatar consulted his mental map, the combined information from all three sources now internalized in ways that seemed to bypass ordinary memory. "There's a formation ahead—the Sleeping Warrior. Rock overhangs that could provide temporary protection."

They pressed forward, the horses struggling against mounting snow and punishing wind. The temperature had plummeted with unnatural speed, turning their breath to crystalline clouds that were immediately torn away by the gale. The ritual markings on their skin burned with unexpected warmth, perhaps the only thing preventing immediate frostbite on exposed flesh.

The Sleeping Warrior materialized from the whiteout like a specter—a massive rock formation that indeed resembled a recumbent giant, complete with a craggy face turned skyward and an arm-like projection creating a natural shelter beneath. They guided their exhausted horses under this stone canopy, the sudden absence of driving snow and wind almost shocking after the storm's assault.

"This isn't natural," Sakura stated flatly, dismounting to check the horses for injury. "The storm formed too quickly. Targeted too precisely."

"The mountain tests us," Baatar agreed, unpacking essential supplies in case they needed to wait out the blizzard. "Or warns us. Or both."

The sheltered space beneath the stone arm was larger than it had initially appeared, extending perhaps fifteen meters into the cliff face. As they led the horses deeper into this natural sanctuary, Baatar's enhanced vision adjusted to the gloom, revealing details that sent a chill through him unrelated to the external temperature.

"We're not the first to shelter here," he observed quietly.

The evidence was scattered throughout the cave-like space—remnants of previous expeditions that had sought refuge from the mountain's wrath. A rusted cooking pot half-buried in silt. Rotted remains of leather packs. Fragments of equipment whose purpose had been obscured by time and decay.

Sakura moved to the deepest part of the shelter, her body language suddenly alert. "Here," she called, voice tight with controlled emotion.

Baatar joined her, his night-adapted vision revealing what had triggered her response. Against the back wall sat the remains of three people—desiccated by the mountain air into mummified forms that retained disturbing detail. They were positioned in a tight circle, backs to each other, as though making a final stand against some approaching threat. Their expressions, preserved in leathery skin stretched over bone, displayed identical terror—mouths open in silent screams, eyes wide with final horror.

"Japanese expedition, 1962," Baatar assessed, noting fragments of clothing and equipment that placed them historically. "Academic researchers from Kyoto University, if I recall the Guardian's records correctly."

"What killed them?" Sakura asked, her professional detachment temporarily overriding ritual identity. "No obvious wounds. No signs of violence or struggle."

Baatar examined the tableau more carefully, noticing details that ordinary perception might have missed. Though the bodies appeared physically intact, there was an inexplicable wrongness about them—as though something essential had been extracted through means that left no visible trauma.

"The guardians spoke of the mountain's hunger," he said softly. "Of its judgment upon those who approach with improper intention."

"You think it... consumed them somehow?" Sakura's scientific skepticism briefly reasserted itself. "That's not physically possible."

"Physical possibility may not be the relevant standard here." Baatar indicated markings on the cave floor surrounding the bodies—intricate patterns scratched into stone that couldn't possibly be natural. "They tried to protect themselves. These are warnings from multiple traditions—Shinto, Buddhist, even elements of Mongolian shamanic practice."

"Ineffective ones, apparently," Sakura observed grimly.

They set up camp as far from the desiccated remains as the shelter allowed, establishing a small fire using the precious fuel they carried. The storm outside had intensified to near-hurricane force, snow and ice particles battering the stone with such violence it sounded like countless tiny fists demanding entrance.

As Baatar prepared a simple meal of traditional Mongolian provisions, Sakura established a protective perimeter—not with modern technology, but with items provided by the guardians. Small totems of bone and sinew. Pouches of herbs placed at cardinal points. Symbols drawn in a paste of minerals and blood upon the stone threshold.

"Will these actually help?" Baatar asked, the rational remnants of Barry Curtis questioning the seemingly superstitious precautions.

"The evidence suggests we should take no chances," Sakura replied pragmatically, nodding toward the mummified researchers. "Whatever approached them, they saw it coming. Had time to attempt protection. Failed."

The implication was clear—they faced threats beyond ordinary understanding, dangers that transcended physical attack. The mountain itself was their most significant adversary, its judgment more consequential than Yamamoto's forces or Blackwood's mercenaries.

As they ate their sparse meal, the storm's voice seemed to change—the mindless howl of wind transforming subtly into something that raised the fine hairs on Baatar's neck. Patterns emerged from the chaos, rhythms that suggested language rather than mere weather.

"Do you hear that?" he asked quietly.

Sakura nodded, her expression revealing she had been tracking the same disturbing shift. "It speaks," she confirmed. "Not in words, but in... intentions."

They listened together, their blood-enhanced perceptions detecting meaning within the storm's voice that ordinary humans would perceive only as elemental fury. The message was not linguistic but nonetheless clear—a warning, a challenge, a statement of ancient rules that would not be violated without consequence.

"It knows why we've come," Baatar translated, the understanding arising from somewhere beyond rational thought. "It... measures our purpose."

"And finds it acceptable?" Sakura asked, her hand unconsciously touching the ritual markings on her face.

"Not rejected," Baatar clarified. "Not yet. We are... permitted to contin-ue, but not welcomed. Tolerated rather than embraced."

The distinction seemed crucially important, though he couldn't have explained why in terms Barry Curtis would have understood. The moun-tain's judgment operated on principles that transcended modern ethical frameworks—ancient, elemental perspectives that categorized human in-tention by standards established long before civilization arose.

As night fell, the storm gradually subsided, its message delivered, its warning implanted in their awareness. Darkness within the shelter became absolute, their small fire the only illumination against a blackness that felt active rather than passive—not merely the absence of light but the presence of something else.

"I'll take first watch," Sakura offered, checking her weapons with habit-ual thoroughness.

"Against what?" Baatar asked, glancing toward the cave entrance where snow had drifted into fantastic shapes. "Yamamoto's forces couldn't pos-sibly track us through that storm."

"Not all dangers approach on feet," she replied cryptically. "The guardians warned of tests beyond the physical. The mountain's judgment takes many forms."

They established a rotation, with each person taking turns to watch while the other rested. Baatar settled into his bedroll, bone-weary from the day's journey yet strangely alert to the shelter's subtle vibrations. The stone itself seemed to pulse with a slow, deliberate rhythm—the heartbeat he had sensed earlier now amplified by direct contact with the mountain's substance.

Sleep, when it came, delivered not rest but vivid dreaming, unlike any-thing Barry Curtis had ever experienced. Baatar found himself moving through the sacred mountains not as a visitor but as an integral compo-nent—perceiving through stone and wind rather than through eyes and ears. He witnessed previous expeditions from the mountain's perspective, understanding its reactions to their intrusions and its judgments on their intentions.

Some it merely deflected—weather shifts, disorienting mists, paths that circled back upon themselves without logical explanation. Others it actively rejected—crevasses opening beneath unwary feet, avalanches triggered by whispered words, strange distortions in space that left expeditions hopelessly lost despite modern navigation equipment.

And a few—those whose intentions carried particular threat—it unmade in ways that defied conventional understanding of life and death. Not killing in any ordinary sense, but a dissolution more complete, a harvesting of essence that left physical husks behind while consuming what animated them.

Baatar jerked awake with a gasp, his body drenched in cold sweat despite the fire's lingering warmth. Sakura was instantly alert, moving to his side with fluid grace.

"What did you see?" she asked, understanding immediately that his reaction stemmed from more than an ordinary nightmare.

"The mountain showed me," he whispered, struggling to translate experiences beyond language into comprehensible terms. "How it protects the tomb. What happens to those it judges unworthy."

"The Japanese researchers?" She glanced toward the mummified remains.

"And others. Dozens of expeditions across centuries." Baatar shuddered despite himself. "It doesn't just kill, Sakura. It... consumes. Incorporates. Their awareness persists within the mountain's consciousness, their knowledge absorbed into its judgment."

The implications were too disturbing to fully process—a form of existence neither life nor death, but eternal subsumption into an ancient entity beyond human comprehension. Those taken by the mountain didn't die in any conventional sense; they became part of what took them, their individual consciousness preserved but subjugated within a vaster awareness.

"The guardians tried to warn us," Sakura observed. "But words were insufficient to convey the reality."

"We still have a choice," Baatar reminded her. "We can turn back. The blood ritual marks us as... potential allies rather than confirmed intruders. The mountain permits our approach but hasn't yet fully accepted our purpose."

The option hung between them—retreat to safety, abandonment of their quest, return to their former identities, and the world they had left behind. For a moment, Barry Curtis resurged within Baatar, the academic's self-preservation instinct clamoring against the madness of continuing into territory that violated everything he understood about reality.

Sakura seemed to sense his internal conflict. "The transformations we've undergone," she said carefully. "They're more than disguise or cultural adaptation. The blood ritual changed us at levels we're only beginning to comprehend."

"Yes," Baatar acknowledged. "Barry Curtis feels increasingly distant. A memory of someone I once was rather than my current identity." He touched the ritual markings on his face, feeling their subtle warmth pulsing in time with the mountain's rhythm. "If we continue, the transformation may become irreversible."

"Would that be so terrible?" Sakura asked, something vulnerable flickering behind her warrior's composure. "Sakura Hirata was forged in vengeance and obsession. Her existence narrowed to a single purpose. Sakura feels... more connected. More complete."

The admission revealed depths to her transformation that paralleled his own. Both had surrendered former identities that had been damaged by trauma and loss. Both had embraced new selves with connections to something larger, something ancient and enduring. The price of return might be higher than merely physical danger.

"We continue," Baatar decided, knowing Sakura had already reached the same conclusion. "Not just to prevent Yamamoto from weaponizing the Book of Gold, but to complete what the mountain has begun in us."

She nodded, satisfied with his resolution. "The storm has passed. We should move while darkness provides cover."

They packed their minimal camp with efficient coordination, leaving no trace of their presence beyond the ancient remains that had greeted their arrival. The horses accepted their burdens with stoic endurance, seemingly recharged by the brief rest despite the supernatural tension permeating their shelter.

Outside, the landscape had been transformed by the storm's passage. Snow blanketed the valley floor, pristine and unmarked, glowing with faint blue luminescence under the light of a moon that seemed impossibly large and close. The air had cleared to crystal transparency, revealing stars in configurations that didn't match any astronomical pattern Barry Curtis would have recognized.

"The sky has changed," Baatar observed, unease prickling along his spine.

"The boundary thins as we approach the sacred peaks," Sakura confirmed, mounting her horse with fluid grace. "What we perceive is increasingly influenced by the mountain's reality rather than our own."

They rode in silence, following a path that existed more in their blood-enhanced perception than physical reality. The valley widened gradually, opening into a basin surrounded by towering peaks that resembled sentinels standing eternal watch. In the center of this natural amphitheater stood a formation that commanded immediate attention—a column of dark stone rising like a massive spear thrust into the earth, its surface covered in carvings too precise to be natural yet too alien to be human.

"The Pillar of Heaven," Baatar identified it from the descriptions of the guardians. "The first true marker on the path to the Mountain of the Sun."

They approached cautiously, dismounting to examine the monolith more closely. Its surface gleamed with an unnatural luster, despite its apparent age; the carvings shifted subtly under direct observation, as though refusing to be fixed in ordinary perception.

"These aren't decorative," Sakura noted, tracing one symbol with careful fingers. "They're functional. Some kind of... mechanism or key."

Baatar consulted his transcribed notes, comparing the symbols to those recorded from the golden sheets. "According to the map, we must activate the pillar to proceed. It marks not just location but intention—announcing our approach to the mountain's awareness."

"Declaring ourselves rather than attempting concealment," Sakura translated practically. "Honesty of purpose rather than stealth."

The procedure required precision and interaction with specific symbols in a particular sequence. Baatar worked methodically, his blood-enhanced understanding guiding movements that Barry Curtis would have found incomprehensible. As he pressed the final glyph, the entire pillar resonated with a deep, subsonic vibration that transmitted through the ground beneath their feet, through their bodies, and into the very air around them.

The mountain had registered their presence.

For several heartbeats, nothing visible changed. Then, with dreamlike gradualness, a path appeared where none had existed before—not through physical transformation of the landscape but through a shift in perception that revealed what had been hidden. A narrow trail winding between two peaks previously separated by impassable terrain, now connected by a route that seemed to exist in multiple realities simultaneously.

"The Way is opened," Baatar said formally, the ritualized phrase emerging from blood memory.

They remounted, leading their horses toward this newly revealed path. As they approached the passage between peaks, Baatar felt resistance—not physical but perceptual, as though reality itself objected to their intrusion.

The air thickened, time stretched, each hoofbeat seeming to echo from multiple locations simultaneously.

"The boundary strengthens," Sakura observed, her voice distorting slightly as though reaching him from a greater distance than the mere feet separating them. "The mountain scrutinizes our approach more intensely."

The sensation built as they entered the narrow pass, becoming almost unbearably intense—a pressure against not just their bodies but their identities, their memories, their very conception of self. Baatar felt Barry Curtis fracturing further, as core memories reshuffled and personality structures realigned to accommodate perceptions beyond the ordinary human capacity.

Then, with shocking abruptness, the pressure vanished. They emerged from the pass into a landscape so alien yet familiar it momentarily stole Baatar's breath. Before them stretched a valley unlike any on modern maps of the Khentii range—a hidden realm that existed separate from ordinary geography, protected by barriers beyond conventional understanding.

And rising from the center of this concealed valley, catching the impossible moonlight like a beacon, stood a peak of distinctive configuration—three ascending ridges converging at a summit that resembled a flame frozen in stone.

"The Mountain of the Sun," Baatar identified it with certainty born of blood rather than scholarship. "The sacred peak beneath which the Khan awaits."

They had reached the outer boundary of their destination, the threshold of the tomb that had remained hidden for eight centuries. But the most dangerous part of their journey still lay ahead—crossing terrain guarded by forces beyond human comprehension, navigating a landscape where reality itself became malleable, and reaching the burial site before either Yamamoto or Blackwood triggered the mountain's most devastating defenses.

And somewhere in that hidden valley, unseen but undeniably present, other expeditions moved with their own purposes—enemies converging on the sacred peak from multiple directions, unwittingly risking catastrophe beyond their understanding.

The race for the Khan's tomb had entered its final, most perilous phase.

Chapter 14: The Watchers

The wind across the Khentii Mountains carried more than the bite of approaching winter—it carried the scent of horses and the distant sound of engines that didn't belong in this sacred wilderness. Barry Curtis crouched behind a weathered boulder, studying the valley below through binoculars. At the same time, Sakura monitored their radio scanner for any electronic communications from their pursuers.

"Three different groups," he murmured, lowering the binoculars with growing concern. "Maybe four."

They had been traveling for two days since leaving Ulaanbaatar, following the ancient caravan routes that led toward the Mountain of the Sun described in the golden map fragments. The journey had started well—clear weather, reliable GPS coordinates, and no sign of immediate pursuit. But as they climbed higher into the sacred range where Genghis Khan was believed to be buried, the situation had changed dramatically.

"The helicopter passed over again twenty minutes ago," Sakura reported, adjusting the frequency dial on their communications equipment. "Same flight pattern as yesterday, but flying lower. They're definitely tracking something."

Barry studied the terrain around them with the eye of someone who had learned to read landscapes for both historical significance and tactical advantage. The Khentii Mountains were a maze of valleys, ridgelines, and hidden passes that had sheltered nomadic peoples for thousands of years. But those same features that provided concealment also created natural choke points where a small force could be trapped by larger, better-equipped pursuers.

"Yamamoto's people?" he asked.

"Has to be. The radio chatter I picked up this morning was definitely Japanese, and they're using military coordination protocols." Sakura packed away the scanner and shouldered her backpack. "But they're not the only ones out there."

That was what worried Barry most. They had expected Yamamoto's Red Lotus expedition to follow them into Mongolia—the man had made it clear he intended to claim the Khan's treasure at any cost. But the electronic signatures and movement patterns Sakura had detected suggested at least two other groups were operating in the region, each with their own agenda and capabilities.

"The tire tracks we found yesterday," Barry said, consulting the detailed topographical map they had been using to navigate. "Military vehicles, but not Mongolian army. Wrong tread pattern, wrong spacing between axles."

"Blackwood's mercenaries," Sakura concluded. "She must have entered the country through a different route, probably with full government cooperation if she's representing British intelligence interests."

They began moving again, following a ridge line that provided good visibility while keeping them out of the most obvious travel corridors. Barry carried the GPS unit that was tracking their progress against the golden map's cryptic geographical references, while Sakura used a handheld thermal scanner to watch for human activity in the valleys around them.

The weather was becoming increasingly hostile as they climbed higher into the mountains. The early winter storm system that had been threatening for days was finally beginning to deliver on its promise, with heavy clouds building against the peaks and the temperature dropping steadily. Snow had already begun to dust the highest ridges, and Barry could feel the barometric pressure changing in ways that suggested serious weather was approaching.

"This could actually work in our favor," he told Sakura as they paused to rest and reassess their situation. "A major storm will ground aircraft and make vehicle movement much more difficult. It levels the playing field between us and anyone with superior equipment."

"Assuming we can survive it ourselves," Sakura replied, checking their cold weather gear. "The forecast called for temperatures dropping to minus twenty Celsius, with winds up to sixty kilometers per hour. That's life-threatening exposure even with proper equipment."

Barry studied their position on the map, calculating distances to potential shelter and weighing the risks of different route options. The golden map's directions were leading them toward a specific valley system that should contain the astronomical markers referenced in the puzzle boxes, but reaching it would require crossing several miles of exposed terrain where they would be vulnerable to both observation and the approaching storm.

"Movement to the south," Sakura announced, studying the thermal scanner's display. "Large group, maybe eight or ten people, traveling in single file about two kilometers away."

Barry raised his binoculars and scanned the indicated direction until he spotted them—figures moving with the patient, efficient pace of people who knew the terrain intimately. Even at distance, their clothing and movement patterns were distinctly different from the military-style expeditions they had been tracking.

"Local nomads," he realized. "But they're not just traveling through the area. Look at their formation—they're conducting a search pattern."

The implications hit both of them simultaneously. The nomadic peoples of the Khentii Mountains had been the guardians of their sacred sites for centuries, passing down traditional knowledge about locations that should remain undisturbed. If word had spread about foreign treasure hunters operating in the region, the local communities would respond with their own protective measures.

"Temujin's people," Sakura said. "The Guardians of the Blue Sky. They're tracking all of us."

That made their situation exponentially more complex. They weren't just being pursued by two groups of well-equipped international treasure hunters—they were being watched by people who knew every trail, every water source, every hiding place in the mountains. People who had been protecting these sites from outsiders for generations and had their own methods for dealing with unwelcome visitors.

"How many groups does that make?" Barry asked grimly.

"Yamamoto's Red Lotus expedition, approaching from the east with helicopter support and military-grade equipment. Blackwood's mercenaries, coming from the south with vehicles and probably satellite communications. Local guardians who know the terrain better than any of us and consider everyone else to be trespassers." Sakura adjusted her pack straps and checked her weapon. "And possibly others we haven't detected yet."

The wind was picking up, carrying the first scattered snowflakes of what promised to be a significant storm. Barry could feel the temperature dropping perceptibly, and the cloud cover was thickening in ways that would soon make helicopter operations impossible. But the same conditions that would neutralize some of their enemies' advantages would also make their own survival much more challenging.

"There," Sakura pointed toward a valley entrance about three kilometers ahead of their current position. "That matches the geographical description from the second puzzle box. The 'Valley of Three Eagles' with the distinctive rock formations."

Barry studied the valley through his binoculars, noting the carved stone markers that were barely visible against the natural rock faces. Ancient Mongolian symbols that confirmed they were approaching the outer boundaries of the burial site's protective perimeter. But reaching the valley would require crossing open terrain where they would be visible to anyone with optical or thermal surveillance equipment.

"We wait for the storm," he decided. "Use the weather as cover to make our final approach."

They found concealment in a natural depression among the rocks, a position that provided some shelter from the wind while giving them clear views of the surrounding terrain. Barry used the time to study the golden map fragments under a tarp that blocked the light from outside observers, while Sakura monitored radio communications and tracked the movement patterns of their various pursuers.

"The helicopter turned back," she reported after an hour of patient observation. "Weather's getting too rough for safe flight operations."

"What about ground movement?"

"The vehicle convoy stopped about five kilometers south of here. Looks like they're establishing a base camp to wait out the storm." Sakura adjusted the thermal scanner's settings to penetrate the increasing precipitation. "But the nomad trackers are still moving. They're not letting weather slow them down."

Barry wasn't surprised. The local people had been living and traveling in these mountains for generations. A early winter storm that would stop modern military expeditions was just another seasonal challenge to be managed with traditional knowledge and equipment.

"The storm will peak around midnight," he estimated, studying the cloud formations and wind patterns. "That's when we move. Zero visibility, impossible tracking conditions, but also maximum danger if we make any mistakes."

As if summoned by his words, the wind intensified dramatically, driving snow horizontally across the mountainside and reducing visibility to less than fifty meters. The temperature plummeted, and Barry could feel the moisture in his breath beginning to freeze. Within minutes, their concealed position had become a genuine winter survival situation.

"Radio chatter has stopped," Sakura reported, huddling closer to share body heat. "Either they've switched to different frequencies, or the weather is interfering with communications."

"Both, probably. This is exactly what we need—a complete communications blackout that forces everyone to operate independently."

They spent the remaining daylight hours preparing for their approach to the valley, checking equipment, reviewing route options, and monitoring the positions of their various pursuers. The storm continued to intensify, transforming the mountainside into a white wilderness where navigation would depend entirely on compass bearings and dead reckoning.

As darkness fell, the wind reached a howling crescendo that made conversation nearly impossible. Snow was now falling so heavily that Barry could barely see Sakura despite sitting less than a meter away from her. But the same conditions that made their situation desperate also provided perfect concealment from anyone trying to track their movements.

"Now," he said, his voice barely audible over the storm.

They began their approach to the Valley of Three Eagles, moving slowly and carefully across terrain that had become treacherous with ice and blowing snow. Barry used a handheld GPS unit to maintain their heading, while Sakura followed close behind, connected to him by a safety rope that would prevent them from becoming separated in the white-out conditions.

The storm was so intense that Barry began to worry they had misjudged the risks. The temperature had dropped well below minus twenty

Celsius, and the wind chill was approaching life-threatening levels. Every step required enormous effort, and ice was forming on their clothing and equipment despite the specialized cold weather gear they were wearing.

But as they struggled through the blizzard, Barry realized they had achieved something remarkable—complete invisibility from their pursuers. No thermal imaging system could penetrate the storm, no aircraft could operate in the conditions, and even the most experienced mountain trackers would be forced to seek shelter rather than continue pursuit.

"There!" Sakura shouted over the wind, pointing toward barely visible shapes looming out of the snow.

The Valley of Three Eagles opened before them, its entrance marked by the distinctive rock formations described in the ancient maps. Even through the storm, Barry could see carved symbols on the stone faces—Mongolian script that warned intruders about the sacred nature of the site and the consequences of disturbing the eternal rest of the Universal Ruler.

They had reached the outer perimeter of Genghis Khan's burial complex, but Barry knew their challenges were just beginning. Somewhere behind them in the storm, multiple groups of determined treasure hunters were waiting for conditions to improve so they could resume their pursuit. And ahead lay whatever defenses the tomb builders had created to protect their greatest secret from exactly this kind of intrusion.

"Shelter first," Barry decided, studying the valley entrance for any sign of natural or artificial protection from the elements. "We need to survive the night before we can worry about finding the tomb."

As they pressed deeper into the valley, the wind began to diminish slightly, blocked by the surrounding ridges. But Barry could see evidence that they weren't the first to reach this location—recent boot prints in the snow, partially filled but still visible, indicating that someone else had found the valley entrance within the past few hours.

"We're not alone," Sakura observed, following his gaze to the tracks.

"No. But in conditions like this, that might not matter. Everyone's focused on survival first, treasure hunting second."

They found shelter in a natural cave that showed signs of recent human occupation—ashes from a small fire, equipment impressions in the sandy floor, and the lingering scent of modern camping fuel. Someone had used this exact hiding place very recently, possibly within the last day.

"Whose camp?" Sakura asked, examining the evidence with the trained eye of someone who had learned to read human activity like a tracking expert.

Barry studied the boot prints and equipment marks, trying to match them with the various groups they knew were operating in the region. "Local nomads, I think. The fire was built using traditional methods, and there's no evidence of modern camping gear."

"Which means the guardians are already here. They're watching the valley entrance, waiting to see who shows up looking for the Khan's tomb."

As they settled in to wait out the storm, Barry realized that their situation had become even more complex than he had anticipated. They weren't just racing against other treasure hunters to find a historical site—they were walking into a confrontation that involved people who considered themselves the legitimate protectors of their cultural heritage against foreign intruders.

The storm continued to rage outside their shelter, but Barry knew it was only providing temporary concealment. When the weather cleared, they would find themselves at the center of a convergence that had been building for months—multiple groups with conflicting agendas, all focused on the same ancient secret, all prepared to use whatever force necessary to claim their prize.

Somewhere in the darkness beyond the storm, the watchers were waiting.

Chapter 15: The False Tomb

The morning sun cast long shadows across the Khentii Mountains as Barry Curtis crouched beside what appeared to be the discovery of a lifetime. Carved into the face of a granite cliff, partially concealed by centuries of accumulated debris and vegetation, was an entrance that seemed to pulse with historical significance. The elaborate Mongolian script flowed across the stone lintel in characters so perfectly preserved that they might have been carved yesterday.

"This is it," Sakura whispered beside him, her breath forming small clouds in the thin mountain air. "The coordinates from both puzzle boxes lead directly here."

Barry studied the entrance through his binoculars, noting every detail. The carved symbols were indeed authentic—classical Mongolian script from the 13th century, invoking the protection of the Eternal Blue Sky and warning that "here lies he who conquered the world." But something about the entire setup made his historian's instincts prickle with unease.

"It's too perfect," he murmured.

"What do you mean?" Sakura lowered her binoculars and looked at him with concern. They had been traveling for three days through increasingly treacherous terrain, staying ahead of their pursuers through a combination of local knowledge and sheer determination. The stress was showing on both of them.

"Look at it objectively," Barry said, pointing toward the entrance. "We're following an 800-year-old treasure map to one of the most closely guarded secrets in human history. And we find it marked with a stone archway that practically screams 'Important Burial Site Here.'"

Sakura frowned, studying the entrance with fresh eyes. "You think it's a decoy?"

"I think the Mongols were too smart to mark their greatest Khan's resting place with obvious signage." Barry adjusted his position behind the boulder that concealed them from the valley below. "Remember, they went to extraordinary lengths to hide Genghis Khan's burial site. They killed everyone who worked on the tomb, then killed the soldiers who killed the workers. Does that sound like people who would advertise the location with carved inscriptions?"

Despite his reservations, Barry couldn't deny the mathematical precision of their discovery. The astronomical alignments referenced in the golden map sheets pointed directly to this location. The seasonal water markers they had followed through the mountain caves emerged from underground springs barely a hundred meters from the entrance. Even the local topography matched the cryptic geographical references encoded in the puzzle boxes.

"But the coordinates are exact," Sakura argued. "My mother spent years cross-referencing the astronomical data with known Mongolian burial practices. This has to be the right place."

Barry lowered his binoculars and studied the valley below them. There was no sign of their pursuers yet, but he knew that wouldn't last long. Yamamoto's expedition had been gaining ground steadily, and Blackwood's mercenaries were somewhere in the region as well. They had perhaps hours before this remote valley became a battlefield.

"Maybe you're right," he conceded. "But we approach this very carefully. If I'm wrong, we don't want to damage anything. If I'm right..." He left the sentence unfinished.

They spent another twenty minutes observing the site from their concealed position, noting wind patterns, animal tracks, and any other details that might provide clues about the entrance's true nature. Barry was particularly interested in the vegetation growing around the carved stones—some plants thrived in areas of human disturbance, while others avoided them entirely.

"The lichen patterns are wrong," he said finally. "See how the growth stops in a perfect circle around the entrance? That suggests the stone has been recently cleaned or altered."

Sakura pulled out the journal her mother had kept during her research into the map fragments. "According to this, the tomb builders were known to create false sites to mislead grave robbers. But they would have been designed to look authentic from the outside."

"Exactly. Which means the only way to know for sure is to go inside."

They began their descent toward the cliff face, moving carefully across loose scree and patches of early snow. The approaching winter had already begun to change the mountain's character—what had been merely challenging terrain a week ago was now potentially deadly. Ice formed in the shadows where the sun couldn't reach, and the wind carried a bite that promised serious cold to come.

The entrance was even more impressive up close. The carved archway stood nearly eight feet tall, with intricate details that spoke of master craftsmen working at the height of the Mongol Empire's power. Barry ran his fingers along the inscriptions, translating the classical script in his mind.

"'Here rests the Universal Ruler, he who brought the world under one sky,'" he read aloud. "'Let his enemies tremble even in death, for his spirit watches over the sacred mountains.'"

"It sounds authentic," Sakura observed.

"Too authentic. It's exactly what you'd expect to find at Genghis Khan's tomb—which is precisely why I don't trust it." Barry examined the entrance more closely, noting how the carved stones fit together. "Look at the mortar between these blocks. It's been repaired recently, within the last century."

Beyond the archway, a stone corridor extended into darkness. The walls were lined with more carved inscriptions, and Barry could see the faint outline of what appeared to be a burial chamber deeper inside. Everything about the site suggested it was exactly what they had been seeking.

"We'll need lights," Sakura said, adjusting the LED headlamp she had borrowed from their mountaineering supplies. "And we should rope ourselves together in case there are hidden shafts or unstable floors."

Barry agreed, and they spent several minutes preparing for their descent into the tomb. He carried the digital camera that would document their discoveries, while Sakura brought the portable ground-penetrating radar unit they had acquired in Ulaanbaatar. Whatever they found inside, they would need proof that would satisfy both academic institutions and the various governments that would inevitably become involved.

The entrance corridor was exactly what Barry would have expected from a 13th-century Mongolian burial site. The walls were covered with scenes depicting the great Khan's conquests—carved reliefs showing mounted warriors sweeping across vast steppes, cities burning in their wake, tribute bearers kneeling before the Universal Ruler. The artistic style was consistent with the period, and the level of detail was extraordinary.

"This is incredible," Sakura whispered, her voice echoing off the stone walls. "Look at these battle scenes. They're like a historical record carved in stone."

Barry nodded, but his unease was growing stronger with each step. The corridor was too well-preserved, too clean. Eight centuries of weather, earthquakes, and natural settling should have left their mark, but the passage looked as if it had been completed yesterday.

They reached a junction where the corridor split into three directions. Ancient symbols marked each passage—a wolf, a horse, and an eagle. Barry consulted the notes from both puzzle boxes, trying to match the symbols with the astronomical references encoded in the golden map sheets.

"The eagle passage leads toward the main burial chamber," he determined. "According to the map, that's where we'll find the Khan's body and the complete Book of Gold."

They followed the eagle passage deeper into the mountain, their headlamps creating a small bubble of light in the encompassing darkness. The air was remarkably fresh for such a deep underground space, which Barry noted as another anomaly. Ancient tombs typically developed distinctive atmospheric conditions over the centuries.

The passage opened into a circular chamber dominated by a raised stone platform in the center. On the platform sat what appeared to be a golden sarcophagus, elaborately decorated with scenes of mounted warfare and cosmic symbolism. Surrounding the central burial were smaller platforms holding grave goods—weapons, armor, jewelry, and scroll cases that might contain the legendary military and administrative knowledge of the Mongol Empire.

"My God," Sakura breathed. "We actually found it."

Barry approached the sarcophagus cautiously, noting how the gold seemed to gleam despite the centuries of supposed burial. His historian's eye catalogued the details—the craftsmanship was exquisite, the symbolism was appropriate for the period, and the overall layout matched descriptions from Chinese and Persian historical sources.

But something was still wrong.

"Sakura, bring the radar unit over here," he called. "I want to scan beneath the sarcophagus."

She activated the ground-penetrating radar and began sweeping it across the burial platform. The device's screen showed the expected signatures of stone construction and metal objects, but there was something else—a hollow space directly beneath the chamber that extended much deeper than the tomb itself.

"There's a void under the floor," Sakura reported. "It looks like... a natural cave system?"

Barry studied the radar readings, his suspicions crystallizing into certainty. "This isn't the real tomb. It's a decoy built over a natural cave system."

"How can you be sure?"

"Because the real Genghis Khan's burial site wouldn't have been built in a location where grave robbers could tunnel up from below." Barry examined the sarcophagus more closely, looking for signs of how it might be opened. "The Mongols were too security-conscious for that. This whole site is designed to fool people exactly like us."

As if summoned by his words, a low grinding sound began to echo through the burial chamber. Ancient mechanisms hidden within the walls were activating, triggered by their presence or their radar scanning. The sound grew louder, accompanied by the creak of stone moving against stone.

"What's happening?" Sakura demanded, her hand moving instinctively toward her weapon.

Barry spun in a circle, trying to identify the source of the mechanical sounds. "The tomb is activating its defenses. We need to get out of here, now!"

The grinding grew louder, and Barry could see cracks beginning to appear in the chamber walls. Whatever mechanism the tomb builders had installed was designed to seal the false burial site permanently once it had been discovered and explored by intruders.

"The entrance!" Sakura pointed toward the passage they had used to enter the chamber. A massive stone block was descending from the ceiling, moving to seal the opening completely.

They ran toward the closing entrance, but Barry could see they wouldn't make it in time. The stone block was moving too quickly, and they were too far from the opening. He grabbed Sakura's arm and pulled her toward one of the side passages that led deeper into the tomb complex.

"This way! There might be another exit!"

The side passage was narrower than the main corridor, and they had to move single-file through carved tunnels that seemed to twist and branch in all directions. Behind them, the sound of collapsing stone echoed through the mountain as the false burial chamber sealed itself forever.

"The whole place is coming down," Sakura said, looking back at the cloud of dust and debris that was following them through the passages.

Barry consulted his compass, trying to maintain their sense of direction as they navigated the maze of tunnels. The tomb builders had created an elaborate system of false passages designed to trap and kill intruders, but they must have included some means of escape for the workers who built the defenses.

They found it in the form of a narrow shaft that angled upward toward what Barry hoped was the surface. The opening was barely wide enough for a single person, and they would have to climb using handholds carved into the stone walls.

"You go first," Barry told Sakura. "If this doesn't lead to the surface, at least one of us needs to be in position to find another route."

Sakura began climbing, her mountaineering experience evident in the efficient way she found purchase on the carved handholds. Barry followed, listening to the continuing sounds of collapse echoing from the chambers below them.

They climbed for what felt like hours but was probably only twenty minutes, their muscles burning with the effort of hauling themselves up the narrow shaft. Barry's shoulders scraped against the stone walls, and he could feel cold air beginning to flow down from somewhere above them.

Finally, Sakura's voice echoed from above. "I can see daylight!"

They emerged from the shaft through a carefully concealed opening among a pile of natural boulders, nearly five hundred meters from the false tomb's main entrance. Barry looked back toward the cliff face where they had begun their exploration and saw that the elaborate archway had completely disappeared beneath a cascade of fallen stone.

"The whole entrance has been sealed," he observed. "Anyone who follows our tracks will find nothing but a rock slide."

Sakura sat heavily on a nearby boulder, and Barry noticed for the first time that she was favoring her left arm. "You're hurt."

"It's nothing serious. I scraped it against the shaft wall during the climb." She rolled up her sleeve to reveal a deep gash along her forearm that was bleeding more heavily than she had indicated.

Barry examined the wound with concern. "This needs proper medical attention. We need to find shelter and treat this properly before infection sets in."

The afternoon sun was already beginning to sink toward the western peaks, and the temperature was dropping rapidly. They were at high altitude in an increasingly hostile environment, with multiple groups of armed enemies somewhere in the region, and now Sakura was injured.

But despite their immediate difficulties, Barry felt a growing sense of optimism. The false tomb had been an elaborate deception, but it had also provided them with crucial information. The real burial site was somewhere else entirely, hidden by a different and more sophisticated form of concealment.

"We need to completely rethink our approach," he told Sakura as he helped her bandage the wound with supplies from their emergency kit. "The tomb builders were even more clever than we gave them credit for. They didn't just hide the burial site—they created an elaborate decoy to mislead anyone who managed to follow the map this far."

"So where is the real tomb?"

Barry looked out across the mountain landscape, studying the peaks and valleys with fresh eyes. "I think we've been approaching this from the wrong direction entirely. The false tomb was designed to be found by people following the astronomical alignments. But what if the real tomb is hidden using completely different principles?"

As they began their careful descent from the collapsed false tomb site, looking for shelter where Sakura could rest and recover, Barry's mind was already working on the puzzle. The tomb builders had demonstrated a level of sophistication that exceeded even his expectations. Finding Genghis Khan's real resting place would require more than following ancient maps—it would require thinking like a 13th-century Mongol who was determined to keep the world's greatest secret hidden forever.

Behind them, the sealed entrance to the false tomb remained as silent and mysterious as the mountains themselves, its deception complete and its purpose fulfilled even eight centuries after its creation.

Chapter 16: Storm Sanctuary

The storm came without warning—not a gradual buildup from natural weather patterns, but an immediate, overwhelming assault from a clear sky. One moment, stars blazed with unnatural brightness above the Mountain of the Sun; the next, dark clouds boiled into existence, covering the heavens with supernatural speed.

"We need shelter," Baatar shouted over the sudden howling wind. "Now!"

Sakura hung half-conscious in his arms, blood still seeping through improvised bandages despite his best efforts. He had managed to descend from their precarious ledge through sheer determination, his transformed physiology granting strength and coordination beyond ordinary human limits. But even blood-enhanced capabilities had boundaries, especially with an injured companion depending entirely upon him.

The first lightning strike hit the mountain's peak with unnatural precision, splitting one of the three distinctive ridges with explosive force. Thunder followed instantly, not a distant rumble but a physical concussion that drove Baatar to his knees. Around them, the valley's terrain transformed under assault from elements that seemed deliberately targeted rather than randomly destructive.

"Not natural," Sakura murmured, consciousness briefly returning through sheer willpower. "Mountain defends... creates barriers..."

Baatar understood immediately—this storm represented the sacred peak's active defense, a response to multiple expeditions approaching with improper intent. The mountain wasn't merely a collapsing false tomb to protect what lay beneath; it was reshaping the external environment to isolate intruders from their goal.

He scanned the valley with desperate intensity, enhanced vision penetrating sheets of rain now falling with impossible density. Nothing offered immediate shelter—no caves visible in nearby rock formations, no natural overhangs large enough to provide protection from elements assaulting them with almost sentient malice.

Lightning struck again, closer this time; the flash illuminated something Baatar had missed in the initial assessment—a small structure nestled against a distant rock outcropping, almost invisible against the surrounding terrain. A herder's shelter, likely abandoned with the valley's increasing isolation from ordinary reality.

"There," he decided, gathering Sakura's limp form closer against the increasingly violent wind. "We can reach it."

The journey, which should have taken perhaps twenty minutes, extended into a grueling ordeal as the storm actively opposed their progress. Wind shifted direction with impossible precision, always blowing directly against their advance. Rain transformed to stinging ice pellets that struck exposed skin with deliberate cruelty. The ground beneath their feet changed consistency with each step—mud giving way to slick stone, then to shifting gravel that threatened to spill them into newly formed crevasses.

"The mountain tests... commitment," Sakura gasped during a brief moment of consciousness. "Don't... surrender."

Baatar pressed forward with grim determination, one agonizing step after another, Sakura's weight growing heavier as his own strength diminished under constant assault. The storm intensified proportionally to their advance, as though calibrating its fury precisely to the threshold of their endurance without quite pushing beyond breaking point.

After what felt like hours but might have been mere minutes—time itself distorted within the mountain's domain—they reached the small structure. It was indeed a traditional Mongolian herder's shelter, constructed from materials that suggested decades of abandonment yet showing minimal decay. Stone foundations supported walls of wooden planks, weathered to a silvery patina, while the roof combined sod and animal hides, preserved through means that defied the ordinary understanding of material deterioration.

Baatar shouldered open the door, which swung inward with resistance, suggesting disuse rather than deliberate barricade. Inside, a single room offered a primitive sanctuary—dirt floor swept clean by the previous occupant, a small stone hearth at the center, and a basic sleeping platform against the far wall. No windows interrupted the shelter's protective envelope; only a smoke hole in the roof provided a connection to the outside world.

He laid Sakura carefully on the sleeping platform, her breathing shallow but stable, transformed physiology fighting to repair damage that would have killed an ordinary human instantly. Blood had stopped flowing from the most severe external wounds, suggesting that internal healing processes were already addressing the most critical injuries.

The storm's fury redoubled as they found sanctuary, lightning striking repeatedly around the shelter's perimeter with precision that couldn't possibly be coincidental. Wind howled through the smallest cracks in wooden walls, finding a voice that almost formed words in an ancient language beyond ordinary comprehension. The mountain was speaking directly to them, its message hovering just beyond conscious understanding.

Baatar quickly established essential survival measures. The hearth contained ancient ashes alongside neatly stacked firewood that showed no sign of rot despite apparent age—another impossibility that no longer registered as particularly remarkable within the mountain's domain. He started fire with practiced motions that Barry Curtis had never learned, but Baatar performed with instinctive familiarity.

As golden light filled the small space, further anomalies became apparent. The shelter's interior dimensions seemed subtly wrong—angles connecting slightly differently than the external structure should allow, corners existing in spatial relationships that defied Euclidean geometry. Not dramatic enough to register immediately as impossible, but creating subconscious wrongness that ordinary humans would interpret as supernatural dread.

"The shelter exists partially between realities," Baatar realized, blood-enhanced perception detecting what ordinary senses would miss. "Like everything within the mountain's domain, it occupies multiple states simultaneously."

This explained the structure's unlikely preservation despite apparent abandonment. Time itself functioned differently here, flowing according to the mountain's conscious manipulation rather than ordinary physical laws. The shelter might have been empty for decades in conventional chronology, yet it remained perfectly preserved through its partial existence in an alternate reality.

Sakura stirred on the sleeping platform, pain drawing her back to consciousness despite her body's attempt to retreat into a state of unconscious healing. "Where...?" she managed, eyes struggling to focus.

"Safe, for now," Baatar answered, moving to examine her injuries more thoroughly now that they had shelter and light. "The mountain provided sanctuary, though not without testing our resolve first."

He carefully removed improvised bandages from her shoulder, revealing wound that simultaneously horrified and fascinated his transformed

consciousness. The damage was catastrophic by ordinary medical standards—compound fracture exposing shattered bone, muscle and tissue
traumatized beyond conventional healing, blood vessels torn in patterns
that should have resulted in immediate exsanguination.

Yet already her transformed physiology was implementing extraordinary
repairs. Bone fragments visibly shifted toward proper alignment as he
watched, severed blood vessels seeking reconnection with their neighbors,
and damaged tissue regenerating at a cellular level, visible to his enhanced
perception. The blood ritual had changed them more fundamentally than
either had fully comprehended until this moment of crisis revealed capabilities beyond ordinary human potential.

"The damage is severe," he told her with academic precision rather than
emotional distress. "But your transformed physiology is implementing
repairs that would be impossible for ordinary humans. Recovery will be
faster than conventional medicine would predict, though still requiring
time we may not have."

"How long... until I can move?" Sakura asked, pragmatic concerns overriding personal distress, even in the most extreme circumstances.

"Unknown," Baatar admitted. "The blood ritual altered our fundamental biology in ways I don't fully understand. Hours rather than days,
perhaps, but celestial alignment occurs tomorrow night. Timing will be...
challenging."

He began proper medical care with supplies salvaged from their minimal equipment—cleaning wounds with antiseptic that seemed woefully
inadequate given the injury's severity, splinting shattered bones that were
already beginning the supernatural healing process, administering pain
medication that likely paled before biochemical changes already occurring
within her transformed physiology.

Throughout this intimate medical intervention, Sakura maintained stoic composure despite obvious agony. Only once did vulnerability break
through professional facade—when Baatar was forced to manipulate bone

fragments back into approximate alignment before accelerated healing could fuse them incorrectly.

"Blossom," she gasped as pain peaked beyond even her formidable tolerance. "I see her..."

Baatar paused, something within him responding to a name that seemed simultaneously familiar and distant—part of identity receding with each hour of their transformation. "What do you mean?"

"Dreams," Sakura managed between ragged breaths as pain gradually subsided to a manageable level. "Since the blood ritual... she comes to me in dreams. Guides me. Warns me."

The admission carried weight beyond its literal meaning. Sakura—whose tactical pragmatism defined her operational approach—acknowledging mystical communication that defied rational explanation represented a significant shift in perspective. The transformation was affecting not just their physical capabilities but their fundamental worldview and relationship with reality itself.

"What does she tell you?" Baatar asked, continuing medical care while monitoring her responses for signs of delirium rather than genuine experience.

"That we've misunderstood..." Sakura's eyes grew unfocused, her voice taking on a quality that suggested she had accessed a memory existing beyond ordinary consciousness. "The tomb isn't merely a physical location... it's doorway between realities. The Khan isn't simply buried... he's transitioned."

These concepts aligned with blood knowledge that had been gradually emerging in Baatar's transformed consciousness—understanding that transcended rational scholarship, connecting directly to truths preserved through ritual rather than academic documentation. The guardians had hinted at a similar perspective, though never articulating it as directly as Sakura now expressed.

"The false tomb was designed to eliminate those seeking merely physical discovery," he acknowledged, securing the final bandage over her reconstructed shoulder. "The true burial site exists partially beyond ordinary reality, accessible only through a proper approach at precise astronomical alignment."

"Underground rivers," Sakura said suddenly, eyes snapping back to focused clarity. "Blossom showed me in dreams. The true approach comes from below, through water channels that connect multiple realities."

Baatar's blood memory resonated with this revelation, as fragments of knowledge assembled into a coherent understanding that had previously eluded him. He reached for the leather-bound journal containing his transcribed notes from the combined maps, examining information with new perspective inspired by Sakura's dream-communication.

"Here," he indicated a specific notation that had seemed contradictory until this moment. "Reference to 'the path that flows between worlds' and 'entrance through the mountain's tears.' I interpreted these as poetic metaphors, but they're literal descriptions of underground water systems."

The fire's golden light illuminated the journal's pages as they studied the combined information with transformed understanding. Symbols previously categorized as decorative revealed themselves to be precise hydrological maps. Astronomical notations revealed not only celestial positioning but also the temporal relationship between star alignments and subterranean water flow. Everything connected with elegant precision that transcended coincidence.

"The rivers rise when proper stars align," Baatar realized, tracing a pattern across the leather map. "Creating a temporary pathway to the burial chamber that exists between ordinary reality and... something else."

"Not temporary," Sakura corrected, her voice stronger as extraordinary healing continued accelerating. "Transitional. The pathway always exists, but human perception can only detect it during specific alignments. Like quantum state collapsing into observable reality only under certain conditions."

The explanation revealed depths to her understanding that surprised Baatar—technical knowledge merged with mystical perspective in a way that transcended both scientific materialism and supernatural belief. Their transformations were creating a hybrid consciousness that integrated seemingly contradictory frameworks into a coherent perspective, one that transcended ordinary human cognition.

Outside, the storm continued its supernatural assault, lightning striking with impossible frequency yet never hitting the shelter directly. Wind screamed with almost-human voices, forming words in an ancient language that hovered just beyond comprehension. Rain transformed repeatedly between liquid, ice, and forms that defied conventional categorization—droplets that appeared to move against gravity, crystalline structures that remained suspended in air rather than falling to earth.

"The mountain isolates us," Sakura observed, following his attention to the storm's continued fury. "Creates barriers between different expeditions approaching the tomb."

"Preventing direct confrontation while final judgment forms," Baatar agreed. "Yamamoto's forces, Blackwood's mercenaries, ourselves—all separated by environmental conditions manipulated directly by the mountain's awareness."

This realization carried strategic implications that they immediately recognized. The storm wasn't merely a random destructive force, but a precisely calibrated intervention designed to isolate different groups from each other, while the mountain formulated a specific response to each expedition's intention. Their enemies couldn't directly attack while supernatural weather created impenetrable barriers between different approaches to the sacred peak.

Yet isolation offered only a temporary advantage. The storm would eventually subside once the mountain had completed its evaluation and implemented its judgment. When that occurred, direct confrontation would become possible again—likely just as celestial alignment created access to the true burial chamber.

"We need to locate the underground river entrance before the storm ends," Baatar concluded, consulting the combined maps again. "When weather barriers dissolve, Yamamoto's forces will implement systematic search patterns to locate us."

"They've had time to establish a perimeter around the mountain's base," Sakura noted with tactical assessment that transcended her injured condition. "Multiple teams are implementing grid-search protocols with advanced technology. Our window for undetected movement will be extremely limited once the storm subsides."

Baatar spread the maps across the dirt floor, firelight casting dramatic shadows across their ancient surfaces. With a transformed perception, he detected patterns previously hidden from ordinary observation—hydrological systems rendered in ink that changed color when viewed from different angles, topographical features that shifted position depending on a precise perspective, and astronomical notations that referenced star positions impossible in ordinary celestial mechanics.

"The river entrance should be here," he indicated, pointing to a location approximately two kilometers from their current position. "Where these three tributary systems converge beneath an extended ridge formation. According to these notations, water level rises precisely as specific stars align, creating a temporary pathway to the chamber existing between ordinary reality and alternate state."

"Timing?" Sakura asked, already calculating a tactical approach despite the injuries that would incapacitate an ordinary human for weeks.

"Alignment occurs tomorrow night, approximately four hours after sunset," Baatar determined from astronomical notations. "Window remains open perhaps thirty minutes before celestial positioning shifts enough to collapse accessible pathway."

"Narrow operational parameters," she observed with professional assessment rather than emotional concern. "Especially considering my current physical limitations and probability of enemy interception."

Her clinical self-evaluation might have seemed disturbing, given the ordinary human suffering and catastrophic injury. However, their transformations had altered their relationship with physical damage, creating a perspective that recognized the body as an operational tool rather than a fundamental identity. Sakura calculated the impact of her injuries on mission parameters using the same detached assessment she might apply to an equipment malfunction.

"Your healing rate exceeds anything medically documented," Baatar noted, monitoring visible regeneration continuing within her damaged shoulder. "Transformed physiology implements cellular reconstruction approximately fifty times faster than ordinary human healing. You should regain basic mobility within hours, though full recovery will require a longer duration."

"Sufficient for operational necessity," she decided with characteristic pragmatism. "The mountain provided this shelter for a specific purpose—recovery interval before final approach to true tomb."

Baatar nodded agreement, their shared understanding transcending need for extensive discussion. The storm's supernatural intensity, the shelter's impossible preservation, their enhanced healing capabilities—all represented deliberate intervention rather than random circumstance. The mountain was actively participating in their journey, although it remained uncertain whether it was acting as an ally or merely a neutral arbiter.

As if responding to this assessment, the storm's character subtly shifted outside. Lightning continued striking with an impossible frequency, but the pattern changed from a random distribution to geometric precision—bolts forming a perfect circle around the shelter's location, creating a barrier that would prevent any outside force from approaching. Wind maintained its howling intensity but altered harmonic structure, forming sounds that increasingly resembled ancient Mongolian ritual chanting rather than merely a natural phenomenon.

"The mountain acknowledges our purpose," Baatar observed, recognizing patterns that transcended coincidence. "Not an alliance in the conventional sense, but... provisional acceptance of our approach."

"Conditional approval," Sakura translated practically. "Dependent on maintaining proper intent through the final phases of the journey."

She attempted to sit upright, her willpower transformed, overriding the physical damage that would render an ordinary human completely immobile. Baatar moved to assist, supporting her weight as she achieved vertical position with a grimace that revealed pain transcending even her formidable tolerance.

"You should continue resting," he suggested, academic assessment rather than emotional concern. "Accelerated healing requires energy conservation for optimal efficiency."

"Time constraints override medical optimization," she countered with tactical precision. "I need to test functional capacity to accurately calculate operational parameters for tomorrow's approach."

With his assistance, she managed to stand briefly before weakness forced her to return to a seated position. The demonstration revealed both extraordinary recovery that has already been implemented and significant limitations that still restrict movement. Her transformed physiology had repaired immediately life-threatening damage. Still, it required additional hours to restore the functional mobility necessary for the final approach to the tomb.

"Progress exceeds reasonable expectation," Baatar acknowledged, helping her back to a comfortable position on the sleeping platform. "But full operational capacity remains approximately twelve to fourteen hours distant based on current regeneration rate."

"Acceptable timeline," she decided after a brief calculation. "Celestial alignment occurs in approximately twenty hours. Sufficient margin for necessary recovery before final approach."

Their pragmatic assessment completed, something shifted in the shelter's atmosphere. The fire's light seemed to change quality, flames acquiring a subtle blue undertone that transformed ordinary illumination into something otherworldly. Shadows cast against rough walls deepened beyond natural darkness, suggesting depths that extended into spaces that couldn't physically exist within the shelter's limited dimensions.

Sakura noticed the change immediately, her enhanced perception detecting subtle wrongness before her conscious mind could process specific alterations. "Something approaches," she said quietly, hand moving instinctively toward the weapon despite physical limitations. "Not physical presence. Something... else."

Baatar felt it too—consciousness pressing against reality's normal boundaries, awareness seeking contact through means that transcended ordinary perception. Not hostile in the conventional sense, but alien enough to trigger instinctive caution even in their transformed perspective.

"The mountain reaches for us," he realized, blood knowledge providing context ordinary experience couldn't supply. "Or something within the mountain. Something awakened by our presence and purpose."

The fire flared suddenly, flames leaping toward the ceiling before stabilizing at an unnatural height, burning with a blue-white intensity that shouldn't be possible from ordinary wood. Within this transformed illumination, shadow patterns formed across walls—not random light effects, but deliberate shapes assembling into recognizable script. Ancient Mongolian characters appeared in a flowing sequence, forming a message that Baatar translated through blood knowledge rather than academic study.

"The worthy approach through trials has been completed. The final threshold awaits those who grasp the truth beyond appearances. Blood calls to blood when stars align."

The message held significance beyond its literal meaning, connecting to fragments of understanding that had been gradually emerging through their transformation. The blood ritual hadn't merely enhanced physical capabilities and perception; it had created a genuine connection to lineage stretching back centuries—consciousness preserved through ritual means rather than merely genetic inheritance.

"Blossom," Sakura whispered, her eyes fixed on specific shadow formation that seemed more substantial than the surrounding patterns. "She's here."

Baatar followed her gaze, enhanced perception, detecting what ordinary senses would miss entirely. Within the shadow-script flowing across the rough wall, one pattern maintained greater consistency—a humanoid figure composed of darkness deeper than mere absence of light. Not clearly defined in conventional visual terms, but conveying an unmistakable impression of feminine presence, observing them with focused attention.

"The mountain allows her to reach across the boundary," he said quietly, understanding emerging from blood knowledge. "Those preserved within its awareness can manifest under specific conditions."

"Not preserved," Sakura corrected with certainty transcending rational knowledge. "Transitioned. Like the Khan himself. Existing partially beyond ordinary reality but maintaining connection to physical world through means we're only beginning to comprehend."

The shadow-presence seemed to respond to this acknowledgment, its form becoming momentarily more defined—features briefly resolving into a recognizable configuration that indeed suggested Blossom Hirata's appearance. Not a detailed representation but an essential impression, identity distilled to a fundamental pattern rather than specific physical characteristics.

Sakura extended her hand toward the manifestation, transformed perception allowing interaction that would be impossible for ordinary human consciousness. "Sister," she said simply, the single word carrying weight beyond its conventional meaning.

The shadow responded, extending a corresponding appendage that connected briefly with Sakura's outstretched fingers. Not physical contact in the ordinary sense, but genuine interaction between consciousnesses existing in different states of reality. Information is transferred through means that transcend conventional communication, with knowledge flowing directly between awareness rather than through symbolic language or physical sensation.

Baatar observed with academic fascination that such a manifestation might occur in an ordinary human, transcending the potential for fear. Their transformations had altered not just physical capabilities but also their fundamental relationship with reality itself, allowing for the acceptance of experiences that would previously have seemed impossible or supernatural.

The contact lasted perhaps three heartbeats before the shadow-presence withdrew, its form gradually losing definition as it reintegrated with flowing script covering the walls. The fire returned to normal illumination, its flames reducing to an ordinary height and color as the supernatural communication concluded.

Sakura's expression revealed rare vulnerability as the connection severed. "She showed me," she said quietly. "The true approach. The river's path. What awaits within the burial chamber?"

"What did you see?" Baatar asked, recognizing genuine communication rather than hallucinatory experience triggered by injury and trauma.

"The Book isn't merely a physical object," she answered, struggle evident as she attempted to translate direct consciousness-transfer into conventional language. "It's... a repository of awareness. Knowledge preserved in a form transcending ordinary documentation. Accessible only to those who approach with understanding beyond mere physical perception."

This aligned with blood knowledge gradually emerging in Baatar's transformed consciousness—understanding that the burial chamber contained something far more significant than merely historical artifacts or ancient technology. The true treasure preserved within the mountain's domain existed partially beyond ordinary reality, its nature comprehensible only through a perspective that transcended the conventional materialist framework.

"And Yamamoto seeks to weaponize this knowledge," he said grimly, implications becoming clearer with each revelation. "To extract technical information without understanding the foundational context. To exploit power without wisdom to guide its application."

"The consequences would transcend conventional catastrophe," Sakura confirmed, her expression revealing genuine concern beneath tactical assessment. "Not merely advanced weapons technology but fundamental disruption of the boundary between different states of reality. Damage extending beyond physical destruction to alteration of consciousness itself."

The storm outside intensified again, lightning striking with renewed fury as if responding directly to their discussion. The mountain was listening to their exchange, evaluating their understanding of what they sought, judging worthiness based on comprehension rather than merely stated intention.

"We need to reach the river entrance before Yamamoto's forces locate it," Baatar decided, calculating a tactical approach based on information transferred through Sakura's supernatural communication. "The storm provides temporary isolation, but when it subsides, they'll implement systematic search patterns with advanced technology."

"They're already searching," Sakura noted, transformed perception extending beyond shelter's physical boundaries. "I can sense them—twenty-two individuals in coordinated teams, methodically mapping terrain despite supernatural weather conditions. Their equipment partially functions despite the mountain's interference."

This represented a significant threat beyond immediate tactical concerns. Suppose Yamamoto's technology could partially overcome the mountain's defensive measures. In that case, his expedition might succeed where countless others had failed across centuries. Modern equipment, combined with ruthless determination, could potentially breach the protective boundaries that had preserved the Khan's burial chamber for eight hundred years.

"Rest while opportunity exists," Baatar instructed, helping Sakura into a more comfortable position on the sleeping platform. "Your injuries require additional recovery time before attempting the final approach. I'll monitor the situation and prepare necessary equipment."

She accepted this tactical assessment without argument, transformed consciousness recognizing operational necessity despite warrior instinct that might otherwise reject temporary vulnerability. Within minutes, her breathing pattern shifted to indicate healing trance rather than ordinary sleep—consciousness partially withdrawn to focus internal resources on accelerated regeneration.

Baatar maintained vigilance beside the fire, monitoring both Sakura's extraordinary recovery and the storm's supernatural patterns outside their shelter. The mountain was reshaping valley's geography with each lightning strike, terrain transforming to create barriers between different expeditions approaching the tomb. Ridges appeared where previously flat ground had existed. Crevasses opened along likely approach routes. Water features shifted position with each thunderous concussion.

Yet, despite these environmental manipulations, he sensed Yamamoto's forces continuing their methodical progress through the transformed landscape. Their technological advantages partially overcame supernatural barriers, allowing advances that should have been impossible under ordinary circumstances. The mountain's defenses—while formidable—had not anticipated modern equipment and the systematic approach employed by the Red Lotus expedition.

Time passed with elastic inconsistency within the shelter's unusual temporal field. The fire burned without consuming fuel at a normal rate, flames maintaining steady illumination despite limited wood supply. Shadows continued to form occasional patterns across the rough walls, although they never again achieved the coherent communication witnessed earlier. Outside, the storm maintained its supernatural intensity, defying normal weather progression; its fury was precisely calibrated to create specific environmental conditions rather than merely causing random destruction.

Sakura's healing continued at an extraordinary rate; damaged tissue visibly regenerating when Baatar checked the bandages periodically. Bone fragments knitted together at an unprecedented speed, severed blood vessels reconnected with precision that defied medical understanding, and muscle and connective tissue rebuilt cellular structure with efficiency surpassing anything documented in the scientific literature.

By what might have been midnight—though conventional timekeeping had limited meaning within the mountain's domain—she awakened from healing trance with significantly improved condition. Movement remained painful but functionally possible, having undergone a transformed physiology that had implemented repairs that would require months for an ordinary human.

"Status report," she requested immediately upon regaining consciousness, tactical assessment overriding personal comfort even in recovery.

"The storm continues with undiminished intensity," Baatar informed her with precise efficiency matching her operational focus. "Yamamoto's forces maintain methodical search patterns despite supernatural intervention, currently concentrated approximately one kilometer southwest of our position. Your physical recovery exceeds predicted parameters, suggesting operational mobility will be possible within four to six hours."

She absorbed this information with characteristic pragmatism, already calculating tactical implications for their approach to the river entrance.

"The storm will subside approximately two hours before celestial alignment," she stated with certainty derived from transformed perception rather than conventional meteorological understanding. "Creating a narrow window for undetected movement toward the true tomb entrance."

"You perceive this directly?" Baatar asked, recognizing a knowledge source that transcended rational deduction.

"Blossom showed me," Sakura confirmed without hesitation or embarrassment—a significant shift from her previously rational perspective. "The mountain's defensive measures follow precise pattern aligned with astronomical progression. When specific stars reach certain positions, environmental manipulation concludes to allow final judgment implementation."

This information aligned with the blood knowledge that was gradually emerging in Baatar's transformed consciousness. The mountain's apparently supernatural interventions actually followed mathematical precision beyond ordinary human comprehension—not random or arbitrary, but calculated with accuracy that transcends the conventional understanding of natural phenomena.

They used the remaining hours of enforced isolation productively—studying combined maps with a transformed perception that revealed details previously hidden from ordinary observation, preparing the minimal equipment required for the final approach to the river entrance, and monitoring Sakura's continued extraordinary healing and Yamamoto's methodical advance through the supernaturally altered landscape.

By what conventional timekeeping would identify as early morning—though dawn's normal progression remained obscured by the storm's unnatural darkness—Sakura had regained sufficient mobility for basic operational function. Movement remained visibly painful despite her formidable tolerance. Still, transformed physiology had implemented repairs that transcended medical possibility for ordinary humans.

"We should prepare for immediate departure when storm subsides," she decided, testing recovered mobility with controlled movements that revealed both extraordinary healing and remaining limitations. "Yamamoto's search pattern will bring his teams within visual range of our position within approximately three hours based on the current progression rate."

"The river entrance lies two kilometers northeast," Baatar reminded her, indicating a specific location on the combined maps. "Across exposed terrain that provides minimal concealment once supernatural weather conditions dissolve."

"The mountain will provide sufficient distraction during the transition period," Sakura stated with certainty derived from her communication with Blossom's manifestation. "Not direct intervention but... adjustment of perception. Those seeking with conquest in their hearts will experience subtle misdirection during the critical movement window."

Again, this information aligned with the blood knowledge that was gradually emerging through Baatar's transformation. The mountain's defensive measures operated on multiple levels simultaneously—physical manipulation of the environment, alteration of perceptual frameworks, adjustment of consciousness itself for those entering its domain. Not an omnipotent intervention but a sophisticated system designed to test worthiness through graduated challenges rather than merely preventing the approach entirely.

Outside, the storm's character began a subtle transformation—lightning strikes shifted from geometric precision to a more random distribution, the wind's harmonic structure changed from recognizable chanting to less coherent howling, and the rain's supernatural variants gradually returned toward more conventional precipitation. The mountain was preparing to transition from active environmental manipulation to more subtle judgment implementation.

"It begins," Baatar observed, gathering their minimal equipment with efficient preparation. "The storm will dissipate within approximately ninety minutes based on the current transformation rate."

"Leaving a narrow operational window before Yamamoto's forces converge on this location," Sakura concluded, already preparing for imminent movement despite injuries that would immobilize an ordinary human. "We move immediately when weather barriers dissolve sufficiently for practical transit."

They completed final preparations with coordinated efficiency that transcended the need for extensive communication—transforming consciousness into an operating harmony developed through shared experiences and blood connection. When the storm's supernatural intensity finally began to noticeably decrease, they were positioned at the shelter's entrance, ready for immediate departure toward the river entrance, which represented the final approach to the true burial chamber.

"Remember," Sakura said quietly as they prepared to exit their temporary sanctuary, "what awaits isn't merely physical discovery but a transitional threshold. The tomb exists partially beyond ordinary reality. Our approach requires a perspective transcending the conventional materialist framework."

"The blood ritual prepared us for this transition," Baatar acknowledged, understanding emerging from transformed consciousness rather than rational deduction. "We perceive already what ordinary humans would miss entirely. The final threshold merely extends the transformation already underway since our first contact with the guardians."

With this shared understanding, they stepped from the shelter's protection into a gradually subsiding storm—not retreating from supernatural manifestation, but advancing toward a consciousness that transcended ordinary human comprehension. The mountain awaited their approach with a judgment that would determine not merely success or failure, but a fundamental transformation beyond anything they had experienced thus far.

The true tomb of Genghis Khan—and the knowledge it contained—lay just hours away, accessible only through underground rivers that connected different states of reality when proper stars aligned in configurations impossible within conventional astronomy. Their journey had reached its most critical phase, with enemies closing in from multiple directions and time dwindling toward an astronomical alignment that would open a pathway between worlds for a brief window of opportunity.

The final approach had begun.

Chapter 17: The Underground Path

The storm's final throes provided temporary concealment as they navigated exposed terrain between the herder's shelter and their destination. Mist clung to the valley floor in unnatural patterns, forming corridors and barriers that seemed deliberately positioned rather than randomly distributed. Overhead, the clouds retained a supernatural darkness, despite what should have been mid-morning sun; occasional lightning still illuminated the Mountain of the Sun with brief, spectral flashes.

"Movement to the west," Sakura warned, her transformed senses detecting what ordinary human perception would miss entirely. "Two teams, coordinated search pattern, approximately eight hundred meters distant."

Baatar nodded, altering their route slightly to maintain maximum concealment within the dissipating mist. Sakura moved with grim determination despite injuries that would incapacitate ordinary human for weeks, her transformed physiology implementing repairs that defied medical understanding. Still, pain etched itself in tight lines around her eyes, in careful control of each breath, in occasionally uneven stride quickly corrected through sheer willpower.

"How much farther?" she asked, the question itself revealing strain beyond her usual stoic endurance.

"Five hundred meters," Baatar indicated ridge formation ahead where three nearly invisible watercourses converged beneath an extended stone outcropping. "The river entrance should be located precisely where those tributary systems meet underground."

Their progress remained deliberately measured—not the direct approach instinct demanded, but a circuitous route utilizing the remaining weather effects for maximum concealment. Yamamoto's teams continued their methodical search pattern to the west, while Blackwood's remaining mercenaries maintained their position on the northeastern ridge, likely regrouping after sustaining losses during the mountain's defensive measures.

As they approached the convergence point, topography shifted from relatively flat terrain to increasingly vertical rock formations—not merely natural geology but deliberately shaped features displaying subtle evidence of ancient human modification. Weathered carvings decorated seemingly random boulders, visible only to a transformed perception that detected patterns ordinary human consciousness would interpret as natural erosion.

"These mark the path," Baatar observed, fingers tracing weathered indentation that formed precise astronomical notation when viewed with blood-enhanced vision. "Guides for those who approach with proper preparation. Invisible to those seeking conquest in their hearts."

The carvings grew more numerous as they neared the convergence point, transitioning from isolated markers to a coherent system that guided worthy seekers toward the entrance while misleading those with improper intentions. Even with a transformed perception, the patterns remained challenging to follow—requiring constant adjustments of perspective, viewing angles that shifted with each step, and interpretations dependent on a precise mental state while observing.

"The mountain tests awareness even in final approach," Sakura noted, her transformed understanding recognizing deliberate challenge rather than merely difficult navigation. "Requires constant adjustment of perception rather than a fixed frame of reference."

They reached the apparent convergence point—an unremarkable depression surrounded by weathered rock formations that ordinary observation would dismiss as a natural geological feature. No obvious entrance presented itself; no cave mouth or fissure suggested passage into the mountain's interior. Just stone and scree, seemingly random arrangement offering no indication of significance.

"The combined maps indicate entrance precisely here," Baatar said, consulting a mental impression of transcribed notes with increasing concern. "Yet nothing visible suggests an access point to the underground river system."

Sakura studied the formation with intensity that transcended ordinary vision, her transformed perception seeking patterns beyond conventional observation. "The entrance doesn't exist continuously in ordinary reality," she stated after several moments. "It manifests only when properly perceived by those with appropriate preparation."

This aligned with the gradual emergence of blood knowledge through their transformation—understanding that certain thresholds existed conditionally rather than continuously, becoming accessible only when approached with a specific mental framework and perceptual capability. Not magical portals in the conventional fantasy sense, but transitional boundaries between different states of reality that ordinary human consciousness would neither perceive nor access.

"We need to align perception with a proper frame of reference," Baatar realized, studying surrounding rock formations with transformed vision. "The carvings don't merely mark a path—they create a perceptual key when viewed in the correct sequence."

Together, they traced carved patterns across weathered stones, following sequence that gradually revealed itself through blood-enhanced understanding. Not linear progression but an interconnected network requiring simultaneous comprehension from multiple perspectives—challenge that would prove impossible for consciousness constrained by conventional observational limitations.

As they completed proper perceptual sequence, reality shifted subtly around them. Not a dramatic transformation, but an adjustment in the fundamental relationship between observation and existence. Stone formation that had appeared solid moments earlier now revealed a dark opening approximately one meter in diameter—an entrance descending at steep angle into the mountain's interior. Not a newly created passage, but a previously existing access point, their consciousness could now properly perceive.

"We found it," Baatar said with quiet triumph that transcended academic discovery. "The river entrance."

The opening emitted a cold draft carrying complex scents that defied ordinary categorization—water flowing through ancient stone, minerals found nowhere in surface geology, and biological processes operating without sunlight for centuries. But beneath these physical components lay something else. This subtle vibration registered directly on consciousness, rather than through conventional sensory apparatus, communication beyond language or sound.

"The mountain acknowledges our approach," Sakura translated, her transformed perception interpreting signals ordinary humans would never detect. "Not welcome in a conventional sense, but... recognition of worthy attempt."

They prepared for underground passage with efficient precision—activating small, luminescent devices provided by guardians that produced light without a conventional power source, securing minimal equipment in waterproof containers, and checking weapons that would function reliably in a transitional environment where modern technology became increasingly unreliable.

"Yamamoto's teams are changing search pattern," Sakura noted, final check of external environment revealing tactical shift in their pursuers' movement. "Their equipment must have detected something—they're converging toward this general area with increased urgency."

"We need to move immediately," Baatar decided, calculations balancing multiple urgent factors. "The entrance will become undetectable again once we've passed through, but they might locate our position through other technological means."

Sakura nodded in agreement, recognizing the transformed perspective that operational necessity still outweighed physical limitations, despite them still restricting optimal performance. Without further discussion, they entered the narrow opening, Baatar leading with careful movements that acknowledged the passage's confined dimensions and unpredictable stability.

The descent proved immediately challenging—a narrow shaft dropping at nearly a forty-five-degree angle, with the surface alternating between slick stone and crumbling material that threatened to collapse under their weight. Transformed physiology provided a crucial advantage—strength and coordination beyond ordinary human capability, perception that detected structural weaknesses before weight triggered catastrophic failure, and reflexes that adjusted to changing conditions with impossible speed.

After perhaps thirty meters of precarious descent, the shaft opened into larger chamber where evidence of ancient human modification became unmistakable. Walls bore elaborate carvings executed with precision that defied the technological limitations of 13th-century craftsmanship—astronomical charts depicting star positions impossible in Earth's conventional sky, mathematical notations expressing relationships beyond ordinary geometry, and writing systems combining multiple ancient languages into a symbology that transcended conventional communication.

"The original tomb builders," Baatar identified with academic precision, transformed by blood knowledge. "Not merely Mongol craftsmen but... something more. Individuals with perception beyond ordinary human limitation."

"Blood-marked ones," Sakura translated the inscription that seemed to shift between multiple languages as they observed it. "Consciousness transformed through ritual, similar to what we experienced with guardians. Individuals selected for the ability to perceive beyond conventional reality."

They studied the chamber with a transformed vision that detected details ordinary human perception would miss entirely. The carvings contained information beyond their superficial appearance—knowledge embedded within mathematical relationships between different elements, communication encoded in precise spatial arrangements rather than merely symbolic representation, and understanding accessible only through a perceptual framework that transcended conventional observation.

"These aren't merely historical records or decorative elements," Baatar realized, academic expertise enhanced through blood transformation. "T hey're... instructional framework. Teaching tools for consciousness transitioning between different perceptual states."

"Preparation for what awaits deeper within the mountain's interior," Sakura agreed, her tactical assessment recognizing strategic purpose behind apparent artistic expression. "The tomb builders created a graduated system to transform consciousness of worthy seekers before the final threshold."

From the initial chamber, three passages extended deeper into the mountain's interior—each bearing distinctive markings that suggested different purposes or destinations. They consulted the combined maps again, determining that the central passage aligned with the route indicated in astronomical notations and hydrological markers.

"This way," Baatar indicated, pointing to the central opening, where a subtle vibration suggested moving water somewhere beyond immediate visibility. "The underground river should lie approximately fifty meters along this route."

The passage descended at gentler angle than initial shaft, its surfaces showing both natural formation and deliberate modification—sections where flowing water had carved stone over millennia interspersed with precisely hewn segments displaying tool marks preserved with impossible clarity after eight centuries. The juxtaposition created an impression of collaboration between natural processes and human intention, rather than merely an artificial construction imposed upon the environment.

As they advanced, illumination from their guardian-provided devices revealed increasingly elaborate modifications to the passage walls—carvings that transitioned from relatively simple astronomical notations to complex systems combining multiple knowledge frameworks into an integrated representation. Mathematics merged with linguistics, astronomy with biology, physics with metaphysics—disciplinary boundaries dissolving into unified understanding beyond conventional categorization.

"The tomb builders perceived reality without artificial distinctions modern consciousness imposes between different knowledge domains," Baatar observed, academic understanding transformed through blood knowledge. "They recognized fundamental unity underlying apparent separation between different phenomena."

"Practical application rather than merely philosophical perspective," Sakura noted with characteristic focus on operational implications. "These aren't abstract concepts but functional technologies operating through principles beyond conventional understanding."

The sound of moving water grew steadily more pronounced as they continued deeper into mountain's interior. First distant murmur barely perceptible even to enhanced hearing, gradually intensifying to an unmistakable indication of substantial volume flowing with considerable force.

The passage itself changed character as they advanced—ceiling height increasing dramatically, walls displaying evidence of periodic submersion, and the floor transitioning from a relatively smooth surface to irregular terrain clearly shaped by powerful water flow during seasonal variations.

After approximately fifty meters, the passage opened abruptly into vast cavern whose dimensions challenged comprehension even with enhanced perception. Their illumination devices barely penetrated the darkness extending in multiple directions beyond their effective range, creating an impression of boundless space rather than merely a large underground chamber. Below, at least twenty meters beneath a narrow ledge where passage terminated, an underground river flowed with impossible force—water black as obsidian moving with speed and volume that shouldn't exist within mountain's interior without external source feeding constant supply.

"The river that flows between worlds," Baatar identified it from the guardians' descriptions and map notations. "Not merely a physical watercourse but a boundary between different states of reality."

The river's surface reflected their illumination with unnatural properties—light not merely bouncing off the water but seeming to penetrate before returning, altered in its fundamental characteristics. Colors shifted beyond the normal spectrum, patterns formed that couldn't result from ordinary physical reflection, and movements occurred across the surface that defied the hydrodynamic principles governing conventional fluid behavior.

"How do we proceed?" Sakura asked, conducting a tactical assessment that immediately identified practical challenges beyond philosophical implications. "No obvious path along river course, and water itself appears... problematic for direct navigation."

Baatar studied the cavern with transformed perception, seeking details ordinary observation would miss entirely. After several moments, he indicated a narrow ledge extending along the cavern wall approximately one meter above water level—not immediately obvious due to strange optical properties within the vast space, but a navigable route following river's course deeper into the mountain's interior.

"There," he pointed toward a partially concealed path. "Ancient hand-holds carved into the wall confirm intentional route rather than natural formation."

Descending to river level required careful navigation down a near-vertical rock face with minimal hand and foot holds—a challenge that would prove impossible for ordinary humans but merely difficult with their transformed capabilities. Sakura's injuries complicated descent, her extraordinary healing still incomplete despite accelerated regeneration beyond medical possibility. Yet she managed, with characteristic determination, to transform pain into a tactical parameter rather than a debilitating limitation.

They reached the narrow ledge with cautious precision, immediately noting strange properties affecting stone this close to river's surface. The rock itself seemed partially transitional—solid when directly contacted but visually unstable, appearing to shift between different states when observed peripherally rather than through direct focus. Standing upon it created a sensation of simultaneously occupying multiple positions, as though physical form extended beyond ordinary spatial limitations into adjacent possibilities.

"The boundary effect intensifies with proximity to river," Baatar observed, academic assessment maintaining precision despite increasingly strange phenomena. "We're experiencing bleed-through from transitional zone between different states of reality."

"Operational implications?" Sakura asked, transforming metaphysical observation into tactical consideration with characteristic pragmatism.

"Our perception will become increasingly unreliable according to conventional standards," he explained, knowledge emerging from blood memory rather than rational deduction. "We need to trust transformed awareness rather than ordinary senses as we proceed deeper into the transitional zone."

They moved along a narrow ledge with careful precision, each step requiring complete attention due to both physical precariousness and increasingly strange perceptual effects. The river flowed beneath them with unnatural consistency—no variation in current despite what should be irregular channel, no normal sound pattern produced by water moving against confining surfaces, no expected spray or moisture despite considerable velocity.

As they advanced deeper along the underground course, carved symbols appeared on the cavern walls with increasing frequency—not merely decorative elements or historical records, but functional markers creating a perceptual framework necessary for successful navigation through the transitional environment. Following their guidance required constant adjustment of consciousness, shifting between different observational modes as conventional perception became increasingly inadequate for accurate interpretation of surroundings.

"The carvings aren't merely informational," Sakura noted, transformed understanding recognizing patterns beyond ordinary significance. "They're... calibration mechanisms. Tools for adjusting consciousness to function within the transitional zone."

"The tomb builders created a graduated system preparing worthy seekers for final threshold," Baatar agreed, his own perception shifting through multiple frameworks as they processed carved instructions. "Each stage requires fundamental adjustment rather than merely additional knowledge."

After what might have been minutes or hours—time itself becoming increasingly elastic within the transitional environment—the narrow ledge terminated at a small chamber cut directly into the cavern wall. Unlike previous spaces that display both natural formations and human modifications, this room had been created entirely through deliberate excavation—a perfect cube approximately five meters on each side, with walls covered entirely with carvings of extraordinary complexity and precision.

"Rest point for those navigating the underground path," Baatar identified it from combined map notations and blood knowledge. "Transitional space where consciousness can stabilize before proceeding deeper into the boundary zone."

They entered gratefully, Sakura's extraordinary endurance finally showing signs of strain as injuries and continuous perception adjustments demanded increasing energy. The chamber's unusual geometry created a stabilizing effect within the transitional environment—reality conforming more closely to conventional physics within a precisely defined space, allowing for a temporary respite from the increasingly disorienting phenomena experienced along the river course.

"How much farther to burial chamber?" Sakura asked, conducting a tactical assessment while maintaining priority despite physical limitations and perceptual challenges.

Baatar consulted a combined mental impression from maps and blood knowledge, incorporating calculations that took both physical distance and transitional adjustments into account for accurate estimation. "Approximately one kilometer following the river course, but distance becomes increasingly meaningless within the deep transitional zone. Duration of journey depends more on consciousness adjustment than physical movement."

"And celestial alignment occurs in approximately six hours," she noted, internal chronometry maintaining precision despite elastic temporality within the mountain's domain. "Creating a narrow operational window for final approach once alignment establishes access to true burial chamber."

They used brief rest periods productively—checking equipment functionally, increasingly unpredictable within a transitional environment, consulting combined maps with transformed perception to reveal de-

tails previously hidden, monitoring Sakura's continued healing, and exchanging observations about increasingly strange phenomena encountered along the underground path.

"The river itself isn't merely water," Baatar noted, transforming academic observation into practical intelligence. "Its composition changes progressively as we advance, transitioning between different states of matter
according to principles beyond conventional physics."

"Explaining why actual burial chamber remains inaccessible except during precise celestial alignment," Sakura concluded with tactical application
of metaphysical observation. "The river's transitional properties intensify when specific stars occupy certain positions, temporarily stabilizing
boundary between different states of reality."

This aligned with the gradual emergence of blood knowledge through
their transformation—understanding that the Khan's burial chamber existed partially beyond ordinary reality, accessible only when an astronomical alignment temporarily stabilized the boundary between different states
of existence. Not a magical portal in the conventional fantasy sense, but a
scientifically comprehensible phenomenon operating according to principles beyond current human understanding.

After a brief recovery period, they continued their journey along the
underground river course, following a narrow ledge that occasionally disappeared entirely, forcing precarious transitions across challenging terrain
with only carved handholds preventing a fatal fall into the transitional
water below. The river itself changed character as they advanced deeper
into the mountain's interior—its surface displaying increasingly strange
properties that defied conventional hydrodynamics, color shifting through
the spectrum beyond the ordinary visual range, and sound alternating
between complete silence and complex harmonics that conveyed information directly to consciousness rather than through conventional auditory
processing.

The cavern's dimensions expanded beyond reasonable geological possibility, creating an impression of space larger inside than the mountain itself could possibly contain. Their illumination devices penetrated darkness with decreasing effectiveness, as light seemed to be absorbed by the environment, operating according to different physical principles than those of ordinary reality. Only their transformed perception allowed for continued navigation, enabling them to detect paths and hazards through means that transcended conventional vision.

"We're approaching a significant threshold," Baatar observed, as the carved symbols along the passage walls increased dramatically in both frequency and complexity. "These markings indicate transition to deeper boundary zone where ordinary physical laws become increasingly optional rather than mandatory."

"Explaining why previous expeditions failed despite occasionally reaching this far," Sakura noted with tactical assessment. "Without proper perceptual framework, navigation becomes impossible beyond this point, regardless of technological advantages or physical capabilities."

The next section of underground path presented immediate evidence supporting this observation. The ledge they followed split suddenly into multiple versions of itself—not merely branching paths but simultaneous variations occupying the same physical space, each apparently solid yet passing through others without interaction. Selecting the correct version requires perception operating beyond ordinary visual processing, a consciousness capable of distinguishing between overlapping realities without conventional reference points.

They navigated this impossible terrain through transformed awareness rather than ordinary sense interpretation, blood-enhanced perception detecting subtle differences between various manifestations that would remain completely invisible to conventional human consciousness. Not merely choosing between multiple physical paths but selecting specific reality-state from overlapping possibilities simultaneously occupying the same apparent location.

"The mountain tests perception rather than merely physical capability," Baatar noted as they successfully traversed a particularly challenging section where ledge existed in at least seven different states simultaneously. "Requiring consciousness operating beyond ordinary human limitations regardless of technological assistance or equipment quality."

"Yamamoto's forces would fail regardless of preparation or determination," Sakura agreed, tactical assessment recognizing absolute advantage their transformation provided. "Even with blood ritual, navigation requires continuous adjustment, impossible for consciousness still anchored in a conventional physical framework."

As they advanced deeper along the underground course, evidence of the original tomb builders became increasingly apparent, despite the passage of eight centuries. Tools abandoned during construction remained perfectly preserved within a transitional environment where ordinary temporal progression operated differently than in the surface world. Inscriptions retained impossible freshness, appearing recently carved rather than weathered by centuries. Occasional personal items—drinking vessels, clothing fragments, and simple jewelry—demonstrated human presence beyond merely a professional construction team, suggesting that an entire community was involved in creating the sacred space.

"The tomb builders lived here during construction," Baatar realized, academic understanding enhanced through blood knowledge. "Not merely a working expedition but an intentional community establishing permanent presence within a transitional environment."

"Creating graduated adaptation rather than merely physical structure," Sakura translated with practical application. "They transformed themselves through prolonged exposure to boundary conditions, becoming increasingly capable of functioning within the transitional zone between different states of reality."

This understanding contextualized the strange architectural decisions evident throughout the underground path—spaces designed for habitation rather than merely functional construction, areas clearly intended for communal gathering rather than simple work requirements, and sections demonstrating ceremonial purpose beyond practical necessity. The tomb builders had created a complete society operating partially outside ordinary reality, establishing a permanent community within a transitional environment.

They continued along an increasingly strange passage where physical laws became progressively more advisory than mandatory. Gravity operated inconsistently, sometimes allowing brief periods of effectively weightless movement across otherwise impassable gaps. Light behaved according to principles beyond conventional optics, occasionally forming solid-seeming structures that could temporarily support weight despite apparent immateriality. Sound transmitted information directly to consciousness without ordinary auditory processing, conveying complex concepts through harmonic relationships rather than symbolic language.

After what might have been hours or merely minutes—temporal progression increasingly meaningless within the deep transitional zone—they reached a section where the underground river widened dramatically into a lake-like expanse, whose opposite shore remained invisible despite their enhanced perception. The narrow ledge they had followed terminated completely, offering no obvious continuation along the apparent shoreline.

"The maps indicate final approach requires water transit at this point," Baatar noted, consulting combined mental impression with increasing certainty. "We must cross the transitional boundary directly rather than merely following alongside."

"Through water that isn't merely a physical substance," Sakura observed with justified concern, transformed perception detecting properties far beyond ordinary liquid composition. "Submersion would expose us directly to transitional effects without protective boundary ordinary physical environment provides."

The implications were immediately disturbing, even to their transformed consciousness. Until this point, they had experienced boundary phenomena while maintaining physical presence primarily within conventional reality. Direct immersion in a transitional substance would expose them to effects beyond anything they had encountered thus far, potentially altering their consciousness in ways that exceeded even their extensive preparation.

"The celestial alignment approaches," Baatar noted, internal chronometry maintaining precision despite elastic temporality within transitional environment. "Approximately three hours until stars reach positions necessary for accessing true burial chamber."

"Leaving no alternative approach," Sakura concluded with characteristic pragmatism despite evident concern. "We proceed through water and accept consequent transformation as necessary condition for completing journey."

They secured the remaining equipment with methodical efficiency, ensuring nothing would be lost during the imminent transition, whose effects remained impossible to predict with certainty. The final check confirmed that weapons would function reliably within the deep transitional zone, emergency supplies were necessary for potential contingencies, and protective measures were in place against environmental conditions beyond ordinary human tolerance.

"Together," Sakura said quietly, reaching for his hand in what had become a ritual gesture at significant thresholds.

Their fingers intertwined as they approached the water's edge, the strange surface reflecting their transformed appearances with properties that defied conventional optics. Ripples formed without apparent cause, patterns emerging that conveyed information directly to consciousness rather than through ordinary visual processing. The water itself seemed to observe them with awareness that transcended physical limitations, assessment flowing from a substance that existed simultaneously as a liquid medium and a conscious entity.

"The river acknowledges our approach," Baatar translated, understanding emerging from blood knowledge rather than rational interpretation. "Not merely a physical boundary but... transitional consciousness existing between different states of reality."

They stepped forward together into water that simultaneously embraced and transformed them—not merely physical submersion, but a fundamental shift in the relationship between consciousness and reality itself. The boundary between internal awareness and the external environment dissolved immediately, creating a perception unconfined by ordinary physical limitations or conventional sensory frameworks.

As the transitional substance enveloped them completely, Baatar experienced immediate confirmation of academic speculation transformed through blood knowledge. The underground river wasn't merely a physical watercourse, but a direct manifestation of the boundary between different states of reality—not a metaphorical description, but a literal identification of a substance existing simultaneously in multiple conditions. Immersion exposes consciousness directly to transitional effects that are ordinarily filtered through the protective barrier of conventional physical existence.

Their journey through the underground path had reached a critical threshold; consciousness had transformed beyond ordinary human limitations as they approached the final boundary separating conventional reality from the true burial chamber, which existed partially beyond the physical world. Ahead lay the tomb of Genghis Khan—not merely a historical monument but a transitional space where the greatest conqueror in human history had transcended ordinary existence eight centuries earlier, preserved within a state beyond conventional life or death.

And within that impossible space lay the Book of Gold—knowledge preserved in a form that transcended ordinary documentation, an understanding capable of transforming human consciousness beyond current evolutionary limitations or destroying civilization entirely, depending on the approach and intention of those who sought its secrets.

The underground path had led them to the ultimate threshold, beyond which nothing would remain unchanged—neither themselves nor the world to which they might eventually return.

Chapter 18: The Rival's Arrival

T he ancient carved marker protruding from the cave wall seemed to pulse in the beam of Barry's headlamp, its weathered symbols confirming what the golden map had promised. After hours of navigating the treacherous underground passages, they had finally reached the outer approaches to Genghis Khan's burial complex. The air itself felt different here—thicker, charged with an almost electrical tension that made the hair on Barry's arms stand on end.

"This is it," he whispered to Sakura, running his fingers along the carved surface. "The marker stone mentioned in your mother's notes. We're less than a mile from the tomb entrance."

Sakura crouched beside him, her LED light illuminating additional symbols carved into the cave floor. Despite her injured shoulder, she had maintained their punishing pace through the flooded passages and unstable tunnels. Her face showed the strain, but her eyes burned with determination.

"The water marks on the walls," she said, pointing to mineral deposits that formed distinctive patterns. "They match the descriptions in the second puzzle box. The seasonal floods create a natural calendar system."

Barry studied the formations she indicated. The limestone had been sculpted by centuries of flowing water into organic shapes that resembled flowing script. But as he examined them more closely, he realized they weren't random at all—they formed a deliberate pattern that corresponded to astronomical observations recorded on the golden sheets.

"Brilliant," he murmured. "The tomb builders used the cave's natural flooding cycle as part of their security system. You can only approach the burial chamber at certain times of year when the water level is low enough."

"And we're here at exactly the right time," Sakura added. "Three weeks before the winter freeze locks everything up until spring."

The sound of their voices echoed strangely in the passage, as if the cave system were much larger than it appeared. Barry was about to comment on the acoustic properties when a different sound reached them—the distant splash of someone moving through water, coming from the direction they had traveled.

Both of them froze, their lights automatically dimming as they pressed against the cave wall. Barry's hand moved instinctively to his pistol while Sakura drew her knife with fluid silence. They had been careful to cover their tracks, but someone with the right equipment and expertise could still follow their route through the underground system.

The splashing grew closer, accompanied by the low murmur of voices speaking in Japanese. Barry felt his stomach drop as he recognized the professional cadence of military communications. Yamamoto had found them.

"How many?" Sakura breathed into his ear, her voice barely audible.

Barry strained to listen, counting the different voices and trying to estimate numbers based on the sound of movement through water. "At least six, maybe eight. They're being careful, but they're moving fast."

"We could go deeper into the system," Sakura suggested. "Try to reach the tomb entrance before they catch up."

Barry shook his head, studying the carved markers around them. "These warnings aren't just decorative. The passages ahead are designed to be death traps for anyone who doesn't know the proper sequence. We need time to decode them properly, not a running gun battle."

The voices were close enough now that Barry could make out individual words. Yamamoto was indeed leading the group, issuing quiet orders to his men as they navigated the flooded sections. But there was something else in his tone—an urgency that suggested he wasn't just pursuing them for the treasure.

"Dr. Curtis!" Yamamoto's voice suddenly echoed through the passage, no longer attempting concealment. "I know you can hear me. We need to talk."

Barry and Sakura exchanged glances. There was no point in hiding now—Yamamoto's men would have thermal imaging equipment that would locate them within minutes.

"What do you want, Yamamoto?" Barry called back, keeping his weapon ready.

"I want what you want—access to the Khan's tomb. But I have something you need to hear first."

"We're listening."

The sound of splashing grew closer until Barry could see the reflected glow of LED lights on the wet cave walls. Then Yamamoto himself appeared around a bend in the passage, flanked by four armed men in tactical gear. But what made Barry's blood run cold was the fifth figure—an elderly Mongolian man with his hands bound behind his back.

"Temujin," Sakura whispered.

The leader of the Guardians of the Blue Sky looked older than when they had last seen him, and there was blood on his traditional robe. But his eyes still held the fierce pride of a man descended from conquerors, and he met Barry's gaze with a slight nod of acknowledgment.

"Dr. Curtis, Miss Hirata," Yamamoto said formally, as if they were meeting at an academic conference rather than in a flooded cave beneath a Mongolian mountain. "I apologize for the dramatic circumstances, but time is not on our side."

"Let him go," Barry said, his weapon trained on Yamamoto's chest. "Whatever you want from us, he's not part of it."

Yamamoto smiled coldly. "On the contrary, he is very much part of it. You see, Mr. Temujin here has been most informative about the final approaches to the tomb. His society has maintained detailed records of the defenses for over eight centuries."

"I told them nothing," Temujin spoke for the first time, his accented English clear despite his obvious injuries. "The Khan's secrets die with me."

"Perhaps," Yamamoto conceded. "But his granddaughter was more... cooperative."

Barry felt Sakura tense beside him. The implications of Yamamoto's words hit them both simultaneously—the Red Lotus hadn't just captured Temujin. They had taken hostages from his entire family.

"You bastard," Sakura snarled, starting to move forward before Barry caught her arm.

"Wait," he whispered, then addressed Yamamoto directly. "What do you want?"

"Simple cooperation. You have the golden map and the expertise to decode the tomb's defenses. I have the manpower and equipment to deal with any obstacles we encounter. Together, we can reach the burial chamber safely."

"And if we refuse?"

Yamamoto's expression didn't change, but one of his men raised a radio to his lips and spoke quietly in Japanese. Within seconds, a child's voice could be heard crying in the background of the transmission—a little girl calling for her grandfather.

Temujin's stoic composure cracked for the first time. "Saikhan," he whispered. "She is only seven years old."

"Your choice, Dr. Curtis," Yamamoto said. "Help me reach the tomb, and the girl and her family are released unharmed. Refuse, and..." He shrugged eloquently.

Barry lowered his weapon slowly, his mind racing through the possibilities. Everything in him rebelled against cooperating with the man who had ordered the deaths of Sakura's family, but the lives of innocent people hung in the balance.

"How do we know you'll keep your word?" he asked.

"You don't. But consider the alternative."

Sakura was vibrating with barely controlled fury. "He's lying. The moment we help him reach the treasure, he'll kill all of us."

"Probably," Barry agreed quietly. "But right now, those hostages are our primary concern."

Before Yamamoto could respond, a new sound echoed through the cave system—the distinctive crack of high-powered rifles being fired in the distance. All of them froze as the reports echoed and re-echoed off the stone walls.

"What the hell—" one of Yamamoto's men began.

The radio in Yamamoto's hand crackled to life, urgent Japanese voices reporting contact with an unknown force. Barry caught enough words to understand that Yamamoto's rear guard was under attack.

"Blackwood," Sakura realized. "Her mercenaries must have followed the same route we did."

Yamamoto's face went pale as he listened to the radio reports. His carefully planned approach was falling apart as his men reported heavy casualties and professional military tactics being used against them.

"How many?" Yamamoto barked into the radio.

The response came through heavy static, but Barry could make out enough to understand that Sarah Blackwood had brought at least a dozen heavily armed mercenaries into the cave system. They were advancing rapidly, eliminating Yamamoto's perimeter guards with ruthless efficiency.

"This changes things," Yamamoto said grimly. "We need to move deeper into the system immediately."

"Like hell," Barry replied. "Release Temujin and we'll consider it."

"You're not in a position to negotiate!" Yamamoto snapped, but his voice carried an edge of desperation. The sound of gunfire was getting closer, punctuated by the occasional explosion of what sounded like grenades.

Sakura stepped forward, her knife held in a reverse grip that spoke of serious training. "You want our help? Prove your good faith. Let the old man go."

Yamamoto hesitated, clearly calculating odds and options. His radio crackled again with reports of his men falling back under heavy fire. Whatever force Blackwood had brought was systematically clearing the cave passages behind them.

"Sir!" one of his operatives called out. "Thermal imaging shows at least twelve contacts advancing through the flooded sections. Military formation, professional equipment. They'll reach this position in less than ten minutes."

Barry could see Yamamoto weighing his options. He needed Barry's expertise and Sakura's knowledge of the map fragments to navigate the tomb's defenses, but he also needed to maintain control of the situation. The approaching mercenaries were forcing his hand.

"Very well," Yamamoto said finally. He gestured to one of his men, who cut Temujin's bonds. "But understand—at the first sign of treachery, the hostages die."

Temujin rubbed his wrists where the ropes had cut into them, his eyes never leaving Yamamoto's face. "The spirits of this place do not look kindly on those who threaten children," he said quietly.

"The spirits will have to wait their turn," Yamamoto replied. "Right now, we have more immediate concerns."

As if summoned by his words, the sound of automatic weapons fire erupted from the passage behind them. Muzzle flashes reflected off the wet cave walls, and Barry could hear the distinctive whine of ricocheting bullets.

"Move!" Yamamoto ordered his men. "Into the deeper passages. Now!"

But as they began advancing toward the ancient markers that guarded the approach to the tomb, a new sound reached them—the electronic beeping of motion sensors being triggered. Blackwood's mercenaries had deployed advanced surveillance equipment throughout the cave system.

"They know exactly where we are," Sakura realized. "This isn't a pursuit anymore. It's a coordinated assault."

Barry studied the carved warnings on the cave walls, their ancient symbols promising death to those who approached the Khan's resting place without proper knowledge. The tomb builders had created multiple layers of defense to protect their emperor's remains, but they could never have anticipated a three-way battle between modern treasure hunters.

"The passage splits ahead," he told the group. "According to the map, there are three possible routes to the burial chamber. But only one is safe."

"Then you'd better choose correctly," Yamamoto said, his weapon now drawn as the sound of approaching mercenaries grew louder.

Temujin stepped closer to Barry, his voice low but urgent. "The markers speak of more than just physical traps, Dr. Curtis. The tomb has guardians that are not of this world."

Before Barry could ask what he meant, the cave erupted in gunfire as Blackwood's advance team rounded the bend behind them. Professional soldiers in full tactical gear opened fire immediately, their weapons equipped with laser sights that cut through the cave's darkness like deadly red threads.

"Take cover!" Barry shouted, diving behind a natural stone formation as bullets chipped fragments from the cave walls around them.

Yamamoto's men returned fire, their muzzle flashes strobing in the confined space. But Barry could see they were outgunned and outmaneuvered. The mercenaries were using military tactics designed for urban combat, advancing in coordinated teams while laying down suppressing fire.

"This way!" he called to Sakura and Temujin, pointing toward the passage marked with the most elaborate warning symbols. "We have to reach the tomb before they overrun us!"

As they ran deeper into the mountain, the sounds of battle echoing behind them, Barry realized that their desperate race to reach Genghis Khan's treasure had become something far more dangerous—a running gun battle in passages designed to kill intruders, with innocent lives hanging in the balance.

The ancient warnings carved into the cave walls seemed to pulse in the strobing light of muzzle flashes, as if the Khan's spirit itself was awakening to defend its eternal rest from those who would disturb it for greed and power.

Behind them, the battle raged on as three forces converged in the darkness beneath the sacred mountain, each driven by their own desperate motivations toward a confrontation that would determine not just who claimed the treasure, but who would survive to tell the tale.

Chapter 19: Unlikely Alliance

The final threshold pulsed with impossible energies—not merely a physical boundary but a transitional membrane between different states of reality. As they approached this shimmering barrier, the temporary alliance that had brought them to this point dissolved with chilling predictability.

Blackwood moved first, her tactical assessment having obviously concluded that eliminating competition before entering the burial chamber represented an optimal strategy, regardless of potential collaborative benefits. Without verbal command, her remaining mercenaries deployed with military precision despite environmental degradation affecting their specialized equipment. Two positioned flanking coverage while two others targeted Yamamoto's group directly, weapons utilizing principles beyond conventional firearms, yet clearly designed for lethal application.

"Predictable betrayal," Yamamoto noted with clinical detachment, despite the immediate threat; his remaining team members formed a protective configuration despite visible cellular deterioration. "Cooperation maintains fictional status until tactical advantage presents itself."

The first shot came from a mercenary positioned behind a crystalline formation that shouldn't exist within ordinary geological possibilities—energy weapons discharging with a distinctive harmonic rather
than a conventional explosive report. The blast struck one of Yamamoto's
few surviving team members with catastrophic effect, body collapsing into
component elements as though cellular structure had been fundamentally
disrupted rather than merely damaged.

Chaos erupted instantly within confined space directly before the transitional threshold. Yamamoto's remaining personnel returned fire with
equipment that similarly transcended conventional weaponry, despite
obvious technological degradation within the boundary environment.
Blackwood's mercenaries advanced with coordinated precision despite deteriorating conditions, their specialized suits providing protection beyond
ordinary body armor while enabling enhanced mobility within transitional gravity fluctuations.

Baatar pulled Sakura behind a massive crystalline formation as energy discharges crossed the confined space with destructive intensity, transforming perception and allowing tactical assessment that transcended ordinary human capability, despite chaotic conditions. The
guardians—Temujin and Khulan—similarly sought cover, their movements suggesting intimate familiarity with the transitional environment,
despite their captive status during the approach journey.

"The threshold destabilizes," Sakura observed, transformed perception
detecting fluctuations ordinary human consciousness would miss entirely.
"Celestial alignment reaches critical maintenance threshold within approximately fifteen minutes."

This assessment established an absolute temporal parameter beyond
factional conflicts or individual survival considerations—a window of opportunity closing, regardless of combat outcome or tactical advantage established during the current confrontation. If all parties remained engaged
in a three-way conflict until alignment was concluded, the burial chamber

would become inaccessible to everyone, regardless of their preparation methodology or technological advantage.

The situation deteriorated further as transitional effects intensified throughout the approach chamber—gravity fluctuating between different intensity levels without warning, light behaving according to principles beyond conventional optics, and ambient temperature shifting through impossible ranges within microseconds. Most concerning, the threshold itself displayed increasing instability—its boundary between different reality states becoming increasingly permeable in unpredictable patterns, rather than maintaining consistent transitional properties.

"We need cover," Baatar decided, identifying a narrow passage extending along the chamber's western perimeter where crystalline formations provided partial protection from energy weapon discharges. "Temporary defensive position until tactical reassessment possible."

They moved with transformed coordination, transcending ordinary human limitations, their physical capabilities enhanced through blood rituals, providing an advantage within a chaotic environment, despite lacking the technological compensation utilized by competing factions. The guardians followed with similar efficiency, despite obvious distress at witnessing the conflict directly before the sacred threshold; their movements suggested training that extended beyond merely ceremonial practice, despite their advanced age and captive status during the approach journey.

From their new position, strategic assessment became possible despite continuing combat between Yamamoto's team and Blackwood's mercenaries. The engagement displayed a disturbing asymmetry, despite apparent technological parity—Blackwood's personnel demonstrated combat efficiency, suggesting extensive experience within transitional environments, despite obvious equipment limitations. At the same time, Yamamoto's remaining team members exhibited increasing disorientation, beyond mere physical deterioration, as boundary effects intensified throughout the chamber.

"Blackwood's operatives have previous exposure to transitional environments," Sakura observed with professional assessment transcending obvious concern. "Their neural adaptation suggests multiple prior experiences despite lacking blood ritual transformation."

"Indicating operation history beyond publicly documented expeditions," Baatar concluded, implications creating disturbing expansion of threat assessment beyond the current tactical situation. "Potentially including successful extraction from similar transitional sites despite official records indicating no such accomplishments."

This realization transformed strategic calculations regarding competing factions—Blackwood's team represented a greater long-term threat than previously assessed, given their operational experience within transitional environments, despite technological limitations similar to those affecting Yamamoto's personnel. The British operation clearly possessed institutional knowledge that transcended individual expedition capabilities, suggesting a systematic exploration of transitional sites beyond public awareness or official documentation.

The conflict's dynamic shifted abruptly as Yamamoto implemented an unexpected tactical adjustment—his remaining team members concentrated fire on chamber's ceiling rather than directly engaging Blackwood's mercenaries. The strategy produced an immediate environmental effect, as crystalline formations shattered with cascading destruction, massive fragments descending upon mercenary positions with a devastating impact, despite their enhanced mobility and protective equipment.

Two of Blackwood's operatives disappeared beneath a crystalline avalanche, their specialized suits providing insufficient protection against the massive geological displacement despite the transitional environment's properties. Blackwood herself narrowly escaped a similar fate, her extraordinary reflexes suggesting an enhancement beyond ordinary human capability, despite lacking visible technological augmentation or ritual transformation.

The chamber's reconfiguration created a momentary combat pause as the remaining combatants assessed the dramatically altered tactical environment. Massive crystalline debris divided the approach space into separate sections, creating natural barriers between different factions while simultaneously restricting movement toward the transitional threshold, now partially obscured behind geological displacement.

Yamamoto utilized this temporary disruption with decisive efficiency, directing his sole surviving team member toward Baatar and Sakura's position despite obvious risk from potential hostility. His movement suggested a deliberate approach rather than random combat displacement; the trajectory was calculated to establish communication possibilities despite the continuing threat from Blackwood's remaining mercenaries regrouping behind the crystalline barrier on the chamber's opposite side.

"Temporary alliance represents mutual survival opportunity," Yamamoto stated without preamble upon reaching position behind the crystalline formation concealing Baatar's group. "Blackwood's team demonstrates operational experience within transitional environments beyond either your ritual transformation or our technological compensation."

"Creating an asymmetric threat profile regardless of numerical parity," Sakura translated with professional assessment transcending obvious skepticism. "Their extraction methodology potentially threatens burial chamber integrity beyond mere archaeological competition."

"Correct assessment," Yamamoto acknowledged with clinical precision despite deteriorating physical condition evident in microscopic desynchronization affecting his movements. "Their equipment configuration suggests extraction prioritizing technological documentation rather than cultural preservation or historical recording."

This observation aligned with concerns emerging from Baatar's transformed perception regarding Blackwood's true objectives—not merely recovering artifacts or documenting historical significance but extracting specific technological information with practical application potential re-

gardless of cultural context or archaeological importance. The approach
represented a fundamental threat to the burial chamber's integrity, beyond
competitive expedition dynamics or factional priority claims.

"You propose cooperative engagement against Blackwood's team,"
Baatar stated, rather than asked, transforming perception to detect intention beyond verbal communication.

"Temporary operational alignment until extraction threat neutralized,"
Yamamoto confirmed with tactical precision, suggesting a genuine strategic assessment rather than a merely manipulative proposal. "Individual
objectives resume priority after shared obstacle eliminated, with threshold
crossing sequence determined by engagement contribution rather than
arbitrary allocation."

The proposal represented a rational response to the tactical situation,
despite obvious trust limitations and fundamental objective conflicts between different factions. Blackwood's demonstrated operational experience within transitional environments created a threat profile that exceeded either ritual transformation advantage or technological compensation
capability when considered individually, potentially requiring a combined
methodology to neutralize it effectively.

"Threshold stability continues degrading," Temujin interjected with evident concern transcending factional conflicts. "Celestial alignment maintains viable transition for approximately twelve minutes before mathematical completion terminates access possibility regardless of individual
positioning or tactical advantage."

This temporal assessment established an absolute parameter beyond
negotiation capability or strategic preference—a window of opportunity
closing, regardless of alliance formation or combat outcome. If Blackwood's extraction methodology threatened the integrity of the burial
chamber, as Yamamoto suggested, preventing her team from crossing
the threshold represented a priority that transcended individual objective
competition or factional advantage.

"Limited operational coordination until Blackwood's team neutralized," Sakura decided with professional assessment, suggesting contingency planning rather than genuine trust. "Threshold crossing sequence determined by practical contribution assessment rather than predetermined allocation."

"Acceptable parameter," Yamamoto acknowledged with equal precision, his deteriorating physical condition clearly secondary to strategic objective despite cellular dissolution visible even to ordinary observation. "Tactical integration is required immediately, given temporal limitations and environmental degradation."

This provisional agreement established a temporary alliance based on pragmatic necessity rather than genuine cooperation, with both parties maintaining obvious reservations despite recognizing a mutual advantage against a shared threat within severely constrained temporal parameters. The arrangement represented a tactical calculation rather than a trust relationship, with strategic assessment transcending ideological differences or competing objectives, given the immediate survival requirements.

While verbal exchange established formal parameters, Sakura implemented additional security measures with professional efficiency, transcending obvious observation—her fingers moving with transformed precision as she separated miniature devices from the equipment secured within her clothing. The objects themselves appeared unremarkable, despite representing guardian technology that went beyond conventional electronic surveillance. Their design utilized principles that combined ritual preparation with material properties responsive to blood-transformed perception.

With subtle movements disguised within ordinary positional adjustment, she attached these devices to Yamamoto's clothing and equipment—placement suggesting tracking functionality rather than merely surveillance capability, technology utilizing principles beyond conventional electronic monitoring despite appearing physically unremarkable.

The implementation occurred with efficiency, suggesting extensive prior experience, despite her lack of obvious technological specialization within her professional background.

Tactical integration proceeded with professional coordination, despite obvious trust limitations—Yamamoto's surviving team member provided a technological assessment of Blackwood's remaining capabilities based on equipment observation during the initial engagement, while Sakura contributed strategic analysis derived from a professional background enhanced through transformed perception. Baatar supplied environmental interpretation utilizing academic knowledge transformed through blood ritual, while Temujin and Khulan provided critical information regarding threshold stability and transitional effects, despite their obvious reluctance to assist individuals who threatened the integrity of sacred sites.

"Blackwood's remaining mercenaries utilize multi-spectrum adaptive shielding," Yamamoto's technician reported with clinical precision despite visibly accelerating cellular dissolution. "Protection prioritizes energy weapon discharge rather than physical impact or environmental degradation."

"Creating vulnerability to kinetic application despite energy resistance," Sakura translated with the immediate tactical application. "Crystalline formations provide both projectile source and environmental disruption capability when properly utilized."

This assessment established an engagement methodology that transcends conventional combat approaches or technological dependency—utilizing transitional environment properties rather than merely deploying brought weapons or equipment, which are increasingly unreliable within boundary conditions. The strategy represented adaptation rather than mere application, a perception-guided approach rather than a predetermined tactical doctrine, regardless of environmental conditions.

As alliance members prepared for coordinated engagement, Blackwood's team initiated a preemptive assault with disturbing efficiency, despite reduced personnel and equipment degradation. Energy discharges with a harmonic signature, suggesting principles beyond conventional directed energy weapons, struck crystalline formations providing cover for an alliance position. The molecular structure was destabilized upon impact, rather than merely fracturing due to physical force.

"They're attempting to eliminate cover before implementing a direct approach," Sakura observed with a professional assessment that transcended obvious concern. "Standard tactical doctrine for numerically disadvantaged force with superior individual capability within a hostile environment."

"Threshold destabilization accelerates with weapons discharge," Temujin warned with evident distress despite captive status. "The boundary between different reality states responds to energy application with increasing permeability disruption regardless of intentional targeting."

This observation created additional tactical consideration beyond immediate combat engagement—weapons utilization potentially threatening threshold stability regardless of intentional targeting or specific application methodology. The situation required an approach that transcended conventional force application or technological deployment, utilizing the properties of the transitional environment rather than merely imposing external capabilities that were increasingly unreliable within these boundary conditions.

"We need environmental engagement rather than direct confrontation," Baatar decided, recognizing that transformed perceptions would be missed entirely by ordinary tactical assessment. "The chamber itself provides a response mechanism beyond conventional weapon application or technological deployment."

This strategic direction aligned with the understanding emerging through blood transformation—recognizing that transitional environments responded to intention beyond merely physical interaction, with reality itself becoming partially malleable through properly focused consciousness, rather than merely manipulable through external force application. The approach represented a fundamental advantage unavailable to technologically dependent expedition members, regardless of the sophistication of their equipment or operational experience within similar conditions.

Implementation required coordination that transcended verbal communication or explicit instruction—transforming perception to allow direct interaction between blood-ritual participants and their consciousness, despite lacking the technological integration utilized by competing factions. Baatar, Sakura, and the guardians established a connection that transcended ordinary sensory exchange, with understanding flowing through direct awareness interaction rather than merely symbolic language or conventional communication methods.

Through this enhanced coordination, they identified critical nodes within crystalline formations where properly applied force would trigger a cascade effect throughout the chamber's structure—not merely physical displacement but a fundamental property transformation as the transitional environment responded to precisely directed intention, rather than merely external manipulation. The approach utilized principles beyond conventional physics or ordinary geological understanding, guiding application rather than merely determining outcome based on force magnitude or direction.

Yamamoto observed this coordination with evident appreciation, despite lacking direct participation capability; his scientific background clearly recognized methodology beyond conventional tactical integration or ordinary strategic cooperation. His contribution manifested through precise technological application—remaining equipment was reconfigured to amplify intentional focusing rather than merely generating an independent effect, regardless of environmental response.

The combined approach produced an immediate environmental response that transcended the ordinary cause-and-effect relationship or conventional physical interaction. Crystalline formations throughout the chamber began resonating with a harmonic frequency that matched the consciousness intention projected through blood-transformed perception, responding to focused awareness rather than merely external force application, regardless of technological sophistication or equipment capability.

The effect propagated with increasing intensity as different formations established synchronization beyond ordinary vibrational physics or conventional resonance principles. The crystal structure transforms from an apparently solid material to a transitional state, sharing properties with the threshold boundary itself. Reality becomes fluid, rather than merely matter changing phase, existence responding to consciousness rather than physical laws determining behavior, regardless of the observer's intention.

Blackwood recognized danger with a professional assessment that transcended ordinary tactical evaluation; her expression revealed understanding that went beyond mere combat experience or operational knowledge in transitional environments. "Fall back!" she commanded with urgency, suggesting genuine comprehension rather than merely precautionary response. "They're triggering an environmental cascade beyond shielding parameters!"

Her warning came too late for effective implementation, as crystalline resonance reached its critical threshold throughout the chamber's structure. Reality itself seemed to shudder as transitional properties propagated beyond ordinary containment parameters; the boundary between different existence states temporarily dissolved as consciousness intention manifested through environmental responses, rather than merely physical interactions or technological applications.

The effect enveloped Blackwood's remaining mercenaries, despite their specialized equipment and obvious operational experience in similar conditions. Their protective suits provided insufficient isolation from the environment, directly responding to their consciousness and intention beyond technological compensation capabilities. Reality itself was restructuring around them according to principles that transcended conventional physics or ordinary material properties.

The mercenaries didn't die in any conventional sense—no blood, no visible trauma, no ordinary biological failure despite obvious existential termination. Instead, they simply ceased maintaining a consistent physical presence within ordinary reality parameters—forms becoming increasingly transparent before dissolving entirely into a transitional environment, existence redistributed according to principles beyond conventional understanding or the ordinary observational framework.

Blackwood herself narrowly escaped a similar fate through an extraordinary reaction speed, suggesting an enhancement beyond ordinary human capability, despite lacking visible technological augmentation or ritual transformation. Her movements displayed precision that exceeded professional training or combat experience, with trajectory calculations incorporating transitional environment properties rather than merely ordinary physics or conventional spatial relationships.

"The threshold!" Temujin's warning carried an urgency that transcended factional conflicts and combat considerations. "Celestial alignment reaches termination phase within approximately seven minutes! Transition possibility concludes regardless of individual positioning or tactical advantage!"

This temporal assessment established an absolute priority beyond remaining engagement considerations or strategic positioning—a window of opportunity closing, regardless of combat outcome or factional advantage. Blackwood's team had been effectively neutralized, despite her individual escape, fulfilling the primary objective established during the temporary alliance formation, regardless of the remaining interpersonal distrust or competing expedition goals.

"We proceed immediately," Baatar decided, transformed perception detecting threshold destabilization beyond ordinary observational capability.

"Sequential crossing according to original agreement, with contribution assessment determining priority allocation."

"Acceptable parameter," Yamamoto acknowledged, despite obvious calculation regarding potential advantage from prioritized crossing sequence. "Though practical assessment suggests transformed individuals demonstrate the greatest probability for successful transition given environmental conditions and threshold instability."

This observation represented a rational evaluation rather than a merely self-serving interpretation—blood-transformed individuals clearly demonstrated enhanced capability within a transitional environment compared to technologically dependent expedition members, regardless of equipment sophistication or operational experience. The assessment established crossing sequence based on practical success probability rather than merely competitive advantage or factional priority.

They approached the threshold with coordinated movement, despite remaining interpersonal tension and obvious objective conflicts—maintaining a temporary alliance that functioned despite fundamental distrust and competing expedition goals. The boundary itself had changed dramatically during the combat engagement—no longer merely a shimmering membrane between different reality states, but an actively fluctuating transition zone where existence itself became increasingly conditional rather than absolute, perception determining manifestation rather than merely observing independently existing phenomena.

Crossing required perception beyond ordinary human consciousness, regardless of technological assistance or equipment capability—awareness capable of maintaining a coherent self-concept while navigating a space where reality itself became negotiable rather than merely externally determined. Blood-transformed individuals possessed a significant advantage within such conditions, as ritual preparation provided the perceptual framework necessary for a successful transition, despite lacking the technological compensation utilized by competing expedition members.

"We maintain physical contact during crossing," Baatar instructed, knowledge emerging from blood memory rather than merely academic understanding or expedition experience. "Consciousness connection ensures cohesive transition regardless of individual perceptual variations or navigational discrepancies."

This methodology established a practical approach that transcends factional differences or competitive objectives—mutual survival dependency despite remaining distrust or continuing intention conflicts. The temporary alliance had transformed from a merely tactical arrangement to an existential necessity, given environmental conditions and threshold instability, with cooperation representing a pragmatic requirement rather than genuine trust or authentic collaboration.

As they prepared for the final approach to the actively fluctuating threshold, Baatar became aware of movement beyond the crystalline debris that partially concealed the chamber's opposite side. Blackwood had repositioned herself despite losing her entire mercenary team; determination clearly transcended ordinary expedition leadership or conventional archaeological ambition. Her expression revealed calculation beyond mere survival consideration or competitive positioning—strategic assessment incorporating variables beyond obvious tactical situation or immediate environmental threats.

"This isn't finished," she called across the intervening space, her voice carrying precision that suggested training beyond ordinary communication or conventional leadership experience. "What awaits beyond the threshold transcends individual expedition capability regardless of preparation methodology or technological advantage."

"Yet you continue pursuit despite team elimination and equipment degradation," Yamamoto observed with clinical assessment transcending obvious adversarial positioning.

"Some prizes justify extraordinary risk beyond rational calculation or conventional cost-benefit analysis," Blackwood responded with disturbing sincerity despite professional detachment. "The Book contains knowledge worth any individual sacrifice or personal consequence regardless of immediate survival probability."

This exchange revealed a concerning insight into Blackwood's true motivation—not merely a professional obligation or organizational directive, but a genuine belief that transcended ordinary expeditionary purpose or conventional archaeological objectives. Her determination suggested a commitment beyond rational assessment or strategic calculation, a conviction that created persistence, transcending ordinary human limitations despite catastrophic tactical setbacks and obvious environmental dangers.

"Threshold stability reaches critical minimum," Temujin warned with urgency transcending factional conflicts or interpersonal tensions. "Transition requires immediate implementation regardless of remaining tactical considerations or strategic positioning."

This assessment established an absolute temporal parameter beyond negotiation capability or preference adjustment—a window of opportunity closing, regardless of complete threat neutralization or comprehensive tactical resolution. Blackwood represented a continuing danger despite temporary isolation and equipment degradation; her determination suggested persistence beyond rational assessment or conventional limitations, regardless of current disadvantage or obvious environmental threat.

"We cross now," Baatar decided, transformed perception detecting threshold fluctuation beyond ordinary observational capability. "Maintaining physical and consciousness connection throughout transition regardless of individual perception or experiential variation."

The unlikely alliance approached its final threshold with a coordinated movement, despite obvious tensions and fundamental objective conflicts—temporary cooperation maintained functional parameters despite interpersonal distrust and competing expedition goals. What awaited beyond the transitional boundary would determine not merely archaeological discoveries or historical documentation, but potentially the future development of human civilization, depending on which faction successfully extracted the knowledge preserved within the transitional environment for eight centuries.

The tomb of Genghis Khan—and the Book of Gold it contained—waited beyond reality's edge.

Chapter 20: The River of Death

Transition through the threshold defied rational description—not merely physical movement between locations, but a fundamental shift in the relationship between consciousness and reality itself. Baatar experienced existence without dimensional limitation, perception unbound from ordinary constraints, awareness expanding beyond conventional understanding before collapsing suddenly back into a corporeal form with jarring finality.

When coherent perception returned, they stood within a space that shouldn't exist in ordinary reality—a vast cavern extending beyond the limits of vision, despite appearing to be part of the mountain's physical structure. Illumination emerged from substance rather than a source, ambient light radiating directly from the surrounding environment without an identifiable origin or conventional propagation methodology. Most significantly, everything within this impossible space conveyed an unmistakable impression of deliberate design, despite lacking obvious construction evidence—architecture emerging directly from reality manipulation rather than merely physical assembly or conventional building techniques.

"The inner sanctum," Temujin whispered with reverent awe, despite his captive status, his voice carrying a mixture of profound respect and genuine concern. "Threshold between ordinary existence and the Khan's final transition state."

The alliance members who had successfully navigated threshold crossing remained in the physical contact formation established before the transition—transformed individuals maintaining a conscious connection, despite overwhelming disorientation, and technological dependents clinging desperately to ritual-adapted companions, despite obvious philosophical objections or ideological conflicts. This arrangement had enabled a collective transition despite threshold instability and fluctuating boundary conditions, with mutual survival dependency transcending factional differences and competing objectives.

Yamamoto maintained remarkable composure despite catastrophic cellular degradation, visible even to the naked eye—microscopic desynchronization affecting physical movement, and tissue transparency revealing internal deterioration beyond the technological compensation capability. His sole surviving team member displayed similar degradation, though accelerated beyond the leader's condition; consciousness clearly struggled to maintain coherent function despite the physical structure failing within an environment operating according to principles beyond conventional biological compatibility.

"Remarkable preservation state," Yamamoto observed with clinical precision, despite an obviously deteriorating condition, as scientific assessment maintained priority despite a personal physical crisis. "Environmental stasis transcending ordinary temporal progression or conventional degradation parameters."

This observation represented genuine insight rather than merely distracting commentary—the cavern displayed preservation beyond archaeological possibility or conventional conservation methodology; everything within this impossible space maintained its condition, suggesting a suspension outside ordinary temporal progression rather than merely environmental isolation or physical protection. The effect transcended normal stasis or ordinary preservation techniques, representing a fundamental relationship with time itself that extends beyond conventional scientific understanding or ordinary physical principles.

Their collective assessment was interrupted by a sound that shouldn't exist within an enclosed subterranean chamber—water flowing in immense volume and considerable force somewhere beyond their immediate visual range. Not an ordinary hydrological system but something fundamentally different—liquid showing properties beyond conventional matter behavior or ordinary fluid dynamics, substance operating according to principles transcending normal physical laws.

"The River of Death," Temujin identified with unmistakable dread despite previous ceremonial composure, transformed perception, clearly detecting aspects beyond ordinary sensory capability. "Final boundary between the approach sanctuary and the Khan's true resting place."

The designation triggered an immediate insight within Baatar's transformed consciousness—understanding that emerged directly from the ritual connection, rather than merely from academic learning or expedition research. The River represented a literal transition between different existence states, rather than merely a physical boundary or geographical obstacle; it was a substance flowing between realities, rather than merely through a physical channel or conventional geological formation.

"It carries more than merely physical matter," he explained, knowledge emerging from blood memory beyond ordinary academic understanding or expedition experience. "Consciousness itself becomes fluid within its flow, identity dissolving without proper preparation or appropriate protective methodology."

"Creating transportation challenge beyond conventional navigation capability or ordinary crossing technique," Sakura translated with practical assessment transcending obvious concern, tactical analysis maintaining priority despite extraordinary circumstances.

This evaluation established an immediate operational requirement that transcended factional differences or competitive objectives—river crossing represented a survival challenge rather than merely an archaeological obstacle, regardless of individual expedition goals or organizational priorities. The alliance maintained a functional necessity despite fundamental distrust and obvious intention conflicts, as mutual dependency transcended interpersonal tension and philosophical disagreement.

They followed the ambient sound with cautious progression, traversing the cavern with movements that suggested a ceremonial approach rather than merely physical advancement. The environment itself seemed responsive to their presence, subtle variations in ambient illumination tracking their movement with awareness, suggesting consciousness beyond mere physical properties or ordinary material characteristics. Most disturbing, temperature fluctuated in patterns matching their emotional states, rather than merely physical proximity or conventional thermal distribution. The environment responded directly to their psychological condition, beyond ordinary physical interaction or conventional environmental sensitivity.

After what might have been minutes or hours—temporal progression increasingly meaningless within a space that existed partially outside ordinary reality—they reached the river's physical manifestation with collective shock, transcending individual preparation or factional differences. The waterway defied conventional hydrological possibilities, despite initially appearing as an ordinary underground river—a channel carved through stone with flowing liquid following gravitational principles, despite its subterranean location lacking an obvious source or destination.

Closer examination revealed profound anomalies beyond ordinary observational capability—water that was simultaneously transparent and opaque, depending on the viewing angle, and a surface that reflected impossible images from locations that couldn't physically exist within the current environment. The flow direction occasionally reversed momentarily without disrupting the overall current progression or general movement pattern. Most significantly, occasional objects floated past, despite lacking physical substance visible to ordinary perception—forms that suggested consciousness imprints rather than merely material debris or conventional river contents.

"Previous expedition members," Temujin explained with evident distress despite ceremonial training or ritual preparation. "Those who attempted crossing without proper methodology or appropriate protective measures. Their physical forms dissolved within transitional substance, consciousness imprints remaining within flow despite corporeal dissolution or identity dispersion."

This revelation created immediate existential dread, transcending rational assessment or conventional fear responses—threats representing fundamental identity dissolution rather than merely physical danger or ordinary mortality risk. The River presented a challenge beyond conventional survival threats, regardless of technological protection or physical capability; the environment directly affected consciousness itself, rather than merely the corporeal form or biological function.

"Crossing methodology?" Yamamoto inquired with remarkable composure, despite visibly accelerating cellular degradation, and maintained strategic assessment as a priority despite a personal physical crisis.

"The guardians traditionally utilize specialized vessels constructed from materials existing simultaneously within different reality states," Temujin replied with obvious reluctance despite providing critical information. "Craft designed through principles combining ritual preparation with physical construction techniques beyond conventional engineering methodology or ordinary manufacturing capability."

"No such vessels present within current environment despite obvious crossing requirement," Sakura observed with tactical assessment transcending apparent obstacle magnitude or immediate solution absence. "Suggesting alternative methodology necessary given available resources and operational constraints."

This evaluation identified an immediate strategic challenge that transcended factional differences and competitive objectives—river crossing represented a collective problem rather than merely an individual obstacle, regardless of expedition affiliation or organizational priority. The alliance maintained functional necessity despite fundamental distrust and obvious intention conflicts, as shared problem-solving requirements transcended interpersonal tension or philosophical disagreement.

Their collective assessment was interrupted by a sound from the river itself—not merely flowing liquid, but something fundamentally different, with harmonic patterns suggesting communication beyond conventional auditory phenomena or ordinary acoustic properties. The water itself seemed to possess a consciousness that transcended mere physical substance or ordinary environmental characteristics, with awareness directed specifically toward its presence rather than merely ambient noise or random sound variation.

"The River acknowledges our approach," Baatar translated, understanding emerging directly from blood memory beyond ordinary linguistic capability or conventional communication interpretation. "It... questions our worthiness beyond mere physical presence or ordinary intentional assessment."

"Indicating potential negotiation capability despite apparent environmental obstacle or physical barrier limitation," Yamamoto observed with scientific precision, transcending obvious metaphysical implications, while analytical assessment maintained priority despite deteriorating physical conditions.

This observation represented genuine insight rather than merely desperate speculation—the River demonstrated properties suggesting consciousness beyond ordinary material limitations or conventional physical constraints, with awareness potentially responsive to appropriate communication methodologies, despite appearing as merely an environmental obstacle or geographical barrier. The possibility represented a potential solution beyond conventional engineering approaches or ordinary technological applications, offering communication that crossed opportunities despite obvious physical impossibilities or apparent navigational challenges.

"Blood-transformed individuals demonstrate the greatest probability for successful communication given perceptual framework compatibility and ritual preparation advantages," Yamamoto noted with clinical detachment, despite an obvious self-interest limitation. The analysis represents a genuine tactical assessment rather than merely a manipulative suggestion.

This evaluation established immediate operational direction, transcending factional differences and competitive objectives—transforming individuals who attempted communication while technological dependents provided support, despite obvious capability disparities and methodology variations. The alliance maintained functional necessity despite fundamental distrust and obvious intention conflicts, complementary capability application transcending interpersonal tension or philosophical disagreement.

Baatar and Sakura approached the river's edge with ceremonial movements that emerged directly from blood memory, beyond conscious learning or explicit instruction. These ritual gestures communicated intention beyond ordinary physical signaling or conventional symbolic representation. Temujin and Khulan provided guidance through subtle indications, despite their captive status, as expertise informed their approach methodology without explicit direction or verbal instruction. Yamamoto and his sole surviving team member maintained a protective perimeter despite deteriorating physical conditions, while technological systems monitored the surrounding environment, despite increasing functional degradation and a reduction in operational reliability.

The ritual communication produced an immediate environmental response that transcended ordinary cause-and-effect relationships or conventional interaction parameters. The river's flow pattern changed with deliberate alteration, suggesting a conscious adjustment rather than a mere physical response or ordinary hydrological variation. Surface formations appeared where none had existed previously; structures resembling stepping stones emerged directly from the liquid, despite lacking a solid composition or conventional material properties. These forms existed simultaneously as both substance and void, depending on the perceptual framework or observational methodology.

"The River provides passage for those demonstrating appropriate respect and necessary understanding," Baatar interpreted, knowledge emerging directly from blood memory beyond ordinary communicative comprehension or conventional linguistic translation. "Stepping stones exist within a perceptual framework established through ceremonial acknowledgment and intentional recognition."

"Creating temporary crossing opportunity dependent upon continuous ritual maintenance and consistent perception application," Sakura translated, with practical assessment transcending obvious metaphysical implications, while tactical analysis maintained priority despite extraordinary circumstances.

This evaluation established an immediate operational methodology that transcended factional differences and competitive objectives—requiring continuous ceremonial maintenance despite apparent physical manifestations or visible structural presence. The alliance maintained functional necessity despite fundamental distrust and obvious intention conflicts, with collective implementation overcoming interpersonal tension and philosophical disagreement.

"Physical connection maintains critical importance during crossing attempt," Baatar instructed, knowledge emerging from blood memory beyond ordinary expedition experience or conventional navigation expertise.

"Consciousness provides structural integrity rather than merely physical properties or conventional material characteristics."

This methodology established a practical approach that transcends factional differences or competitive objectives—mutual survival dependency despite remaining distrust or continuing intention conflicts. The temporary alliance had transformed from a merely tactical arrangement to an existential necessity, given environmental conditions and crossing requirements, with cooperation representing a pragmatic requirement rather than genuine trust or authentic collaboration.

They formed a physical connection chain with transformed individuals positioned strategically throughout the sequence—Baatar leading with direct perceptual access to stone manifestations, Sakura positioned centrally, providing stability through transformed physicality and enhanced perception, and guardians placed between technological dependents, offering protection through ritual knowledge and ceremonial expertise. The arrangement maximized the collective survival probability despite variations in individual capabilities or methodological differences, with cooperation representing a practical necessity rather than genuine trust or an authentic alliance.

The crossing began with deliberate progression, transcending ordinary physical movement or conventional positional advancement. Each step required perceptual adjustment beyond ordinary visual assessment or conventional spatial recognition, consciousness directly affecting manifestation stability rather than merely observing independently existing phenomena. The stones themselves responded to individual perception with alarming variability—solid when approached with the appropriate ceremonial framework, but dangerously insubstantial when contacted with an inadequate understanding or insufficient ritual recognition.

"Maintain ceremonial focus regardless of apparent physical stability or visible structural integrity," Baatar instructed as they advanced cautiously across impossible stepping stones. "Perception determines manifestation rather than merely observing independent existence or predetermined physical properties."

This guidance represented a critical methodology beyond conventional navigation instruction or ordinary crossing techniques—consciousness directly affecting physical reality, rather than merely experiencing an externally determined environment or independently existing conditions. The approach required continuous adjustment beyond ordinary attention maintenance or conventional focus application, as perception actively created a pathway rather than merely identifying a predetermined route or pre-existing structural sequence.

Their progression continued with precarious advancement despite increasing environmental resistance and growing instability in manifestation. The river itself seemed to resist their crossing with deliberate opposition, transcending ordinary hydrological properties or conventional fluid dynamics. Current patterns shifted with apparent intention, despite lacking obvious direction or visible guiding intelligence. Most concerning, the stepping stones became increasingly transparent with each successive position, manifestation requiring greater perceptual effort despite identical ceremonial methodology or consistent ritual application.

"The River tests commitment beyond merely physical capability or ordinary navigational skill," Temujin explained, despite obvious distress at witnessing an inappropriate approach to sacred boundary. "Crossing difficulty increases deliberately with each advancement regardless of technical proficiency or procedural correctness."

This assessment presented an escalating challenge that transcended factional differences and competitive objectives, crossing a progressively increasing difficulty threshold regardless of individual capability or collective methodology. The alliance maintained its functional necessity despite fundamental distrust and obvious intention conflicts, with mutual dependency superseding interpersonal tension or philosophical disagreement.

Disaster struck halfway across when Yamamoto's sole surviving team member experienced catastrophic cellular dissolution, beyond the technological compensation capability and physical endurance limitations. His deteriorating condition reached a critical threshold without warning indication or preliminary destabilization, the body suddenly losing coherent structure despite equipment attempting desperate preservation or system implementing emergency stabilization protocols.

The team member's dissolution created an immediate chain reaction throughout the physical connection sequence—structural integrity was compromised despite ceremonial maintenance or ritual continuation, and the perceptual framework was disrupted despite conscious focus or intentional stabilization. The stepping stone beneath his position vanished instantly upon physical structure failure, creating a sequence disruption that threatened the entire crossing attempt, despite the remaining individual's stability or continued ceremonial maintenance.

Yamamoto himself maintained remarkable composure despite witnessing the final team member's dissolution and experiencing immediate personal danger—analytical assessment implementing instantaneous response despite catastrophic circumstances or overwhelming environmental conditions. His reaction transcended ordinary human capability, despite lacking ritual transformation or blood enhancement. Scientific understanding enabled immediate comprehension, even in the face of apparent metaphysical phenomena or seemingly supernatural manifestations.

"Cut physical connection to maintain remaining sequence integrity," he instructed with clinical precision, despite personal peril, prioritizing strategic assessment to ensure collective survival over the implications of individual sacrifice. "Disruption containment requires immediate isolation regardless of personal consequence or individual survival probability."

The instruction represented genuine tactical insight rather than merely desperate self-sacrifice or a heroic gesture—connection severance necessary for preserving the sequence despite abandoning the individual to the river's transitional properties or the consciousness-dissolving effect. The assessment demonstrated a remarkable understanding, despite lacking ritual preparation or blood transformation, as scientific comprehension transcended ordinary observational limitations or conventional analytical frameworks.

Baatar made an immediate decision, transcending factional differences and competitive objectives—accepting personal risk despite the temporary nature of the alliance or the limited parameters of cooperation. With transformed movement transcending ordinary human limitations, he released the main sequence connection while establishing a separate tether to Yamamoto's position, creating an independent rescue system despite compromising personal stability or endangering the overall crossing integrity.

"Maintain primary sequence progression regardless of our position or movement success," he instructed Sakura, using a transformed communication that transcended ordinary verbal exchange and conventional linguistic limitations. "Complete crossing represents priority beyond individual survival or personal safety consideration."

This direction established an operational priority that transcended factional differences and competitive objectives—mission completion, despite obvious risk or apparent danger, took precedence over personal survival. The transformed individuals demonstrated commitment beyond ordinary human limitations, despite lacking technological assistance or equipment dependency, and blood enhancement enabling capabilities that transcended conventional physical parameters and ordinary biological constraints.

The primary sequence continued with crossing progression, as Sakura maintained ceremonial leadership despite obvious concern for separated individuals or visible apprehension regarding the divided crossing attempt. Simultaneously, Baatar implemented a desperate rescue methodology despite a precarious position or unstable structural support, transforming capability to enable impossible movement despite lacking a conventional support system or ordinary stabilization mechanism.

Yamamoto's position deteriorated rapidly as the dissolution of stepping stones accelerated beyond the capability of ceremonial compensation or perceptual stabilization methodology. The structure beneath him became increasingly transparent at an alarming rate, its manifestation failing despite his remarkable scientific comprehension and extraordinary analytical capabilities. Without ritual transformation or blood enhancement, his perception lacked the fundamental framework necessary for manifestation maintenance despite intellectual understanding or conceptual comprehension.

Baatar reached him precisely as the final structural integrity failed completely, transforming his reflexes to enable impossible timing despite chaotic conditions or environmental instability. His enhanced physiology provided him with strength beyond ordinary human capability, even in awkward positioning or under mechanical disadvantage. Blood transformation enabled impossible rescues, despite conventional physical limitations or ordinary biological constraints.

The moment of contact produced an unexpected transfer of consciousness, transcending ordinary physical interaction and conventional interpersonal connection. Baatar experienced immediate perception sharing with startling intensity—Yamamoto's scientific understanding flooded transformed awareness with extraordinary clarity, an analytical framework providing conceptual structure beyond ritual knowledge or ceremonial information. Simultaneously, blood memory transferred critical components, despite lacking ritual preparation or ceremonial implementation, and transformed consciousness by sharing essential elements, despite incomplete transmission or partial connection establishment.

This mutual exchange created a temporary hybrid awareness that transcended individual limitations, regardless of methodological differences or variations in preparation. Baatar's ritual transformation provided physical capabilities that exceeded ordinary human limitations, despite lacking a scientific framework or analytical structure, while Yamamoto's scientific understanding offered conceptual comprehension that surpassed ceremonial knowledge, despite lacking physical enhancement or biological transformation. Together, they established a temporary functional entity that transcended individual capability limitations, regardless of the preparation methodology or enhancement variation.

With hybrid capability transcending individual limitations, they implemented impossible movement across dissolving stepping stones, despite lacking a conventional support structure or ordinary stabilization mechanism. The progression defied physical possibility, despite apparent gravitational constraints or obvious structural absence, as consciousness directly manipulated reality parameters, despite lacking a complete ritual framework or full ceremonial implementation. Their movement represented a genuine violation of physics rather than merely skillful navigation or extraordinary athleticism, with awareness directly affecting environmental conditions rather than merely operating within established parameters or predetermined limitations.

They reached the far shore precisely as the primary sequence completed the standard crossing, transforming timing to enable impossible synchronization despite separate movement patterns or independent progression methodologies. The collective alliance reformed with an immediate reassessment, transcending factional differences and competitive objectives—shared survival experiences creating temporary cohesion despite fundamental distrust or obvious intention conflicts.

Yamamoto displayed remarkable adaptation despite experiencing a catastrophic event or near-dissolution, incorporating a scientific framework with new understanding in an extraordinary manner, despite lacking ritual preparation or a ceremonial background. His assessment of Baatar transcended previous evaluation parameters or preliminary capability estimation, an appreciation demonstrating genuine recognition rather than merely tactical calculation or strategic positioning.

"Your intervention demonstrated commitment beyond factional limitations or alliance temporary parameters," he acknowledged with precision, suggesting sincere evaluation rather than merely manipulative communication or strategic positioning. "Hybrid perception sharing provided critical information transcending conventional knowledge transfer or ordinary communication methodology."

This acknowledgment represented a genuine reassessment rather than merely a tactical adjustment or strategic recalibration—recognition that transcended the limitations of previous understanding or preliminary evaluation parameters. The experience had transformed relationship dynamics beyond the original alliance formation or initial cooperation parameters, creating a shared consciousness that created connection, transcending ordinary interpersonal interaction or conventional collaborative frameworks.

Their collective recovery was interrupted by a sound from behind—water movement suggesting an approach, despite the river's apparent impassability or the obvious difficulty of crossing. The entire alliance turned with a simultaneous realization that transcended factional differences and individual priorities, transforming their perception to identify threats before conventional visual confirmation or ordinary observational verification.

Sarah Blackwood emerged from the river with impossible grace, despite lacking ritual transformation or blood enhancement; the movement suggested technological compensation beyond the current understanding of the alliance or the present knowledge of the expedition. Her specialized equipment displayed capabilities that transcended conventional engineering parameters or ordinary technological limitations, systems that enabled an impossible transition, despite lacking ceremonial methodology or ritual protection.

"Impressive crossing methodology despite obvious technological dependency or equipment reliance limitation," she observed with professional assessment transcending obvious adversarial positioning, analysis suggesting genuine appreciation rather than merely tactical calculation or strategic positioning.

Her appearance created immediate tension, despite previous alliance formation or temporary cooperation, as competitive objectives reasserted priority despite shared survival experiences or mutual assistance histories. The truce maintained provisional functionality despite fundamental distrust and obvious intention conflicts; pragmatic necessity transcended interpersonal tension and philosophical disagreement.

"The burial chamber lies ahead," Baatar stated with transformed perception, detecting pathways beyond ordinary observational capability, consciousness identifying routes invisible to conventional human awareness or normal visual processing. "Final approach requires specific methodology regardless of individual preparation or factional affiliation."

This assessment revealed a continuing mutual dependency, despite competing objectives or adversarial positioning, where cooperation was a pragmatic necessity rather than a genuine expression of trust or authentic collaboration. The unlikely alliance maintained functional parameters despite fundamental distrust and obvious intention conflicts; shared challenges transcended interpersonal tension and philosophical disagreement.

As they prepared for the final approach toward the burial chamber containing Genghis Khan's eternal resting place and the Book of Gold, with its reality-transforming knowledge, carved warnings appeared along the passage walls with increasing frequency and alarming specificity. The inscriptions utilized language that transcended ordinary linguistic categorization or conventional communication methodologies, meaning they were transferred directly to consciousness despite lacking conventional symbolic interpretation or ordinary translation capabilities.

"Those who approach with conquest in their hearts will find dissolution beyond physical death or ordinary existence termination," Baatar translated, understanding emerging directly from blood memory beyond ordinary linguistic capability or conventional translation methodology. "The Khan's guardian consciousness judges worthiness beyond stated intention or external presentation, essence evaluation transcending deception capability or dissimulation possibility."

This warning created immediate existential consideration, transcending factional differences and competitive objectives—a final approach representing a fundamental identity assessment rather than merely a physical challenge or an ordinary obstacle. The alliance maintained functional necessity despite fundamental distrust and obvious intention conflicts, as shared danger overrode interpersonal tension and philosophical disagreement.

They stood together before the final passage leading directly to history's greatest archaeological discovery and potentially civilization's most dangerous knowledge repository, an unlikely alliance forged through shared survival despite competing objectives and fundamental distrust. What awaited within the burial chamber would determine not merely the success of the expedition or the quality of archaeological documentation, but potentially the trajectory of human consciousness evolution, depending on which faction successfully accessed the knowledge preserved within the transitional environment for eight centuries.

The River of Death had claimed its victims, tested their worthiness, and allowed passage—but the true judgment still awaited within the Khan's final resting place.

Chapter 21: The Hall of Warriors

The passage beyond the underground river opened into darkness so profound that their headlamps seemed to be swallowed by it. Barry Curtis pressed forward cautiously, his boots splashing through the last few inches of the deadly current they had barely survived. Behind him, the reduced expedition—now consisting of himself, Sakura, Yamamoto, and four remaining Red Lotus operatives—moved with the careful coordination of people who had learned to trust each other's competence, if not their motives.

"The air is different here," Sakura observed, her voice echoing strangely in the vast space ahead of them.

Barry paused to test the atmosphere, noting the subtle shift from the damp, mineral-scented air of the river passages to something drier and more complex. There was an underlying chemical tang that made his nostrils burn slightly—not unpleasant, but distinctly artificial.

"Preservatives," he said, the realization hitting him like a physical blow. "The tomb builders used chemical preservation techniques."

Yamamoto stepped beside them, his tactical flashlight cutting a stronger beam through the darkness. "What kind of preservatives?"

"Mercury compounds, probably. Mixed with other minerals." Barry's voice carried growing excitement and apprehension in equal measure. "The Chinese historical accounts mention that Genghis Khan's tomb contained rivers of mercury to prevent decay and ward off grave robbers. I always assumed it was metaphorical."

As they advanced into the chamber, their combined lights began to reveal the scope of what lay before them. The space was enormous—a natural cavern that had been carved and shaped into a ceremonial hall easily the size of a cathedral. But what commanded their attention were the figures standing in perfect formation throughout the vast space.

"Terracotta warriors," breathed one of Yamamoto's men in accented English. "Like the ones found with China's First Emperor."

Barry approached the nearest figure, his historian's eye cataloguing details with growing amazement. The warrior stood exactly six feet tall, clothed in scaled armor that appeared to be made of actual metal rather than clay. The craftsmanship was extraordinary—every detail of the face was individually sculpted, from the weathered features to the determined expression. A spear was held at the ready, and a sword hung at the figure's side.

"Not terracotta," Barry said quietly. "Look at the hands."

Sakura moved closer, studying the warrior's exposed flesh with her LED light. What she saw made her step back involuntarily. "Those are real fingers. Mummified, but real."

The implications hit them all at once. This wasn't a ceremonial army of clay soldiers built to accompany the Khan into the afterlife. These were actual warriors—hundreds of them—who had been preserved through some ancient process that had maintained their physical forms for eight centuries.

"My God," Barry whispered. "They really did it. They killed everyone who worked on the tomb, then preserved the soldiers who did the killing as eternal guardians."

Yamamoto raised his binoculars, scanning the rows upon rows of pre-served warriors that extended beyond the reach of their lights. "How many do you estimate?"

"Hard to say. Could be a thousand, maybe more." Barry moved to examine another figure, noting variations in armor style and weaponry that suggested different military units. "They represent the Khan's entire honor guard—Mongol cavalry, Chinese siege engineers, Persian archers, captured European knights. It's a museum of 13th-century warfare."

The chemical smell was growing stronger as they moved deeper into the hall, and Barry noticed that several of Yamamoto's men were beginning to cough. The preservative compounds that had maintained the warriors for centuries were still active, creating an atmosphere that was increasingly toxic to living humans.

"We need to be careful here," he warned. "These chemical preservatives could be dangerous in high concentrations."

But Yamamoto was no longer listening. He had approached one of the warriors—a figure in elaborate gold-inlaid armor who appeared to be a high-ranking officer—and was examining the precious metals with undisguised avarice.

"Look at this craftsmanship," Yamamoto said, his voice taking on the tone Barry had learned to associate with dangerous obsession. "The gold alone must be worth millions, and that's just one figure."

"Don't touch anything," Barry warned sharply. "We don't know what triggers the preservation system. Disturbing these figures could release more toxic compounds."

Yamamoto ignored him, reaching out to test the weight of a golden torque around the warrior's neck. The moment his fingers made contact with the metal, the chamber's atmosphere changed dramatically.

A low hissing sound began to emanate from hidden vents in the walls and floor, and the chemical smell intensified exponentially. Barry watched in horror as wisps of what appeared to be metallic vapor began rising from the preserved bodies, creating a glittering fog that caught and reflected their lights in ominous patterns.

"Gas masks!" Sakura shouted, pulling her emergency breathing apparatus from her pack. "Everyone, now!"

Barry struggled with his own mask as the toxic fog thickened around them. Through the transparent visor, he could see that the preserved warriors seemed to be changing—their mummified flesh was reacting to the sudden release of additional preservative compounds, causing visible chemical processes that made them appear to move in the shifting light.

"What have you done?" he demanded of Yamamoto, his voice muffled by the gas mask.

"I barely touched it!" Yamamoto's reply was defensive, but Barry could see he was continuing to examine the warrior's equipment even as deadly vapors swirled around them.

One of the Red Lotus operatives—a man Barry knew only as Chen—suddenly collapsed, his breathing apparatus either malfunctioning or inadequate to filter the concentrated chemicals. Sakura immediately moved to help him, dragging the unconscious man toward what appeared to be cleaner air near the chamber's entrance.

"The whole preservation system is designed to kill intruders," Barry realized, studying the patterns of vapor release. "Disturbing any of the warriors triggers a defensive mechanism that floods the chamber with toxic compounds."

The fog was growing thicker, creating an almost solid wall of metallic vapor that made it impossible to see more than a few feet in any direction. Barry could hear the other members of their group coughing and struggling to breathe despite their protective equipment.

"We need to get out of here," Sakura called from her position near the fallen operative. "These masks aren't designed for prolonged exposure to mercury vapor."

But as Barry looked around the chamber, he realized their options were severely limited. The passage they had used to enter was now completely obscured by the toxic fog, and the natural air currents in the chamber were distributing the poisonous compounds throughout the entire space.

"There has to be another way out," he said, more to himself than to the others. "The tomb builders would have needed escape routes for the workers who installed this system."

He began moving systematically along the chamber walls, feeling for hidden openings while fighting off the effects of chemical exposure. His head was beginning to swim, and he could feel a metallic taste building in his mouth despite the gas mask's protection.

Yamamoto, meanwhile, had become completely fixated on the treasures surrounding them. Despite the deadly atmosphere, he was moving from warrior to warrior, cataloguing valuable items with the single-minded focus of a man who had found his life's greatest prize.

"Yamamoto!" Barry shouted through his mask. "You're going to kill us all!"

"Look at this!" Yamamoto held up what appeared to be a jeweled dagger he had taken from one of the preserved figures. "These aren't just guards—they're a treasury! Each warrior is carrying a fortune in precious metals and gems!"

His greed was making him reckless, and Barry could see that every item he touched was triggering additional releases of toxic vapor. The preservation system had been designed to respond to any disturbance with increasingly lethal countermeasures.

"Put it back!" Barry commanded. "The more you disturb, the worse this gets!"

But it was too late. Yamamoto's systematic looting had triggered what appeared to be the chamber's ultimate defense mechanism. Ancient bronze pipes hidden throughout the walls began releasing not just preser-

vative vapor, but what Barry recognized as an early form of chemical warfare—compounds designed to kill quickly and thoroughly.

"Run!" Sakura screamed from somewhere in the toxic fog. "Find an exit,
now!"

Barry stumbled through the deadly mist, using the preserved warriors as
landmarks while searching desperately for any opening that might lead to
cleaner air. The chemical exposure was affecting his coordination, making
each step a struggle against growing disorientation.

He found what he was looking for almost by accident—a narrow gap
between two warriors that revealed a passage carved into the natural rock
wall. Air was flowing from the opening, suggesting it led to a different part
of the cave system where the toxic compounds were less concentrated.

"Here!" he called to the others. "Emergency exit!"

Sakura appeared first, dragging the still-unconscious Chen through the
deadly fog. Two of Yamamoto's remaining men followed, their gas masks
fogged with condensation that made them look like goggled ghosts. Finally, Yamamoto himself emerged from the toxic cloud, his arms loaded with
golden artifacts and precious weapons despite the mortal danger they were
all facing.

They squeezed through the narrow passage one by one, leaving the hall
of warriors to its chemical defenses. The passage led to a natural cave chamber where the air was cleaner, though still carrying traces of the preservative
compounds that permeated the entire tomb complex.

Barry collapsed against the cave wall, pulling off his gas mask to breathe
the relatively clean air. His head was pounding from chemical exposure,
and he could feel the metallic taste of mercury poisoning coating his
tongue.

"Is everyone accounted for?" Sakura asked, checking on Chen, who was
beginning to regain consciousness.

"Tanaka didn't make it out," reported one of Yamamoto's men. "The gas
got him before he could reach the exit."

Barry looked back toward the passage they had used to escape, knowing that somewhere in the toxic fog behind them, another man had died for the sake of an 800-year-old treasure hunt. The preservation system that had maintained the warriors' eternal vigil had claimed yet another victim.

"This is what the warnings meant," he said to Yamamoto, who was still clutching his stolen artifacts. "The tomb doesn't just contain the Khan's treasure—it's a elaborate death trap designed to kill anyone who tries to claim it."

Yamamoto studied the golden dagger in his hands, its blade still gleaming despite eight centuries of burial. "Every great prize requires great risk, Dr. Curtis. These warriors have been guarding their treasures for eight hundred years. Now they belong to whoever is strong enough to take them."

"And how many of your men are you willing to sacrifice for that strength?" Sakura demanded.

Before Yamamoto could answer, the sound of stone grinding against stone echoed from somewhere deeper in the cave system. The tomb's defenses were still active, responding to their presence with mechanisms that had been designed by master engineers who understood both human nature and the art of killing.

"The chamber is sealing itself," Barry realized. "Just like the false tomb. Once the preservation system is triggered, it's designed to contain the threat permanently."

They could hear the grinding growing louder, accompanied by the hiss of escaping gases and the rumble of shifting stone. The hall of warriors was transforming itself into a permanent tomb for anyone unlucky enough to be trapped inside.

"We can't go back," Sakura observed. "Whatever lies ahead is our only option now."

Barry studied the cave passage that extended deeper into the mountain, knowing that each step forward took them further from any possibility of retreat. The tomb builders had created a system of escalating challenges designed to test anyone who sought the Khan's resting place. They had survived the river of death and escaped the hall of warriors, but greater trials undoubtedly lay ahead.

"The warriors were just the outer guard," he said, consulting the golden map fragments that had brought them this far. "According to the inscriptions, there are three more chambers before we reach the actual burial site."

"Then we keep moving," Yamamoto declared, his voice still carrying the excitement of a man who had seen unimaginable treasure and was determined to claim more.

As they began moving deeper into the tomb complex, Barry couldn't shake the image of the preserved warriors standing eternal watch in their toxic sanctuary. They had been living men once—soldiers who had served their Khan in life and been condemned to serve him in death. Now they were guardians of a secret that had already cost too many lives, both ancient and modern.

Behind them, the grinding of stone continued as the hall sealed itself forever, taking its deadly secrets and its fortune in artifacts with it. Ahead lay mysteries that would test not just their courage and intelligence, but their very humanity in the face of power that had once ruled half the world.

The Khan's tomb was revealing itself to be more than just a burial site—it was a testament to an empire's determination to keep its greatest secrets, no matter the cost in human lives.

Chapter 22: The Three Trials

The passage beyond the Hall of Warriors narrowed into a corridor carved with such precision that the walls seemed to flow like water frozen in stone. Barry's headlamp illuminated inscriptions in multiple scripts—Mongolian, Chinese, Persian—all repeating the same message according to his rough translations: "The worthy shall be tested thrice."

"The map," Sakura said, unfolding the golden sheets they'd photographed. "It shows three symbols before the final chamber. A mountain, a star, and an eagle."

"Strength, wisdom, and courage," Barry interpreted. "Classic trial structure. The Khan's engineers drew from multiple traditions."

Yamamoto pushed past them, impatient. His team had been reduced to eight men after the Hall of Warriors, where two had succumbed to the toxic atmosphere despite their masks. "Enough academic discussion. We move forward."

The corridor ended at a circular chamber, smaller than the previous halls but more intricately decorated. The floor was a mosaic depicting the Mongol Empire at its height, with each conquered territory rendered in a

different colored stone. At the far end stood a door that defied comprehension.

It wasn't simply large—it was monumental. Two massive stone slabs,
each twenty feet high and seemingly as thick, blocked the passage. Where
they met in the middle, a complex mechanism of interlocking gears and
counterweights was visible, all carved from solid rock.

"The Trial of Strength," one of Yamamoto's men muttered.

Barry studied the mechanism. "It's not just about brute force. Examine
the gear ratios and pulley systems. This is a mechanical advantage on a scale
I've never seen."

Carved handholds were positioned at various heights on both doors,
with grooves in the floor showing where teams of men would stand. Above
the doors, an inscription in Mongolian made Barry's blood chill.

"What does it say?" Sakura asked, noting his expression.

"'The mountain moves not for one, but yields to many united.' And
below that... a warning. The doors will only remain open for a count of
one hundred heartbeats."

"Then we work together," Yamamoto ordered his men. "Positions!"

They arranged themselves at the handholds—four men per door, with
Barry and Sakura joining to even the numbers. The stone was cold beneath
their hands, worn smooth by centuries but still solid.

"On three," Yamamoto commanded. "One... two... three!"

They pulled. At first, nothing happened. Then, with a grinding that
seemed to come from the earth itself, the massive doors began to part. The
mechanism engaged, gears turning, counterweights dropping, mechanical
advantage multiplying their efforts a hundredfold.

But it was still barely enough. Barry's muscles screamed as they fought
against the tonnage of stone. Beside him, one of Yamamoto's men—already weakened from the toxic air—suddenly convulsed and fell.

"Keep pulling!" Yamamoto roared.

The doors were now halfway open, revealing a passage beyond. But with one man down, the balance was off. The door on their side began to slow, then stop, then reverse.

"Someone has to go through!" Barry shouted. "Before they close!"

Yamamoto didn't hesitate. He abandoned his position and dove through the narrowing gap, followed quickly by three of his men. The sudden loss of manpower caused the doors to close more quickly.

"Move!" Sakura yelled.

Barry, Sakura, and the remaining men scrambled through as the doors slammed shut with earthshaking finality. One man didn't make it—his scream cut short by tons of stone.

They lay gasping on the floor of the next chamber, taking inventory. Yamamoto's team was down to six, plus Barry and Sakura. The businessman showed no remorse for the man they'd lost.

"The weak fall, the strong continue," he said coldly. "Get up. We have two more trials."

The second chamber was dominated by a raised platform in its center. Upon it sat an armillary sphere of breathtaking complexity—bronze rings within rings, covered in astronomical markings, with jade and gold inlays marking celestial bodies. The ceiling above was painted with constellations, some familiar, others alien.

"The Trial of Wisdom," Barry breathed. "It's beautiful."

"It's a lock," Yamamoto corrected. "The passage forward is there—" He pointed to another sealed door. "This mechanism opens it."

Barry climbed onto the platform, studying the sphere. It was similar to Chinese armillary spheres, but with Mongol modifications, Islamic mathematical notations, and even what appeared to be Greek astronomical symbols. A true synthesis of knowledge from across the conquered world.

"The inscription here," Sakura called from the base. "It says 'The star-reader must show the sky of the Khan's last breath.'"

"August 25th, 1227," Barry said immediately. "The accepted date of Genghis Khan's death. But the sky as seen from where?"

He began manipulating the sphere's rings, aligning them to show the night sky from that date. But each adjustment affected the others in complex ways. This wasn't just astronomy—it was a three-dimensional puzzle of incredible sophistication.

"Hurry up," one of Yamamoto's men growled. "We don't have all day."

"You can't rush this," Barry snapped. "One wrong alignment and—"

A hidden mechanism clicked. Suddenly, jets of flame erupted from the walls, forming a cage of fire around the platform. Barry threw himself flat as the heat washed over him.

"The punishment for error," Yamamoto observed with academic detachment. "Continue, Dr. Curtis. Unless you'd prefer to burn."

Barry forced himself to focus despite the sweat pouring down his face. The flames receded but didn't extinguish—a constant reminder of the price of failure. He thought back to his studies, to the astronomical knowledge the Mongols had collected.

"Not just the date," he muttered. "The location. The Khan died near the Yellow River, but his body was transported..." He adjusted the rings to account for the latitude of the Khentii Mountains. "And the time. Mongol astronomers marked time differently than the Chinese..."

Ring by ring, calculation by calculation, he built the correct configuration. The sphere was heating up from the surrounding flames, burning his hands, but he couldn't stop now.

"There!" The final ring clicked into place. The sphere began to rotate on its own, faster and faster, creating a hypnotic pattern. The flames died, and the sealed door ground open.

But as Barry climbed down from the platform, exhausted, he noticed something. The sphere's rotation was accelerating beyond its mechanism's apparent limits. Cracks appeared in the ancient bronze.

"Run!" he shouted.

They sprinted for the door as the armillary sphere exploded behind them, sending bronze shrapnel ricocheting off the walls. Another of Yamamoto's men, too slow, took a fragment in the leg and went down screaming.

"Leave him," Yamamoto ordered.

"We can't—" Sakura began.

"We can and will." Yamamoto's gun appeared in his hand. "Move, or join him."

They had no choice. The wounded man's cries followed them into the third chamber, where they stopped short at the sight before them.

A chasm split the floor—fifty feet across, depth unknown. Spanning it was a bridge, but calling it that was generous. It was a series of stone pillars, each topped with a platform barely two feet square, arranged in a zigzag pattern across the void. Between each pillar was a gap of six to eight feet—jumpable, but only just.

"The Trial of Courage," Yamamoto said unnecessarily.

"It's suicide," one of his men protested. "One slip and—"

"Then don't slip." Yamamoto studied the pattern. "Dr. Curtis, your archaeological expertise. Is there a trick to this?"

Barry examined the pillars, noting the wear patterns and stress marks. "No trick. Just nerve. But look—" He pointed to the far side. "There's a mechanism there. Once someone crosses, they can extend a proper bridge for the others."

"Then who goes first?" Yamamoto asked, though his eyes were already calculating.

"I'll do it," Sakura said quietly. "I have the training."

"No," Barry protested. "I can't let you—"

"You can't stop me." She was already removing her pack, lightening her load. "Besides, you need to be alive to read whatever's in the final chamber."

She approached the edge, studying the distances, the angles. Then, without warning, she sprinted forward and leaped.

Her form was perfect—a gymnast's grace combined with a warrior's precision. She landed on the first pillar, barely pausing before jumping to the next. Zigzagging across the chasm, she made it look almost easy.

But as she reached the middle, something changed. The pillars began to vibrate, a harmonic resonance building through the stone.

"The weight!" Barry realized. "It's designed to detect the crossing. The vibrations will—"

The pillar Sakura had just left crumbled into the abyss.

"Move!" Barry shouted.

Sakura needed no encouragement. She accelerated, jumping desperately from pillar to pillar as each one began to fail behind her. It was no longer a careful crossing but a race against cascading destruction.

She almost made it. The final jump was the longest, and the pillar was already shaking when she launched herself forward. Her fingers caught the edge of the far side, but her grip was slipping—

Barry didn't think. He backed up, got a running start, and threw himself across the first gap. Behind him, he heard Yamamoto cursing, his men shouting, but all that mattered was reaching Sakura before she fell.

He jumped from pillar to pillar, muscle memory from college track serving him well. The vibrations were building again, the ancient mechanism preparing to claim more victims. He reached the far side just as Sakura's grip failed, catching her wrist and hauling her up.

Together, they scrambled to the mechanism—a wheel that, when turned, extended stone slabs from the walls to form a solid bridge. They cranked it desperately as the remaining pillars continued to fall.

The bridge locked into place just as the last pillar crumbled. Yamamoto and his four surviving men rushed across, all pretense of dignity abandoned.

They all collapsed on the far side, gasping. The trials had taken their toll—three more of Yamamoto's men lost, the survivors exhausted and demoralized. But they had passed. Ahead, a final passage led toward what could only be the tomb itself.

"The Khan tested everything," Barry said, helping Sakura to her feet. "Strength of body, clarity of mind, courage of spirit. Those who failed were judged unworthy."

"Spare me the philosophy," Yamamoto snarled, though he looked shaken. "We're through. That's what matters."

But as they entered the final passage, Barry wondered if they had truly passed the trials or merely survived them. The Khan's tests seemed designed not just to weed out the unworthy but to transform those who succeeded. They had entered as a group driven by greed and ambition. What were they now?

The answer awaited in the chamber ahead, where the greatest conqueror in history kept his final secrets. They had proven their strength, wisdom, and courage.

Now they would discover if that was enough.

Chapter 23: Betrayal in the Dark

The echo of the ancient bridge mechanism grinding to a halt still reverberated through the chamber as Barry helped Sakura onto solid ground. His hands were raw from the rope, and his shoulders burned from the strain of their crossing. Around them, the survivors of Yamamoto's expedition stood catching their breath, their headlamps creating wild shadows on the carved walls.

"Remarkable," Yamamoto said, removing his glasses to clean them with deliberate care. His voice carried an odd note that made Barry's instincts prickle. "Three trials designed by warriors dead for eight centuries, and yet they functioned perfectly. The Khan's engineers were truly masters of their craft."

Barry kept his hand near Sakura's elbow, ready to move. Something in Yamamoto's posture had shifted. Throughout their forced alliance, the Red Lotus leader had maintained a facade of scholarly cooperation, but now, having passed the trials, that mask was slipping.

"We should keep moving," Sakura said, her voice steady despite her exhaustion. "Blackwood's mercenaries won't be far behind."

"Oh, I think not." Yamamoto replaced his glasses and smiled—a cold expression that never reached his eyes. "Tanaka, Yoshida."

Two of his men stepped forward, assault rifles rising with practiced efficiency. The other surviving Red Lotus operatives followed suit, forming a semicircle that trapped Barry and Sakura against the chasm they'd just crossed.

"Predictable," Sakura muttered in Japanese.

Barry's hand moved toward the pistol at his hip, but Yamamoto tutted disapprovingly. "Dr. Curtis, please. After all we've been through together? Simply place your weapons on the ground. Slowly."

"You need us," Barry said, not moving. "The final gate—"

"Will require your expertise, yes. But not your independence." Yamamoto's smile widened. "You see, I've been studying you both during our journey. Your methods, your reasoning. I believe I can complete your work once you've... served your purpose."

"The same way Nakamura believed he could?" Sakura's voice dripped contempt. "How did that work out for him?"

Yamamoto's expression darkened. "My mentor was a visionary betrayed by his trust in others. I won't make the same mistake." He gestured sharply. "Disarm them."

Tanaka stepped forward, rifle trained on Barry's chest. The chamber's ancient acoustics amplified every footstep, every breath. Barry could feel Sakura coiling beside him, ready to spring, but the odds were impossible. Six armed men in a confined space with no cover—

The explosion came from behind Yamamoto's group.

The carved entrance they'd passed through erupted in a shower of stone and dust as Blackwood's mercenaries blasted their way in. The concussion knocked everyone off balance, headlamp beams swinging wildly in the sudden chaos.

"Contact rear!" one of Yamamoto's men shouted before a burst of automatic fire cut him down.

Barry grabbed Sakura and dove behind a fallen stone column as the chamber erupted into a firefight. Muzzle flashes strobed in the darkness, turning the ancient space into a nightmare of light and shadow. Bullets sparked off stone, sending chips flying like shrapnel.

"The ladder!" Sakura hissed, pointing to crude handholds carved into the wall. They led up to a ledge that ran along the chamber's perimeter—probably used by the original builders for maintenance.

They scrambled upward as gunfire erupted below. Barry could hear Blackwood's crisp British accent shouting orders, competing with Yamamoto's rapid-fire Japanese. A round whined past his ear, and he pressed himself flat against the stone.

Reaching the ledge, they crawled along it as the battle raged below. In the strobing muzzle flashes, Barry could see Yamamoto's men had taken cover behind pillars and fallen stones, returning fire at the mercenaries crowding through the entrance.

"There!" Sakura pointed to an opening in the far wall—another passage leading deeper into the complex.

They'd made it halfway when a new sound cut through the gunfire: the distinctive whump-whump-whump of a helicopter. But that was impossible—they were deep underground.

The sound grew louder, and Barry realized it was echoing through some kind of ventilation shaft. Ropes dropped from a hole in the ceiling he hadn't noticed before, and figures in tactical gear began fast-roping down into the chaos.

"Japan Intelligence Service!" a voice boomed through a megaphone in accented English. "All parties cease fire immediately!"

"Kenji," Sakura breathed. "He actually came."

The new arrivals moved with surgical precision, their weapons spitting controlled bursts. They wore night-vision goggles, giving them a massive advantage in the flickering darkness. Barry watched one of them put two rounds center-mass into a mercenary who'd been drawing a bead on their position.

"Go, go, go!" Sakura urged, pulling Barry toward the passage.

They'd almost reached it when Yamamoto himself appeared from below, mantling up onto their ledge with surprising agility for a man his age. His glasses were gone, and blood ran from a cut on his forehead, but his eyes burned with fanatic determination.

"You won't deny me!" he snarled, drawing a knife from his belt.

Sakura moved to intercept, but the ledge was too narrow for proper footwork. Yamamoto's blade flashed in the darkness, and she barely deflected it with her forearm, crying out as it opened a gash through her jacket.

Barry didn't think. He simply charged, slamming into Yamamoto with his shoulder. They went down in a tangle of limbs, the knife skittering away across stone. Yamamoto was stronger than he looked, fingers finding Barry's throat with murderous intent.

Stars exploded across Barry's vision. He could hear Sakura calling his name, hear the ongoing firefight below, but everything was growing distant. His hand scrabbled desperately across the stone, finding something—a loose rock. He brought it up in a short arc, connecting with Yamamoto's temple.

The Red Lotus leader's grip loosened, and Barry sucked in a desperate breath. Yamamoto tried to rise, swaying, and Barry kicked out, catching him in the chest. The man windmilled his arms for a moment, eyes wide with realization, before toppling backward off the ledge. His scream was cut short by a wet impact below.

"Barry!" Sakura helped him to his feet, blood running down her arm. "Can you move?"

He nodded, still gasping. Below, the firefight was dying down. The Japanese intelligence operatives had established fire superiority, systematically eliminating or capturing both Red Lotus and mercenary forces. Barry caught a glimpse of Blackwood trying to retreat back through the blasted entrance before two operatives tackled her to the ground.

A figure in tactical gear looked up at them, lifting his night-vision goggles to reveal a young Japanese face. "Hirata-san! This way, quickly!"

More ropes dropped from above. As they were hauled up through the ventilation shaft, Barry could hear Kenji coordinating the mop-up operation below. Professional, efficient, and perfectly timed. He wondered how long the man had been tracking them, waiting for the perfect moment to intervene.

They emerged into cold mountain air and a dawn sky painted in shades of rose and gold. The helicopter sat on a relatively flat section of mountainside, rotors still turning. Medics rushed forward to tend to Sakura's arm.

"Dr. Curtis." Kenji approached, removing his tactical helmet. He was younger than Barry had expected, perhaps early thirties, with intelligent eyes that missed nothing. "I apologize for the dramatic entrance, but when we detected the explosions, we had to move quickly."

"How did you—" Barry started.

"Find you?" Kenji smiled slightly. "Sakura-san has been remarkably clever with her tracking devices, but we've had our own assets in place. When three separate armed groups converge on a sacred mountain, it tends to draw attention."

"The tomb," Sakura said as a medic wrapped her arm. "We still need to—"

"Will remain secure," Kenji assured her. "My team will hold this position until you've completed your archaeological work. The Japanese government has no interest in plundering Mongolia's heritage. We simply wanted to ensure the Red Lotus could never weaponize whatever lies within."

Barry looked back at the ventilation shaft, thinking of the chaos below, the bodies of those consumed by greed and violence. "Yamamoto is dead. So are most of his men."

"And Blackwood is in custody," Kenji confirmed. "She'll have much to answer for, to multiple governments." He paused, studying them both. "You've done well to survive this long. But the hardest part may still be ahead. Are you prepared to continue?"

Barry met Sakura's eyes. Despite her injury, despite everything they'd been through, he saw the same determination that had carried them this far. They'd come too far to turn back now.

"We're ready," he said.

Kenji nodded. "Then let's finish what you started. My men will secure a perimeter and ensure no one interferes. The tomb's secrets will be yours to discover—and to protect."

As medics finished treating their injuries, Barry looked out across the Khentii Mountains bathed in morning light. Somewhere beneath their feet lay the tomb of the greatest conqueror in history, waiting behind one final gate. Yamamoto's betrayal had failed, Blackwood was neutralized, and they had unexpected allies.

But Barry had learned enough about the Khan's defenses to know the mountain itself wasn't finished with them yet. The trials had been tests of worthiness. Whatever lay beyond the final gate would be the true measure of whether they deserved to stand in the presence of Genghis Khan.

"Barry," Sakura said softly, flexing her bandaged arm. "What Yamamoto said about studying us, learning our methods..."

"He was wrong," Barry said firmly. "He thought he could take shortcuts, use force and betrayal instead of understanding. The same mistake every treasure hunter makes." He gestured toward the shaft. "Shall we go finish this properly?"

Sakura smiled—the first genuine smile he'd seen from her since her sister's death. "Together."

As they prepared to descend back into the mountain with Kenji's team providing security, Barry felt a strange sense of completion. Not an ending, but a circle closing. Blossom had started this journey with her sacrifice.

Now her sister would help complete it, not for greed or glory, but for knowledge and truth.

The sun climbed higher, painting the ancient peaks in shades of gold that seemed to echo the precious metal that had drawn so many to their deaths. But Barry knew now that the real treasure wasn't gold—it was the chance to touch history, to preserve it, and to ensure it served wisdom rather than warfare.

The Khan's tomb awaited, and with it, the final chapter of their journey into the heart of one of history's greatest mysteries.

Or normal functional boundaries.

Chapter 24: The Final Gate

The descent back into the mountain felt different with Kenji's team securing their path. LED work lights had replaced the chaotic swinging of headlamps, but the ancient stones seemed to pulse with anticipation. Yamamoto walked between two guards, his hands zip-tied, blood still seeping from the gash on his forehead where Barry's rock had struck him.

"You should have killed me when you had the chance, Dr. Curtis," Yamamoto said, his voice eerily calm despite his injuries. "You still don't understand what we're dealing with."

"Keep moving," Kenji ordered, prodding him forward with his rifle.

The passage beyond the chamber narrowed, forcing them to proceed single file. The walls here were different—smoother, more carefully worked, with intricate patterns that seemed to shift in the moving light. The temperature dropped noticeably with each step deeper into the mountain.

"Construction's changing," Sakura observed, running her fingers along the seamless stonework. "No tool marks. It's like the rock was melted into shape."

They emerged into a circular chamber that stole the breath from everyone present. The space was a perfect sphere carved from living rock, fifty
feet in diameter. But it was the far wall that commanded attention—a
massive, circular door that appeared to be made from a single piece of
stone, black as obsidian and veined with gold, which seemed to pulse with
its own light.

The door was covered in concentric rings of symbols—Mongolian
script, Chinese characters, Persian text, Arabic numerals, and scripts Barry
couldn't immediately identify. At the center was an indentation shaped
like a multi-pointed star, surrounded by astronomical markings of extraordinary complexity.

"The final gate," Barry breathed. "It's not just a door—it's a monument
to knowledge itself."

Yamamoto laughed, a harsh sound that echoed off the curved walls.
"Knowledge? You naive fool. It's a lock designed by the greatest minds of
the 13th century. And you think you can solve it in minutes?"

"Barry," Sakura said, studying the mechanisms. "These astronomical
markings—they're familiar."

"Multiple calendar systems," Barry confirmed, moving closer. "All synchronized to specific celestial events. The Mongols didn't just conquer
territories—they absorbed their knowledge, their ways of marking time."

Kenji's men took defensive positions around the chamber while Barry
and Sakura examined the door. Blackwood was brought in, her mercenaries either dead or captured. She watched the proceedings with calculating
eyes, saying nothing.

"The puzzle boxes," Barry said suddenly. "Sakura, we need both of them.
The indentations here—they match the jade keys."

She carefully removed both boxes from her pack. As she set them on the
carved pedestal before the door, a low vibration ran through the chamber,
felt more than heard.

"You're making a mistake," Yamamoto said, straining against his bonds. "The Red Lotus has studied the legends for generations. There are defenses you can't imagine—"

"Quiet," Kenji snapped. But Barry noticed the nervous glances his men were exchanging.

"No, let him talk," Barry said without looking away from the door. "What defenses?"

"The Khan was no fool," Yamamoto said. "He knew grave robbers would come. The door isn't just locked—it's trapped. One wrong move and this entire chamber becomes a tomb."

"He's trying to psyche us out," Sakura said, but Barry heard the doubt in her voice.

"Am I?" Yamamoto's smile was cold. "Tell me, Dr. Curtis—why do you think no one has succeeded in eight centuries? Luck? The Soviets found this place in the 1960s. Sent in a full archaeological team. They were found a month later at the base of the mountain, their minds gone, babbling about golden warriors and the voice of the Khan."

Barry's hands hesitated over the puzzle boxes. The astronomical calculations swirled through his mind, but now doubt crept in. What if there were multiple correct combinations, but only one that wouldn't trigger defenses?

"Barry," Sakura said softly. "We've come too far to stop now."

He nodded, focusing on the patterns. "The alignment markers—they're showing specific dates. Here, this configuration of Mars and Jupiter—it would only occur every twelve years in the Mongolian calendar."

"The year of the Horse," Yamamoto supplied, surprising them. "1227. The year the Khan died."

Barry looked at him sharply. "You know the solution?"

"Pieces of it. Fragments passed down through the Red Lotus." Yamamoto's expression was unreadable. "But knowledge and understanding are different things. You have the boxes, the astronomical training. Perhaps together—"

"Absolutely not," Kenji interrupted. "He stays restrained."

"Then we all die here," Yamamoto said simply. "The door requires three elements: the two keys, yes, but also a specific vocal component. A phrase in old Mongolian that must be spoken at the exact moment of alignment."

"You're lying," Sakura accused.

"The inscription along the third ring," Yamamoto nodded toward the door. "Can you read it, Dr. Curtis?"

Barry studied the text, his heart sinking. It was in an archaic form of Mongolian script, but he could make out enough. "It's... a warning. And instructions. 'Speak the Khan's true name as the stars align, or the mountain shall reclaim its own.'"

"The Khan's true name," Blackwood spoke for the first time. "Not Temüjin, not Genghis Khan. The secret name given by his mother, known only to his closest family."

"Which died with them," Barry said.

"Did it?" Yamamoto's eyes glittered. "The Red Lotus has preserved many secrets. Free my hands, let me help with the alignment, and I'll give you the name."

"This is a trick," Kenji warned.

But Barry was already doing the calculations. The mechanism was far more complex than he'd initially thought. It would take at least three people to manipulate the boxes and the surrounding controls simultaneously.

"We need him," Barry admitted reluctantly. "But—" He turned to Kenji. "Keep multiple guns on him. Any sudden moves—"

"Understood." Kenji nodded to his men, who trained their weapons on Yamamoto as one of his guards cut the zip-ties.

Yamamoto rubbed his wrists, then approached the door with something approaching reverence. "The first box aligns with the solar calendar, here."

He showed them a series of indentations. "The second with the lunar. But both must be turned in sequence with these outer rings."

They worked in tense cooperation, Barry calling out astronomical positions while Yamamoto and Sakura manipulated the mechanisms. The concentric rings began to rotate, symbols aligning in patterns that seemed to dance before their eyes.

"Almost there," Barry said. "The final position should be—"

"Now!" Yamamoto suddenly shouted. But instead of betraying them, he spoke a phrase in ancient Mongolian, his voice ringing with surprising power: "Temüjin Yesukhei Baghatur!"

The chamber filled with a sound like a thousand bells chiming at once. The golden veins in the door blazed with light, and the massive stone began to move. Not swinging open, but irising like a camera aperture, the center spiraling outward in a hypnotic pattern.

"You actually helped us," Sakura said, stunned.

Yamamoto's expression was unreadable. "The Red Lotus serves a purpose greater than any individual. The Khan's legacy must be preserved—or destroyed. Either way, it cannot remain hidden forever."

Through the expanding opening, they could see a passage lined with sheets of gold, leading to a chamber beyond. The air that flowed out was cool and dry, carrying a scent like old incense and preservation spices.

"Move in carefully," Kenji ordered. "Watch for—"

A grinding sound cut him off. The door mechanism had stopped expanding and now seemed to be cycling through a different pattern.

"It's on a timer," Barry realized. "We have maybe ten minutes before it seals again."

"Then let's not waste them," Yamamoto said, and before anyone could stop him, he strode through the opening.

"Stop him!" Kenji shouted, but Yamamoto was already disappearing down the golden passage.

They rushed after him, Barry clutching the puzzle boxes, knowing they might need them again. The passage walls were covered in gold sheets inscribed with text in a dozen languages—a library made of precious metal.

They emerged into a vast chamber that defied imagination. And there, at its heart, sat the one sight that made even Yamamoto stop in his tracks.

The preserved body of Genghis Khan, enthroned in gold, waiting as he had waited for eight centuries.

Chapter 25: The Burial Chamber

The chamber seemed to exist outside of time. Carved from a single massive block of dark stone, its domed ceiling stretched fifty feet overhead, covered in a map of the night sky rendered in precious gems. But it was the figure on the throne that commanded absolute attention.

Genghis Khan sat as if he had merely paused in contemplation. His preservation was beyond extraordinary—the techniques used made Egyptian mummification look primitive. His skin had a subtle sheen, like wax but somehow more lifelike. He wore simple clothes—a fur-lined deel and felt boots—but they showed no sign of age. His eyes were closed, his expression one of intense concentration, as if he were solving some great problem that required eternal thought.

"Impossible," Blackwood breathed. She had been brought in with the others, still under guard. "Eight centuries, and he looks like he died yesterday."

"Not died," Yamamoto corrected, his voice filled with an almost religious awe. "Transformed. Look at his hands."

The Khan's hands rested on the arms of his golden throne, and Barry saw what Yamamoto meant. The fingernails had continued growing slightly, and there was a subtle tension in the fingers, as if they might move at any moment.

"Some kind of suspended animation?" Sakura suggested, though she sounded unconvinced.

"The Chinese alchemists searched for immortality elixirs," Barry said, unable to look away from the figure. "The Islamic scholars preserved bodies with compounds we still don't fully understand. What if the Khan's advisors combined their knowledge?"

Around the throne, arranged with mathematical precision, lay the accumulated treasures of the Mongol Empire. But these weren't mere gold and jewels—this was a collection of knowledge. Scrolls in sealed tubes, books bound in strange materials, clay tablets that looked ancient even by 13th-century standards. The walls were lined floor to ceiling with golden sheets covered in minute text.

"The Altan Debter," Kenji's voice was hushed as he pointed to an ornate box on a pedestal at the Khan's feet. "The Secret History of the Mongols."

"More than that," Barry said, recognizing scripts and languages. "Look—Sanskrit texts, Greek scrolls, Arabic treatises. This isn't just Mongol history. It's the collected knowledge of every civilization they conquered."

Yamamoto had moved to one side of the chamber, examining what appeared to be weapons displayed on racks. "These shouldn't exist," he said, his usual composure cracking. "This is... it looks like a early firearm, but the design is all wrong. And these containers—"

"Don't touch anything," Kenji warned sharply. "We don't know what—"

A sound like a grinding stone interrupted him. They all turned to see the entrance beginning to close.

"The timer," Barry said. "We need to—"

"No." Yamamoto's voice was firm. "We're exactly where we need to be." He turned to face them, and his expression had changed. The awe was gone, replaced by fanatic determination. "Do you understand what this place is? It's not just a tomb. It's an arsenal. A library of destruction."

"Yamamoto," Kenji raised his weapon. "Step away from those containers."

"The Khan conquered the known world with horses and bows," Yamamoto continued, ignoring the threat. "But look what he chose to hide. Greek fire was improved by Chinese alchemists. Poisonous gases from Persian recipes. Mechanical devices from Damascus workshops." His hand moved toward one of the sealed containers. "The Red Lotus has waited generations for this moment."

"Don't!" Barry shouted, but Yamamoto had already grasped one of the ceramic vessels.

The moment his hand touched it, the chamber responded. A low vibration built through the floor, and dust began falling from the ceiling. The gems in the sky map above flickered like stars coming to life.

"What did you do?" Sakura demanded.

"Activated the final defense," Yamamoto said with grim satisfaction. "The Khan knew human nature. Greed would bring robbers here, but it would also be their doom. The chamber is designed to protect itself."

A cracking sound echoed through the space. In the walls, previously invisible seams began to appear. Water—impossibly—began seeping through.

"There's no water source at this elevation," one of Kenji's men said, voice tight with fear.

"Underground river," Barry realized. "Diverted and held back by ancient mechanisms. That's why the passages had those drainage channels—this whole complex can flood."

The entrance was nearly sealed now, just a narrow gap remaining. More water began flowing, not seeping but pouring from widening cracks.

"Everyone out!" Kenji ordered. "Move!"

"Not without the Book," Barry said, rushing toward the pedestal.

"Leave it!" Sakura grabbed his arm. "It's not worth dying for!"

"This is human history," Barry insisted, pulling free. He reached the pedestal and carefully lifted the ornate box containing the Altan Debter. It was heavier than expected, made of gold and jade and meteoric iron.

Yamamoto laughed, a sound edged with madness. "Take it then. But know that you're taking only what the Khan allows. The real treasures—the weapons, the formulas—they'll die with me."

The water was ankle-deep now and rising fast. The entrance had closed to barely a foot wide. Kenji's men were squeezing through one at a time.

"Yamamoto, come on!" Even now, Barry couldn't simply leave a man to die. "There's still time!"

"Time?" Yamamoto looked at the throne where Genghis Khan sat unmoved by the chaos. "I've had eight hundred years. The Red Lotus has passed this duty from generation to generation, and I will not be the one who fails."

He smashed another container, and a greenish gas began seeping out. The smell was acrid, burning.

"Gas masks!" Kenji shouted. "Everyone out NOW!"

Barry clutched the box containing the Secret History and ran for the entrance. Sakura was already through, turning back to help pull him through the narrow gap. Behind them, he could hear Yamamoto chanting in Mongolian, his voice echoing off the flooding chamber walls.

They squeezed through just as the door sealed completely. The grinding of stone was drowned out by the sound of rushing water behind the barrier. The entire mountain seemed to shudder.

"The structural integrity," one of Kenji's engineers said, checking his instruments. "The flooding is causing shifts in the rock. We need to get out—the whole complex could collapse."

They ran through passages that were already beginning to crack and shift. Ancient mechanisms, disturbed by the flooding, ground to life.

Stone blocks fell from the ceiling, and walls that had stood for centuries began to buckle.

Behind them, muffled by tons of stone, they could hear explosions. Whatever chemicals Yamamoto had released were reacting with the water, or with each other.

"Faster!" Kenji urged.

They reached the chamber where the mechanical guardians stood, but the figures were toppling as the floor cracked beneath them. One fell across their path, and they had to climb over its metal form. In the strobing light of their headlamps, Barry saw that beneath the armor was an intricate framework of gears and counterweights—a clockwork soldier centuries ahead of its time.

Another explosion, closer now. A wall of hot air rushed past them, carrying the scent of chemicals and age.

They burst from the cave system just as a section of the mountain collapsed behind them. The ground shook, and avalanches of stone poured down the slopes. In the pre-dawn light, they could see the entire face of the mountain changing, sealing the tomb more thoroughly than any human hand could have managed.

Barry collapsed on the ground, still clutching the box containing the Altan Debter. His clothes were soaked, and his lungs burned from exertion and chemical fumes. Around him, Kenji's team was conducting a head-count and checking for injuries.

"Yamamoto?" Sakura asked, though they all knew the answer.

"Buried with his obsession," Kenji said grimly. "Along with whatever weapons he was so eager to claim."

"The Khan's final victory," Barry said, looking at the mountain. "He knew someone would eventually break through his defenses. So he made the tomb itself the last guardian. Let greed trigger its own punishment."

Blackwood, who had survived the escape, laughed bitterly. "All of this—the deaths, the fortunes spent—for one book?"

"Not just a book," Barry corrected, looking at the box in his hands. "The true history of an empire, written by the victors themselves. The story the world has never heard."

As dawn broke fully over the Khentii Mountains, they sat among the rubble of their escape and watched the mountain settle into its new configuration. Somewhere beneath millions of tons of rock and water, Genghis Khan still sat on his golden throne, his secrets safe once more. The chemical fires would burn out, the waters would find their level, and the mountain would sleep again.

But in the box Barry held lay words written in gold, waiting to tell their story after eight centuries of silence. It was enough. It had to be enough.

"We should go," Kenji said finally. "My government will want a full debriefing. And Dr. Curtis, that book—"

"Will be studied properly," Barry assured him. "With international oversight and full academic transparency. The Khan kept his weapons. The least we can do is share his words."

As helicopters arrived to evacuate them, Barry took one last look at the transformed mountain. Yamamoto had been wrong about one thing—they hadn't taken only what the Khan allowed. They had earned what they had through wisdom, rather than greed, and cooperation rather than betrayal.

The Book of Gold would reveal its secrets in time. And perhaps that had been Genghis Khan's plan all along—to test not just the courage of those who sought him, but their worthiness to receive his legacy.

The mountain had judged them and found them acceptable. Barely.

Chapter 26: The Khan's Curse

The box containing the Altan Debter sat between them in the helicopter, wrapped in protective cloth and secured in a climate-controlled case. Barry couldn't stop glancing at it, still hardly believing they had escaped with even this much. Below them, the Khentii Mountains retreated into morning mist, keeping their secrets.

"Status report," Kenji spoke into his headset. "What's the situation at the tomb site?"

His expression darkened as he listened to the response. He switched to speaker so they could all hear.

"Sir, we're detecting continued seismic activity centered on the collapse zone. Temperature readings are... anomalous. Whatever chemical reaction Yamamoto triggered, it's still ongoing beneath the rubble."

"Casualties?" Kenji asked.

"Yamamoto is confirmed lost. Two of our men have chemical burns from exposure to the gas, but they'll recover. Blackwood's surviving mercenaries are in custody. We also have three bodies recovered from the initial firefight."

Barry thought of Yamamoto, choosing to die with the weapons he'd sought for so long. The man had been a fanatic, a killer, but in those final moments, he'd seemed almost peaceful. As if being buried with the Khan's secrets was a form of honor.

"There's something else, sir," the voice continued. "The local herders are reporting strange phenomena. Lights in the mountains at night. Sounds like... singing."

"Singing?" Sakura asked.

"The old Mongolian funeral songs, they say. But there's no one there."

Kenji switched off the speaker. "Trauma and suggestion. These mountains are sacred to the locals. After what happened, their minds are creating—"

"Maybe," Barry interrupted. "Or maybe Yamamoto was right about one thing. That tomb was more than just a grave. It was designed to protect itself, to respond to threats." He looked out at the mountains. "Who knows what other mechanisms we triggered?"

"Speaking of protection," Kenji said, his tone becoming official. "Dr. Curtis, Ms. Hirata—we need to discuss the book."

Barry's hand moved instinctively to the case. "We've been through this. The Altan Debter belongs to the academic community, to historians—"

"I'm not talking about confiscating it," Kenji assured him. "But you must understand the implications. This isn't just a historical document. It's the private records of Genghis Khan, potentially containing military strategies, technological insights, information about the locations of other sites like the one we just left."

"You mean other tombs," Sakura said. "Other weapons caches."

"Exactly. The world isn't ready for a treasure hunt on that scale. Think of what just happened—three different groups trying to claim one site. Now multiply that by dozens, maybe hundreds of locations across Asia and Europe."

Barry opened his mouth to argue, then closed it. He thought of the mechanical guardians, the chemical weapons, the advanced devices he'd glimpsed in the tomb. All of it from the 13th century or earlier. What else had the Mongols hidden?

"What do you propose?" he asked finally.

"A joint commission," Kenji said. "Japanese intelligence will work with UNESCO, major universities, and the Mongolian government. The book will be studied, but carefully. Information will be released gradually, with anything potentially dangerous classified until we better understand the implications."

"Censorship," Barry said flatly.

"Wisdom," Kenji countered. "You're an archaeologist, Dr. Curtis. You know the damage looters can do to historical sites. Now imagine those looters armed with specific information about locations containing weapons we don't even understand."

"He has a point," Sakura said quietly. "Think about what my sister died for—keeping one map out of the wrong hands. This book might contain dozens of such maps."

Barry was quiet for a long moment, watching the landscape pass below. Finally, he nodded. "All right. But I want guarantees. Full academic access to the historical content. Publication rights for anything that doesn't pose a security risk. And the Mongolian people must benefit from any discoveries about their heritage."

"Agreed," Kenji said. "We'll draw up formal protocols when we reach Ulaanbaatar."

The rest of the flight passed in exhausted silence. Barry dozed fitfully, dreaming of golden walls covered in text, of the Khan's preserved face, of water rising in ancient chambers. He woke to find Sakura watching him with concern.

"You were calling out," she said softly. "In Mongolian, I think."

"I don't speak Mongolian," Barry said, disturbed.

"You were saying 'Temüjin Yesukhei Baghatur.' Over and over."

The name Yamamoto had spoken to open the door. Barry shivered despite the warmth of the helicopter cabin.

They landed at a secure facility outside Ulaanbaatar as the sun reached its zenith. Medical teams were waiting, along with officials from multiple governments. Barry was reluctant to let the book out of his sight, but Kenji assured him it would only be moved to a climate-controlled room where they could begin preliminary examination.

While Sakura's arm was properly treated, Barry was debriefed by a succession of intelligence officers, diplomats, and academics. He told the story again and again, each time remembering new details. The precision of the preservation techniques. The impossible mechanisms. The way the Khan's face had seemed to watch them even with closed eyes.

It was evening before he was allowed to see the book again. In a sterile room with perfect lighting and multiple cameras recording, he donned white gloves and carefully opened the box.

The Altan Debter lay before him, its cover of black leather and gold unmarked by age. With reverent care, he opened it to the first page.

The metal foil pages were covered in minute script, so fine it required magnification to read clearly. The first section was in classical Mongolian, written in the vertical script. But as he turned the delicate pages, he found sections in Chinese, Persian, Arabic, and languages he couldn't identify.

"It's not just a history," he breathed. "It's a compilation. Look—this section appears to be about metallurgy. This one is astronomical calculations. And here—" He paused, frowning. "These diagrams look like architectural plans, but for what?"

Sakura leaned closer, careful not to touch the pages. "Those measurements—they're using a unit system I don't recognize."

"Because it's not from Earth," a new voice said.

They turned to see Dr. Erdene Batbold enter the room. But that was impossible—Yamamoto's men had killed him in Virginia.

"You're dead," Barry said flatly.

The man smiled. "Dr. Batbold is indeed dead. I am his brother, Dr. Ganbold. I apologize for the deception, but I wanted to see your reaction." His expression grew serious. "My brother sent me copies of his research before he died. He believed the Mongols had access to knowledge that predated known civilization."

"That's absurd," Kenji said.

"Is it?" Ganbold moved closer to the book, studying the diagrams Barry had found. "These architectural plans match no known building techniques. The mathematical principles they demonstrate weren't 'discovered' by Western science until the 20th century. And these astronomical charts show celestial bodies that weren't officially observed until we had powerful telescopes."

"You're suggesting what—ancient aliens?" Barry's skepticism was clear.

"I'm suggesting," Ganbold said carefully, "that human civilization is older and more complex than we admit. The Mongols conquered lands that had been continuously inhabited for millennia. They had access to libraries and scholars from cultures that preserved knowledge from even earlier times. Some of that knowledge was... unusual."

He pointed to a particular page. "This describes a weapon that projects 'heaven's fire' across great distances. The proportions and materials match no known medieval weapon. But they do match theoretical designs for directed energy weapons."

"Theoretical designs from when?" Sakura asked.

"The 1960s. Soviet military research. Which raises the question—did they develop these ideas independently, or did they have access to historical sources we don't know about?"

Barry felt a chill run down his spine. He thought of the devices in the tomb, the things that looked like firearms but wrong, the containers of chemicals that shouldn't have existed.

"The sphere," he said suddenly. "There was a metal sphere in the box with the book. It projected a map showing locations across the empire."

Ganbold's eyes sharpened. "Where is this sphere?"

"Secured," Kenji said firmly. "And it will remain so until we better understand what we're dealing with."

"You must let me examine it," Ganbold insisted. "If it's what I think it is—"

An alarm cut through the room. Red lights began flashing, and Kenji's radio crackled to life.

"Sir, we have a situation. The artifact in Containment Room 3—it's activated on its own."

The sphere. Barry exchanged glances with Sakura as Kenji barked orders into his radio.

"It's projecting again, sir. But not the map this time. It's... it appears to be text. Streaming text in multiple languages. The data rate is incredible—our systems can barely record it all."

"Is it dangerous?" Kenji demanded.

"Unknown, sir. But the energy readings are climbing. And—" A pause. "Sir, the text it's displaying. Some of it matches what's in the book Dr. Curtis is examining. But it's showing pages he hasn't reached yet. Pages that seem to be... instructions."

"Instructions for what?" Barry asked, though he was afraid he already knew.

"Weapons, sir. Detailed schematics for weapons. And something else—coordinates. Hundreds of them. Locations all across Asia and Europe. If these are other sites like the tomb—"

"Shut it down," Kenji ordered. "Cut power to the entire room if you have to."

"We've tried, sir. It's drawing power from somewhere else. The sphere itself seems to be the source."

Barry closed the Altan Debter carefully. "It's connected. The book and the sphere—they're parts of a whole. The Khan didn't just hide his treasures. He created a system, a network of information."

"Which is now activating," Ganbold said. His face was pale. "Probably triggered by the tomb's destruction. A failsafe to ensure the knowledge survives even if the physical locations are lost."

"Can we stop it?" Kenji asked.

"Do we want to?" Ganbold countered. "This is the accumulated knowledge of the Mongol Empire at its height. Scientific, military, cultural—"

"And dangerous," Sakura interrupted. "You didn't see those weapons. You didn't see Yamamoto's face when he realized what was in that tomb. Some knowledge is too dangerous to release."

Another alarm joined the first. Kenji's expression grew even grimmer as he listened to his headset.

"What now?" Barry asked.

"Satellite surveillance of the tomb site. The chemical reaction we detected—it's not dying down. It's spreading. The entire mountain is showing thermal blooms. And the seismic activity is increasing."

"The Khan's curse," Ganbold said quietly. "The legends say that disturbing his rest would bring catastrophe. We thought it was superstition, but what if it was a warning about literal defenses?"

"We need to evacuate the area," Kenji said. "Get any civilians clear—"

The lights went out. Emergency power kicked in a second later, bathing everything in a red glow. In the distance, they could hear shouting, the sound of running feet.

"The sphere?" Barry asked.

Kenji listened to his radio, his expression growing more concerned by the second. "It's not just projecting anymore. It's... broadcasting. Electromagnetic pulses are interfering with our equipment. And the information it displayed before we lost video—" He looked at them with something like fear. "It wasn't random. It was targeted. Names, dates, locations. Like it was identifying specific people and places."

"Broadcasting to whom?" Sakura asked.

Before anyone could answer, the building shook. Not an earthquake, but a single sharp jolt, as if something massive had struck the earth. Through the reinforced windows, they could see a pillar of light rising from the direction of the Khentii Mountains.

"The tomb site," someone said unnecessarily.

The pillar of light pulsed once, twice, then faded. But in its wake, the sky seemed different. The stars were brighter, and there were patterns in them that Barry had never seen before.

"What have we done?" he whispered.

Ganbold was at the window, his face reflecting the strange new starlight. "We've awakened something. The question is whether it's a blessing or a curse."

"Or both," Sakura said quietly. She stood beside Barry, her hand finding his. "The Khan conquered the world with knowledge as much as swords. Maybe this is his final conquest—forcing us to face knowledge we're not ready for."

In the distance, sirens were beginning to wail. The modern world was responding to something ancient and impossible. And at the center of it all sat a book written in gold and a sphere that pulsed with its own light, holding secrets that had waited eight centuries to be revealed.

The Khan's curse, Barry realized, wasn't death or destruction. It was truth—dangerous, transformative truth that would change everything they thought they knew about history, about technology, about the world itself.

And there was no putting it back in the tomb.

As emergency protocols activated around them and the world began to grapple with the impossible, Barry thought of Genghis Khan sitting eternal on his golden throne. Even in death, the great conqueror had won a final victory. Not through weapons or armies, but through the one force more powerful than both:

Knowledge that could not be unlearned.

The curse had only just begun.

Chapter 27: Collapse

The emergency command center in Ulaanbaatar had descended into controlled chaos. Multiple screens showed satellite feeds of the Khentii Mountains, where the pillar of light had emanated just minutes before. The thermal blooms Kenji had mentioned were spreading outward from the tomb site in concentric circles, like ripples in a pond.

"Radiation?" Barry asked, watching the expansion with growing dread.

"Negative," a technician reported. "But we're reading massive electromagnetic disturbances. Every electronic device within fifty kilometers of the site is experiencing interference."

"The nomadic families," Dr. Ganbold said urgently. "There are herders in those mountains. They need to be evacuated."

Kenji was already coordinating with local authorities, but the conversation was clearly not going well. "They're refusing to leave," he reported. "The elders say the mountain is reclaiming what was taken. They're calling it the Khan's awakening."

Another screen flickered to life, showing the containment room where the sphere was held. The device was floating three feet off the ground, spinning slowly, its surface covered in flowing patterns of light. The electromagnetic pulses it emitted were visible as waves of distortion in the air.

"Energy output is increasing exponentially," someone reported. "At this rate, it'll overload every system in the building within an hour."

"Then we move it," Kenji decided. "Get a shielded transport ready—"

"No." The voice came from the doorway. Sarah Blackwood stood there, flanked by guards but somehow looking more like their leader than their prisoner. "You move that sphere, and you'll trigger something far worse."

"Get her out of here," Kenji ordered.

"Wait," Barry said. Something in Blackwood's expression—not greed or cunning, but genuine fear—made him pause. "What do you know?"

She stepped into the room, ignoring the weapons trained on her. "My employer wasn't just interested in treasure, Dr. Curtis. They'd found references to the sphere in Soviet archives. Tests done in the 1960s on similar artifacts found in Siberia."

"Similar artifacts?" Ganbold leaned forward intently.

"Three of them. All smaller than this one, all found near sites connected to the Mongol Empire." Blackwood's usual composure cracked slightly. "The Soviets tried to study them. Two of the research facilities were completely destroyed. Officially blamed on reactor accidents, but the real reports told a different story."

"What happened?" Sakura asked.

"The spheres created a resonance. The more they tried to contain or move them, the stronger it grew. Eventually..." She gestured at the screens showing the expanding disturbance. "But those were small. This one—if it follows the same pattern—"

An alarm cut through her words. On the satellite feed, they watched as a section of mountain simply ceased to exist. Not collapsed or exploded—it flickered and vanished, leaving a perfectly spherical void in the rock.

"Dimensional instability," Ganbold whispered. "The theoretical papers suggested it was possible, but—"

"Theoretical?" Barry grabbed his arm. "What papers? What are you talking about?"

"Research into non-Euclidean geometries in ancient architecture. Some scholars believed certain structures were designed to manipulate space-time on a quantum level. But it was considered fringe science—"

Another section of mountain vanished. The void was growing.

"The tomb wasn't just trapped," Barry said, understanding flooding through him. "It was designed to remove itself from reality if breached. And we triggered it."

"The flooding, the chemical reactions—they were just the beginning," Blackwood confirmed. "The real defense was always this. Complete erasure."

"How do we stop it?" Kenji demanded.

"The Soviets couldn't," Blackwood said simply. "They lost entire installations. Hundreds of people simply... gone."

Barry's mind raced. He thought of the astronomical alignments on the tomb door, the precise calculations required to open it. "The sphere. It's not causing this—it's responding to it. They're connected across distance, quantumly entangled."

"So if we destroy it—" Kenji began.

"You'll accelerate the collapse," Ganbold interrupted. "Breaking the connection could cause a cascade failure. The dimensional void could expand exponentially."

On the screens, they watched the void claim another chunk of mountain. But now something else was happening. Light was bending around the edges of the void, creating visual distortions that hurt to look at directly.

"We need the book," Barry said suddenly. "The Altan Debter. If the Khan's engineers built this system, they must have included shutdown protocols."

"Or warnings to never activate it in the first place," Sakura pointed out.

But Barry was already moving back to the clean room where they'd left the golden book. The others followed, even Blackwood, though the guards kept weapons trained on her.

The book lay open to the page they'd been examining. Under the emergency lighting, the golden pages seemed to glow with their own luminescence. Barry began turning pages frantically, looking for anything that might relate to the defenses.

"Here," Ganbold pointed to a section in Persian. "It's talking about 'the final guard, which consumes even memory.' That could be—"

The building shook. Not from impact, but as if reality itself hiccupped. For a moment, Barry could have sworn he saw through the walls, glimpsed impossible geometries beyond.

"The effect is spreading," a technician reported, voice tight with fear. "We're detecting dimensional anomalies throughout the city. Small ones, but growing."

"There!" Sakura pointed to a diagram near the back of the book. It showed a sphere identical to theirs, surrounded by mathematical equations and what looked like musical notations. "It's a harmonic sequence. The sphere responds to specific frequencies."

"To activate or deactivate?" Barry asked.

"Unknown. The text is in a dialect I don't recognize."

"I do." Blackwood stepped forward. "It's Tangut—the language of the Western Xia. They were one of the first kingdoms the Mongols destroyed completely. May I?"

Kenji nodded reluctantly. Blackwood studied the text, her brow furrowing. "It's not a shutdown sequence. It's... a tuning protocol. The sphere needs to be synchronized with something. But with what?"

Another reality fluctuation. This time, Barry definitely saw through the walls. Beyond them was not the city of Ulaanbaatar but a vast plain under an alien sky. The vision lasted only a second, but it left him gasping.

"The other spheres," he said. "The ones the Soviets found. Where are they now?"

Blackwood's face went pale. "One was destroyed in the testing. One was lost when the facility collapsed. The third..." She hesitated. "My employer has it."

"Where?" Kenji grabbed her shoulder. "Where is it?"

"London. In a private collection. But it's been dormant for decades—"

"Not anymore," Ganbold said, looking at his phone. "I'm getting reports of electromagnetic anomalies in London. Centered on—" He looked up. "The British Museum district."

"Your employer," Barry said. "They knew this would happen. They wanted to activate the network."

"No," Blackwood insisted. "They wanted to study it, to understand the technology. They never intended—"

The lights went out again. This time, the emergency power didn't activate. In the darkness, the only illumination came from the golden pages of the book and, filtering through the walls, the pulsing light of the sphere in its containment room.

"We need to get to that sphere," Barry said. "If we can input the harmonic sequence—"

"Through the electromagnetic interference?" Kenji asked. "Even if we could get close enough, our equipment is failing."

"Then we do it the old way," Sakura said. She held up the book, pointing to the musical notations. "These are meant to be sung. The Mongolian throat singing—it produces multiple harmonic frequencies simultaneously."

"You're suggesting we sing to an alien artifact while reality collapses around us?" Kenji's skepticism was clear.

"Do you have a better idea?"

Another fluctuation. This time, part of the floor simply wasn't there for a moment, revealing a drop into swirling nothingness. Reality reasserted itself, but cracks were spreading through the walls—not physical cracks, but fractures in space itself.

"We need someone who can perform the sequence," Barry said. "Traditional Mongolian throat singing at the precise frequencies—"

"The herders," Ganbold interrupted. "The ones refusing to evacuate. Some of them still know the old ways, the sacred songs."

"Then we go to them," Barry decided. He turned to Kenji. "Can your helicopters fly through the interference?"

"Unknown. But staying here isn't an option." Kenji made his decision. "Everyone to the roof. We evacuate to the mountain, try to reach the herders before—"

The building lurched. Not sideways or up and down, but in a direction that didn't have a name. When it stabilized, they were no longer in the same room. The walls were the same, but through the windows, instead of Ulaanbaatar at night, they could see the Khentii Mountains in daylight.

"Spatial displacement," Ganbold breathed. "We're being pulled toward the epicenter."

"Then we better hurry," Barry said, clutching the book. "Because if the void reaches us before we can stop this—"

He didn't need to finish. They all understood. The Khan's final defense wasn't just destroying his tomb. It was unmaking reality itself around it, erasing not just the physical location but the very possibility of it ever having existed.

As they raced for the roof and the uncertain safety of the helicopters, Barry thought again of Genghis Khan on his golden throne. Had he known what his engineers were creating? Had he understood that his final legacy would be not conquest but annihilation?

The sphere's light pulsed faster, and reality continued its slow collapse around them. They had perhaps an hour before the effect became irreversible.

Time to save the world with a song eight centuries old, written in gold by a dead conqueror's hand.

The mountain was calling them home.

Chapter 28: The Mountain's Judgment

The helicopters struggled against electromagnetic interference that turned their instruments into useless displays of static. They flew by sight alone, navigating through a sky that flickered between day and night, where stars appeared in impossible constellations and clouds moved in directions that defied meteorology.

Below them, the Khentii Mountains were transforming. The expanding void had claimed three peaks entirely, leaving spherical absences in reality that hurt to perceive. Around these voids, the landscape rippled like water, solid rock flowing in patterns that belonged to fever dreams rather than geology.

"There!" Ganbold pointed through the chaos. "The herders' camp. They haven't moved."

Indeed, in a valley that somehow remained stable amid the dimensional storm, a collection of traditional gers stood in a perfect circle. Smoke rose from their center, and Barry could see figures standing in formation, facing the collapsing mountain.

The pilot fought to land, the helicopter bucking against forces that had nothing to do with wind. They hit hard, skidding across grass that shifted between green summer growth and winter brown with each flicker of unstable time.

Barry clutched the Altan Debter as they disembarked. The herders didn't turn at their approach, continuing their low, rhythmic chanting. At their center stood an ancient woman, her face weathered by decades of mountain wind, her eyes milky with cataracts—yet she seemed to see them perfectly.

"You bring the golden words," she said in accented English. "Good. The mountain has been calling for them."

"You knew we were coming?" Sakura asked.

"The Khan told us in dreams. For three nights, the same vision. The thieves would wake the mountain's hunger, but the scholars would bring the song to make it sleep again." She held out her hands for the book. "Show me."

Barry opened to the page with the harmonic notations. The old woman studied them, running gnarled fingers over the golden surface. Then she laughed—a sound like wind through stone.

"Clever, clever Khan. He wrote the song of unmaking, but also the song of mending. Two voices needed—one to sing the world apart, one to sing it together." She looked at her fellow herders. "We know the first voice. Our ancestors have sung it to keep the mountain calm. But the second voice..."

"Must come from outside," Barry realized. "Someone not of the steppes. The Khan's message—even in destruction, cooperation is required."

The old woman nodded. "Can any of you sing?"

"I can," Blackwood said quietly. Everyone turned to stare at her. "Oxford choir. I sight-read music fluently."

"The treasure hunter becomes the savior," the old woman mused. "The Khan appreciates irony."

Another pulse of wrongness swept over them. The ground beneath their feet existed in three different seasons simultaneously. One of the helicopters simply ceased, leaving only a helicopter-shaped hole in the air.

"We're running out of time," Kenji said urgently.

The old woman began organizing quickly, positioning the herders in a specific pattern around Barry and Blackwood. "You must stand at the center. Hold the book between you. When we begin the first voice, you"—she pointed at Blackwood—"must find the harmony and sing the counter-melody written in gold."

"How will I know—" Blackwood began.

"The mountain will teach you. If it finds you worthy."

They took their positions. Barry held one side of the book, Blackwood the other. Around them, the herders began to hum, a low vibration that seemed to come from the earth itself. Then, one by one, they added their voices to the throat singing—multiple tones from each singer, creating harmonics that made the air itself ring.

The effect was immediate. The chaotic flickering of reality began to slow, as if the song was giving time a rhythm to follow. However, the void continued to expand, now visible as a dark sphere consuming the sacred mountain.

"Now," the old woman commanded.

Blackwood looked at the notations and began to sing. Her voice was clear, trained, but at first, it clashed with the herders' tones. The dissonance made the instability worse—cracks of nothingness spider-webbed across the ground.

"Feel it," the old woman urged. "Don't think. The mountain is listening. Show it your true self."

Blackwood closed her eyes. Barry watched her face transform as she let go of her careful control. When she sang again, it was different—raw, honest, carrying all the greed and ambition that had driven her here, but also something else. Regret. Wonder. A genuine awe at touching something greater than profit or power.

The harmonics shifted, aligned. The two vocal streams intertwined like DNA strands, creating something entirely new. The golden pages of the book began to glow, and that light spread outward, pushing back against the encroaching void.

But it wasn't enough. The void had consumed too much, grown too strong.

"We need the sphere," Barry said. "Its resonance—if we could synchronize it—"

"Already coming," Ganbold pointed skyward.

The sphere was approaching, flying under its own power, leaving a trail of bent light. It descended to hover above their circle, pulsing in rhythm with the song.

"Sing to it," the old woman commanded. "Both voices, together. Show the Khan's spirit that his children have learned to speak as one."

The herders intensified their throat singing, the multiple harmonics creating a sound like the mountain itself groaning. Blackwood's voice soared above it, following the golden notations but also improvising, finding spaces between the written notes where East and West could meet.

The sphere's pulsing synchronized with their rhythm. Light began to flow from it—not the harsh electromagnetic pulses from before, but something softer, warmer. The light touched the edges of the void and solidified them, like cauterizing a wound in reality.

Slowly, impossibly, the void began to shrink.

But the effort was taking its toll. One of the elderly herders collapsed, his voice cutting off. The harmonic pattern wavered, and the void surged forward hungrily.

Sakura stepped into his place. She didn't know the traditional songs, but she had heard her sister humming Mongolian melodies during their research. Her voice was untrained but true, adding just enough support to maintain the pattern.

Then Kenji joined, his bass tones reinforcing the foundation. Ganbold added his voice, chanting mathematical equations in a rhythmic tone. Even the surviving members of Kenji's team began to hum, wordlessly supporting the greater song.

The void's advance slowed, stopped. Began to reverse.

Barry couldn't sing—he needed both hands to hold the book steady as its pages turned of their own accord, revealing new notations, new patterns. But he felt part of the song nonetheless; his heartbeat aligned with the rhythm, and his breath matched the pauses.

The sphere descended lower, its light now blinding. Through that radiance, Barry thought he saw a figure—translucent, ancient, wearing the simple clothes of a Mongol warrior. Genghis Khan, or his echo, or perhaps just the mountain's memory of him. The figure watched them with eyes that held eternity, then slowly nodded.

Judgment rendered. Worthy.

The void collapsed in on itself with a sound like the universe sighing. The dimensional instabilities smoothed out, reality reasserting its proper structure. The sphere's light faded to a gentle glow, then went dark entirely, falling inert to the grass.

The song ended, voices trailing off one by one. In the sudden silence, they could hear normal sounds again—wind through grass, distant birds, their own ragged breathing.

"It's done," the old woman said. She looked exhausted but satisfied. "The mountain sleeps again. The Khan's test is finished."

Barry looked toward the Khentii peaks. Where the void had been, the mountain stood whole again—but changed. The entrance to the tomb was gone, not sealed but absent, as if it had never existed. The entire face of the mountain had been remade, smoother, more natural. No trace remained of their passage.

"The weapons, the gold, all of it—" Blackwood began.

"Where it belongs," the old woman interrupted. "With the Khan, in the place between dream and waking. You were judged and found worthy—not to claim his treasures, but to prove they should remain hidden."

"But we still have this," Barry held up the Altan Debter. "The history, the knowledge."

"The parts humanity is ready for," Ganbold said, picking up the inert sphere. "This, I think, should be studied very carefully. Or perhaps not at all."

"Bury it," the old woman advised. "Deep and far from here. Some gifts are too great to accept."

As Kenji called for extraction—their remaining helicopter responding sluggishly but functionally—Barry took a last look at the transformed mountain. They had come seeking treasure and found something far more valuable and terrifying: proof that some knowledge was too dangerous for any one person or nation to possess.

"What will you tell the world?" Sakura asked.

"The truth," Barry said. "That we found evidence of Genghis Khan's tomb, but it was destroyed in a seismic event. That we recovered one book of historical significance, which will be studied with full international cooperation."

"And the rest?" Blackwood asked. "The weapons, the dimensional technology, the other sites the sphere revealed?"

"Never happened," Kenji said firmly. "My government will classify everything. As will yours, I suspect, Ms. Blackwood."

She nodded slowly. "My employer... former employer... will be disappointed. But after what we've seen, perhaps that's for the best."

The old woman approached Barry one last time. "The Khan's spirit asked me to give you a message. He says the greatest conquest is knowing when not to conquer. You understood this. That is why the mountain let you live."

As they boarded the helicopter, Barry clutched the golden book—their only tangible proof of an adventure that had nearly ended the world. Behind them, the herders were already breaking down their camp, preparing to move to winter pastures as if nothing had happened.

The mountain stood silent and whole against the sky, keeping its secrets once more. But Barry knew that somewhere beneath those peaks, Genghis Khan still sat upon his golden throne, surrounded by wonders and terrors that humanity might never be ready to face.

The judgment had been rendered. They had passed—not by claiming victory, but by accepting defeat. Not by taking the treasure, but by ensuring it remained hidden.

As the helicopter rose into a sky that was blessedly, normally blue, Barry thought he heard an echo of the great song they had sung—a harmony between old and new, East and West, greed and wisdom. It was the sound of the world healing itself, of reality choosing to continue.

The mountain had judged them worthy of survival.

It was enough.

Chapter 29: The Guardians' Blessing

The safe house in Ulaanbaatar was modest—a two-story building in an older district where foreigners rarely ventured. Temujin had arranged it through his network, the Guardians of the Blue Sky, and it was here that the survivors gathered to decide what came next.

Barry sat at a low table, the Altan Debter before him wrapped in silk. The golden book seemed heavier now, weighted with the knowledge of what they'd witnessed. Across from him, Temujin poured milk tea with steady hands, as if dimensional voids and reality collapse were everyday occurrences.

"You have seen what few are meant to see," Temujin said, his weathered face grave. "The mountain tested you, and you chose wisdom over greed. This is why you still breathe."

"Your people," Sakura said, cradling her own tea. "The herders who helped us—will they be safe?"

"They are already gone," Temujin replied. "Scattered to the four winds as is our way. In a week, it will be as if they were never there. The old woman you met—she is my grandmother. She has waited seventy years to sing that song."

"She knew this would happen?" Barry asked.

"We have always known someone would eventually breach the tomb. It is the way of things—what is hidden will be sought, what is sealed will be opened." Temujin's eyes moved to the wrapped book. "But the Khan was wise. He made the treasure itself the final judge of who was worthy to possess it."

Kenji entered from the secure communication room, his expression troubled. "I've spoken with my superiors. The official story is being prepared. Seismic activity caused by illegal excavations resulted in the deaths of several international criminals. No mention of the tomb, the artifacts, or... the other events."

"And the sphere?" Ganbold asked. He had barely left the device alone since they'd recovered it, studying its now-inert surface with a mixture of fascination and fear.

"Will be transported to a joint research facility," Kenji said. "Somewhere very remote, with representatives from multiple nations. We'll study it carefully, but any findings will be classified at the highest levels."

"You're assuming it will let you," Blackwood said. She sat apart from the others, technically still a prisoner but treated more like a reluctant ally after her role in saving them all. "The Soviets thought they could study their spheres too."

"Which is why we'll be extremely cautious," Kenji assured her. "Your cooperation in providing your employer's research data would be appreciated."

She nodded slowly. "I'll give you everything. After what we saw... some things should remain buried."

Temujin stood and moved to a wall hanging—a beautiful piece depicting the Mongol Empire at its height. He pushed it aside to reveal a modern safe, which he opened with practiced movements.

"The Guardians have protected the Khan's legacy for eight hundred years," he said, removing several rolled scrolls. "Not just the tomb, but other artifacts, other knowledge. These are copies of texts our brotherhood has preserved—historical accounts, philosophical treatises, scientific observations. Nothing dangerous, but valuable for understanding the true Mongol Empire."

He placed the scrolls before Barry. "You have earned the right to share these with the world. The secret of the tomb's location dies with us, but the history, the culture—this should be known."

Barry unrolled one of the scrolls carefully. It was written in classical Mongolian, but he could make out references to astronomical observations, descriptions of foreign lands, what looked like medical treatments.

"These are incredible," he breathed. "Primary sources from the Khan's own scholars."

"There is more," Temujin said. He produced a small jade seal. "This marks you as a friend of the Guardians. Should you ever return to Mongolia, show this to the right people, and you will find doors open to you. Archives, oral histories, sites no outsider has seen."

"I'm honored," Barry said, accepting the seal. "But why trust me with this?"

"Because you did not try to take what was not offered," Temujin replied simply. "The mountain could have given you everything—weapons, gold, power beyond imagining. Instead, you accepted what it chose to give and helped seal away the rest. This shows wisdom."

A knock at the door interrupted them. One of Temujin's men entered and whispered urgently in his ear. Temujin's expression darkened.

"We have a problem," he announced. "Government forces are conducting searches throughout the city. Not Mongolian—Chinese. They're looking for foreigners matching your descriptions."

"How did they—" Kenji began.

"The electromagnetic event was visible from space," Ganbold said. "Every intelligence agency in the world will be trying to understand what happened here."

"Which means you need to leave. Now." Temujin moved with sudden urgency. "We have a route prepared, but it must be tonight."

They gathered their few possessions quickly. Barry secured the Altan Debter in a specially designed case, while Ganbold reluctantly surrendered the sphere to Kenji's team for separate transport. Blackwood was given a change of clothes and temporary documents—her cooperation had earned her that much trust.

"What about you?" Sakura asked Temujin as they prepared to leave.

"The Guardians will endure as we always have," he said. "In the shadows, in the margins, keeping the secrets that must be kept. But you—you have a different role to play."

He led them through back alleys to a nondescript van. The driver was one of his men, face hidden beneath a hood. As they climbed in, Temujin pulled Barry aside.

"A warning, Dr. Curtis. You carry the Khan's words now. They will change you, as they change all who read them deeply. Do not let the knowledge consume you as it did Yamamoto."

"I'll be careful," Barry promised.

"Be more than careful. Be wise." Temujin pressed something into his hand—a small leather pouch. "Mongolian soil from the sacred mountain. When the burden becomes too great, hold this and remember: some treasures are too heavy for any one person to bear. Share the load."

The van pulled away, leaving Temujin standing in the shadows. Through the rear window, Barry watched him fade into the darkness, another secret keeper in a land full of them.

The ride to the border was tense. Twice, they had to detour around checkpoints, the driver navigating by routes known only to smugglers and nomads. Sakura dozed fitfully against Barry's shoulder, exhausted by their ordeal. Kenji maintained radio contact with his team, coordinating their extraction.

"My government has arranged transit through Russia," he explained quietly. "A military flight from Irkutsk. You'll be in Tokyo by morning, then connections home."

"What about her?" Barry nodded toward Blackwood.

"That depends on her cooperation. And yours, Dr. Curtis. My superiors are concerned about the book. They want assurances it won't be used to locate other sites."

"It won't," Barry said firmly. "I'll publish the historical content—the cultural information, the philosophical texts. But anything that could lead to weapons or dangerous technology gets sealed."

"And if other governments pressure you? If they offer funding, resources, anything to get access?"

Barry thought of the void consuming reality, of the terror in all their eyes as existence itself threatened to unravel. "Then I remind them what happened when we opened one tomb. The Khan's other secrets can stay buried."

They reached the border as dawn broke. The crossing was unofficial—a gap in the fence known to locals, guards who looked the other way for the right price. On the Russian side, unmarked vehicles waited to take them to the airport.

As they transferred vehicles, Sakura's phone buzzed. She answered in rapid Japanese, her expression cycling through surprise, relief, and concern.

"That was my handler," she said after hanging up. "Japanese intelligence wants a full debrief. They're also offering you a position, Barry. Consultant on historical threats. It seems you've impressed them."

"I'm an archaeologist, not a spy," Barry protested.

"After this week, is there a difference?" she asked with a tired smile.

The flight to Tokyo was quiet. Military transport didn't offer much comfort, but it was secure. Barry spent the time studying some of Temujin's scrolls, marveling at the detail—accounts of daily life in the Mongol court, descriptions of engineering projects, philosophical debates between Chinese Confucians and Islamic scholars.

"This alone will revolutionize Mongol studies," he told Ganbold, who was reading over his shoulder. "Primary sources we thought were lost forever."

"The Guardians kept them safe," Ganbold mused. "Makes you wonder what other brotherhoods are out there, protecting what secrets."

"Let's hope we never need to find out," Kenji said darkly.

Tokyo's Haneda Airport was a shock after the wilds of Mongolia. The press of humanity, the neon lights, the constant motion—it all seemed surreal after their experiences. Kenji's people whisked them through diplomatic channels to a secure hotel.

"This is where we part ways," Kenji announced. "Dr. Curtis, Ms. Hirata—you'll have escorts to your homes. Dr. Ganbold, I believe the Mongolian embassy is expecting you. Ms. Blackwood..." He paused. "Your cooperation has been noted. British intelligence will handle your debriefing. I suggest you continue being helpful."

"I intend to," Blackwood said. She turned to Barry. "For what it's worth, I'm sorry about your friend. The first Ms. Hirata. She was just supposed to be leverage, not—"

"Don't," Barry cut her off. "Just... don't."

She nodded and was led away by stone-faced agents.

That evening, Barry and Sakura had one last meal together in the hotel restaurant. The normal sounds of clinking dishes and quiet conversation seemed impossibly mundane.

"What will you do now?" Sakura asked.

"Write," Barry said. "Publish what I can. Try to make sense of it all. You?"

"I have my sister's foundation to run. And..." She hesitated. "My government wants me to continue working with their historical security division. It seems other sites in Japan might have connections to what we found."

"Be careful," Barry warned. "Temujin was right. This knowledge is seductive."

"I know." She reached across the table to touch his hand. "But someone has to stand guard. To make sure the next Yamamoto or Blackwood doesn't succeed where we chose to fail."

Later, as Barry packed the precious scrolls and the even more precious golden book, he thought about the journey that had brought him here. It had started with grief, with a desperate need to complete Blossom's work. But it had become something more—a test not just of courage but of wisdom.

The Khan had built his tomb as a trap for the greedy and ambitious. But he'd also built it as a gift for those wise enough to recognize that some victories were too costly to claim. The book Barry carried was proof of that wisdom—history without the power to repeat its darkest chapters.

As his plane lifted off the next morning, carrying him back to a life that would never be quite normal again, Barry fingered the pouch of sacred earth Temujin had given him. The Guardians had blessed him with their trust, but also with their burden. He was a keeper of secrets now, a guardian in his own right.

The golden book sat secure in its case, holding the words of an empire. But the real treasure, Barry realized, was the knowledge of when to stop seeking, when to let mysteries remain mysterious, when to choose wisdom over glory.

The mountain had judged them and found them worthy.

Now came the harder test: living up to that judgment in a world that would always hunger for secrets better left buried.

Chapter 30: Unfinished Business

The train rumbled through the darkness of the Trans-Siberian Railway, carrying Barry and Sakura away from Mongolia and toward what they hoped would be safety. Kenji had arranged this route as a more discreet alternative to flying. Still, three days into their journey, Barry couldn't shake the feeling that they were being watched.

"You feel it too," Sakura said quietly, joining him in the narrow corridor outside their compartment. She had changed into practical clothes—dark jeans, boots, a jacket that concealed the knife Barry knew she carried.

"Since Irkutsk," he confirmed. "Someone got on there. Maybe more than one."

They had thought the Red Lotus died with Yamamoto in the tomb, but evil organizations rarely disappeared so neatly. The survivors would want revenge—and the golden book Barry carried.

"Should we contact Kenji?" Sakura asked.

"The satellite phones in the compartment. But if they're listening..." Barry trailed off. They both understood. Any call for help would confirm their location and what they carried.

A door opened down the corridor. A Japanese businessman emerged, adjusting his tie. Nothing suspicious, except Barry had seen him in three different cars over the past day, always in different clothes.

"Dining car," Sakura suggested loudly. "I'm hungry."

They moved through the swaying train, Barry carrying the innocu-ous-looking briefcase that held the Altan Debter. He'd memorized several of the historical accounts from Temujin's scrolls during the journey, in-cluding one that might prove useful—a tactical manual written by Subu-tai, the Khan's greatest general.

The dining car was half full, mostly Russian businessmen and a few tourists. They took a table by the window, ordering tea and watching the Siberian forest flash by in the darkness.

"Two cars back," Sakura said without looking. "The businessman. And the woman who got on at Krasnoyarsk."

Barry had noticed her too—athletic build, always reading but never turning pages. "Red Lotus?"

"Or freelancers hired by survivors. Does it matter?"

"Subutai wrote about fighting on restricted terrain," Barry said, keeping his voice conversational. "Ships, narrow passes. He said the key was to control the transition points."

"The spaces between train cars," Sakura translated. "Force them to come at us one at a time."

"Exactly. But first, we need to know how many—"

The lights went out.

The train's emergency lighting kicked in a second later, bathing every-thing in red. In that moment of darkness, Barry heard movement—quick, purposeful, closing in.

"Kitchen," Sakura hissed, already moving.

They burst through the service door as the first shots shattered the din-ing car windows. The kitchen staff scattered, shouting in Russian. Barry grabbed a pot of boiling water from the stove, throwing it behind them as two figures appeared in the doorway.

The scalding water bought them seconds. They raced through the kitchen into the next car—sleeping compartments, doors locked, passengers presumably cowering inside.

"They'll try to pin us between teams," Barry said, breathing hard. "Some ahead, some behind."

"Then we don't run in a straight line." Sakura tried a compartment door. Locked. She produced thin metal tools from her pocket, working the lock with practiced efficiency.

More shots, muffled by the train's clatter. Their pursuers were being cautious now, not wanting to alert the whole train.

The lock clicked open. Inside, a terrified Russian family huddled on the bunks. Sakura spoke rapid Russian, gesturing to the window. The father's eyes widened, but he nodded, starting to work on the window latch.

"You're not thinking—" Barry began.

"Roof," Sakura confirmed. "Unless you have a better idea?"

The window came free, letting in a blast of icy air. The train was doing maybe sixty kilometers per hour—survivable, if they were careful. Sakura went first, flowing up onto the roof with acrobatic grace. Barry passed the briefcase up, then followed more awkwardly, with the Russian father actually boosting him up.

The roof of a moving train in Siberia at night was a special kind of hell. Wind tore at them, threatening to pluck them off like leaves. Ice made every step treacherous. But it also made them nearly impossible targets.

They crawled forward, Barry clutching the briefcase like his life depended on it—which it probably did. Behind them, shouts indicated their pursuers had discovered their escape route.

"There!" Sakura pointed ahead.

A service ladder led down between cars. They could re-enter the train several cars ahead of their pursuers. But as they approached, a figure climbed up to block their path.

The woman from Krasnoyarsk was steady on the roof despite the wind. In the moonlight, Barry saw the tattoo on her neck—a red lotus blossom.

"Keiko Tanaka," she said, voice carrying despite the wind. "Yamamoto-san was my uncle. You killed him."

"He killed himself," Sakura replied, shifting into a combat stance despite the treacherous footing. "Chose death over wisdom."

"He chose honor over surrender." Tanaka drew a blade—not a modern tactical knife but a traditional tanto. "As do I."

The two women circled each other on the narrow roof, death waiting on either side. Barry pressed himself flat, trying to stay out of the way while protecting the briefcase.

Tanaka struck first, her blade flashing in the moonlight. Sakura deflected with her own knife, steel ringing against steel. They fought with a fluid grace that seemed to defy the wind and motion, each perfectly balanced despite the impossible conditions.

A shot cracked past Barry's head. The businessman and another pursuer had made it onto the roof behind them. Barry remembered another passage from Subutai's manual—when outnumbered, use the terrain.

He waited until the train approached a curve, then kicked out at an ice-covered section of roof. The sheet of ice broke free, sliding backward like a frozen projectile. The businessman tried to dodge, lost his footing, and vanished over the side with a scream.

His partner opened fire, forcing Barry to roll dangerously close to the edge. The briefcase skittered across the icy metal, stopping just short of falling.

Meanwhile, Sakura and Tanaka's duel had intensified. Both women bled from minor cuts, their breath misting in the frigid air. Tanaka had skill, but Sakura had something more—a reason to survive beyond revenge.

"Your uncle understood in the end," Sakura said, deflecting another strike. "The tomb's secrets were too dangerous. That's why he chose to seal them."

"Lies!" Tanaka pressed her attack, but grief made her reckless.

Sakura saw the opening. Instead of striking with her blade, she grabbed Tanaka's wrist, using the woman's momentum against her. For a moment, Tanaka teetered on the edge of the roof.

"It doesn't have to end like this," Sakura said. "The Red Lotus can choose a different path."

Tanaka's eyes showed a moment of doubt. Then the remaining gunman fired, the bullet catching her in the shoulder. The impact spun her off the roof into the darkness.

"No!" Sakura lunged forward, but it was too late.

The gunman advanced, weapon trained on them. But he'd forgotten the first rule of fighting on a train—watch for tunnels.

The concrete wall of a tunnel mouth took him at chest height, the impact brutal and final. Barry and Sakura pressed themselves flat as the tunnel roof rushed by inches overhead, emerging into open air gasping and shaking.

They were alone on the roof now, but the train was slowing—approaching a station. They needed to get back inside before anyone saw them.

"The briefcase," Barry said, crawling toward it.

"Leave it," Sakura grabbed his arm. "It's not worth—"

"History has to survive." He stretched out, fingers just reaching the handle as the train lurched around another curve.

They made it down the service ladder as the train pulled into a small station. Back inside, they looked like disaster victims—clothes torn, faces cut by wind and ice, hands blue with cold. But they were alive, and the golden book was safe.

A conductor found them, exclaiming in Russian. Sakura spun a story about opening a window that got stuck, forcing them outside to close it. The man clearly didn't believe it but seemed unwilling to pursue the matter. The less he knew, the safer he was.

In their compartment, they found a message slipped under the door. A single line in Japanese: "The red lotus blooms in blood, but also in wisdom."

"Tanaka," Sakura said. "She survived."

"Will she come after us again?"

"I don't think so. She had her chance at revenge and chose to let us go." Sakura touched the shallow cut on her cheek. "Maybe some of the Red Lotus can change after all."

They spent the rest of the journey in watchful silence, taking turns sleeping. No more assassins appeared, but Barry couldn't shake the feeling they were still being observed. Not hunted, exactly, but evaluated.

At the Chinese border, their transit was surprisingly smooth. Too smooth. Someone had cleared the way, ensuring that no inspections or questions would be asked about the diplomatic case Barry carried.

"Guardian angels?" Sakura wondered as their new train pulled away from the border.

"Or someone who wants us to reach our destination," Barry replied. "The question is why."

The answer came in Beijing. As they waited for their flight in a diplomatic lounge, an elderly Chinese man approached. His suit was expensive but understated, his manner that of a scholar rather than a spy.

"Dr. Curtis, Ms. Hirata. I represent certain interests within the Chinese government. We are aware of your recent... adventures."

Barry tensed, but the man raised a peaceful hand.

"We do not seek the book or the tomb's location. In fact, we applaud your decision to let such secrets remain buried. The Middle Kingdom has its own hidden dangers, things better left undisturbed."

"Then what do you want?" Sakura asked.

"To offer our assistance in your future research. And to make a request." He produced a photograph—an ancient stone tablet covered in multiple scripts. "This was found in Xinjiang Province. The Mongolian text mentions 'the Khan's warning to the southern kingdoms.' We hoped you might provide insight."

Barry studied the image. He recognized some phrases from the Altan Debter, references to weapons that should never be used, places that should never be opened.

"The Khan wasn't just hiding his own secrets," Barry realized. "He was containing others. Things he found during his conquests that were too dangerous even for him."

"Precisely. The Mongol Empire was built on pragmatism. They preserved useful knowledge and destroyed or contained that which threatened the world itself." The old man smiled sadly. "Perhaps that is the Khan's greatest legacy—knowing when to stop."

He left them with a business card—just a name and an email address. "Should you encounter other such warnings in your research, we would be grateful to know. Some doors, once opened, cannot be closed again."

Their flight was called. As they gathered their belongings, Sakura asked, "How many others know? How many groups are out there, keeping these secrets?"

"More than we imagined," Barry said. "The Guardians in Mongolia, this Chinese group, whatever's left of the Red Lotus, Kenji's organization..."

"A shadow world of secret keepers," Sakura mused. "And now we're part of it."

They boarded the plane carrying the weight of that knowledge along with the golden book. The Red Lotus might be broken, but the real challenge was just beginning. They had proven themselves worthy of the Khan's secrets by choosing not to claim them all.

Now they had to prove worthy of the ones they had taken.

As the plane lifted off, Barry thought of Tanaka, somewhere below, choosing wisdom over revenge. The Chinese scholar, offering cooperation instead of confrontation. Of all the groups that might be watching, waiting, judging.

The unfinished business wasn't just with their enemies. It was with history itself, with knowledge too dangerous to fully reveal but too important to lose.

The game of Genghis Khan, which had started eight centuries ago, was still being played. And Barry and Sakura had just become major pieces on the board.

Chapter 31: The Reckoning

The conference room, located on the forty-second floor of the United Nations building in Geneva, offered a panoramic view of Lake Geneva and the Alps beyond. It was neutral territory in the truest sense—a place where governments could meet without any one nation claiming dominance. Barry stood at the window, watching boats leave white wakes across the blue water, trying to find calm before the storm was about to break.

"They're ready for you," Sakura said from the doorway. She wore a conservative business suit, her arm fully healed but still occasionally stiff. The past two weeks of preparation had been exhausting—encompassing legal briefings, security protocols, and media training.

Barry adjusted his tie, feeling out of place in the formal wear. The briefcase containing the Altan Debter sat on the conference table, sealed with diplomatic locks from five different nations. "How many?"

"Seventeen countries sent representatives. UNESCO, the World Bank, three major universities, and..." She paused. "About forty journalists in the media room are watching via closed circuit."

"Forty?" Barry's stomach tightened. They'd known word would leak eventually, but the speed had been breathtaking. Within days of their reaching safety, rumors had exploded across the internet. Satellite images of the dimensional event. Seismic data from the mountain's transformation. Fragments of radio chatter about ancient tombs and the collapse of reality.

"It's better this way," Sakura assured him. "Controlled disclosure. We tell our version before the conspiracy theorists run completely wild."

Kenji appeared beside her, looking tired but satisfied. "The security arrangements are complete. No recording devices allowed in the main presentation. The journalists will receive approved footage and transcripts only."

"And Blackwood?" Barry asked.

"Cooperating fully with British intelligence. She's provided all her employer's research data. In exchange, she's been granted immunity for her role in helping prevent... the incident."

The incident. That's what they were calling the near-collapse of reality. Barry wondered what euphemism would eventually make it into the history books.

Dr. Ganbold entered, carrying a stack of papers. "I've finished the preliminary analysis of the safe historical sections. Nothing about weapons, dimensional technology, or site locations. Just pure history—governance, philosophy, cultural exchange."

"The Mongolian government?" Barry asked.

"Has agreed to the terms. Fifty percent of any publication revenues go to a cultural heritage fund. The original book remains in Mongolia after study, housed in a new secure facility with international oversight."

It had taken delicate negotiations to reach this point. Every nation with a historical connection to the Mongol Empire sought access, priority, and control. The compromise satisfied no one completely, which probably meant it was fair.

"Time," Kenji said simply.

They filed into the main conference room, where diplomats and academics waited with barely concealed anticipation. Barry recognized some faces from news footage—the Chinese cultural minister, the head of the Russian Archaeological Institute, the director of the British Museum. Power and knowledge gathered in one room, all wanting what he carried.

The Secretary-General's representative, a stern Swiss woman named Müller, called for order. "Dr. Curtis, the floor is yours."

Barry opened the briefcase with the required keys, revealing the Altan Debter in its climate-controlled case. Even through the protective glass, the golden pages seemed to glow. A collective intake of breath swept the room.

"Ladies and gentlemen," Barry began, his lecturer's instincts taking over. "What you see before you is the complete Secret History of the Mongols, written on gold foil, preserved for eight centuries. It contains firsthand accounts of the empire's expansion, philosophical texts from multiple traditions, and scientific knowledge from across the known world."

He clicked a remote, bringing up prepared slides on the screen. "What it does not contain—and I want to be absolutely clear about this—is the location of Genghis Khan's tomb. That site was destroyed in a seismic event that claimed multiple lives, including several international criminals who were attempting to loot it."

"Destroyed?" The Russian representative leaned forward. "Our satellites detected anomalous energy readings suggesting something far more complex than mere seismic activity."

Barry had rehearsed this answer. "The tomb incorporated advanced architectural techniques that created unusual resonance patterns when disturbed. The resulting structural collapse was... comprehensive."

Not a lie, technically. The tomb had incorporated advanced techniques. They had created resonance. The collapse had been comprehensive. He just left out the parts about dimensional voids and reality nearly unraveling.

"And the other artifacts mentioned in leaked reports?" the Chinese minister asked with studied casualness. "A sphere of unknown origin? Weapons beyond their time?"

"Exaggerations and misunderstandings," Kenji interjected smoothly. "The criminals involved made wild claims to attract buyers for their illegal enterprise. A few unusual historical items were recovered but proved to be of purely archaeological interest."

Müller restored order. "Dr. Curtis, please continue with what the book does contain."

Barry clicked through more slides, showing translated excerpts. "The historical content is remarkable. We have accounts of the kurultai—the Mongol assemblies where policies were debated democratically. Descriptions of the yam, the postal system that connected the empire. Medical texts combining Chinese, Islamic, and European knowledge."

He showed a page of astronomical calculations. "The Mongols didn't just conquer—they synthesized. This section contains observations from Chinese astronomers verified against Greek mathematics and Islamic star charts. They were creating a unified understanding of the cosmos."

"And the philosophical texts?" asked a professor from Oxford.

"Extraordinary. Debates between Buddhist monks and Daoist sages, mediated by Islamic scholars, recorded by Christian scribes. The Mongol court was perhaps the most intellectually diverse gathering in human history."

For an hour, he presented carefully selected excerpts. The room's mood shifted from suspicion to genuine academic excitement. These were scholars and diplomats who understood the value of historical knowledge, even stripped of its more dangerous elements.

"Questions?" Müller asked when Barry finished.

They came in a flood. How would access be determined? What about translation rights? Would the original be available for spectroscopic analysis? Barry and his team fielded them all, sticking to their prepared positions.

Then the British Museum director asked the question they'd dreaded: "Dr. Curtis, given the remarkable preservation of this artifact, might there be other sites of similar historical value? The Mongol Empire was vast, after all."

Barry met his gaze steadily. "The Altan Debter contains historical accounts, not treasure maps. Any references to other locations are vague at best, often metaphorical. The Mongols were poets as much as warriors."

"But surely—"

"The book will be fully available for study," Barry interrupted. "Scholars can draw their own conclusions. But I would remind everyone that the illegal excavation of the tomb site resulted in deaths and significant geological damage. Some secrets are better approached through careful scholarship than shovels and dynamite."

The warning was clear. The room subsided into murmurs.

After the main presentation, smaller meetings filled the remainder of the afternoon. The Mongolian delegation was satisfied with the arrangements for the heritage fund. The Chinese quietly withdrew their requests for priority access in exchange for assurances that certain passages would be handled "sensitively." The Russians sought assurances regarding certain historical claims to their territories.

"Politics," Ganbold muttered during a break. "Eight centuries later, and they're still fighting the Khan's wars."

"At least they're fighting with words, not swords," Sakura observed.

The media briefing was simpler. Barry gave a prepared statement about the discovery, showed approved images of some golden pages, and took no questions. The journalists were frustrated, but the security was absolute.

That evening, as Geneva settled into twilight, the core team gathered in Barry's hotel suite. The official work was done, but the actual decisions remained.

"The Japanese government is satisfied," Kenji reported. "The incident is classified, the sphere is secured for study, and you've both been granted honorary positions with our cultural security division."

"The Guardians send their approval," Ganbold added. "Temujin particularly appreciated your emphasis on careful scholarship over treasure hunting. Several universities are already planning legitimate archaeological surveys in Mongolia, with full government cooperation."

"And the Red Lotus?" Barry asked.

"Scattered. Some seeking revenge, others..." Kenji paused. "We've had quiet contacts. Tanaka survived, as you suspected. She's gathering the younger members, the ones who joined for the philosophy rather than the power. They may become something new. Something better."

"From a criminal organization to a historical society?" Sakura sounded skeptical.

"Stranger transformations have happened. The Mongols themselves went from conquerors to preservers of culture. Perhaps their modern followers can do the same."

A knock at the door interrupted them. Barry opened it to find Müller standing in the hallway.

"Dr. Curtis, I apologize for the intrusion. Might I have a private word?"

She entered, declining the offered tea, and got straight to the point. "The UN Secretary-General has been fully briefed on the... complete events in Mongolia. The classified version."

Barry tensed. "And?"

"He's creating a new sub-committee. Quietly, of course. To monitor and respond to what we're calling 'anomalous historical sites.' Places where the past might pose very real dangers to the present." She studied him carefully. "He'd like you to consider serving as a consultant."

"I'm an archaeologist, not—"

"Not what? Someone who prevented a dimensional collapse? Who chose wisdom over greed when faced with weapons that could destabilize the world?" Müller smiled slightly. "Dr. Curtis, you're exactly what we need. Someone who understands that not all knowledge should be unleashed."

"What about Sakura?" Barry asked. "We're a team."

"The offer extends to Ms. Hirata as well. Her skills would be invaluable."

Barry looked at Sakura, who gave a subtle nod. "We'll consider it," he said.

"That's all we ask." Müller stood to leave, then paused. "Oh, one more thing. The sphere you recovered? Initial studies suggest it's not unique. There may be dozens scattered across the old empire. Dormant for now, but if they're connected as we suspect..."

"You want us to find them," Sakura said. "Before someone else does."

"Find them, study them, and most importantly—keep them from being activated." Müller's expression was grave. "The world survived one near-catastrophe. We might not be so fortunate next time."

After she left, the team sat in silence. The weight of what they'd stumbled into—what they were being asked to continue—settled over them like a heavy blanket.

"It never ends, does it?" Barry said, finally. "We seal one tomb, and a dozen more wait to be discovered."

"The Khan's final strategy," Ganbold mused. "He scattered his weapons too widely to ever be fully contained. The best we can do is stay ahead of those who would misuse them."

"Then that's what we do," Sakura said firmly. "We know the dangers now. We've seen what happens when greed meets power. If we don't stand guard, who will?"

Barry thought of Blossom, whose death had started this journey. Of Yamamoto, choosing burial over retreat. Of Tanaka, possibly finding redemption. Of the herders who sang reality back together. Of all the unnamed people who might suffer if the wrong person found the wrong artifact.

"Alright," he said. "We continue. But on our terms. Full transparency with the committee, protection for local populations, and always—always—the choice to seal rather than reveal."

"The Guardians' way," Ganbold approved. "Temujin will be pleased."

They raised glasses of wine—a toast to survival, to wisdom, and to the strange path ahead. Outside, the lights of Geneva sparkled like earthbound stars, a modern city built on centuries of negotiation and compromise.

The reckoning was over. The Altan Debter would share its safer secrets with the world. The Mongolian people would benefit from their heritage. The dangerous knowledge would remain classified, protected by a new generation of guardians.

But Barry knew this was not an ending. It was a transformation. From treasure hunters to secret keepers. From academics to defenders against the darkness that lurked in humanity's past.

The golden book sat in its case, pages full of wisdom and warning in equal measure. Tomorrow, it would begin its journey to Mongolia, to a secure facility where scholars could study it safely.

Tonight, though, it served as a reminder. The past was never truly past. It waited, patient and powerful, for those brave or foolish enough to seek it.

Barry and Sakura had sought it, survived it, and chosen to protect the world from it.

The reckoning was complete. The real work was just beginning.

Chapter 32: New Beginnings

The fall sun streamed through the tall windows of Barry Curtis's new office at Georgetown University, casting golden rectangles across the mahogany desk where ancient scrolls lay carefully preserved under climate-controlled glass. Six months had passed since he and Sakura had emerged from the Mongolian mountains with fragments of the legendary Altan Debter, and the academic world was still reeling from the implications of their discovery.

"The carbon dating results came back this morning," Sakura announced as she entered the office, carrying two cups of coffee and a manila folder thick with laboratory reports. She had traded her field clothes for a tailored blazer and dark slacks. However, Barry could still see the alertness in her eyes that marked her as someone who had faced death and learned to value life accordingly.

"Good news or challenging news?" Barry asked, accepting the coffee with the grateful smile of a man who had grown accustomed to having a partner he could trust completely.

"Both." Sakura settled into the chair across from his desk, a piece of furniture that had become as much hers as his over the past months. "The scrolls are definitely 13th century, contemporary with Genghis Khan's reign. But the metallurgy described in them is at least two centuries ahead of what we thought was possible for the period."

Barry studied the laboratory reports, his excitement growing with each technical analysis. The Hirata Foundation for Historical Research—the organization they had established using the substantial reward the Mongolian government had provided for their cultural preservation efforts—had spared no expense in authenticating their discoveries.

"Advanced metallurgy, sophisticated astronomical calculations, engineering principles that wouldn't be rediscovered in Europe for generations," he mused. "The Khan's scholars really were documenting knowledge from every civilization they conquered."

"And synthesizing it into something new." Sakura pulled out a translation she had been working on, covered with her precise handwriting. "This section describes a navigation system that combines Chinese magnetic compass technology with Persian astronomical charts and what appears to be original Mongol innovations in cartography."

The foundation had become their life's work—a research institute dedicated to studying the historical documents they had recovered and protecting similar cultural treasures around the world. Barry's academic reputation, damaged by his involvement with treasure hunters and international incidents, had been completely restored by the scholarly significance of their findings. More importantly, he had found a purpose that combined his love of history with a commitment to preserving cultural heritage for future generations.

"Speaking of navigation systems," Sakura said, consulting her tablet, "we have the UNESCO conference call at three, and the National Geographic interview at five. The documentary team wants to review our recreation of the Khan's court ceremony."

Barry glanced at the appointment calendar that had become significantly more complex since their return from Mongolia. The foundation regularly consulted with museums, universities, and government cultural agencies around the world. Their expertise in historical preservation and ancient security systems had made them surprisingly valuable to institutions trying to protect irreplaceable artifacts.

"Any word from Temujin?" he asked.

"He's doing well. The Guardians of the Blue Sky have officially recognized our foundation as honorary protectors of Mongolian cultural heritage." Sakura smiled, an expression that had become more frequent as the months passed. "He says the spirits of the sacred mountains are pleased that the Khan's wisdom is being used to preserve rather than plunder."

The phone rang, interrupting their review of the day's schedule. Barry's assistant—a graduate student named Michael who had proven remarkably adept at managing both scholarly research and the occasional security concern—announced that Dr. Elizabeth Chen from the Smithsonian was calling about a potential collaboration.

"Dr. Curtis," came the familiar voice of one of the world's leading experts in Central Asian archaeology. "I hope you and Miss Hirata are well. I'm calling because we've encountered something that I think might interest you."

"What kind of something?" Barry activated the speakerphone so Sakura could participate in the conversation.

"We've been studying artifacts recovered from a recently discovered 13th-century site in Kazakhstan. The preliminary analysis suggests connections to the same historical network you documented in your Mongolian findings. But there are also references to much older civilizations—possibly Scythian or even earlier."

Barry and Sakura exchanged glances. Their success with the Khan's scrolls had led to numerous requests for consultation on similar historical mysteries, but most proved to be either authentic but mundane, or sensational but fraudulent.

"What makes you think there's a connection?" Sakura asked.

"Astronomical calculations that match the precision level you found in the Altan Debter fragments. And symbol sets that appear to reference the same geographical network of sacred sites." Dr. Chen paused. "There's also evidence that someone else has been investigating these connections. Someone with resources and expertise comparable to your own."

The implication was clear—they weren't the only ones following the threads of ancient knowledge that connected historical civilizations across vast distances and centuries. Other treasure hunters, possibly including surviving elements of organizations like the Red Lotus, were pursuing similar discoveries.

"We'd be happy to consult on your findings," Barry said. "Can you send us the preliminary reports?"

"Already on the way to your secure server. But Dr. Curtis, Miss Hirata—be careful. Some of the people asking questions about this site have backgrounds that concern our security advisors."

After Dr. Chen disconnected, Barry and Sakura sat quietly for a moment, both thinking about the implications. Their foundation had provided them with a respectable, scholarly way to continue pursuing historical mysteries, but they both knew that the kind of discoveries they specialized in would always attract dangerous attention.

"We should visit her today," Sakura said suddenly.

Barry didn't need to ask who she meant. Every few weeks, they made the drive to Arlington National Cemetery to visit Blossom's grave. It had become a ritual that honored her memory while allowing them to discuss the dangers and responsibilities that came with their work.

The cemetery was quiet in the late afternoon light, with only a few other visitors moving among the white headstones that stretched across the rolling hills. Blossom Hirata's grave was marked with a simple stone that identified her as a cultural preservation specialist who had died in the service of international understanding. This description was both accurate and carefully vague about the circumstances of her death.

"I brought copies of the latest translations," Sakura said, placing a folder beside the small bouquet of flowers they had brought. "I thought she'd want to see how her work led to everything we've accomplished."

Barry knelt beside the headstone, feeling the familiar mixture of gratitude and regret that accompanied these visits. "She would be proud of what you've become. The foundation, the research, the way you've used her sacrifice to build something meaningful."

"We've built something meaningful," Sakura corrected. "This only works because we can trust each other completely. That's what she gave us—not just the map, but the understanding that some things are worth risking everything to protect."

They stayed for nearly an hour, talking quietly about their current research, their plans for the foundation's expansion, and their ongoing efforts to ensure that cultural treasures remained in the hands of the people who created them rather than private collectors or criminal organizations.

As they walked back toward their car, Sakura's phone buzzed with a message notification. She glanced at the screen, then stopped abruptly.

"What is it?" Barry asked.

"Message from an unknown sender. Encrypted, but using our foundation's public key." She opened the message, her expression growing more serious as she read. "Barry, look at this."

The message was brief but intriguing:

"Dr. Curtis and Miss Hirata - Your work with Mongol historical documents has come to our attention. We represent parties interested in similar research regarding Roman archaeological sites. Specifically, locations where Eastern and Western ancient knowledge may have intersected. If you are interested in a consultation that could prove mutually beneficial, please respond to this message. Time may be a factor."

Attached to the message was a single image—a photograph of what appeared to be an ancient Roman seal, intricately carved with symbols that combined Latin inscriptions with mathematical notations that looked suspiciously familiar.

"Those astronomical calculations," Sakura said, studying the image on her phone's screen. "They're using the same computational methods we found in the Khan's scrolls."

Barry felt the familiar tingle of historical excitement mixed with apprehension. "Which means someone in the Roman Empire had access to the same network of ancient knowledge that the Mongols later incorporated into their own records."

"Or," Sakura added thoughtfully, "someone today has access to both Roman and Mongol sources and is putting together connections that span continents and centuries."

They reached their car, but neither made any move to get inside. The message represented exactly the kind of opportunity that had led them to their greatest discoveries—and their greatest dangers.

"We don't have to respond," Barry said, though his tone suggested he was already calculating the possibilities. "The foundation is successful, we're making genuine contributions to historical scholarship, and we're not actively being hunted by international criminal organizations. We could have a normal, safe, academically respectable life."

Sakura smiled, the expression carrying both affection and mischief. "Dr. Curtis, in the six months we've been working together, when have either of us ever chosen the safe option when there was a mystery to be solved?"

Barry laughed, realizing that she was absolutely right. They had both discovered that their greatest fulfillment came not from security, but from pursuing knowledge that could change humanity's understanding of its own history. The foundation had given them the resources and legitimacy to continue that pursuit. Still, it had never diminished their appetite for the next great discovery.

"Besides," Sakura continued, "Blossom spent her life following threads that connected different civilizations and historical periods. Suppose there really is a network of ancient knowledge that links Roman, Mongol, and possibly other cultures. Don't we owe it to her memory to investigate?"

Barry looked back toward the cemetery where Blossom's headstone stood among thousands of others who had died in service to ideals larger than themselves. The foundation they had built was successful and respectable, but it had always been intended as a platform for exactly this kind of investigation.

"All right," he said finally. "But we do this carefully. Full background checks on whoever sent this message, complete security protocols, and no commitments until we understand exactly what we're dealing with."

"Agreed. But Barry?" Sakura's expression grew more serious. "I have a feeling this is going to be bigger than anything we've encountered before. If someone has been collecting ancient knowledge from multiple civilizations, they're not doing it for academic purposes."

As they drove back toward Georgetown, the sun setting behind them and the mysterious message still glowing on Sakura's phone, Barry felt the familiar mixture of anticipation and concern that marked the beginning of a new adventure. The foundation had given them stability and purpose, but it had also prepared them for exactly this moment—when the next great mystery presented itself and challenged them to risk everything in pursuit of truth.

The Kane's tomb had taught them that some secrets were worth any price to preserve or uncover. Now, it seemed, history was offering them another chance to test that conviction against the forces that would use ancient knowledge for modern power.

"What do you think?" Sakura asked as they pulled into the university parking garage. "Roman archaeological sites, Eastern and Western knowledge intersections, time-sensitive consultations. Does it sound familiar?"

Barry smiled, feeling more alive than he had in months. "It sounds like the beginning of our next case."

The foundation's work would continue, their academic careers would flourish, and their commitment to cultural preservation would remain unwavering. But beneath the respectable surface of scholarly research, they both knew they were preparing for another journey into the dangerous territory where history, greed, and human nature intersected in ways that could change the world.

As they walked toward the building that housed their offices, Sakura's phone buzzed again with another encrypted message. This time, the sender had included coordinates and a single line of text that made them both stop in their tracks:

"What the Khan knew, Caesar discovered first."

Epilogue: The Next Mystery

T hree months later

The package arrived on an ordinary Tuesday morning, delivered by a courier who didn't wait for a signature. Barry found it propped against his apartment door when he returned from his morning run along the Potomac, its weight and shape immediately commanding attention.

In his kitchen, coffee cooling forgotten, he examined the parcel. The brown paper wrapping was modern, but what lay beneath was anything but. A wooden box, old enough that the grain had darkened to near-black, sealed with burgundy wax that bore an impression he recognized from his classical studies, the eagle of the Roman Senate.

His hands trembled slightly as he reached for his phone. "Sakura? You need to see this."

She arrived within twenty minutes, still wearing the tactical gear from her morning training session with Kenji's team. Her eyes widened when she saw the seal.

"That's authentic," she said, leaning close to examine it. "The wax formula, the pressure depth—this was made with an actual Roman seal matrix."

"Which should be impossible," Barry said. "Those were destroyed when Rome fell. The Senate made sure of it."

"The Senate," Sakura repeated thoughtfully. "Not the emperors. Interesting distinction."

Barry carefully broke the seal with a heated knife, preserving as much as possible for later analysis. The box opened on silent hinges to reveal two items: a scroll wrapped in oiled cloth and a folded piece of modern paper.

The note was brief, written in English with a fountain pen:

Dr. Curtis—

Your work in Mongolia has not gone unnoticed by those of us who guard older secrets. The Khan was not the first to face the terrible choice between power and wisdom. He learned from those who came before, just as you must now learn from him.

What the Khan knew, Caesar discovered first.

And what Caesar discovered, Alexander glimpsed.

And what Alexander glimpsed, the Pharaohs buried.

The chain of guardianship stretches back to humanity's dawn, each civilization adding their own locks to doors that must never be opened. You have proven worthy to know this truth. The question is whether you are ready to accept its burden.

The scroll contains a fragment of the Acta Senatus Arcana—the Secret Acts of the Senate. Translate it carefully. Share it with no one beyond your circle of trust. And prepare yourself for what must come next.

The dragons you guard in the East have siblings in the West. They stir in their sleep.

—A Friend in Rome

Barry and Sakura exchanged glances. In the months since Mongolia, they'd received various overtures from groups claiming ancient knowledge. Most were cranks or treasure hunters. This felt different. The authentication details, the specific references to their classified work—someone with real knowledge had sent this.

"Should we call Kenji?" Sakura asked.

"Not yet. Let's see what we're dealing with first."

Barry carefully unrolled the scroll. The papyrus was perfectly preserved, though he suspected through modern conservation techniques rather than ancient ones. The Latin text was in an archaic form, but readable:

In the year of the consulship of Marcus Licinius Crassus and Gnaeus Pompeius Magnus, the Senate convenes in secret session to address the matter of the Thracian Devices.

Let it be recorded that the general Julius Caesar, fresh from his victories in Gaul, has reported the discovery of certain mechanisms in the ruins beneath Alesia. These devices, of design similar to those found in the Alexandrian vaults and reported by our agents in the Parthian lands, pose a threat to the natural order.

The Senate commands that these devices be transported in secret to the vaults beneath the Temple of Vesta, there to join the other abominations collected in our centuries of conquest. Let no citizen speak of them. Let no record be made in the public acta. Let the Vestals guard them with their sacred flames, as they have guarded the Palladium and the other remnants of the world before.

Furthermore, the Senate acknowledges receipt of communication from the Eastern Kingdoms regarding similar discoveries. We concur with their proposal: each civilization shall guard its own terrors, sharing only the knowledge needed to maintain the seals.

By unanimous vote, the Senate declares: Some victories are too terrible to claim. Some knowledge is too dangerous to wield. We are not the first to learn this lesson. We pray to all gods that we shall not be the last.

Barry set down the scroll, his mind racing. "The Thracian Devices. The Alexandrian vaults. The 'world before.'"

"And communication with Eastern Kingdoms," Sakura added. "China? The early Mongol tribes? Who else knew?"

"Everyone, apparently. Or at least every civilization that reached a certain level of power." Barry stood and began pacing, his lecturer's instincts kicking in. "Think about it. Rome conquered most of the known world. They would have found things, just as the Khan did. Ancient weapons, lost technologies, artifacts from civilizations we don't even remember."

"And they chose to hide them rather than use them," Sakura continued. "Just like the Khan. Just like us."

"The Vestals," Barry muttered, pulling books from his shelf. "Guardians of the sacred flame, sworn to virginity and service. Historians always wondered why they were so important, why violating their temple meant death. What if they weren't just keeping a flame burning?"

"They were guarding a vault," Sakura finished. "Like the Mongolian Guardians, like Kenji's organization. Another link in the chain."

Barry found what he was looking for—a map of ancient Rome. "The Temple of Vesta was destroyed and rebuilt multiple times. But the underground chambers..." He traced the location. "They were never fully excavated. The Italian government declared them too unstable in the 1920s and sealed them."

"Convenient," Sakura observed. "Want to bet someone in the Italian government knows exactly why they're sealed?"

They spent the next hour researching, cross-referencing the scroll's contents with historical records. Every search led to more questions. The Thracian Devices—what were they? The Alexandrian vaults—the famous library had burned, but what lay beneath? The "world before"—before what?

"We need to tell the others," Barry finally decided. "Kenji, Ganbold, the UN committee. This is bigger than just us."

"Agreed. But Barry..." Sakura held up the modern note. "Whoever sent this chose us specifically. They could have gone through official channels, but they didn't. Why?"

Before Barry could answer, his laptop chimed. A new email, no sender address, subject line: "For your eyes only."

The message was simple: a set of GPS coordinates and a date two weeks away. The coordinates, when mapped, showed a location in Rome—specifically, directly above where the Temple of Vesta's underground chambers would be.

"They want to meet," Sakura said.

"Or it's a trap."

"Only one way to find out." She smiled, and Barry was reminded of her sister—that same mix of caution and excitement when facing a mystery. "Besides, we were due for a vacation. I hear Rome is lovely in the fall."

Barry looked at the scroll, the note, the mysterious coordinates. Six months ago, he would have been terrified. Now, he felt only the familiar thrill of a puzzle waiting to be solved. Mongolia had changed him, transformed him from a simple archaeologist into something more. A guardian, yes, but also an explorer of the spaces between history and myth, between what was recorded and what was hidden.

"I'll book the flights," he said.

As Sakura made secure calls to their allies, Barry carefully stored the Roman artifacts. His apartment had become a small museum of secrets—the jade seal from Temujin, photographs of the Altan Debter, maps marked with sites they'd secured or still needed to investigate. Now these Roman pieces joined the collection, another link in a chain stretching back through time.

He thought of Genghis Khan on his golden throne, preserving weapons too terrible to use. Of Roman senators voting to hide what they'd found rather than wield it. Of all the unnamed guardians through history who had chosen wisdom over power.

The dragons were stirring, the note had said. In the East, they'd managed to keep them sleeping. But if the Roman connection was real, if there were Western dragons equally dangerous...

"Flights booked," Sakura announced. "Kenji's arranging secure transport for the artifacts. Ganbold is checking his Mongolian sources for any mentions of Roman contact. And..." She paused. "Tanaka sent a message through channels. The new Red Lotus has information about Roman expeditions to the East. She's willing to share."

"The enemy of my enemy," Barry mused.

"Or perhaps just someone else who understands that some secrets are too dangerous for any one group to hold."

That night, Barry stood on his balcony as he had three months before, but his thoughts were no longer on the past. The future stretched before them, full of mysteries that spanned continents and millennia. Each answer they found led to ten new questions. Each secret they secured revealed ten more waiting to be discovered.

But he was no longer alone in this work. Sakura stood beside him, a partner forged in the crucible of near-disaster. Behind them stood a growing network of guardians—some official, some shadow, all united by the understanding that humanity's greatest achievements were often its most dangerous.

"Ready for another adventure?" Sakura asked, joining him on the balcony.

"With you? Always."

She laughed. "Careful. This one might make Mongolia look like a training exercise."

"Then we'd better start preparing."

As the lights of Washington glittered below, Barry felt the weight of the Roman seal in his pocket, a tangible reminder that their work was far from over. What the Khan knew, Caesar discovered first. And what Caesar discovered...

How deep did this rabbit hole go? How many civilizations had faced these same choices? How many had failed where others succeeded?

In two weeks, they would begin finding out.

The adventure that had begun with a sister's death and a golden map had become something greater—a calling that spanned centuries and civilizations. Barry and Sakura had proven themselves in the mountains of Mongolia. Now Rome awaited, with its own tests, its own secrets, its own dragons sleeping beneath ancient stones.

They would face whatever came next together, armed with wisdom earned through sacrifice and the knowledge that some victories lay not in conquering, but in protecting.

The game that Genghis Khan had played, that Caesar had played, that countless unnamed guardians had played throughout history, continued.

And Barry Curtis and Sakura Hirata were ready for the next move.

To be continued in: The Golden Book III: Caesar's Dragons.

Coming Soon: The Golden Book III — The Wolf of Empire

W hat the Khan guarded, Caesar first uncovered...

After uncovering the lost tomb of Genghis Khan and preserving its secrets from the world, Dr. Barry Curtis and Sakura Hirata have finally found peace—or so they thought.

But when a mysterious Roman scroll arrives bearing a cryptic message and an imperial seal lost to history, their quiet life is shattered once more.

"The key lies beneath the ashes."

From the windswept ruins of Hadrian's Wall to the hidden vaults beneath Vatican City, Barry and Sakura are thrust into a race against time to uncover a lost alliance between two of history's greatest empires. Beneath layers of myth, betrayal, and ancient warcraft lies a secret so powerful it could reshape the narrative of Western civilization—and unlock a weapon long buried in the dust of forgotten dynasties.

As rival factions emerge—secret orders, rogue scholars, and powerful elites—one truth becomes clear:

The empires never died. They simply went underground.

With love deepening and danger closing in, Barry and Sakura must rely on each other more than ever to solve a puzzle two thousand years in the making.

History is written by the victors. But the truth was hidden by the survivors.

Also by Donald J. Wright

Novels

Lilith's Garden

ASIN: B0DQX8ZWD9

The Terraforming Protocol ASIN: B0FHBVY1QS

ASIN: B0DNY8Z3WB

The Prometheus Protocol

ASIN: B0DLHFF79M

13th Moon Book I

ASIN: B0DGNTV533

13 Moons: Legacy of the Guardians Book II

ASIN: B0FDYNP7WP

Killer Ice

ASIN: B0F1G6HVMR

The Ghost Code

ASIN: B0F4FGQMG5

The Golden Book

ASIN: B0DXQGMFL8

Tomorrow

ASIN: B0FFTS4C39

The God Equation
ASIN: B0FGZFNZTD
THE QUANTUM SCHISM:
ASIN: B0D1N9RHMQ
The Quantum Alchemist:
ASIN: B0FD43QCDB
The Quantum Heart:
ASIN: B0F9YZTRVG
The Codex Protocol:
ASIN: B0F1Z1XH89
THE QUANTUM ECHO
ASIN: B0F6KWPGG2

Non-Fiction
Beyond Climate Debates
ASIN: B0DZB8CB7K
Diamonds Under Fire
ASIN: B0CDYSTBLL
The Handbook of Lab-Created Diamonds
ASIN: B0D8V4X3CW
The Diamond Revolution
ASIN: B0FHBVY1QS
Eternal Shine
ASIN: B0DQX8ZWD9
Globe Treasure Hunting
ASIN: B0DF6RN4H8

www.ingramcontent.com/pod-product-compliance
Lightning Source LLC
Chambersburg PA
CBHW022143010726
47493CB00002B/320